Clinton Smith has spent much of his life writing advertising, documentaries and fiction. His commercials have won thirty Australian and international awards, his short stories several more. His shoots have taken him to many countries and people as diverse as Edward De Bono and Ronnie Barker have fronted his campaigns. For twenty years, he wrote the classic King Gee workwear campaign that featured the slogan, 'If they were any tougher, they'd rust.' He became a partner in his own agency then retired to write thrillers. His books are extensively researched using his military contacts and the first two have been optioned for film.

Very Best
wishes
Clin Smith

Also by Clinton Smith

THE FOURTH EYE

THE GODGAME

EXIT ALPHA

CLINTON SMITH

HarperCollins*Publishers*

HarperCollins*Publishers*

First published in Australia in 2003
by HarperCollins*Publishers* Pty Limited
ABN 36 009 913 517
A member of the HarperCollins*Publishers* (Australia) Pty Limited Group
www.harpercollins.com.au

HarperCollins*Publishers*
25 Ryde Road, Pymble, Sydney, NSW 2073, Australia
31 View Road, Glenfield, Auckland 10, New Zealand
77–85 Fulham Palace Road, London W6 8JB, United Kingdom
Hazelton Lanes, 55 Avenue Road, Suite 2900, Toronto, Ontario M5R 3L2
and 1995 Markham Road, Scarborough, Ontario M1B 5M8, Canada
10 East 53rd Street, New York NY 10022, USA

National Library of Australia Cataloguing-in-Publication data:

Smith, Clinton, 1938– .
  Exit alpha.
  ISBN 0 7322 7579 2.
  1. Intelligence officers – Fiction. 2. Intelligence
  service – Fiction. I. Title.
NZ823.2

Cover and internal design by Darian Causby
Typeset in 11.5/15 Sabon by HarperCollins Design Studio
Printed and bound in Australia by Griffin Press on 80gsm Bulky Book Ivory

5 4 3 2 1   03 04 05 06

Contents

1

CREVASSE

ANTARCTIC PLATEAU, 1973

The thermometer on his parka read minus 40 degrees centigrade. Whiteout and wind chill made the glacier a featureless hell. Since the split had appeared in his boot-top he'd tried everything to patch it. If they kept on like this, he'd lose his toes.

One thing was certain in Antarctica. Everything was ten times harder and more dangerous. The 'A' factor, they called it. The smallest mistake could kill.

Chafed by his harness, anxious about his foot, cursing the man ahead of him, Cain struggled on. They were on powder snow now, had cleared the sastrugi, thank God. But there could be crevasses here.

Zuiden, far ahead all morning, was now a speck at the end of his sledge tracks, his more powerful body better at hauling 200 pounds. He'd stopped at the top of a rise to probe with the spike of his ice axe.

Cain plodded towards him, straining to see through his goggles. In this undefined, unrelieved whiteness it was hard to spot slumps. The danger wasn't the centre of a snow bridge. You had to watch for the fault line at the edge. Plumes blew from ridges. The wind was rising fast.

Last night in the snapping tent he'd hunched beside the Primus, shaken frost from between his double layer of socks, checked his foot. Two toes — spongy, painful.

'Amputation time,' Zuiden said through salami and peas.

'You'd like that, wouldn't you?'

'Another Paki cripple. So what? You black bastards are a dime a dozen.'

Why the fixation on skin colour? He wasn't even that dark. He'd been told his mother had been Caucasian, his father Pakistani. Zuiden's parents were Dutch students. So bloody what? They'd never known their parents. Why did deadshits like Zuiden make such comments?

They were manhauling far south of Alpha with a rendezvous point but no backup. EXIT cadets sank or swam. They were both twenty-four years old. Training continued seventeen hours a day and seven days a week for twenty years — special forces techniques and streaming for specific operations. For Cain, that included a liberal education that Zuiden ridiculed, probably from envy.

He slogged on through squeaking snow, beard frozen, eyelids encrusted. They were nearing the crest where the ice flow would change direction. The second hour was up. His turn to lead.

He drew level with the Dutchman. 'Time to rope up.'

'Got to crap.' Zuiden's overmitts hung from their harness. He struggled with zips.

Cain unhitched himself from the sledge and pulled the coiled safety-rope from under the strapping. It was secured to the eyelet at the rear and he'd tied the prusiks last night when they'd pitched camp. He tossed the coil on the snow, removed his mitts, tied a figure-eight in the shorter end and snapped it into his harness karabiner.

He glanced at Zuiden — freezing his arse off, squatting behind the windbreak of his sledge. Turds, in this place, remained preserved for ever. You were supposed to shit in the tent just before you took it down but the bastard hadn't managed it this morning.

'Wind's getting up.' Cain's fingers were already numb and he wanted to keep moving to stop heat draining from his limbs. He hitched up to the sledge again, replaced his hands in the clumsy gauntlets and walked an idle step forward to probe the drift with the spike of his axe.

The bridge must have been a mere crust.

Like an unlocked trapdoor, it dropped.

He fell in a cloud of snow, arms out, feet kicking air, expecting the sledge to smash down on top of him, expecting a 100 foot fall.

Then he jerked, stopped, dangled against a glacial-blue ice wall. Below him, the fissure widened to a bottomless blue-black void.

The cascading snow stopped. He hung in tomb-like silence, blood pounding in his ears. What had snagged him? He pushed back his frosted hood, peered up.

The lip was 15 feet above. The fibreglass sledge was jammed 8 feet down the slot on an irregular projection of ice. He was hanging from the sledge poles. If the sledge slipped, he died.

He yelled up.

No answer.

Jesus.

He yelled again, disoriented, shocked.

In this limbo-land, half the effort was psychological. He had to pull himself together, think.

The safety-rope hung slack beside him. If the main coil was still above the lip Zuiden could belay it. Perhaps he was doing it now. But the crap would have cost him — like everything on this continent cost you. His hands wouldn't be warm for half an hour.

He yelled, 'Zuiden.'

He'd lost his ice axe. The strap had come off his wrist. He checked for damage. Nothing seemed broken. The harness cut into his thighs but he wore no crampons so had no forward spikes to kick into the undercut wall.

One prusik hung near his side — a small diameter loop of rope tied to the main one with a sliding hitch that jammed under load. The other was attached to his harness. In theory, you used the loops to inch your way up the rope. In practice it was hard. Although he was strong, Antarctic gear was heavy. You really needed other men above, using an improvised pulley system.

And if he yanked the safety-rope, he'd jerk the coil into the crevasse.

Sweet Jesus, Brahma and Allah. Zuiden had to belay him or he was dead.

'Zuiden!' He shrieked it.

Nothing.

He hung, helpless, chilled by the smooth walls. It was hard to look up. Ice on his face mask had stuck to his hood halfway around. Zuiden would need to anchor himself off, then take up the slack and belay.

At last a masked, goggled and hood-shrouded head appeared above the lip.

Cain yelled, 'Belay the rope.'

The shape went. Cain waited, losing sensation in his limbs, inertia pooling warmth in his core. Soon he'd shake with cold and his hands would be senseless meat.

A jerk.

Ice particles pattered on his hood.

The sledge had slipped and he'd dropped 3 inches down the face.

He dangled from the poles, scared to breathe.

Zuiden's hood again, a dark triangle, snow building on one side. 'Okay. You're anchored off.'

Cain pulled on the rope. 'You could have taken up the slack.'

'You do it.'

'Bastard. You're supposed to winch me up.'

'Suck arse.' The hood disappeared.

Cain cursed and raved. The deadshit didn't care if he fell.

He pulled on the live rope. Still slack. Each time he pulled, he had to slide the prusiks higher — the one attached to his harness, and the other longer loop for his foot.

Was it anchored off at all? Or had Zuiden just decided to leave him? He wouldn't put it past the bastard. Although his jammed sledge held much of the food, Zuiden's had the vital tent and stove.

Yes, the black-hearted swine would enjoy arriving at the rendezvous alone. They'd question him but have nothing to go on. All evidence would be in the glacier. Entombed.

He kept pulling until the rope hung like a lift cable loop far below. Perhaps the shit hadn't anchored off at all. He mightn't even be up there — could have left.

Cursing, heart pounding, he dragged on the rope.

A jerk as it took up.

He gasped with relief.

He worked a foot into the long loop and slowly added weight, saw the knot jam and kink the rope. As he stood in the stirrup-like loop the cutting pressure of the harness eased. Next problem — the sledge poles. They held him down. But if he unbuckled from the sledge, he'd rely entirely on the rope.

He slipped off his gauntlets and fumbled around his hips. He could barely feel his fingers and needed his hands or he was dead. There was no sensation through the gloves he still wore, the silk inner and thick, thermal outer. After a long fiddle, the poles and flexible links hung free.

Shaking with effort, he slid the harness loop high, bent his leg so it took his weight and slid the knot of the foot loop higher. The tension had to be off the knots to move them along the rope. Even then they were hard to dislodge. He had to push the loop against the knot each time to free them.

He rested a moment, exhausted. In this frigid hell, each movement hurt.

He stood in the stirrup loop again. His body weight twisted the rope until the loops twined around it like vines. After he worked the slack knot loose he had to turn it to untangle the loop and the gloves made it as easy as playing a piano with his feet. He hung in the chasm, revolving on the rope, fighting to make the loops work.

'Zuiden,' he bellowed. The sound was absorbed by the ice.

Above him, the loop knots were fraying but the lip was closer at least. Working the loops, he drew level with the sledge then dragged himself up until stopped by the loop secured to its end.

Without help there was no alternative. He'd have to cut the tie to the sledge.

'Zuiden,' he yelled again.

Nothing.

He waited to gain strength, worked the knife from its sheath on his harness strap and sawed at the loop. As the strands gave, the live rope straightened in a spray of ice. Wind moaned above. The weather was getting bad.

The fibreglass sledge hadn't budged and seemed jammed enough to stand on. Now he was half on the rear of the sledge, his head two feet below the crevasse lip.

He slid the loop knots as high as he could to guard against falling back. Thank God for the foothold of the sledge. He rested, panting in the thin air, staring up.

The two feet might as well have been ten. The lifeline had cut into the lip. Zuiden should have put an ice axe handle crossways under the rope but hadn't bothered. A rising gale swirled snow down the slot. How to climb out without help?

Gasping, yelling curses, his beard iced to his face mask, shivering like a wet dog, he pushed the harness loop as high as he could.

He dangled, looking up.

No Zuiden. Just snow blowing across the gap.

The only way to move up was to shorten the foot loop. He'd have to tie a knot in the bight.

With fingers that barely worked, he finally got it done, put his foot in the loop and clutched the rope. When he straightened his leg, his head moved higher than the lip. Snow pelted his face, turning his eyelashes to ice.

'Zuiden, you arsehole.'

His bellow was stolen by the wind.

All his rage at his companion was suddenly in his arms. He clawed at the drift until he could see the rope taut against the ice then chipped a hole with the knife so that he could work a hand around the rope. With one grip secure, he reached far forward, used the blade as an ice spike and dragged himself out of the slot.

He lay prone, close to hypothermia, wind moaning around him, driven snow pounding his hood.

He'd survived the crevasse. Now the blizzard — they called it a blizz — was the threat. The rope was all he could see. Visibility was almost zero.

'Zuiden, I'll bloody kill you.'

He crawled along the rope, reached the anchor, a single snow stake. Zuiden should have anchored twice but obviously didn't give a damn.

He couldn't think properly, didn't know what to do. He had no equipment, just the rope. Should he use it to search in widening circles around the spot? No. He'd slot himself again.

He needed shelter desperately. The wind was strong enough to blow him off his feet. If he'd had a bivvy bag or extra insulation, he could have dug himself into the snow. He realised with terror that he could no longer feel his left foot.

'Jesus,' he whimpered. So this was how you died.

Then, through blasting drift, he glimpsed a yellow smear. An illusion? He crawled ahead.

Yes, a yellow tinge.

The tent!

Relief flooding him, he crawled forward yelling, lurched into a guy-line and turned for the crosswind face. The entrance was meant to be there and Zuiden had done the job by the book — dug in the floor and heaped snow on the valance to stop wind getting underneath. A polar pyramid tent, properly pitched and secured, could withstand the highest winds.

At the end of his strength, Cain got himself inside.

Zuiden sat, legs in his sleeping bag, melting snow on the stove. He didn't bother to look up.

Cain pulled the entrance drawstring tight, dislodging frosted condensation, lay on the cell-bed matting, too weak to move.

Above the snapping of the fabric, the thrumming of the guy-lines and the storm, Zuiden's laconic voice. 'What took you so long?'

'You arsehole. You left me to die there.'

'No point in two croaking. And you'd be stuffed now without the tent.'

'If you'd bloody winched me out, you would've got the tent up faster.'

'This is survival training. Why should I give a stuff?'

'You don't just look after number one, you incredible arsehole shitface ...'

'Edict fourteen. DEATH IS AN ASPECT OF LIFE.'

'Don't quote me the edicts,' Cain roared. 'I've probably lost my bloody foot.'

'Edict six. LOYALTY TO PEOPLE IS WEAKNESS. Down here, your poncy degrees don't cut any ice.'

Cain wanted to sob. With relief? For his foot? He didn't know. But he was damned if he'd do it in front of this callous shit. He was alive at least and able to get warm. And, for once, kerosene fumes were the sweetest smell in the world.

He looked at his damaged left boot, frightened to take it off.

He said, 'An eye for an eye. And a foot for a foot. You heard it here.'

Zuiden sneered and raised a middle finger.

2

SCREAMS AT MIDNIGHT

LAHORE, PAKISTAN, MARCH 1978

Kot Lakhpat Jail. Iron gates sweating and rusted with heat. Filthy cells the sun never found. Iron beds chained to the floor. Cockroaches crawling from the toilet hole. Flies. Stench. Endless merciless mosquitoes.

The man sat on the lice-infested mattress, his body covered with sores. He had lately vomited blood but hadn't told his daughter. They'd let her see him yesterday. He'd trained her well. She hadn't cried.

To guard against a coup, he'd chosen an obsequious buffoon. But the man was sly. Strange how you attracted what you feared.

It was starting again in the courtyard. They began it at midnight so that screams kept the prisoners awake. Each man was spreadeagled on the slanting rack — belly on a bolster, feet in stocks, hands tied above his head. Then they'd flog him with a *lathi*, running at him and striking sideways with full force. He could hear the long cane whistle as it slashed the victim's bare arse, hear the scream, hear the army officer count off the stroke.

He slapped mosquitoes, remembering the meeting with Kissinger last year. The agreement with France on the nuclear reprocessing plant was meant to offset soaring oil prices. But the 'free world', the rumbling voice had explained, wouldn't tolerate an Islamic bomb. Henry had actually threatened him, said he could become 'a horrible example'.

The screams outside had stopped. The prisoner would have fainted. They'd wait for the doctor to check his pulse and revive him with smelling salts.

Kissinger, of course, had also attracted what he feared. America feared fundamentalists and now had one. Zia would play the Islamic card — bruise his head on his prayer mat and enforce the old barbaric laws.

They began flogging the clod again but he was pointlessly, desperately brave — still screamed '*Jiye* Bhutto' with each stroke.

The man sweated in the cloud of insects, listening to the wretch repeat his name.

Long live Bhutto. Ironic. He was born to lead the rabble of course, but his life had hardly been guiltless.

Now only roaches and pain remained.

Zia would hang him within the month.

3

PALACE OF THE PATRIARCH

VENICE, ITALY, AUGUST 1978

The Patriarch of Venice had a kindly, bespectacled face, a brisk, waddling walk and though of average height, seemed shorter. He hurried down the *calle* toward the Piazza San Marco, enjoying the exercise and the freedom of being alone. He'd forsaken his cardinal's red for the cassock of a *bagarozzi* because he hated ostentation, deplored the pomp and wealth of the Church. A shopkeeper called out to him, '*Buon giorno, Eminenza,*' and received a ready smile and wave.

A prominent businessman stopped him, longing for inner contact. Then, constrained by diffidence, talked of the mundane — about local building restrictions that made it impossible to get things fixed or changed.

Luciani nodded and smiled, the lenses of his glasses glinting. 'Would you prefer a hundred and seven churches, half of them closed ... San Marco sinking into the sea ... a congregation of tourists and old people ... ?'

'What can one do? We live in a museum.'

'One does what one can. But one tries to be all one can.'

'Difficult,' the man sighed.

'For me, too.' The gentle smile. 'But I'll keep trying if you will.'

Near the loggia, an old hunched woman, head raised to compensate, recognised the incognito cardinal and shuffled forward to pluck his sleeve. He spoke to her quietly, fumbled inside his coat, pressed bank notes into her hands, blessed her then walked on. She stared after him, astonished, blinded by tears.

He almost skipped across the great square, feeling lighter than a bird, wishing he could sell the palace that entombed him and give the money to some South American church.

At 1.30 pm, after his last appointment, he walked down the echoing passage to his suite. Though sixty-five he still rose at 4.30 am and napped briefly in the afternoon. He removed his shoes with relief, settled back on the bed, thinking about the case of possession reported by nuns in Treviso — a child who seemed the centre of strange phenomena. Ornaments flew off shelves, furniture shook. The tales of repressed and superstitious sisters or something more?

A knock.

'Come in.'

His private secretary entered. He'd replaced the previous one for harping on Church politics — a subject he detested. The man bowed his apologies. 'We've heard the Holy Father's worse. He's semi-conscious. It may only be hours.'

Luciani nodded. It had come. And he would be obliged to join the conclave that elected a new pope. At least there was one thing to be glad about. They'd never choose him.

Twenty days later, after one day's voting, the conclave elected the Patriarch of Venice.

'We felt as if our hands were being guided as we wrote his name on the paper,' Cardinal Hume later remarked.

The bewildered pope said, 'May God forgive you,' and often said during his papacy, 'Why on earth did they ever choose me?'

And once he said, 'I would have done better to say no.'

4

REQUISITION
FOR TWO DEATHS

CHARTRES, FRANCE, 1988

She had the mind of a company receiver, the heart of a leopard seal and the body of a movie star, which she was. She spoke in Urdu, because it was safer. 'So where and how do they kill us?'

The afternoon sun bathed the bed. Cain stroked the coffee-toned skin of her bare breast. 'Tomorrow, we take the TGV back to Paris and book into a small hotel in Rue Vernet, close to the Arc de Triomphe. It has a glass-walled lift. Next day, we take the lift down to the lobby and they hit us with AKRs — make it look authentic by shattering the glass.' Her hand moved down his body. The sex was still a comfort but after five years in Pakistan, they were exhausted by the project and each other. Despite edict eight — OCCUPATIONAL RELATIONSHIPS ARE NO LESS FULFILLING.

She said, 'How will it work?'

'One covers the door. One stays as back-up in the car. Ali makes it look good but fires between us. As we fall, Murchison fires from the stairwell and wounds the man by the door. Ali gets away with the wounded man who's legit. He'll confirm the hit.'

'Elaborate.'

'Be an item on TV that night: Lollywood movie queen and director boyfriend killed by hard-liners in retaliation for steering Zia toward elections.'

'Will it stick?'

'Shaded truth's convincing. Then — debrief and we're clear — praise Allah, the beneficent, the compassionate.'

'And Rahib Badar again becomes Ray Cain, the westerner with shady skin.' She touched his jaw. 'You can grow your Antarctic beard again.'

'And you can take up with a stud in Baloachi robes, observe *mayoon*, suffer two days of ceremonies, gold brocade, full bit, have five children and . . .'

'Patriarchal bastard.' She poked his ribs. 'I think you're a closet fundamentalist.'

They had been loyal to each other as in edict ten: CONSISTENCY IS THE HIGHEST ACHIEVEMENT. An unorganised relationship could be fatal to others in the team. He slid back between her legs, resumed the drowsy thrusts she liked. She murmured, 'After a time, you could miss your dear Rehana.'

The sun had gone from the room. She looked beautiful asleep, like a child. He dressed, gently closed the door, descended the narrow stairs, needing to see the cathedral, the miracle, again. They'd toured the crypt that morning but missed the roof tour. Despite edict twelve, PERSPECTIVE IS STRENGTH, the astonishing building had bored her.

Long shadows stretched across the square. He strolled to the main doors, a fortyish man with a slightly uneven step —

compensation for the lack of three toes on his left foot. His darker skin emphasised his matinee-idol looks, the intelligent eyes, the tinge of grey at his brow. He ignored the tourists. Beside Chartres they didn't exist. He sensed he was being trailed by Murchison or Zuiden from Department S. The S operatives, nicknamed 'surgeons', handled assassinations while D, the 'dentists', his own outfit, replaced people. Usually they worked independently. But sometimes S assisted D. He needed the surgeons now for security, extraction and cleaning. Still, he disliked having Zuiden help him wind up the assignment. Although the swine was a top man now — Grade Three — lost toes weren't easy to forgive.

The cathedral's exterior was a cosmos — alchemy, astrology, its endless elaborations a contrast to the soaring bare interior. Beyond the building he visualised the cathedrals of Antarctica. Ramparts of ice with deep fissures of turquoise and green — some beached with sea-scoured bases, some thundering as they calved.

There, implacable nature. Here, the immortal work of mortals. Vaults, flyers, arcane geometry seeking the essence of God in stone. Unable to reconcile the two, he moved to the carvings near the left-hand door.

Before him, a teaching designed to last for a thousand years. The precise positioning of the sword haft, the folds of material across the belly. *Hara no aru hito.* An invocation moulded in rock.

Someone behind him. 'Rahib Badar?'

He half turned.

Slowly.

Not Murchison or Zuiden.

Where the hell were they?

He surveyed the stranger — a dark man in western clothes, neck bulging from a collarless shirt. Stubble. Liquid eyes. He knew these third-world inter-services types. Young fanatics, swamped by testosterone, who confused murder with a crusade.

So now he was flying solo and about to be hit by a pro. He'd been trained to face such things. But why here? Couldn't life, this once, leave him alone?

'Who are you?'

'You come now.'

He played the affronted tourist. 'What is this?'

A second bargain-basement type with the eyes of a fighting dog edged in. An express-post bag under his armpit shielded something bulky. He held a spray bottle in his latex-gloved right hand. Fentanyl? It used to be a bullet. Things weren't improving.

'We have present for you.'

'Uh-huh.' Cain dropped the act and scratched the side of his chest through his jumper as if thinking. It released the safety on the breastplate-cannon and gave him an even chance.

The man in front of him narrowed his eyes, as if assessing whether it was a signal. If he'd known what Cain had strapped to his chest he would have hit the deck. The cluster of inch-long barrels cradled fat explosive rounds.

Were they Zia's hoods, Cain wondered, or his cronies in the mujahideen? If the regime had sent them, was it known what had happened to the president? Surely not, after the years of preparation he'd put in. Still, it was vital to find out.

As he walked, the thugs flanked him, guiding him back to his hotel. Where were Murchison and Zuiden? Retired?

This way, the orchestrated deaths they'd planned were going to occur two days early — life overtaking artifice. Had they got to Rehana? Please God, no!

There was no one in the cramped lobby. That would have been arranged. The man with the glove removed a burp gun from his bag.

Cain passed the dining room's double glass door and went ahead up the stairs. Time seemed to slow and he felt acutely aware — of the chipped paint, the tired carpet, the sauce smell infusing the walls ...

The bedroom was darker. They didn't put on the light. His eyes had to adjust before he saw the extent of the carnage on the bed. She hadn't gone easily. Tufts of hair lay on the sheet. She was prone, naked, bound to the bed with electrical cord. An iron on the floor explained livid boat-shapes burnt into her skin and the blood-soaked sheet between her legs suggested a fate worse than rape.

Cain, in blind fury, faced the man with the gun square on. The breast-cannon was cruder than a belly gun, its accuracy appalling. To hit a target you had to be kissing it, but at this range he couldn't miss. Exploding bullets had been vetoed by the 1868 Declaration of St Petersburg. But EXIT wasn't bothered with niceties. He'd watched a demonstration round deconstruct the carcass of a pig but had never seen a living body hit.

He fingered his jumper as if itchy, touching the pressor switch on the shoulder strap beneath. The back-plate drove into his plexus, its concussion like a slamming door. He dived to the side, aware that a shot man's hand tightens on a trigger.

The dying man fell on his knees, staring at his gut. The bullet, destructive as point-blank buckshot, had blown a crater in him that dangled offal. He still held the sub-machine-gun, a 9mm Beretta 12 switched to semi, but had forgotten what it was for. Cain took it from him, wheeled.

The other man, splattered, shocked, had taken cover behind the door, was firing an automatic down the stairwell. He didn't know the direction of attack, suspected the landing behind him. By now he'd have tunnel vision, his precision responses gone. Before his secondary reaction came, Cain flicked the Beretta's fire selector to 'R' and sprayed the back of his knees. The man folded against the doorway, toppled.

As he tried to swing his pistol around, Cain said, 'Drop it,' holding the snout of the burp gun an expressive 2 inches from his eye.

His automatic hit the floor and Cain kicked it across the outside landing where it spun against the bannister and slid over the top step. His sense of retribution was made sweeter by clean underpants. He'd wet himself slightly. That was all. The body reacted, no matter how well you were trained. It was unnatural to kill your own species.

'Having fun?' Zuiden's thinning blond hair appeared above the stairs behind the snout of his buttless Ingram.

Cain felt anger and relief. 'Where the hell have *you* been?'

'On the can.' He shot the gutted man in the head.

'How come you're having a dump each time I need you?' He was thinking of his absent toes. 'This crud's your stuff, not mine. Where's Murchison, for Christ's sake?'

Zuiden scooped up the automatic from the stairs. 'Could have been taken out.' He stepped over the second man, who'd never walk again. 'You've done well for a dentist.' He scanned the mess on the bed, replaced his Uzi clone in the soft EXIT snap-flap holster that kept it out of sight beneath his jacket then took the Beretta from Cain, checked it with approval. 'Nice. If you're happy with 500 rpm. So what's going down?'

'Look at her. Good God!' He was starting to shake. 'I don't think they were after information. It looks like payback.'

The surgeon went to the bed. 'She got the big sendoff, all right. You were next cab on the rank.' He returned to the man with pulped knees. 'Squeaky time, pal.' He kicked the maimed legs. A scream of pain.

Cain left him to it. Torture was Zuiden's trade and slaughter his satisfaction. As he listened to the screams, he moved to the bed and placed a finger on the crimson neck. The sight of her turned-away face almost made him puke. Poor love. Christ, she ...

Then he noticed the sheet beside the pillow. A scrawl that looked like a 'Z' that she'd written with her blood.

Zuiden? In on this? Was that why he hadn't fronted earlier? But if the swine was setting him up, why hadn't he just shot him?

He watched the surgeon, muscular back and bald patch, as he crouched over the man by the door. Zuiden held his hand, bending back the fingers, soft-talking like a ministering priest. The man had met his match and knew it.

A background hubbub of panic from the street. The unsuppressed guns must have sounded like an IRA jamboree. A head appeared above the stairs — the shocked face of a woman. A terrified stare. She bolted.

A muffled snap and howl. Zuiden was breaking the terrorist's fingers.

Cain looked away in disgust. Surgeons were appalling bastards. And Zuiden was one of the worst.

He secured the safety catch on the breast-gun, went to check the stairs. 'I'll try and stall the audience.'

'No,' Zuiden grunted. 'If you're seen, you can't have been shot. And now it's best you're dead. If you're shipped out of here in a body bag, we can cancel the Paris number. Get it?'

He knew the man was right. Cleaning strategy was part of his craft. 'But you'll have plods here in a minute.'

'Some local cop used to the quiet life? Would *you* come up?' He'd finished with the man's hands. It hadn't helped. 'This guy's doing it for Allah. I've got to up the amps.' He started working in earnest on the man's shattered legs. Cain looked away, appalled. The victim's noise was terrible. After a minute, the fellow cracked and sang. He knew nothing about the duplication. And he was mujahideen. Zuiden stood up. 'Least you're not blown.'

Cain breathed out.

As Zuiden picked up the Beretta, Cain stood ready with his cannon. If Zuiden had set them up, he'd change the slime to a doughnut.

Zuiden shot the Afghani and the man juddered with the burst. Then he examined the gun, weighing it in his hand. 'Simple but good. Not much muzzle climb on full.' He stared around the room as if he'd mislaid a cup of tea.

Cain wondered why Zuiden felt superior when the Ingrams the surgeons favoured, despite their high rate of fire, were almost antiques. 'What now?'

'We wait for the GIGN. The locals won't front an automatic firefight. They'll cordon off, wait for troops. Stand by for stun grenades and canisters.'

'We have to?'

'Safer than shooting a gendarme in self-defence.' He produced a multi-band transceiver no larger than a beeper. 'With luck I can back them up a bit.'

Zuiden got a signal through. It probably saved their lives. They spent a wary evening with messieurs of the GIGN. The renowned French 'Third Force' wasn't charmed by the scene and the Groupe d'Intervention commander had never been shown a Blue Exemption Card. After much chatternetting on different frequencies clearance was confirmed — not only the exemption for murder and an embargo on investigation but also a requisition for logistic support. The commander's attitude changed from revulsion and suspicion to affront.

Zuiden handled the cleaning of the site, using GIGN cover. Cain, playing dead, was lugged to the chopper in the body bag. They were flown with the corpses to a military compound north of Paris. Then continent-hopping began.

In three hours, they were on a cargo flight to Cairo. After an interminable wait in a baggage bay, they connected with a charter to Somalia.

The Mogadishu terminal was basically a dusty hangar. They slumped on a bench, exhausted, sweating with the heat. The only transport visible was a bullet-pocked truck and bus — both with windscreens shot out — and a white armoured personnel carrier manned by Italians in UN berets. Even children here, Zuiden told him, carried AKs and SARs.

The local contact's khat-chewing sidekick took their civilian clothes with delight, as if assessing how much they would fetch in this Eden of bullets and loot. They were handed unmarked jumpsuits, float coats, foam earplugs and two dry contra-concave objects that once may have been sandwiches.

After another hour they were driven in a buggy far across the tarmac towards droop-bladed US Black Hawks that shimmered like mirages. Unexpectedly, they turned and headed towards a US Navy Grumman E–2C — a mini AWAC capped by a frisbee-like radar dome.

'Hawkeye,' Zuiden said. 'Airborne control centre.' Military things were his bag. He explained that it was packed with electronics and had a five man crew — two pilots and three acronyms — and that a further two carcasses wouldn't help trim and takeoff weight.

'So where are they taking us?' Cain asked.

'A CV in the Indian Ocean?' Zuiden looked puzzled.

'To a carrier?'

'Hawkeyes live on carriers. But carrier transport is a C–2A.' The surgeon ridged his brow and even the ridges seemed muscular. 'Why didn't they reroute a COD?'

'Perhaps we're in for some kind of comms op.'

They walked well clear of the arc marked by a threatening red line on the fuselage, climbed the steps built into the downward-hinged door and entered the dark tube. There was no room for them back with the NFOs so they were told to sit feet first on the floor by the rear bulkhead of the forward electronics compartment. They were handed webbing and told to lash themselves to the equipment racks.

They squeezed in earplugs. The engines ran up, the brakes released and the props chopped air. They powered forward, thrumming, left the ground fast, banked.

Soon Zuiden's head lolled. Cain scrutinised the man's brutal face. Although ominously tough, he was ageing now, not the young Turk he'd been in Antarctica. Both of them forty this year. Mine enemy grows older, Cain thought. It was simple for surgeons — kill or be killed. They were basic types, technicians. But dentists were taught to review their acts — to bear the liberal education and the angst.

He saw Rehana's desecrated body, the man dying on his small-intestine quilt, the screaming mouth-hole of the Afghani.

He closed his eyes but couldn't escape.

Had EXIT transformed the child he'd been into an over-civilised adult — for this?

5

BIRD FARM

PERSIAN GULF

The Hawkeye pilot, a first tour junior, was tense. He was 25 miles out and close to Bingo. He'd asked for an ASAP recover, but the CATCC controllers weren't buying.

A section of Hornets were inbound after practice plugs. So was the tanker. The standard sequence was Hornets first, tanker next, hummer last. And although the unscheduled divert had drained their fuel, mother didn't care. 'Six zero three — climb and maintain angels eleven.'

His copilot said, 'Boat's out to kill us again.' Then his NFO aircraft commander selected the front end to talk options. The back-seat driving only increased the pucker-factor.

Strike finally acknowledged that they'd soon be flying on fumes. They dirtied up and trolled in. Gear and hook down, 6 degrees, airspeed, distance ... You had to come in just above stall and from three-quarters of a mile out, fly the ball. He watched his cross-hairs, concentrated on glide slope, centreline. Wind over deck: 30 knots slightly axial. If they boltered or had to wave off, they'd be below joker. He called up the mole hole. 'Someone tell our guests to hang on.'

As always, the flight deck of the carrier looked like a postage stamp on approach, then got bigger very fast. Landing was the killer. The LSO gave points for each one. Would he score an okay three-wire? Cop a major deviation — turd brown? The hazardous thoughts were back. I have to land this pass. Better to die than look bad. He concentrated on getting in. Cockpit light amber: on speed. You couldn't use instruments even at night. Too much lag, happened too fast.

'Hawkeye, ball.'

Anticipate the burble. Pitch spot-on — tail-down for the hook because the arresting wires were two inches off the deck. Over the ramp — hit power and ...

The plane trapped an uneventful two-wire, was snatched to a stop and his body, as usual, tried to fly through the windshield. He hauled back on the throttles, enormously relieved. As the wire started to drag them aft he raised the hook, braked and wondered how the freight had fared. On a COD they'd be belted into backward-facing seats. But cinched on the floor would represent a definite ouch!

Cain had discovered why naval aircraft design began with the undercarriage and airframe. He'd been slammed so hard on the landing that he was ready for a chiropractor.

'Told you,' Zuiden shouted. 'Hear that? Elaborate wingfold on these. Double-acting hydraulic cylinders, skewed-axis hinges ...'

Surgeons learned and loved all that crud. He didn't share Zuiden's lust for technical detail.

They moved on an unstable surface and finally were released onto acres of slowly pitching deck. Cain breathed in the smell of aviation fuel and diesel — blinked in the sudden glare of sun. Despite his earplugs, the noise was painful. He'd never been on a carrier.

He stared at the matt-blue chocked and chained fighters stacked with folded wings. Green-jacketed maintenance men stood on wing stubs, dwarfed by the forest of angled metal fins. He'd expected elegant plumage for the billions the planes must have been worth but even the cloudy-white Hawkeye looked smarter. He edged around its flat tail section which was labelled DO NOT PAINT.

He followed Zuiden past yellowshirts sorting out a tiedown. One yelled, 'Like where are you going, dudes?' and pointed them toward the island. A sign on it read: BEWARE OF JET BLAST, PROPELLERS AND ROTORS. Cain stared up to sailors watching from the superstructure's catwalks, then at the wingless bridges with their sloping windows. Above it all, antennas and SATCOM domes seemed to scrape the ragged bottoms of the clouds.

He skirted plane-handling equipment, heading for one of the secured-back doors. As he stepped over the sill he lurched against the metal frame and realised how much the huge vessel moved. Inside stood a smart marine corporal who seemed to be some kind of honour guard but they were greeted by a thin lieutenant commander in crisp whites. 'Afternoon, gentlemen. Scott Spencer, NSWC. I'm your nursemaid. And sorry about the transfer. One COD's hauling freight. The other's a hangar-queen.' Creased eyes and a smile. 'Follow me, please.'

The inside of the carrier was a maze of pipes, bulkheads and blasting air vents. The flight deck clamour cross-faded to the racket of air-con fans and the far-off whine of engine turbines. Cain pocketed his earplugs, his body slowly thawing.

They moved along narrow corridors that had the same synthetic nonslip surface as the deck. No portholes, just an architecture of functional steel. Seven levels down and along another corridor they reached a grille guarded by marine sergeants who produced elbow-snapping salutes.

On the floor inside the grille was a red demarcation line

that the sergeant who let them in was careful not to step across. They entered a space featuring two stump-like metal columns and a desk with a VDU, stood facing security cameras as scanners in the columns probed their pockets and aromas.

The woman behind the desk, thirtyish, plain, wore the black cylinder-necked Department S uniform. EXIT? Here? How in hell could they compromise a participating nation's warship? It was as incriminating as displaying a murder weapon as a souvenir.

They handed the woman their Blue Cards. As she glanced up to take his, Cain spotted a flicker of interest. Evoked, he wondered, by his appearance or reputation? The latter, he hoped. It disturbed him to find apparently intelligent women swayed by his looks.

She swiped the cards and waited for her screen to give clearance.

Spencer tapped his foot on the vibrating deck. 'Your security's a piece of work. Be awkward if we hit a mine.'

The woman spun a central locking wheel on the end door, pulled it open. On the other side were the shafts of six retracted dogs and heavy seals.

They stepped over the sill into another corridor. Here no blast from air-con vents. The walls and floor were lined with stainless steel. On each side of the floor were the same padeyes that studded the flight deck but the fittings had been adapted to drainholes. Of the pipes lining the ceiling, two were atypical. One had jets. The other, dispersion nozzles.

Zuiden pointed to a jet. 'Uncle Sam off his nut?'

Spencer nodded. 'This setup's stirred coals on the flag bridge. The rear admiral says he's been suckered.'

Cain couldn't believe it either. This was a permanent installation, a typical EXIT choke point. An incursion force moving through here would end up like beetles in amber. Except that the amber would be a space-filling sticky foam that hardened in five seconds and was far more unpleasant than the product developed by SNL in Albuquerque. When the dissolvent was oversprayed by the second pipe, the foam turned to acid. In half an hour, the only thing left would be pitted weapons and blobs of bone.

As they reached the end hatch the dogs slid back as it was opened from the far side by a uniformed EXIT cadet.

The next space was a vivid contrast — a pastel-coloured vestibule with comfortable casual chairs and a feature carpet with shaped panels in a pleasing design. On the low far wall was emblazoned the main EXIT credo:

WORLD MAINTENANCE IS MORALITY.

The others followed beneath in smaller type — the fourteen edicts expounded to them from near childhood:

2. PREDATORS AND PARTISANS ARE PERNICIOUS.
3. EQUILIBRIUM COUNTERS CONFLICT.
4. THE END DOESN'T JUSTIFY THE MEANS,
    BUT SURGERY AND DENTISTRY ARE PRACTICAL.
5. LOYALTY TO THE CAUSE IS POWER.
6. LOYALTY TO PEOPLE IS WEAKNESS.
7. TRUE SELF-SATISFACTION COMES FROM SERVICE.
8. OCCUPATIONAL RELATIONSHIPS ARE NO LESS
    FULFILLING.
9. EMOTION IS A FORCE, NOT AN ARGUMENT.
10. CONSISTENCY IS THE HIGHEST ACHIEVEMENT.
11. TRAINING LEADS TO COURAGE.
12. PERSPECTIVE IS STRENGTH.
13. AUTHORITY TO KILL IS A PRIVILEGE, NOT A RIGHT.
14. DEATH IS AN ASPECT OF LIFE.

Rhonda and Vanqua were there to welcome them. They made an incongruous pair. A large, thick-waisted woman wearing scuffed flatties and a pantsuit flecked with cigarette ash. Beside her, an elegantly dressed man with a sombre face and a gymnast's body.

Rhonda grasped Cain's hand warmly. She was dowdy as always. Despite her large frame and thick figure, she could scrub up well when she bothered. But she mostly didn't, preferring comfortable disarray. The too-sensual lower lip, the extra chin, the close-cut greying curls, the impish eyes ... He felt a rush of affection for her, hugged her hard.

Her upper-class British drawl, 'Welcome home, Grade Four.'

'I was Three when I left.'

'So your return is more auspicious than your departure.'

He appreciated the upgrade but they both knew it was nonsense. Salary and prestige were irrelevant now. She squeezed his hands again, delighted to see him. 'You're still absurdly good looking. Barely a sign of decay.'

Zuiden had also greeted his department superior. Vanqua assessed them both with sad, intelligent eyes. He still looked super-fit. His only erotic outlet was rumoured to be the gymnasium. He said in his Danish accent, 'Well, you must be tired. You'll need sleep.'

Zuiden yawned. 'Anything to eat?'

Vanqua's sad smile. 'Of course.' His positive words, as always, clashed with his melancholic nature and produced the impression of deceit. He turned to Spencer. 'A basic type, Jan. It's steak and kidney pie today and you're welcome to join us, Commander.'

'You're on.'

Vanqua glanced at Cain but, observing protocol, didn't invite him. He was Rhonda's alone to command.

She asked him. 'Food?'

'Just want to crash.'

'Not till we talk. There's something you need to know.'

6

SUBVERSION

Her den, half sorting room, half command centre, stank of Turkish cigarettes. There were security cabinets, a file-covered desk and casual chairs each side of a small coffee table which supported an overfull ashtray and a dirty whisky glass. One wall of the big stateroom was fitted with a communications console. A vertical AC plasma display showed a map of Pakistan and Afghanistan. Marked on it were the combined-arms Soviet bases at Farah and Shindand — and the border, longer than NATO's central European front, guarded by eighteen Pakistani divisions outnumbered by Indian forces three to one.

Rhonda lifted rubber-band-secured files off chairs and dumped them on the floor, where they slid as the carpet tilted. She sat heavily, legs apart, not demure about her crotch. 'Take the weight off your feet.'

He sat opposite her, very tired now. 'So, you know the worst.' At Cairo, he'd sent an interim report as a burst transmission to COMOPS tagged 'CO Department D'. 'How's Zia?'

'Delighted he wasn't killed in the crash. Allah's will, no doubt.'

'So why in hell are we on this tub?'

'Come away jolly sailors ...' she trilled in her rich contralto, then gestured at the walls. 'Vanqua's obsession. Theta base. I call it his Theta of the Absurd.'

'But we can't have a base on a participating nation's warship. Didn't you tell him to sod off?'

'Not easy. Our Spartan foe — how can I delicately put it without betraying my deep resentments — has the ear.'

'But you've run EXIT since Wolf topped himself.'

'In a temporary/auxiliary capacity. I'm in charge of D. There it officially ends.'

'What are you now? Fifty? He's ... what?'

'Forty-one.'

'So he's nine intakes behind you. He's only been surgeon CO three years. And surgeons are the junior department.'

'Tell that to the Oberkommando Wehrmacht.'

'Christ, Ronnie. You're everything here. I mean ... Shit. Tigon gave you East Germany, Wolf chose you as his successor. And now you take orders from that anal Calvinist?'

'Danes are Lutherans.' She stared around the room. 'Where are my blasted ciggies? Actually I see him more as a Mongolian trotting duck.'

He grinned.

'That's better. PERSPECTIVE IS STRENGTH. I admit I resent being a little lower than his angel.'

'Surgeons can't be senior to dentists. Be the tail wagging the dog.'

'You'll be glad to hear that our Führers haven't entirely suspended common sense. I still run the senior department. But he has final say on strategy. For now.'

'Shit.' He banged the chair, intensely sorry for her.

'Dear heart, if you were funding EXIT, who'd you rather back? A sanitary, humourless, gloom-ridden, virtuous threepenny-bus young man? Or an ultra-poetical, super-aesthetical, sluttish, satirical dyke?' She guffawed. In her youth, she'd been an acclaimed Gilbert and Sullivan actress. He could see her as Buttercup or Lady Jane. 'Name your poison. Hooch or hemlock?'

'I'm trying to give them up.'

'Stuffed if I am.' She got up, found a bottle of Glenfiddich, searched her desk for a second glass, gurgling with monstrous primness, 'And I refuse to drink alone.'

He chuckled. 'That'll be the day.'

She returned with two glasses a third full of straight whisky. 'Alcohol. The only thing God got right.' As she handed over his drink she feigned shock. 'Oh-my-gosh. A dirty glass. What will you *think* of me?'

'I prefer your dirt to Vanqua's hygiene.'

'Remember Lenin's comment about sex? I consider him Vanqua's soulmate. The allusion escapes you?'

'You mean about not drinking from a dirty glass?'

'Bravo.' She scratched her rump. 'Without dirt, no immune response. As for this glass,' she did a dainty shuffle with her hippo body and assumed a little girl's voice, 'I can wipe it with my filthy hanky if you like and smear the yuk further round the rim?'

'Too kind. It's fine.'

She sat again and raised her drink. 'To all sobriety-deprived persons.'

He drank with her and felt the relief it gave his body. 'Hits the spot.' On the wall behind her, he noticed an infrasound panel. Any unauthorised snooper here would activate a low-frequency pulse that liquefied his bowels into a quivering diarrhoeic mess. When EXIT security went critical it took more than body bags. It took mops.

She was gazing at him fondly. 'You're a *very* fine fellow, sir.' She'd become the Fairy Queen in *Iolanthe*.

He remembered the reply. 'I am generally admired.'

'And you *are*, you rotten chick-magnet. I should retro-fit you with a bimbo barrier.'

He fought his tiredness, yawned. 'I still want to know how Vanqua justified this tub?'

'It's what he calls a branch office, may it wither on the vine. Oh, his reasoning's plausible enough.' She sat bolt upright, parodied Vanqua's clipped accent and expression. '"Who can find it in a ship that big far out to sea? And a carrier is a fort."' She was a hilarious mimic. '"It's guarded by a battle group and layered air defences — a shifting location no civilian or insurgent can approach."'

'So what?'

'My argument precisely. Unheeded. The bugger doesn't like me.' She trilled, 'And I can't — tell — why.' She reverted to speech. 'Where are my rotten fags?'

He still didn't understand. 'How could they sanction something that contravenes our charter? We've managed perfectly well for decades with bases in non-participating countries.'

'A comedy for those who think.'

'You're making smoke.'

'Wish I was.' She brushed papers off her desk, looking for cigarettes.

He stared at her keenly. 'They've got to you, haven't they?'

'A bit, silly sausage that I am. Please, dear, don't ... resuscitate my drowning sorrows.' She gulped scotch. 'Remember when we were cadets? That law of Manu? How did it go?'

He dredged his fuzzy mind for the passage. 'A kingdom peopled mostly by Sudras ... filled with ... godless men and deprived of twice-born inhabitants ...'

She joined in: '... will soon wholly perish, stricken by hunger and disease. I'm glad you haven't forgotten.' She drained her glass. 'And a place devoid of balance and humour loses perspective. When people get over serious, stock up on tinned food, candles and pray. Take a man with a severed jocular vein, mix him with despots, senators, pooh-bahs, simmer for some months, and ...'

'Why didn't you cream the bugger?'

'Can one, by impatience, force tight buds to open?' A wicked glance.

'Do I detect a fiendish plan?'

'I'm a serviceable fiend. But quick moves won't work. Despite my *grande aptitude à la patience* it's been like watching paint dry.'

'As long as you haven't conceded.'

'Thought you knew me.'

'I do. So you're pretending to roll over. And then you'll attack from the flank.'

'Perceptive. Now let's talk about you. This is currently a conference venue and you're press-ganged as a keynote speaker. Fifty cadets are dying to meet you. I want you to lecture them, Ray.'

'My God.' He was almost out of it. 'Want a fill-in on the Chartres debacle?'

'You're tired now. Can do that later. I just need you to know that ...' She lit her fag, locked eyes with him, her playful side gone.

'What is it?'

She flicked her hands. 'Sabotage.'

His amazed look. 'Internal?'

A nod.

He could imagine nothing more dangerous. 'Christ.'

'And it takes a peculiar form. No projects damaged. Only people. As if they're feeling their way.'

'Doesn't make sense. If they're inside they can bring down everything. So why haven't they exposed us?'

'Exactly.'

'The Chartres thing. Would it ... ?'

'Not sure. Leave that out for now.' Suddenly she was diamond-hard. 'But in the gross and scope of my opinion, this bodes some strange eruption to our state.'

Did she intend him to make the connection? Something rotten in ... 'The Great Dane?'

'I'm being carefully unspecific. It may not be him, but it's *one* of us. So I may need you to fabricate a ghost.'

'In *here*?'

She nodded. 'Full alert. Be ready to take someone out.'

7

NUDE WITH MIRROR

The cramped cabin they gave him had a fold-down desk, wardrobe and bunk. On the bunk was a towel. He needed a shower, then sleep.

The washroom, four cabins down, vibrated with the ship. When he entered, a naked black woman was facing the mirrored wall, foot on a bench, paring her nails. The mirror reflected her small, high breasts. She looked around and smiled.

It had been a while since he'd been in an EXIT bathroom. In the interests of emancipation, they had been unisex since Wolf's time. Wolf himself had appeared naked among his lowliest cadets and his successor, Rhonda, followed his example — risking comments about her weight and inclinations with majestic unconcern. Vanqua, the closet narcissist, welcomed self-display. His ripped muscles were the talk of the base. But for cadets schooled in traditional cultures, the policy was disconcerting.

Cain smiled back. After spending years in a country where even a bared ankle on a billboard was considered outrageous, he found female flesh refreshing.

He said, 'Hi.'

'Wish I was.'

He slid the towel from his waist, stepped into a booth, ran the shower. The next shower was occupied. Below the half-partition he saw a scrawny female foot.

Its owner must have seen his foot as well, and known about the missing toes. Then she was in beside him — lank bleached hair, gaunt body, drooping shoulders, sagging breasts, and the slim hips he knew well. Her hips and butt were her glory. 'Ray,' she shrieked. 'When did you blow in?'

'An hour ago.'

'About time.'

He kissed her lined face, cradled her wet bottom. 'You don't look a day older.'

'Bulsh.'

If a man's as old as the woman he feels, Cain thought, I'm now fifty. But the pressure of her job had made Pat Newsome look years older. He said, 'What are you doing here? I thought they never let you out of Tassie.'

'We're delegates. I've got to do my number.' She clamped a hand on his penis. 'I suppose a root'd be out of the question?'

He cradled her breasts. 'Still got a soft spot for me?'

The cadet passed them, said dryly, 'Acquainted?'

They went back to his cabin. He was too tired to be much good but it was bliss to be with her again — in a familiar tense body that bucked, jerked, demanded its due. He relished the scrawny feel of her, the swinging breasts, lank thighs. He found her as pleasurable as the gorgeous Rehana. It proved to him that each woman was the dearest, the only person you wished to be with.

At last they lay content, jammed together on the bunk, lulled by the movement of the ship. She said in her Aussie accent, 'Lucky I got in first. You'll be beating them off with sticks.'

'I'm too old for sex-crazed cadets.' He was fading with tiredness. 'How's John? Still down with you at Beta?'

— 37 —

'Yup. In the pink. Always asking about you.'

EXIT had replaced everyone from resistance leaders to presidents but John Paul I was the first pope.

He yawned. 'What's he up to?'

'He writes. Walks a lot. Has a bliss-session at dawn with some of the staff.'

'You talk to him much?'

'No. He's sweet but I find him scary. Makes me feel like an ankle-biter. So — change of subject — getting pensioned-off worry you?'

'Should it?'

'Some take it hard.' A level look from kindly eyes with dark crescents of skin beneath. 'Steponoski's still there — working in the storeroom.'

Steponoski had done the job on Tito. 'Why? She must be worth millions.'

'We're her family, that's why. Poor old bat'll do anything to stay.'

'Perhaps she wants to be near John.'

'Hadn't thought of that.'

'Anyway, I won't hang around.'

She stroked his face. 'What'll you do?'

'Might shoot the odd commercial.'

'Pull the other one. Whatever for? Directing's your cover job. Why fart-arse around selling tampons?'

'It's what I do. You make duplicates of world leaders. I grind out Lollywood mush. Would you rather I teach Punjabi?' He closed his eyes, his body begging for sleep. 'Making movies for illiterate Pakis is hardly creative. Coy sex, violence, daffy heroics, asinine love scenes, mindless songs. I could use a reasonable budget and script.' He was drifting off, pulled his mind back. 'Ron says someone's knocking us off.'

'Yeah. Just dentists. Lovely, tell your ma. Surgeons, strangely enough, don't have probs — still getting smeared in the course of duty, but ...'

He ran his hand along her flank. The skin had seen too much sun. She was head of Duplications and Rhonda's 2IC, so had to know the plot. 'How long is it since you corrupted me?'

'Nineteen years, give or take a century.'

'I'm not much of a security risk. And if you want help with this, you'd better fill me in. Don't need details. Just high concept. The elevator pitch.'

'Can't, love. Classified.' She put a finger on his nose, smiled sadly. 'It's over, Ray. You're yesterday's hero now. Take the loot and give us the flick.'

'I will,' he yawned, out of it.

'Won't miss not being around?'

'Am I getting a whiff of subtext here?'

'It's just that . . . if Ron found you another job . . .'

'What've you two cooked up? Did she send you into the shower on assignment?'

'Just a small short-term job. Grab you?'

'Women!' But he nodded.

'Good-oh.' She patted his bottom. 'I'll slip Ronnie the word. Next question: what's your opinion on psychic phenomena?'

His mind was drifting out of phase. He was in Antarctica again. The dazzling sunlight. The profound silence, peace. His first snore jerked him back.

'Ray? Are you receiving me? Psychic phenomena? True or false?'

'What? It's . . . bullshit.'

She held out her hand. 'How much?'

'A thousand bucks if you can prove it.'

She shook the hand. 'Done. And you *have* been.' She kissed him and left.

8

THETA

The conference room was cramped but equipped with everything from a rear projector to sound and lighting consoles. He'd been told that the audience, young people of all races, were mostly Department D.

As he walked down the aisle, a murmur started and heads turned. He found a front-row chair beside Pat who winked. As he bent to sit, the breast-cannon harness dug into him. He hadn't worn it on a base before.

The department heads sat on the podium like politicians granted equal time. Vanqua, elegant in expensive casual clothes. Rhonda, enduring a dress uncharacteristically clean. Was she on her best behaviour? He doubted it.

Vanqua moved to the lectern first. 'Welcome to Theta. First, I'll introduce our visitors. Commander Spencer many of you know . . .' He motioned the man to stand — which he did, smiling around the room. 'He's attached to the Strategy and Tactics Group of the Naval Special Warfare Center, Coronado, and is our liaison with the CVN. Remember we are guests on this vessel. Unwanted guests.'

Cain noted the 'N' which meant the carrier was nuclear-powered. He suspected the 'Theta of the Absurd' had been positioned as additional reactor shielding.

'Also observing this session are the heads of five intelligence services. And for them, we'll briefly outline what we do.'

He pressed a remote. The lights dimmed and a slide of the EXIT hierarchy appeared. Gone were the prior EXIT directors: Tigon and Wolf. Now it merely showed participating nations: UK — FRANCE — USA — GERMANY — JAPAN.

'EXIT,' Vanqua continued, 'stands for EXTRACTION INTERNATIONAL TASKFORCE. We're funded by a consortium of nations. But funding is all we get. No nation can help us directly or even admit to our existence because it's too politically dangerous.' A bleak stare at the audience. 'So we are not just orphans but outcasts.

'EXIT has two departments,' he continued, 'D and S — who we call dentists and surgeons. Surgeons kill difficult people. Dentists replace difficult people. Sometimes it's better to kill. Sometimes to replace. I am Vanqua. My colleague is Rhonda. Not our real names.' He pointed to the slide. 'I command Department S. And Rhonda commands Department D.'

He switched to a slide of the departmental structure. 'My department's main function is to kill. Its secondary function is to aid Department D operations and protect their agents. My field staff are taught practical and scientific skills and fatal techniques. Training is long, and assignments difficult because many targets are well protected.'

Cain listened without interest, feeling the slight roll of the ship. Pat's fingers brushed his thigh and he closed his hand over hers. They'd seamlessly come together as if they'd never been apart and after the long, dreamless sleep he felt good. His attention drifted back to Vanqua's drone. '...a last point. Field staff of both departments above Grade Two level have

Blue Cards — which signify international kill exemptions. These are unique to EXIT.' He made standing gestures to someone in the front row. 'Jan.'

Zuiden rose.

'And Mr Cain, would you stand?'

Pat withdrew her hand as he reluctantly got up. At least it eased the constriction of the harness.

'These men are senior operatives, one from each department. If they maim or kill they cannot be charged under international agreement, a great advantage for us but also a great responsibility. For EXIT and for them. However you'd be wise not to offend them. Thank you, gentlemen.'

They sat again.

'Next Rhonda will explain her department.' Vanqua resumed his chair.

Rhonda ponderously skipped to the podium. She enjoyed her nonsense. The audience relaxed, settled back, prepared to be beguiled.

'Now that Vanqua has explained things in his vague and equivocal way . . .' She paused to milk the mood. '. . . I'll confuse you more. The distinguished observers here today are obliged to lie for their countries. But at EXIT we don't *have* a country or even a political allegiance as our charter vetoes bias. We're funded to attack excess wherever it appears, independently of factions or national aims.' She smiled broadly at Vanqua.

He shuffled. It wasn't a tack he enjoyed.

She turned back to the half-darkened room. 'You may argue that all action is bias, and impartiality a fiction. EXIT ethics are labyrinthine but to summarise — our foes are avarice, folly, pride and the intoxication of bloodshed.'

Cain spotted the borrowing from Camus but doubted others did.

'Of course, for every problem, there's a solution that's simple, neat and wrong. And our assignments are as easy as picking up mercury with tweezers. *Hinc illae lacrimae.*' She dabbed an imaginary tear.

Energy was building in the room from cadets fighting not to laugh. He wondered how the guests were coping.

'We're called [he was thankful she abstained from 'yclept', one of her absurdities] dentists because a dentist removes decay and fills the hole with something that looks the same but is less harmful. That's what we do with people.'

A question from one of the guests. 'Why not just kill them?'

'I'm glad you asked that. What if a tyrant has henchmen to carry his policies on? He's a hydra — so killing him solves nothing. But replace him with a look-alike who diverts what he's doing and you can steer it in a less harmful way.'

She beamed over the lectern strip-light. 'To make it more complex, our targets can be innocents. There may be, for instance, a scientist with a world-threatening discovery that others in his team could duplicate. So killing him won't fix things. Better to replace him with someone who can subvert his research, cover tracks, lay red herrings. In short — although killing people is generally best practice, sometimes it's too dangerous. Hence, Department D.'

She gazed around the room. 'Perhaps another guest has a question.'

A rumbling voice. The man could have been a cantor. 'What happens to the originals? If you replace someone innocent ...'

'An excellent observation.' She was instantly serious. 'The removed person is held at a secure base *in perpetuum* or until the five nations sign a death warrant. Which often never happens.'

'So it becomes a holding pattern?'

The man was the head of Mossad, Cain decided.

'Worse. The original is tremendously dangerous because he's alive. It's a problem similar to the storing and disposal of nuclear waste. And no — we don't have a solution.'

A drawling voice from the rear of the room and south of Tennessee. 'Like have your fillings ever come loose?'

'Not since God dreamed the universe.'

A muffled female titter.

She completed the answer sensibly. 'We've never been sprung ... Yes sir? You over there.'

A mid-continental accent. 'You say dentist operative is trained different to surgeon, is it?'

'Very differently indeed. It's arts and farts. Or humanities and profanities.' A senior cadet choked trying not to laugh, which set the rest of the room off. The young ones loved it when Ronnie was in form. 'For instance, this very fine fellow ...' She motioned to Cain to stand again. He made gargoyle faces at her but got them back. Once again, he stood. '...is a dentist mark four. You've no idea what he's been through to get to this level.'

He itched to sit but she left him dangling.

'Each potential Department D cadet is adopted at birth. They're assessed for eight years and the selected children are streamed for one location, one assignment. The comparisons with *The Pirates of Penzance* and Fagin are obvious, ludicrous and I hope you'll ignore them. We've all found it painful enough to have no parents without adding ridicule to the mix.'

A murmur of assent through the hall.

'Inducted children are trained for a minimum of twenty years before attaining what we call Protectorships. Mr Cain has been taught in London and Karachi Universities for good reasons. But academic subjects are only a little of what he learned which included diplomacy, comparative religion, English lit and languages. He was also short-course cross-trained by Department S, as are all D cadets, in survival techniques and armed combat.'

Christ, Ron, he thought. Give it a rest.

'Half a lifetime preparing for a future assignment in a specific country. An assignment which may never come — but generally does. And like an astronaut or athlete, he can only do one thing. Why? If you spend your youth training to be a weightlifter, you can't then switch to the high jump. You're too old to retrain —

too specialised. Fortunately, Mr Cain's immensely difficult assignment was a success, as you'll hear when he gives his presentation. Would you care to add anything, Ray?'

He glowered at her mischievous smile. 'If I'd known this was all-singing, all-dancing I would have worn taps.' The ripple of laughter that followed was tinged with admiration. He sat down thankfully. Lord, he thought, I'm some kind of hero here.

The introduction was followed by Pat's astonishing presentation. She had the videos, the before and afters, the secret films of the targets. Each time he'd seen her segment, it was better and more effective. It went into plastic surgery of the face, the body. The radical implants. Hair, diet, iris, fingerprint and dental difficulties. Prime subjects, selection, attitude. Physical and mental re-education. Voice production and acting. The memory factor. Specialists and staffing. Simulation testing. Lead time. And, finally, the grim matter of end-point relief.

At the finish, the stunned audience filed from the room as if retreating from an open coffin.

On tables in the foyer outside were coffee and canapes. Cain waited his turn to get coffee, reading the crowd. Two impressive-looking men he'd identified as observers stood together shaking their heads, barely able to credit what they'd seen.

Pat came over. 'How'd I go?'

'You know damn well.'

Spencer appeared briefly in front of her, jaw flapping for words. 'Oh my gosh,' he finally got out. 'You people. I've never ...'

She said brightly, 'Thorough, aren't we?'

'And I thought naval aviation was tough!' He pumped her hand, drifted away.

She turned to Cain. 'You got quite an intro.'

'Bigger razz than the *Thieving Magpie* overture.'

Rhonda barged up to the table, edging them aside like a runaway refrigerator, 'Having fun?'

'Did you have to do the potted bio?'

She sang, 'And noble lords will scrape and bow, and double them in two. And open their eyes in blank surprise at whatever she likes to do.'

'I saw nothing in the job description about hosannas for superannuated icons.'

'If you could trust job descriptions, there wouldn't be chaos theory.'

A madonna-faced woman entered the room. She had a supermodel's figure. He'd noticed her when she'd stayed behind to cue up the next videos. Rhonda called to her, 'All set up?'

She came over. 'I think so.' Her cutaway top displayed the high lift of her breasts.

'Karen Hunt. Meet John Cain — our great Grade Four.'

'Hello,' Cain said, longing to look at the cleft of exposed smooth skin. With effort he kept his eyes on her face. Smooth brow, beautiful jawline. She made Pat look like her mother.

Rhonda said, 'Karen's one of my best Grade Ones. She's handling The Square.'

He'd heard of it — a pervasive cult already a concern to several governments. 'Must be a blast.'

'She'll be telling you about it next session.'

'Uh-huh.'

'Ron's told me a lot about you,' the woman said. Her voice sounded like a recorded message. He wondered what kind of training had produced her inner deadness. Pat watched his reactions but needn't have worried. Hunt was as sexually approachable as a waxwork.

A glass was tapped and Vanqua, in the centre of the room, raised his hand. 'Now cadets have a work session and observers have one hour free before the next presentation.'

Rhonda turned to Cain, coldly serious again. 'Let's talk.'

9

DEBRIEF

When they were back in her den she said to him, 'You're officially dead. Feel good?'

'Marvellous.'

'And poor Rehana's really dead.' She eased her bulk into a chair. 'A terrible death.'

'And pointless.'

She passed a hand above her head. '*Que?*'

'We get our man installed, then Pak One falls out of the sky.' He sat opposite her, wondering why she didn't see it. 'Was it Beg? He was the only top general not on the plane. The other fifteen died, plus the US Defence Attache. Beg took the chopper, flew over the wreckage. What's your take on it?'

'Yes, tricky one that.' She got up, searching for something. 'There were chemical traces in the cockpit. Could have been poison gas. I'd say the likely lads are Spetsnaz.'

'Moscow knows?'

'That we substituted Zia? No. We think they did it to pay him back for funnelling arms to Afghanistan. Can't blame them. Even Washington was fed up with Zia back in '86. I

— 47 —

know you were fretting because I wouldn't let you switch him sooner. But we had to wait until we were sure about the Russian withdrawal. And now I've got *nicotine* withdrawal. Where the hell are my fags?'

'But he sold off half the arms he got.' His work with Zia and the man's puppet government still rankled. 'That was why he blew up the Ojheri dump before the audit. A few more Stinger missiles he didn't have to account for, tricky bastard. We could have done him six months earlier and got the other half across the border.'

'The Pentagon factored that in — just gave him twice as much.' She dropped from sight to search under the desk.

'Thirty-two years of training. Four and a half more in the field. Then the whole thing up the spout. And you say it's a success?'

'A brilliant success.' Her head popped up. 'You made the switch right on time. Your duplicate dismissed the regime, dissolved the assemblies, announced elections ...'

'And died in a crash ten weeks later with the top brass of the army. Come on, Ron.'

'Dear heart, our last state's still more blessed than the first.' But he still didn't believe her.

'Oh, happy the blossom that blooms on the lea ...' She launched into Sullivan's most joyous confection, the finale of *Ruddigore*, dancing about the room, still looking for fags but lifting piles of folders in time with the refrain. It was a curious sight — this woman who shaped the progress of nations, leaping around like an impala.

She stopped moving and stared at him. 'I'm not just being nice. Honestly. A tremendously difficult switch. And a wonderful result. The first female prime minister of Pakistan.'

'Her government's on the take already. The rip-off mindset in that country's ...'

'But equilibrium's restored.' She laughed. 'Poor wandering one. You still don't believe me, do you? We're *thrilled* with how it's gone.'

'Long as you're happy,' he shrugged. She was the strategist. Despite dregs of doubt, he felt pleased and suspected the alcohol was making him benign. 'The link with the CIA in Islamabad helped. And he was the spitting image, right down to the tombstone teeth.'

She was hunting again. 'Ah! Success has crowned my efforts.' She pounced on a half-crushed pack and came back to her chair. 'Now. A serious question.' She lit the fag and sucked, squinting with satisfaction. 'The feudal heiress from 70 Clifton ... equipped with her own generators, water tanks, security guards and tutored by daddy to rule ... You see, I *do* read your reports. They say she's arrogant and cold.'

'She's a Gemini.'

'Spare me the superstition. Will she stick?'

'If a despot put you under house arrest, smashed around your mother, killed your father, would you face the world with an enchanting demeanour?'

'Daddy Bhutto was no paragon.'

'But she cared for him, needs to vindicate him. She's no pushover either.'

'Attractive, too. Mind you, she's still controlling the media. And there's the chain-smoking, playboy-husband factor. Will she survive?'

He shrugged. 'Why ask me?'

'Don't fudge. What was that Hegel thing? "History teaches us that man learns nothing from history"? You've spent years in the country. Stop being disgustingly coy.' She sucked the fag, eyes narrowed, waiting.

'Okay. You've got a newly married woman with a baby. She's in charge of a broke, illiterate, bazaar-culture theocracy where nothing works, nothing's on time. More guns than sewers, *zamindars*, poverty ... I give her three years.' He shook his head. 'If our man had survived, at least we'd have control.'

'What I've been labouring to explain, dear heart ...' she gulped the last of her scotch, '... is he survived long enough to alter the spin. And the fetching Benazir will do very nicely for now.'

'Long as you're happy.' He sipped his scotch, feeling good.

'So Zia's fixed. But our internal problem isn't. In the next few hours, I may do some inconsistent things. So be warned.'

'Uh-huh.'

'And remember what I told you. Watch your step.'

10

BLOW-UP

Hunt, the drop-dead gorgeous woman with the supermodel body, managed her segment well. She began by showing a video of Gustave Raul, guru of millions and charismatic phoney who, as far as Cain could see, packaged new-age cant as entertainment.

'What this cult trades on,' she told them, 'is a mixture of philosophies arranged in a manipulative way. It takes people's money and turns them into sociopaths. This gives Raul enormous power. He's ruthless but clever. He's now infiltrating bureaucracies and political parties. I think he regards God as his favourite fictional character.' She concluded the survey of her assignment with a tape showing devotees clustered around the master who sat on a kind of throne. Hunt herself sat at his feet, gazing at him intently and oozing carnality, in stark contrast to her attitude on the platform.

'What I've managed to do,' she explained, 'is become his most trusted follower. And yes, I sleep with him, which proved the easy way in.' She cupped her hands beneath her breasts. 'I was trained to regard these as weapons. In my case, they have been. Now many of his manipulations are filtered through me. It's difficult, though. You have to go along with him utterly or he'll pick you. That means a big part of me has to believe his guff. Meanwhile my team's getting things ready to replace him. I can't be specific but ask general questions if you like.'

Several cadets did.

Then unexpectedly Zuiden spoke up. 'You say your primary offensive installation is your tits. So why are you such a prissy bitch with us?'

Cain looked around at him, amazed. Even coming from a crass shit like Zuiden, the comment was out of line. The man was a Grade Three. He knew better than that.

A stunned silence in the room. Zuiden pugnaciously stared at Hunt.

Cain glanced at Vanqua expecting the Dane to pull him into line but the surgeon head sat impassively.

A tic of shock on Hunt's face. Her answer was slow, deliberate. 'When I started here, some people told me that surgeons were degraded thugs and emotionless assassins. I've tried to be more open-minded. Now I wonder why I bothered.'

'Funny,' Zuiden sniggered, 'surgeons see dentists as stuck-up pricks and perverts.' It was a direct hit at Rhonda.

Vanqua was up. 'No name-calling here. Session finished.'

11

BULLET ENTRÉE

Lunch was a war zone. Tables for four with place cards. And at Cain's table, facing each other — Zuiden and Hunt. It could have been avoided. But nothing was done. Cain was opposite Spencer. That, at least, was sane.

Hunt was ice, said nothing. Cain was thankful. Because, if she started, he'd have to defend her against Zuiden. And fronting a senior surgeon was as dangerous as it got.

No one spoke. Spencer was obviously embarrassed but Zuiden seemed to be enjoying himself and attacked his oysters kilpatrick with gusto. He paused between mouthfuls to finally say to Spencer, 'Good grub.' Then he turned to Hunt with the deliberation of a gun turret, stared down her front and said pointedly, 'You know, all I care about is my stomach — and the little thing that hangs on the end of it.'

Cain said, 'Cut it out.'

'Jesus, Cain.' Zuiden's deprecating look. 'Is your hand still up your arse?'

He wasn't ready for the stab of derision and glanced around at Rhonda. She was at the head table, with Vanqua. Why hadn't she handled this?

The almost imperceptible shake of her head warned him to do nothing.

'So tonight,' Spencer said to keep the peace, 'we're going up to vultures row to see the cats on the roof.'

'Cats?' Cain asked.

'Tomcats. F–14s. They're doing night launch and recovery cycles. The trouble is signing you out of this vault because it takes so long. So a few of us go tonight. Tomorrow, we'll take the rest.'

'Sounds good.' He was grateful to the man for heading it off, tried to keep the conversation going. 'The pilots must be hotshots.'

'According to our surveys, they go through several stages. They're hard-chargers up to 250 hours. Around 1200, they get careless. If they don't goon it up and survive to 5000, they get too confident and relax again. Everything to do with fighters is pushing the envelope anyway.'

Zuiden stared at Hunt's cleavage and said to her with a leer, 'They certainly lift and separate. Like to help me lose some zinc?'

She stood bolt upright, slapped Zuiden hard across the face and walked out.

The conversation in the room had stopped. Everyone was watching the scene. Zuiden, now half out of his chair, seemed about to follow and drop her.

'You bloody disgrace. Sit down.' Cain fingered the release off the cannon. If he had to spread the table with the surgeon's guts, he'd do it.

Zuiden looked at him levelly, deciding whether this was it. 'Careful, Cain. Next time it won't just be your toes.'

Cain fought rage, loathing the bastard, choking on what they'd drilled into him. EMOTION IS A FORCE, NOT AN ARGUMENT. No one in the room moved, aghast at the sight of two men who could kill anyone with impunity confronting each other like pit bulls. Finally, Zuiden, one cheek reddening, sat down.

Cain glanced at the head table. Both department heads were immobile. Then Vanqua, with measured action, passed Rhonda a bread roll. The tension in the room dropped one notch and conversation started again.

A waiting steward, shaking with terror, slid a main course under Zuiden's nose. The surgeon regarded it unseeingly as if debating whether to attack.

Spencer cleared his throat. 'You know, on the *Midway* it got so ugly, we had to separate whites from blacks. No-go areas. Perhaps it might work for EXIT departments.'

Zuiden thrust his face round to him. 'What if I separate your head from your neck?'

'So,' Cain said to Spencer, 'I hear you're doing a preamble before my thing.'

Spencer looked at him nervously, sensing the volcano beside him. 'Yes, Rhonda asked me to give a strategic summary before your talk.'

'Well, thank you for that.'

'Well, thank you for that,' Zuiden mimicked. 'You intellectual git. I bet you're pissing your pants.'

Cain stared at the surgeon again. Something was wrong. Zuiden was too well trained for this. The resentments had always been there but they'd suffered each other for years. What had got into the bastard? He murmured, 'Jan. Please don't do this.'

The shock of hearing his first name must have gone deep. Zuiden glanced up as if caught out, then sullenly began to eat his food.

12

ATTACK IN BLACK

Presentations continued through the afternoon and even during dinner when the rumbling-voiced head of Mossad gave a summary on: Small Arms Developments, Unpleasant to Vile. '...lasers as small as rifles that cause irreversible blindness up to a distance of 3 kilometres. And a new white phosphorus grenade that ...'

The details didn't complement dessert.

After the meal, senior staff chaired discussion groups. Cain wanted to work on his speech but was obliged to head a forum of eight awed cadets — including the black woman he'd met in the shower.

When the session finished, she smiled up at him. 'Fantastic to talk to someone who's done it all.'

'Glad it helped.'

'So how was Pat? Good tunes on old fiddles?'

He smiled. 'We go back a long way.'

'Whatever rings your bell.' A flash of coal-dark eyes made it clear. She was available if he wanted her.

Pat's group was breaking up. She raised her eyebrows as he passed.

He shook his head. 'Got to work on the speech.'

She made a face.

'Only time to do it.'

'Well, tomorrow night, you're booked.'

In the glow from his bunk-head light, he scrawled bullet points to use as prompts. After an hour, still unhappy with it, he switched off the light and slept.

Something woke him. The cabin was black except for the crack of light beneath the door. The crack, a slight wedge shape, slowly became a line.

Someone had shut the door.

Someone now in the room.

Only Pat knew his door code and she wasn't coming tonight.

He looked at the corner of the ceiling, searching with peripheral vision for movement. The breast-gun was in a drawer as the straps made it uncomfortable to sleep in. So for years he'd slept with a super-reliable SIG-Sauer automatic by his thigh.

He aimed through the bedclothes to the left of the door. Knife? Gun? Torch beam? In the first 30 seconds you were vulnerable — had to react first.

Nothing came. Whoever it was didn't have night goggles or would have attacked. That gave him the advantage because the other's eyes had to adjust. The intruder also couldn't use his ears, because the ship's noise drowned small sounds.

Cain couldn't see movement so grunted a strategic snore then sat up, thankful for dark skin and blue sheets. He moved to the foot of the bunk, cautiously slid off. Unrelieved blackness. No pale oval of face. Had whoever it was blacked up?

Then he saw — thought he saw — the blackness of the bed intensify. Something lightly brushed his motionless leg.

In an instant he'd fired, repositioned at the crouch.

He heard a gasp.

He was squatting by the door now — hand forward at the high diagonal, gun facing forward from the waist in the touch-and-fire position. Get it wrong and you lost fingers. He'd give it 30 seconds and ...

Another gasp. Christ. It sounded like a woman.

Pat?

Jesus. No!

Jesus bleeding Christ!

He stood up. He'd have to risk the light.

He threw the switch, ducked, aiming at the bed.

He needn't have bothered.

Blood had pooled on the floor and she was almost dead. She'd been shot in the back then had slid off the bed face down. He turned her over, exposing the mess at the front. Through her open mouth bubbled blood. She hadn't needed to blacken her face.

She stared at him wide-eyed.

He said, 'You bloody fool.'

13

LAST HURRAH

Rhonda in a nightdress seemed more physical than Rhonda naked. Her huge boobs hung as if cling-wrapped and from beneath the uneven hem her massive calves ended in feet splayed like tree roots. She scratched her rump, surveying the body on the floor. 'We were grooming her for Nigeria. She was one of our best code-breakers. The door keypad wouldn't stop her. She worked out the sequence.'

He looked at the black woman's gaping face. 'Friend or foe?'

Rhonda shrugged. 'There's no weapon. From what you've said, I'd say it was your fatal charm. She wanted your body and thought you were condition blue. They don't get much fun, after all. She read this as a muck-up time.'

He banged his fist on the bulkhead. 'Shit.'

'I put you on alert. It's just unfortunate.'

'Now I have to face the others and play hero.'

'I'll tell them she's ill — been transferred to the ship's hospital. Zuiden can clean this tomorrow when they're all in the lecture room.'

'Shit, what a stuff-up.'

'You don't mind sleeping with a corpse in the room?'

'It's not that. I feel sorry for her, damn it.'

'Fortunes of war, love. Sweet dreams.'

Spencer prefaced Cain's presentation using rear-projected maps, beginning with a view of the Indian Ocean.

'Most of the Arabian Peninsula's oil bases and population are littoral — within 100 miles of the coast. Before Afghanistan, the Soviets were 700 miles from the Gulf. Now, they're 235. A direct Soviet move on Iran and things get sticky. But right now it's manipulate, not march.'

Cain was grateful for the introduction although it had little to do with what he intended to say. He could still see the dead woman, staring at him from the floor that morning as he'd dressed. He tried to tune the picture out, concerned about yesterday's fracas at lunch and the impression it had given the cadets.

He glanced at Rhonda. Her sober face revealed how important it was to pull things together.

'The North Arabian Sea,' Spencer continued, 'is within range of Soviet aircraft, so our carriers are deployed there to cover any air-strike on the Gulf. Both fleets are in the Indian Ocean projecting forward presence and forward pressure. It's political, vastly expensive and supply lines are long.'

Cain glanced around the room but couldn't see Zuiden. Had Vanqua grounded him or was he cleaning?

Spencer was winding up. 'There's a CentCom stockpile at Oman and they allow recce flights to operate from Masirah. But Diego Garcia's the nearest US base. It can handle carriers but it's a three-and-a-half-day steam from the Gulf. That's the strategic outline. Now let's hear it from the coalface.' He stepped down and Cain mounted the podium.

He surveyed the expectant audience. He had to go for the gut.

'I've just finished my assignment so this is off the cuff. For most of you here, I'm your future. And Rhonda makes that sound impressive. But she's also told you I'm through.'

He looked at the worried faces, the young ones in his 'family'. He took them through his years of training and told them he'd worked for an aim — had suffered the punishing schedule because he believed EXIT's credo to be true.

He moved on to his time in the field, the complexity and detail needed to convince scores of people that an impostor was the person they knew. The need to act a part and probe into the target's life. The need to replace friends with facsimiles, to pay off others. He then gave specifics about the replacement of Zia ul-Haq, the stress, the dangers. The cadets sat enthralled.

He finished with an appeal. A rock was needed to stand against the waves of national selfishness. He believed in EXIT and its credo because he believed in humanity and the attempt to be impartial. As he concluded, several cadets were close to tears. Allah be praised, he'd done it, got the thing back on track. He felt emotional himself. He turned to Rhonda, shrugged. 'Enough?'

She stood up, 'Thank you, Ray,' came forward and hugged him.

The cadets were up. A storm of fervent clapping.

She smiled and gestured for quiet. 'Well, we intended to have questions but we're now over time, so you can talk to him individually later.'

Although the cadets were sitting again, a score of hands waved in the air.

'All right. Three questions?' She looked at him.

He nodded and pointed to an intense-looking Chinese girl. 'Yes?'

'You're at the top. A Grade Four. Now you have to leave. Isn't that an enormous waste of training?'

'It's not restricted to us. It's a typical situation in the services. Consider the captain of this ship. He may have trained all his life for the job and he might hold it … how long, Commander?' He glanced at the sailor.

Spencer piped up. 'Two years.'

He turned back to the girl. 'And remember, when you're my age, you won't have the physical drive you feel now.'

'But won't you miss this?'

He laughed. 'I've slaved nonstop for thirty years. Constant stress. You burn out. Yes … ?'

A Malaysian-looking youth with a punk haircut. 'The thought of killing people still grosses me out. How do you cope when you actually have to do it?'

'Yes.' He paused, last night raw in his gut. 'I've been taught how to kill but it still sickens me. You could say I've absorbed the techniques but not the attitude. The short answer is that combat readiness requires compassion fatigue. But it's a long conversation with many aspects. I'll be glad to discuss it with you privately. Yes … ?'

A thoughtful-looking cadet with a beard. 'One hears rumours that several of our projects aren't quite as impartial as you paint them. There have been instances that don't stack up lately. Has Tigon's vision been subverted?'

A murmur went around the room. Vanqua was standing up quickly.

'Do you have any comment?' the cadet persisted. 'For instance, why are we on a participating vessel?'

Cain locked eyes with him, 'I'm trying to find out.'

His reply wasn't the evasion they expected but a deliberate affirmation. The cadets looked at each other.

'Already too many questions,' Vanqua cut in. 'Enough.'

Zuiden appeared at lunch. After the meal he brushed by Cain and drawled almost admiringly, 'You're some messy sleeper.'

14

CATS BENEATH THE MOON

Dinner was early that evening to accommodate the first
tour of the ship. Spencer handed half of them security
tags and told them to sign out. As Cain joined the line of
cadets he saw the sandy hair of Zuiden ahead.

Then Hunt joined the line in a jumpsuit that fitted her
disturbingly. Were they mad?

He dropped back two places to talk to her. 'Why not
give it a miss till tomorrow?' He flicked his eyes toward
Zuiden.

'I can't. Vanqua insists I go tonight. Something about
things looking right.'

'Rhonda went along with that?'

She nodded.

'Then you'd better stay close to me.'

'She said I had to.'

Great, he thought. Now I'm nurse.

First stop was a tour around the hangar bay conducted by
a black chief petty officer. 'We've got two acres in here but as
you see we don't waste space. Ship's so big no one ever sees

all of it and even if you had your own brother on board, you'd be lucky to run across him in a year.'

Beyond the closely parked, chained aircraft was a vast oval in the hull. A rating stood in the middle of it, outlined against moonlit wave-crests, arms spread wide and down, hands pointing to the deck. A klaxon sounded twice then kept on sounding as a plane with ugly splayed landing gear descended on a huge exterior platform.

'Deck-edge elevator, one of four,' the petty officer yelled. 'Can strike down aircraft in 30 seconds. He pointed out features of the bay. 'Refuelling outlets over there. Hangar control. Bomb-proof doors. Conflag station up near the overhead. Fire control's a big deal here, when you consider all the go-juice and ordinance . . .'

Cain stared at drop tanks cradled in racks far above. He'd noticed that the cadets glanced at him admiringly and found it disconcerting. Hunt stayed by him. Fortunately Zuiden was still up front.

'This is a Tomcat . . .'

The group stopped to examine the fighter which was being maintained by blue-shirted mechanics on a work stand. As questions started Cain walked around the dirty-looking plane, reading instructions written on it. COOLANT ELECTRICAL DISCONNECT. ADAPTOR INSTL. UMBILICAL ACTUATION HOOK. COMMAND SIGNAL DECODER. There were vanes behind the engine exhausts — one set open, one closed.

'What are these for?' he asked.

'Turkey feathers,' the man said. 'New GE engines. You take off closed down. No afterburner. Melt the blast shield. Just military thrust.'

He didn't understand or much care. He touched Hunt's arm and fell back behind a fork-lift to talk to her unheard. 'What exactly did Rhonda say to you?'

'We can't talk here.' She walked ahead.

'This is a Hornet,' their escort explained. 'A strike fighter we convert to attack role by adding weapon racks. Heavy on juice. Always looking for plugs ...'

Cain trailed the group, keeping an eye on Zuiden, who was asking a question about repairs. Their guide was keen to inform him. 'We keep the down birds back this end. Got aircraft shops, spare parts stowage. Engine maintenance astern. Planes are cranky, like babies. When we get to the fantail, you'll see the ...'

Spencer glanced up from his watch. 'Sorry, chief. Pushed for time. Got to get on the roof for the launch. Can we muster them on an elevator?'

They were herded out onto the platform that jutted from the hull. Cain stared at the water creaming below, then up at the great bulk of the ship. Canisters for inflatable life rafts festooned its sides like grapes on a vine. Sponsons, catwalks, splayed safety nets jutting angles and protrusions, made it a citadel overhanging the sea.

The klaxon sounded. They rode up and joined the flat-top. Posts holding a safety cable slid smoothly into the deck. He walked over the cable which fitted into a groove.

'We'll take a short cut through the bomb farm.' Spencer led them behind the island. 'Some climbing ahead. In here.'

'Isn't there a lift?' Zuiden asked.

'Sure, but so small you've got to be married to ride in it.'

'Do we get to see Pri-Fly?'

'They're a bit busy right now.'

They had to climb six levels before they reached the steel walkway high above the flight deck. By then, the vanished sun was a glow on the horizon. Looking down at the now yellow-lighted deck, Cain was surprised to see planes stacked with tails projecting over the sea. He could feel the huge vessel listing to starboard and looked aft to a curving wake. Behind them and to the side, he saw the running lights of a ship and another light far astern.

Spencer said, 'She's coming into the wind. It's no fun being the plane-guard destroyer captain — watching a floating airport charging in every direction. Carriers are notorious for unannounced turns and speed changes.'

'So why don't they communicate?'

'Because the carrier's got this permanent can of worms. And the junior grade lieutenant on the greyhound is too intimidated — too scared to pick up his primary tactical circuit handset and front the admiral. Meanwhile the carrier's fighting the crosswind. For instance, it's okay for launching one plane but out of limits for another in the pattern. So the PIM's out the window because she's got to chase the wind for the birds.'

'Uh-huh.' It was double-Dutch to him. He looked at the organised bedlam below. Hurrying figures carrying flashlights, waving light wands. Power cables festooning the deck, yellow plane-handling equipment being moved into position. A chopper took off further aft. 'What's the significance of the jacket colours?'

'The red guys with the carts are ordies — ordnance.' Spencer pointed down. 'Blue guys are plane handlers, tractor drivers and so on. Purple are "grapes" — fuel guys. Green's catapult and arresting gear crews. Yellow for officers handling the show.'

'And this thing's powered by a reactor?'

'Eight — two for each shaft. Driving thirty-two heat-exchangers. Welcome to the world of the supercarrier — grandest expression of the American Empire.

A PA system roared, 'Stand clear of intakes ... check positioning of huffers ... check again for FOD. Aaaaand ... start 'em up.'

Cain watched, feeling the vibration of the ship. Dim red glows from the cockpits. Plane captains on the deck, waving their blue lights. The whine of a turbine from the deck. Then others, as starter-carts came to life. The racket of the first aircraft engine starting. He took out his earplugs, rolled them into grubs, inserted them.

'Turkeys are cooking.' Spencer inserted his own plugs as

more engines spooled up. The ground crews were checking control surfaces and hydraulic pressures.

Cain glanced along the line of faces gazing down. He poked Spencer, yelled, 'Where's Hunt?'

Spencer got it, more by lip-reading than sound, looked around. Cain walked back along the steel balcony. No Hunt. And no Zuiden. Spencer turned back, shrugged, then went forward through a door at the end of the walkway.

Cain followed him in. The noise level dropped. It was a dimly lit, glassed-in eagles' nest that protruded from the island. The air boss sat on a raised chair in front of intercoms and consoles, controlling the launch.

Spencer asked his assistant, 'Did a big fair-haired man and a woman come in here?'

'No, sir.'

The commander's face tightened. He looked across at Cain. 'Must have gone back down the way we came up.'

Cain said, 'I'm on it.'

He ran back on the walkway to the hatch and half-slid down the ladders, surprising other sailors coming up.

'See a fair-haired guy and a woman come down here?'

'Check.' One rating pointed down. 'Guy was carrying her. Said she'd fainted.'

Zuiden had dropped her on the noisy island walkway without the others even seeing it. Accurate pressure on the carotid sinus was all it took. Cain, using the rails, half-slid down more ladders. If Zuiden was carrying her he wouldn't have got far.

He was on the level below the flight deck before he saw them — at the far end of a passageway running athwart the ship. Beyond hurrying sailors and air-crew, he glimpsed the flash of Zuiden's back with the woman like a sack over his shoulder. He ran after them, past cabins and ready rooms, pushing past the crew.

At the end, the passage split and a ladder rose through a trunk. It was a three-way choice. He took the ladder.

A light trap brought him out into the wind and darkness near the waist of the vessel on the catwalk that ran around the flight deck. He turned away from the sea which foamed 60 feet below the overhang — faced the island across the deck which was level with his chest. It was alive with light-wands and launching planes.

Where the hell were they? Up here? He dodged past reels of hoses, heading forward.

On the deck, a Tomcat — wings spread, flaps set, exhaust gases shimmering — was moving toward the catapult shuttle. As it paused, inching forward, a blast shield rose from the deck behind it.

A yellow-jacketed officer held his wands crossed above his head while red jackets did something to the missiles on the pylons beneath its wings. Last-minute checks. The plane's control surfaces cycled. Cain moved further along the catwalk, trying to ignore the drama on his right.

He saw a sponson below him, beside a column holding what looked like a signalling lamp or searchlight. The small outcrop looked deserted.

Zuiden knew his stuff, had cut loose during the main event. Hunt might not be unconscious, he realised. Perhaps he'd killed her — come here to drop her overboard. No, he couldn't be up here. There were green-clad sailors further forward — a launch or recovery crew — and Zuiden wouldn't have gone near them. The bastard wasn't on the catwalk and now could be anywhere in the ship.

Another jet was waiting behind the shield while the first one ran up, the power of its engines depressing the nose wheel strut. The roar was visceral.

White flame thundered from the Tomcat's tailpipes. He covered his ears as the sound became unbearable. The plane's port and starboard lights came on and the white light on the tail. The crouching catapult officer swung his yellow wand in an arc to the deck, then brought it up to the horizontal like a lunging fencer. A green light winked out near a control bubble further forward. As steam slammed against the catapult pistons the aircraft rocketed down the rail, twin furnaces of flaming orange and, in three seconds, was flung off the deck.

Cain had instinctively ducked, found himself facing tie-down chains hooked from a rail and a red fire extinguisher labelled CARBON DIOXIDE. He rose, padded back through drifting steam, wondering how much hearing he'd lost.

As he passed the jutting sponson, he thought he saw movement. Was someone there?

He craned over to see more, could just make out a shape that looked like a boot.

Then a sailor appeared on the sponson — a burly black man who crouched and pulled at something. A flash of teeth but his voice was drowned by the racket from the deck. He seemed to be dragging on a second man's legs — a man who lay prone on the grid. As the man was pulled back, he twisted. A man with fair hair, a pale stalk protruding from his pants.

Zuiden — with his dick out.

Cain vaulted over the catwalk rail and dropped to the platform below, landing beside the sailor a second too late. Zuiden, still down, had hooked one leg behind the man's foot and smashed the other into his knee. As the sailor toppled, yowling as his leg collapsed, Zuiden chopped his throat.

Then Zuiden saw Cain and moved inboard as far as he could, aware that Cain's breast-cannon wasn't accurate. He had his pistol out and with his other hand was trying to zip his pants.

Beside him on the grid — the blur of Hunt's splayed body, her top off and her clothes around her knees. The hatch into the hull was open. Zuiden would have closed it but couldn't lock it. And the sailor had stumbled on the scene.

Cain registered it all in a blink. He felt welded to the deck, knew there was nothing he could do. If he moved his hand to the pressor switch, Zuiden would shoot and he'd be dead before the explosive slug went wide.

A launching F–14 shook them with a speech-defying roar. Hunt was stirring, coming around.

He looked at the rock-steady gun. He'd feel the jolt before he saw the barrel flame.

An endless second.

Zuiden's savage grin. He edged toward the hatch — was gone.

15

FALLOUT

Cain went to the salt-sticky rail and looked at the creaming sea far below. It had been close. The sweat on his face was clammy with it. He turned back, stepped over the dead seaman and squatted beside Hunt.

She peered at his face then, felt wind on her flesh, looked down. She saw the sailor's body, stared up at him again, uncomprehending — her full, perfect breasts transformed by moonlight to marble.

He yelled, 'Zuiden.'

She felt between her legs, made a poor attempt to cover herself.

He said, 'Zuiden knocked you out and raped you.'

'That sailor's ...?'

'Dead. Zuiden killed him.'

She breathed heavily, eyes blank.

He got her dressed and helped her through the hatch away from the noise. She leaned against the side of the alleyway as if she might collapse.

*　　*　　*

By the time they were cleared through into EXIT, Hunt was herself again, which Cain didn't consider an improvement. She said, 'I'll handle it from here.'

She left a message in reception for Rhonda then led him along a corridor and keyed a code into the doorpad.

The cabin was larger than his and featured a wider bunk. Its personal compost revealed immediately whose it was. On one wall was a poster in a frame.

The Suffolk Savoyards present
HMS PINAFORE
or
The Lass that Loved a Sailor

Cut-in photographs of cast members included an attractive, dark-haired woman about twenty.

He said, 'You and Ron are an item?'

'Objections?'

'No.'

She sat on the bunk as the door-control clicked and the catch disengaged. Rhonda was in the room, leaning back against the closing door, her good-natured face now grave. She sat beside her lover, petted her, while Hunt told her what she knew.

Cain turned to a railed shelf holding bottles and poured himself a scotch. Above the shelf was a picture of an urchin peeing in a pond. A frog was leaping from the pond in alarm. The caption read: NEVER DRINK WATER.

When he turned back, Hunt was staring at the floor. Rhonda looked at him, livid. 'Well?'

He told his version, ending, 'I cocked up.'

'Wonderful.'

'And the flag bridge won't like him killing one of the crew.'

'Vanqua's problem.'

'I should have topped the bugger at lunch. It was a set-up. Like lunch was a set-up.'

She caressed Hunt's thigh but didn't respond.

'Well, wasn't it?' he insisted.

'Not mine.' She stared at the woman's perfect leg. Hunt sat immobile.

He swigged his drink, jaundiced by both of them. 'I'd say Vanqua put him up to it. The insult in the conference. Then lunch. Then this. Because Zuiden's a deadshit but he's not mad.'

'You need a reality check,' Hunt said.

Cain said, 'Don't flatter yourself. The man's a Grade Three. I chipped him at lunch and he looked guilty. I'd say Vanqua told him to bait you, then poke you.'

'And to kill a sailor?'

'No. He swatted a fly.'

Her smooth brow dimpled to a frown. 'So why would Vanqua put him up to it?'

'To get at Ron.' He stared at his department head. 'Well?'

Rhonda's furious glance. She was back on the job. 'You and Zuiden hate each other — hate each other so much you need each other. So your judgement might be ...'

'Come off it.'

'He doesn't understand you. You don't understand him. And it bothers you both. Because you secretly admire each other. We used to call you Cain and Disable.'

'Spare me the arabesques. What's your point?'

She moved a protective hand to the younger woman's thigh. As far as Cain could see the loving was one-way. 'You're full of theories without substantiation. What if he just wanted to sink the salami?'

'I've given my opinion. The deadshit's porked your girl ... killed a sailor on this ship. Now what do I do about it?'

She stroked Hunt's hair, thinking. 'Be in Room C3 in half an hour. The meeting with Vanqua. Don't volunteer any information unless I prompt you. Clear?'

'Pellucid. But factor this in. The thing in Chartres. Rehana had drawn a "Z" on the sheet in her blood. I thought it might have meant Zia. It could have meant Zuiden — could have meant he'd sabotaged the operation. What if he did the job on Rehana before I got there?'

'Ray, I know you want to help. But we're all upset just now. The best thing you can do is leave the thinking to me and just — stay out of it. That's an order.'

'Shit.' He upended his drink and left.

He walked through the sinews of the boat, cursing her and loving her too. Her attempt to be kind had made him feel old and useless.

Pat's comment echoed in his head. 'It's over, Ray. You're yesterday's hero now.'

Room C3 was barely large enough for the small bolted-down table and six chairs. Vanqua sat at the table's end alone, nodded as Cain came in. 'The exceptional Mr Cain. Please sit.'

Cain sat on a chair at the side, determined to say nothing as instructed.

'So.' His sad face and speculative stare. 'I still have no word of Murchison. What do you know?'

Murchison? What was this? They were back to Chartres discussing Murchison? 'No idea. He wasn't there when it happened. It was a cleaning job and fast ship-out. No time for head checks.'

'Mm.'

Rhonda entered, sat opposite Vanqua, turned to Cain. 'Tell him what happened.'

Vanqua listened to his account, said, 'Yes, yes. I've been informed.'

'And ...?' Rhonda snapped.

'I thought this meeting was a brief on Murchison.'

'Fuck Murchison.'

Their conflict made the air vibrate.

Vanqua gazed at the lagged pipes above and stroked the muscles of his neck. Cain knew five ways to kill him by attacking that neck. The body was so vulnerable when you knew. 'Jan tells me Mr Cain has been indulging his sexual tastes.'

Cain lurched forward. 'What?'

Rhonda put a hand on his arm.

'I suppose you're aware what training her cost us? Millions.'

'Let's get back to the exploits of Zuiden,' Rhonda said.

Vanqua made inconsequential sounds and waved his hands. 'He's been under great pressure, which has now been removed and ... his natural ... exuberance has emerged.'

'Exuberance? What are you? A fucking epistemological realist? Cut the crap.'

'We're talking about a Grade Three.' The surgeon pursed his lips. 'He's purpose-designed — just like Cain. Just as Cain is extraordinary, so is Jan. But in a different way — a destroyer.'

'One you can't control?'

Vanqua tutted. 'No, no.'

'So he had your leave to do it?'

Cain tensed at the remark. She may not have bought his theory, but was trying it for size.

Vanqua's melancholy look became long-suffering. 'No, of course not.' He made placating movements. 'He selected the woman he wanted but killed the man instinctively. I know that was painful for you and I deeply regret it occurred.'

'You think I'm a dope?'

'I beg your pardon?'

'Not everyone who carries a long knife's a cook. Explain the seating arrangements at lunch.'

'I was trying to give an impression of unity. The whole thing's been ... unfortunate.'

'You bet your bippy. This base is now as compromised as the Japanese Constitution.'

'I know. I know.' He bowed his head like a penitent.

'And the navy's going to gut you until you can see your mouth through your ring.'

He looked down, frowning.

'What happens to Zuiden?' Her lips were a line.

'Yes.' He rubbed his eyes with his fingers.

'I suggest you decommission him.'

Vanqua recleared his throat. 'Normally one would. But I'm afraid he's too valuable for that.'

Cain wanted to thump the man. Why didn't Rhonda tell him to get knotted? Then he had the notion that she was playing a role and that what was actually happening here he'd probably never know. He recalled one of the less questionable Hadiths: part of being a good Muslim is leaving alone that which does not concern you.

Vanqua was staring at the centre of the table. 'I'll have him transferred on the first flight out tomorrow. He'll be on special assignment in Bosnia. I've spoken to him severely of course.' He checked his watch and stood up. 'I now have to face the commander of this ship. You can imagine how that will be.' He paused at the door. 'Once again, my sincere apology.'

He left.

Cain stared at the closing door, swung back to Rhonda. 'Hell, why didn't you tell him where to shove it?'

'Yes, that would have been fun.' She smiled, now surprisingly at ease. 'But I need him to wallow in his biography just a tadlet more.'

'He *must* have told Zuiden to do it. Did you see the body language?'

'It certainly walks and quacks like the proverbial broad-billed waterfowl.' Her speculative look. 'But why target the *inamorata*?'

'Because the bugger's out to get you.'

'By attacking Karen? Strategically pointless. And with the sailor dead, he's compromised himself.'

'The killing was a mistake.'

'Agreed. But there's more to this.'

'Whatever the motive, he's your enemy. And that makes him mine.'

She sang, 'The enemy of one, the enemy of *all* is,' then chuckled. 'Did you know that the dragoons' chorus from *Patience* was, shall we say, borrowed from Auber's "Laughing Song"?'

'Ronnie, for God's sake ...'

'Yes, dear?'

'Is this a serious matter or not?'

'It is for the desiccated Dane. For us it's merely a ripple in the current of bliss.'

'Shit, Ron. He fucked your ice maiden and I almost got creamed.'

She smiled. 'At my age, misfortune never causes surprise. You've helped, dear. Truly you have. *Mille grazie.*'

He shrugged. 'How's Hunt?'

'Composed. If she has a heart, I haven't located it. My obsession with glacial women I don't wish to discuss.' She frowned, paused.

'What is it?'

'Vanqua. When he does that hang-dog thing he ... reminds me of ...'

'What?'

'Nothing. It's mad.' She clapped her hands like a maiden aunt confronted with a tray of chocolates. 'Now — enough of head-office intrigue. It's your time to bugger off.' She began to sing again. 'Farewell, my own. Light of my life, farewell,' then grinned at his expression. 'From *Pinafore* of course — and the only octet in the whole of G and S.'

'Is this relevant?'

'Certainly, dear heart. We may need our Savoyard secrets for verification later. There's method in my madness. *Nicht wahr*? Now,' she continued brightly, 'here's your chance to swap your double life for a single one. Pat tells me you want to direct commercials.'

He shrugged. 'Something to do.'

'Outrageous waste of talent. However. You can do anything you like for the rest of your life.'

'Exile, huh?' So this was how the kiss-off happened. He felt emotion building in him. The edict came back: LOYALTY TO PEOPLE IS WEAKNESS. But EXIT was his family and home. And this devious but dear woman was somewhere between his mother and big sister. 'I'll miss you.' He choked on the words.

She reached across and pressed his hands. 'There's no easy way to say goodbye. But your last little job's still to come.'

'Which is?'

'All in good time.'

'And I wanted to see John again.'

'Ah yes. Gianpaolo. You will. But not for a while.' She stood up. 'I want you to stay for the rest of the conference, bask in the adoration of the cadets, talk to them, encourage them, and of course comfort yourself with Pat. Then we'll crank out a new set of credentials and ship you wherever you say. As you're no longer on active service, you'll revert to Condition Blue. Except, as the shit's still in the fan, wherever you are, take care.'

He stood too, fighting the feeling. He'd never imagined it would get to him like this. Leaving her. Leaving Pat. Leaving John. Suddenly it was fact. 'When's this job come up?'

'Eighteen months or more. You in?'

A nod.

'Gives you plenty of time to wind down. And as for the job ... well, you could do it chained to a rock with a vulture eating your liver. Which reminds me, I'd better get back to Pandora and her ...' She gave him a bear hug. 'You have my love.'

He nodded, not trusting himself to speak.

16

ALPHA

ANTARCTICA

The MSA for approaching McMurdo was 15,300 feet. Beyond reporting-point Byrd, the ski-equipped C–130s normally descended to bleak Willy Field's soft-snow skiway. But the levellers and rollers hadn't been working for this flight. When the radar dish on the control tower picked up the plane 90 nautical miles out, the base's HF and VHF stayed mute.

In the elaborate communications complex called Mac Centre, far across field, the overflight was monitored. That was all. No assistance was rendered, no sked kept, no transmission taped. Even recording evidence was prohibited. Because the Hercules was at 20,000 feet, heading to a place that no one at Mac ever named.

To a place roughly equidistant from Amundsen/Scott, Mawson and Vostok.

To the most geographically and politically isolated pinpoint in the world.

To a frigid hell no traverse was cleared to approach.

To a diplomatic nightmare.

The EXIT Alpha base.

Through a sky streaked with green fire, the elderly transport droned, its vapour trail a thin line above the vastness of the rising plateau. Soon it would have to land in blowing snow with a 20-degree, 40-knot crosswind and visibility at 400 metres.

Rhonda had sat for most of the flight on the supplementary crew bunk. She rose and shrugged on her anorak. The noise level with engines running was 128 decibels. She pulled the headset from the ear of the pilot and screamed, 'Don't bend it. We can't afford it.'

The pilot gave the thumbs up to acknowledge.

EXIT's two veteran C–130s were second-hand but they'd been well maintained and progressively upgraded. They had ski landing gear, JATO and every navigational aid including GPS, Omega and the original but excellent N–1 gyro compass. Even with four on the flight deck the crew didn't take Antarctica lightly. The featureless terrain made VMC flying suicidal. A magnetic compass was useless, INS essential. The radar altimeter was supposed to be accurate to 50 feet but the extreme dryness of Antarctica could make its signals doubtful as they could penetrate dry ice and send back a false reading.

Rhonda went down the staircase to the cargo deck and lowered one of the stowable troop seats near the main cabin bulkhead. In full polar gear it was difficult to strap yourself in. Difficult to do much more than fart. The temperature in the near-windowless fuselage had been reduced progressively since takeoff at Christchurch. It was still a sauna near the ceiling but icy at deck level.

Down here, the racket of the turboprops was inescapable. She stared at the two benson tanks and the shipping container secured to the deck. The D model could handle a payload of

25,000 pounds and accommodate the same weight of fuel. The aircraft weighed around 90,000 pounds and gross poundage for ski landings was 125,000. So the extra fuel needed for these flights reduced cargo capacity. Flying transports demanded a symmetry achieved only by exquisite trade-offs.

Vanqua was seated out of sight on the other side of the load. When they were forced to travel like this they tended to ignore each other. As usual he'd spent most of the flight drowsing in the upper bunk, oblivious to the beauty of the floes and, later, of the great peaks glittering with white fire. Apparently his blue-metalled soul preferred slumber to splendour.

She heard the whine of servos as the hydraulics lowered the skis. Their broad undersides were Teflon-coated so that they didn't stick to the ice.

The plane lost altitude, banked and bucked. They didn't have the luxury of external PAR pickup from GCA controllers. They were using ARA, which depended on nylon mesh flags on the boundary of the skiway that reflected the aircraft's radar. The navigator would be feeding heading, distance, pressure and radalt readings to the pilot. And directional changes on final to keep him lined up.

The side of the cabin behind her vibrated with the strain as the creaking airtruck locked on the glide-path. They'd used thousands of pounds of fuel but still would be slithering 60 tonnes of deadweight across the wasteland.

'Hang in there, guys,' she mouthed.

As the skis connected with compressed snow she heard the sizzling crackle and thumps. Even on a prepared surface, these things landed rough.

They were down, had lucked it in.

She was dragged sideways by deceleration as the props reversed thrust. The plane's trailing tempest of snow would now engulf it in a self-made storm. She'd seen these landings many times and they never ceased to amaze her.

The deafening noise of the four engines and the throbbing vibration lessened. She saw the loadmaster now, pulling his balaclava around his goggles. There was a gas turbine compressor inside the port mainwheel bay fairing but number three engine still ran. They weren't shutting right down. It had to be extremely cold.

The loadmaster operated the ramp control panel. The rear cargo door went up. Then the ramp door lowered on two long hydraulic jacks.

Snow. Glare. Biting chill.

They were here.

She saw air-conditioned tractors and a refuelling truck approaching through white mist. They were painted, like the tail of the plane, in distinctive orange and black stripes. A Hagglunds was ready by the plane but, as usual, she refused the ride. She walked in the troughs of its rubber tracks until she came to the first blizz line. She was glad she'd worn the face mask. In these temperatures even a short walk could cause frost nip.

Was Vanqua behind her? Because of the enveloping hood, she had to turn fully round to see him plodding behind her like a wraith. Thou beside me in the wilderness, she thought, annoyed to be tethered to the man.

Through swirling snow, she glimpsed oil drums, pipes and crates. By the time she'd reached the snow ramp, the fur around her hood was ringed with frost. Real fur. The synthetic stuff froze and tried to poke your eyes out. She clumped down to the main entrance. Another visit to the Room of Doom. Both of them had to sign for executions, the final check after five-nation confirmation.

After the initial security scans at the heavily armed entrance guardhouse, the two of them were cleared through.

Vanqua said, 'Chilly,' vapour pouring from his mouth.

She nodded and they walked down the main tunnel. Its walls, rough and dry as concrete, had the sheen of fine plaster and supported sagging electrical cable and insulated plastic water pipes. The temperature in the corridors never rose beyond zero.

The base was dug into the ice cap and covered with arched roofing. Its network of corridors tended to creep sideways so needed frequent repair. Below its three main domes were accommodation blocks made from modular units flown in as kits. As the main holding-block entrance door opened, condensed vapour billowed out like smoke. They went into the boot room, shed their anoraks and felt-lined rubber overboots. In the next annexe, they discarded their gloves, glove liners and two layers of polypropylene. The temperature here, while not warm, was as pleasant as a winter's day. They preferred to keep it at a moderate 12 degrees centigrade. Adam Pohl, the base commander, welcomed them. 'Good trip?'

Rhonda said, 'Beautiful.'

Vanqua shrugged. 'I slept.'

'We're ready,' Pohl said, eager to please. The last of his hair sheltered behind his ears but he sported a neat grey beard — cropped to give a decent air-seal on breathing gear for fire crew drills. In the extreme cold here, facial hair became caked with ice and dripped when you entered the warmth of heated vehicles or huts. Yet some of the Antarctic staff at Alpha still wore beards. And, at Vostok, according to the wags, even some of the women.

Pohl and the base administrative officer escorted them to the table for the signing. She looked down at the three orders, each countersigned five times. The names at the top were famous. One of the men was from the Far East, one from eastern Europe, one an African.

She signed at the bottom of all three sheets then handed the pen to Vanqua. But he had produced his own pen, a palladium-coated Lamy Swift. As he clicked the point down, the clip retreated until flush with the barrel. A reflection of himself, she thought. Form obsessed with function, function followed by fatality. She contemplated his face, the smooth skin, fair hair, muscled neck. He was a good-looking man with the attitude of a monk. His dismal, desiccated nature made him almost unapproachable.

He signed the papers. Pohl and the AO witnessed the signatures. Then she walked with Vanqua and Pohl to the electrocution bay.

It was in a converted container. No separate viewing room, no chair. Witnesses stood around the sides on a rubber mat. In the centre of the floor, raised on four ceramic insulators, was an unpadded wooden slab fitted with leg, arm, chest clamps and a head dome. On the wall was the edict: DEATH IS AN ASPECT OF LIFE.

A shivering man with a lined face and neat moustache lay clamped to the slab. His face, the subject of photographs and video clips for twenty years, was sallow now. His head and calves were shaved and he was naked except for a diaper. The subjects were brought in unclothed because it made handling simpler for the vat. The diaper handled involuntary voiding. The electric current paralysed motor functions but sensory functions continued.

The two surgeons fitted the copper-and-sponge-lined dome to the victim's head. Some of the saline solution dripped down his cheek. They attached the electrodes to each of his calves. The 2400 volts would enter his skull and fork out his legs.

Vanqua asked the man, 'Are you comfortable?'

She glanced at him sourly. The fastidious prick was funny as a bedsore. But perhaps it wasn't intended as derision.

The shackled man's mouth turned down. He ignored it, teeth chattering. The attendants nodded to Pohl and left the room.

There was a small metal box on the wall beside a lever with a rubber handle and gauges showing voltage and amperage. Pohl removed a stethoscope from the box, hung it around his neck and grasped the handle. 'Is the original verified?'

She muttered, 'Verified.'

Vanqua repeated it.

Pohl pushed back his sleeve to see the second hand of his watch.

The condemned man roared, 'I'm cold.'

You'll be warm in a minute, she thought, you genocide-loving hyena.

She nodded.

Pohl closed the contact.

The man's brief scream was choked off as he went into spasm. Fists clenched, back arched, his body slammed against the straps. Steam drifted from beneath the metal cap and his face became a strictured mask. According to the manual, his brain would eventually cook at 60 degrees centigrade. But there was evidence that the skull was a bad conductor — that, while the body burnt, the brain still functioned.

Barbaric, Rhonda thought. But the five powers considered this humane. Wolf had recommended that subjects be stripped and staked in the snow — a solution too sensible for the bureaucratic mind.

The man's face, hands and toes contorted and his sinews stood out against his quickly reddening flesh. His eyes bulged and vomit trickled from his mouth. The skin attached to the electrodes was burning.

Pohl frowned at his gauges. 'Stupid business. The voltage always drops ten per cent and the current goes up as the body gets saturated. Resistance is the problem.'

Vanqua covered his nose with a monogrammed handkerchief. The room now stank.

After two one-minute jolts, Pohl shut off the power and put the stethoscope to the man's chest. He shook his head. The heart still pumped. The man's spasm had relaxed. He shuddered and gasped in a breath.

Pohl went back and threw the switch again.

The body bucked and yellow flame shot from the side of the head. The skin was stretching, the figure swelling as it started to cook.

Rhonda endured the stench by composing a liturgy for electrocutions. How would it go? 'Peace on earthing and good connections to all primary stakes'?

Pohl still stared at his watch.

Blood now spurted from the nose, the skin of the head smoked and began to peel from the skull.

The power was turned off and Pohl checked the heart again. This time it seemed successful but you could never be sure. They'd had two subjects revive before going into the vat. Pohl nodded, shrugged, and they filed from the room. The corpse had to cool before they could move it.

Vanqua refolded his handkerchief. He seemed subdued. Had the events on the carrier sobered him?

After the three originals were done, they had dinner in the mess where Pohl entertained them with a fund of excellent jokes, all clean. He never offended good taste. Despite the nature of their work, EXIT had many decent people.

Well fed, she went to see the 'acid drops'.

The room was a dismal space, bare except for the vat, a chain hoist on an overhead rail and two metal chairs. Two of the originals, hideous in death, were chin-strapped and ready for the hook. The third, neck stretched by his weight, was pulled along the rail until he dangled over the tall alloy tank.

Rhonda sat uncomfortably, sticky-date pudding heavy on her stomach. She knew she ate too much. But with diets, knowledge wasn't power.

Vanqua sat beside her, looking glum. Both department heads had to witness the dissolving and confirm all physical trace had gone.

She nodded and the attendant surgeon pressed a button on the control stalk. He wore protective overalls, acid-resistant boots and a helmet with a visor.

The body was lowered very slowly. A splash would eat through the floor. The air was pervaded by a sharpness that attacked the back of the nose.

As the feet went in, steam rose from the vat. The angled

convex mirror attached to the ceiling was clouded now but later would show nothing but the ends of the corroded harness.

As she watched the body go in, she mused on the events of the year. The Soviet withdrawal from Afghanistan, the ferment in eastern Europe, even China. Developments in Nicaragua, Tunisia, Iran, Iraq. In Angola, Cuba, South Africa, Palestine, Yugoslavia. George Bush now certain to make it in America. An astonishingly volatile time with huge implications for the future. And EXIT, despite internal problems, had done extremely well.

Berlin was her great hope. She wanted the rotten wall down and they were so close now. So close.

Except that EXIT itself was threatened. By the man on her left? She didn't know. Perhaps Cain was right. Perhaps the morose surgeon CO was behind it, destabilising things enough to damage her but not enough to destroy EXIT itself.

Why?

The motive was missing.

Damn it. She still couldn't see it.

The second bloated, charred body was hoisted. She didn't find it disgusting. Here, death wasn't life's conclusion but its salve. She came to this place to excise the rotten tissue of society, just as a doctor might view a necrotic wound seething with sterilised maggots as therapy. She glanced across at Vanqua. He continued to look ahead, nostrils narrowed against the smell.

Minimalist, she thought. For her, few censures were worse.

It was before time, she decided. That meant she had to move now. In this business, timely moves were tardy. What was Zurich Axiom Two? Always sell too soon?

Time to activate the countermeasure — the one she'd hoped, prayed, never to use.

17

CULT

SYDNEY, AUSTRALIA, FEBRUARY 1990

Cain entered the wind tunnel of Walker Street, North Sydney, his tape in his briefcase, his mind half a world away. He'd been in Australia three months, his first time back in sixteen years.

Compared to the subcontinent, it was heaven — although the place had changed. The competition was greater, the traffic a car park, the people sourer, more hounded. And with the increasing depletion of ozone, the sun burnt you in minutes.

He'd begun with a Barrier Reef holiday that made him feel he was spinning his wheels. Although he had money and a life to himself, exile hurt. He felt suspended at the fringe of events. Worse, he was lonely — which he considered adolescent.

As he waited to cross at the lights, he noticed a poster taped to a window.

THE SQUARE.
ABUNDANT LIFE AND THE
SECRET OF SUCCESS.
THE ASTONISHING
GUSTAVE RAUL
IN PERSON
Exhibition Centre, Darling Harbour
Two nights only

Raul — the cult leader? Here?

The lights changed. He walked across. Women glanced at him, eyes lingering. He appraised the pert arses of younger ones ahead. Since coming here he'd been celibate, first happily, now uneasily.

He'd cadged two jobs — corporate videos slung at him by mates who'd once been well paid to train him. These had scored an assignment with the advertising agency he was visiting today. He couldn't show his Pakistan footage. It was irrelevant and would place him. In this hard-bitten industry, florid foreign-language footage would be bizarre. With no show-reel of recent commercials, he was starting almost from scratch. Videos weren't commercials but they were work.

He'd learned film techniques in this city — started as grip, then gaffer's assistant, worked with an editor, done focus-pulling, assistant directing. Now he was back. Funny how things went — not in straight lines but circles. Which explained the disasters of businesses, relationships and nations. He had to stop being philosophical. Today's meeting called for shallowness profound. Get with it, kid, he told himself. Be light, bright and trite.

The lift swished him to the creative floor where he was met by Jojo, their producer, a tall trendoid woman who looked nothing until she smiled.

'Hi. Pre-prod's in Gary's room.' Her superwide mouth peeled back to display racks of teeth. If she'd played pro tennis, she could have swallowed difficult balls. The Associate

— 89 —

CD, a copywriter, head shaved and shirt-sleeves rolled high, rose and shook Cain's hand with what he supposed to be a vice-like grip. He was the standard truculent arsehole with self-image invested in his body — a type he'd been taught to disable in seconds. 'It's below-the-line crud. We're in hand-holding mode with the client and he has this subsidiary. You with it? Here's the hardware.' He slung across brochures for a range of mobile towers.

Cain scanned them. *Four lever operation at pivot frame with overriding foot-operated dead-man switch. Maximum working height — 40 metres ...*

'We're right for crane shots.' Jojo flashed teeth. 'I see it as perspective shots and great low-angle stuff.'

The writer glared at Cain for assent.

He said what they wanted to hear, lukewarm about the job.

The woman dealt papers around. 'Working call sheet and rough agenda. Talent. Location. Gear ...'

After the session, he waited in her cubbyhole while she went to copy papers for him. Pinned to her partition was a poster for the Gustave Raul circus.

She returned, saw him looking at it. 'You into that?' She produced a paperback from her drawer. 'One of his books. It's great.'

He glanced at the title: *Live Selfishly and Love It.*

'I'm going tonight. Want to come?'

The impulsive type, he wondered, or did it mean she was available? She looked flat as a board but he had the drive of a nail gun. 'Sure.'

There were no booked seats and the car park was a trial but she was impressed with his leased BMW. By the time they entered the cavernous place and found the open section, the only seats left were high up from the stage. Once they sat, she turned to him.

'It's so nice to go out with someone.'

'No current attachment?'

'Been a bit of a desert. You?'

'No one at the moment.'

Her flicker of delight.

He took her hand which felt like a collection of small screwdrivers and applied his matinee-idol smile. She chattered happily, her letterbox mouth an intriguing gash. '...most have gone freelance or got jobs in production houses. So I'm one of the few in-house producers. Now tell me about you.'

The houselights faded, sparing her his cover story.

A synthesised dirge began as they projected starscapes on a black expanse. Three women in flowing costumes came on, entwined in a languorous gymnastic display. He wondered if Karen Hunt was here — and if she'd replaced Raul with his duplicate yet.

As the tempo increased, a floating throne slowly moved forward bearing a man in a golden tunic with compelling eyes emphasised by make-up. It was an excellent illusion. Some in the audience gasped. A pale youth in the next row clasped his hands and sobbed.

The chair reached the front of the stage, hovered over the dancers. They raised supplicant arms then retreated as it lowered to the floor. The man rose from the chair, walked forward, bowing, and the faithful erupted with acclaim.

Cain wondered how anyone could take this nonsense seriously and hoped his companion despised mass psychosis. But her engaging teeth were sheathed, her eyes transfixed. Not, he decided, a critical companion.

After the tumult subsided, Raul began to speak in a deep, convincing voice, augmented by throat mike. His stock in trade was a fixed smile and Wagnerian body language. 'So things will never get better? Never change? Don't be so sure. Did any of you suspect the Berlin Wall would come down? That Mandela would be freed? Life — *can* — change.'

With help from EXIT it can, he thought. The man went on with his sales pitch. Interest, motivate, authenticate. He was gaining acceptance by hooking onto the international bandwagon. 'Everyone here is able to control their lives. Even as you sit there, you're making your future. Your thoughts, moods, attitudes are creating what will happen. You' — pregnant pause — 'are your destiny.'

'That's one of his themes,' Jojo whispered and squeezed his hand.

'Because,' Raul continued, 'there's no time. The sense of time lies in the mind itself. We live either in memory or anticipation. But we can make our world right now. As you are — so you become.' Another stagy pause. 'Do you realise what this means? You are either your greatest friend or your most implacable enemy. You.'

Raul was starting to sound like another health-and-wealth heretic. He wondered if Hunt was in the audience and scanned heads in the front rows. Then a three-quarter profile of a bearded man caught his eye. No jug ears. And the hair wasn't straight, but something in the cast of cheek and brow ...

Murchison, the other surgeon shadowing them in Chartres — now written-off as missing in action? If it was, they'd fixed the ears.

No, he thought. Too far-fetched. But he pinpointed the silhouetted head.

Raul had the audience hanging. 'The secret of supra-personal work is unconditional surrender. It's the connection with the overmind that brings us what we need.'

Predictable, Cain thought. Concepts borrowed by a hollow man.

'But all traditions say you have to destroy yourself. Why should I destroy myself? Aren't my wants, wishes important? If not for myself, who for then?'

Sighs from the rows. No, this wasn't health and wealth. More like fame and power. The man was pitching his distortions at the aggrandisement of the personal self. Feeding personal indulgence. It worked every time.

As he talked, barely clad women filed onto the stage behind him, began to chant as their mentor added an amplified stage whisper. 'Do you hear where that sound is coming from? Yes. Yes. The overmind is none other than yourself.'

The chanting ended. As the women exited stage left Hunt entered, carrying a scroll. She looked virginal, dramatic, gorgeous. Some in the audience clapped.

Raul said, 'I've asked one of my senior assistants to read from transcripts transmitted to me. Listen carefully.' He stood aside.

She read in her impersonal voice: 'There is no empty space in the universe — simply a vastness of vibrating energy. We are manifested foci in this vastness. But, more truly, we are repositories of energy connected with each other as towns are connected by roads, as muscles are connected with nerves, as planets are connected by gravity. So you — YOU — can control your destiny absolutely.'

She had some assignment, he thought — the obscuring of truth with facts. Raul knew his stuff. Propaganda was best at catching geese.

'That's Karen,' his companion whispered. 'The most accomplished of the young ones. He's grooming her. Isn't she stunning? I'd kill for her figure.'

Cain was still assessing Raul. Had she done the job on him? He doubted it.

When the lights came up at interval, he rechecked the Murchison lookalike who was now waiting to join the crowd of uncriticals jamming the aisle.

The fuzz disguised it and the ears. But it was the same surly expression, the same hulking body movement. Christ. Had Vanqua been feeding them a line?

Did Hunt know the surgeon was here? If not, she was in trouble.

Then he remembered.

It wasn't his war any more.

18

TEETH AND BONE

After the show, as they crossed the road to a bistro, he watched how her coathanger body moved — then watched her intriguing mouth sip cappuccino. She asked him what he thought of Raul.

'As far as I can see, most people can only assimilate truth as a lie. So only distortions of great teachings became popular. Raul's a huckster.'

'But what he says works.'

'Because it strengthens the surface grasping part of a person. He's preaching self-development. It's nothing to do with transformation.'

'You've lost me.'

On the way to the car, they encountered a commotion of minders and groupies ushering Raul and Hunt into a limousine. He tried to hurry past but Hunt spotted him, looked away quickly. He looked away too, knowing it could be fatal to stare.

He sensed rather than knew that someone had detached from the group and heard steps behind them in the car park.

He looked back once, saw a youngish man with staring eyes. He decided not to handle it there, with an uninvolved woman beside him.

As they drove to her St Leonards apartment, he spotted the tail, an ageing Volvo with a side-light out — a cardinal sin for night work. The guy was either incompetent or stuck with an *ad hoc*. Either way, Cain thought, he could wait.

She invited him up to show him the view. At least that was her excuse. The place was a security block and even if the man could locate the apartment, it had a fire-rated door with steel frame, keycard access and chain. No, the bugger could cool his heels and, later, he'd be tired, bored, sloppy.

Her balcony, one of dozens in the cliff-like building, had a nightscape of the CBD above glittering railway tracks. Like most well-paid Aussies with insecure jobs she'd reassured herself by buying concrete.

She responded to his casual touches. 'Would you like to stay?'

There was something about the way her lips peeled back as if threatening to reveal the whole skull that he found oddly kissable. So he kissed her several times. She relaxed in his arms, looking blissful, then led him to the bed.

She wanted to paw him but he had the holster to dispose of. When she went to the bathroom, he undressed, shoving it under the bed, and got beneath the covers feeling vaguely disgusted with himself. He'd brought condoms — standard EXIT practice when sleeping with those not checked.

She came back naked. Her body, outlined by the moon, mimicked its terrain — night-bleached prominences and deep craters. Her thin shoulders revealed clavicles like tie-rods. Her breasts were little more than nipples. Muscles lay beneath the skin of her long arms and flanks like cords. She felt like a wrapped skeleton as she snuggled beside him — a warm, bony opportunity, teeth sheathed now, eyes a little wary.

He took her slowly, gently, first exploring her in the semi-darkness — feeling the contours under his hands as if she were a form of Braille. He kissed her many times, sliding his tongue around her teeth, then mouthed down the washboard of her ribs. He'd never had a woman so thin.

The delicate cleft between her legs soon responded to his fingers. She began to tremble then twisted as he worked her closer to her need.

For the first time in months the warmth of a woman enclosed him. He cradled her tenderly, grateful. She came quickly, whimpering and shuddering.

Then he turned her on her side and entered her from behind, caressing the ridges of her backbone, fondling her chest. He turned her again and held her arms pinned above her head as the frustration of months left him in a second. They chatted for a while and he thought of the man below in his car. Then she clamped long legs and arms about him like a spider cocooning a moth. He made love to her more roughly and they ended on the floor.

He asked her to set her alarm for four, saying he had an early location survey. 'Sparrow-fart start and I've got to go home first. Sheet-metal shoot.' She'd know there were half-hour windows for car shoots, dusk and dawn.

He slept and was woken by the alarm. She barely stirred as he dressed.

He kissed her. 'I'll ring you.'

'Please.'

She'd let him into the basement car park with her door card. The mesh shutter was only half up when he gunned the BMW out. If his tail was contemplating homicide, it would have been a difficult shot. Pros used a souped car with driver and an automatic weapon with suppressor. An iced Vovo with one occupant? Amateur hour. Still, it was healthy to be careful.

He headed toward his unit in Killara. There was little traffic so early apart from interstate trucks, but he made sure the car behind didn't lose him. The guy was brazenly following.

He stopped at Lindfield beside the supermarket, loosened the SIG-Sauer in the holster under his arm. It was a beautiful limited-issue weapon, not yet generally released — highly accurate and with a double-action trigger for immediate first shot potential. He hadn't fired it in anger but it was sweet on the pistol range.

Far under the seat, secured by plastic clips, was his ugly PSM. Unlike the finely made Swiss pistol, the CIS weapon was obsolete. But it had a bottlenecked 5.45mm cartridge able to penetrate fifty-five layers of Kevlar. He decided against taking it. This tyro was no Jack Flak.

He left the car and hurried into a lane. There were large-wheeled garbage bins for cover. The back entrances of shops one side. A blank wall on the other.

The car came around the corner, pulled up just beyond the lane. The driver got out, walked to the entrance of the lane, hands wide of his body. He'd grown breasts, wore jeans.

It was Hunt, looking drawn and tired.

She said, 'I'm alone.'

He holstered the SIG. 'Come here.'

She walked out of the street-light's glare. He wondered how long she'd been waiting. She must have swapped with the man, sent him back in her car and stayed with the Volvo to be sure that he'd keep her in sight.

He said, 'You trying to kill us?'

'Don't start. It's enough for one day.'

'So what the hell's this?'

'I need to know what's going on.'

'*Nothing's* going on.'

'Then why are you in Sydney? Now?'

'Sydney, KL, Tokyo. Who cares where I am? I did training here — like the place. Where am I supposed to be? Back in Karachi?'

'But you were there last night.'

'I was chatting up a bird. It was her idea to go. Nothing to do with you.'

'God.' She slumped on the kerb, arms around her knees. 'All I need.'

He crouched in front of her. 'Who was the drop-kick in the car?'

'One of the faithful.' A toneless comment.

'Why didn't you send one of ours?'

'Couldn't at the time. And I trust him. He won't ask questions.'

'Are you daft?' Christ, he thought, she's lost it. 'You're a Grade One, remember? CONSISTENCY IS THE HIGHEST ACHIEVEMENT? TRAINING LEADS TO COURAGE? Get with it.'

'Yes,' she spat. 'I'm not you — the great Grade Four. I'm just a Grade One with a bloody Grade Three job.'

'The ice-maiden in meltdown mode? Getting punchy?'

'I'm just so — tired.'

Cold-faced bitch, he thought. Did you think it was going to be easy? Then he remembered the words of a Sufi. Words echoed later by Tolstoy, curiously enough, perhaps because sublime ideas were limited. The sage, asked by a disciple 'Who is dearest to you in the world?' had replied, 'He who sits in my presence.'

It reminded him what a shit he was. He sat beside her, said quietly, 'Grade One's tough. We've all felt this, you know. And Ron's given you a biggie. You're discovering you're human. We're not gods.'

'*You're* supposed to be.'

'Give me a break. Look, you've managed so far. You're going to make it.'

She covered her face with her hands. Her shirt wasn't fully buttoned and he was staring into paradise regained. At least one part of her didn't need support.

He waited, hard experience telling him how she felt — no family but EXIT, years of punishing study, the terrors of a complex assignment. Despite the endless training, pressure had crippled many people.

'Heard from Ronnie?'

'No, fuck her. She got me into this mess.'

'She always knows what she's doing. If she trusted you with this, you can hack it.'

'Don't try to patch me up, Cain. I'm stuffed.'

There wasn't much he could do for her and her crisis was draining him too. 'Stuffed or not, you've *got* to go on. What's the deal on Murchison?'

The hands came down. 'Who?' Hard eyes staring at him.

'Murchison. A Grade Three surgeon. He was there tonight. Are you running him?'

She scowled, brain in overload, trying to take it in.

God, she didn't know! He could hear Rhonda's voice again, telling him to stay out of politics. Odd when he'd spent years undermining a dictatorship.

She breathed out, straightened. 'I don't know anything about him.'

'Then watch it. He's a big guy. Lurching walk. Wavy hair now. Beard. Around forty. If you spot someone like that, steer clear.'

A nod.

'And next time you contact Ron, tell her about tonight. Tell her I saw Murchison there. Are you reading me?'

A nod.

'And tell your guy you lost me in traffic. And have a cover-line for tonight.'

'I have. I'm not dumb, Cain.'

'You were close to it last night, young lady.'

'Jesus,' she snapped, 'you sound like my big brother.'

'Near as you'll get.' He stood up, sad for them all.

She rose, wearing the strange frown that didn't score her face.

He gripped her shoulders. 'You're beautiful, clever, great and doing a fantastic job. I saw you doing it tonight. You're also an appalling stroppy bitch and we all think you're marvellous. And it's not forever, you know. Not far to go ...'

She screwed up her eyes.

Poor Ronnie, he thought. She'd been a sitting duck for this one. Someone dispassionate, gorgeous, brilliant — even conveniently bent.

He gave her a Ronnie-strength bear hug, turned her to face the mouth of the lane then pushed her gently like a wind-up toy.

She reached the corner, turned, eyes bright. He looked at her amazed. Her tears were as unexpected as the thunder of a glacier cracking. Pressure couldn't force them from her. But kindness had.

'Thank you. Brother.'

He heard her get back in the car and leaned against a bin, exhausted.

He'd been free of women and EXIT for three months. Now this.

He'd had a night.

19

ENCOUNTER AT 3000m

SOUTH ISLAND, NEW ZEALAND, NOVEMBER 1990

The ridge was near the summit and there was little room to move. They'd rerigged the hang-glider for the sixth time that day and its pilot was ready for another charge into space.

The cameraman looked up from the Arri's eyepiece to assess the sky. Clouds were closing in but an approaching hole promised sun. 'Should get five.'

The assistant checked the mag. 'Two hundred feet.'

They were shooting at twenty-four frames. A foot equalled sixteen frames. Meant they had around two minutes twelve seconds left. It was enough to see the glider against the peaks before it spiralled to the slopes far below.

'Okay,' Cain said. 'We'll roll till we run out.'

He checked the launch slope and lugged a camera case further out of shot. In the thin air and knee-deep snow, the effort left him out of breath. He left the crew fussing with the miniature camera clamped to an upright of the glider's trapeze and plodded to the top of the spine.

The chopper was perched on a knoll just down from the ridge, framed against the snowscape of peaks. It was a Hughes 500 turbo hired from the Queenstown base and hadn't stopped chugging all day. Up here, they didn't shut down. He pressed the lever on the walkie-talkie. 'We're going again in five.'

The pilot opened the egg-shaped cabin's door and gave a visual thumbs up.

The script was simple. Video: a hang-glider, painted with an aftershave insignia, soaring against snowy mountain peaks. Then super pack shot and slogan. Audio: a rock track.

There were no peaks this majestic in Australia and they couldn't afford a European shoot. So they shot spots like this in New Zealand. The local production company swore there'd be snow on the Aspirings in November. They were right. It looked like Nepal.

Cain turned back, checked the clouds. They'd got great stuff in the can this morning but now they seemed about to be weathered.

The DOP and assistant were back behind the Arri and the sun was almost in the break. The glider pilot held the nose up, touched his helmet, ready.

'Standing by,' the DOP called.

The spine was flooded with crystalline light.

'Okay for exposure.'

'Turn over.'

'Rolling.'

No 'speed' call. They weren't recording sound.

'And ... action.'

The madman ran down the slope, avoided ankle-snapping holes and launched himself into space.

They kept rolling until they ran out while he soared against the peaks. Then he was too low, too distant.

The DOP straightened. 'Good stuff there.'

The assistant fussed with the camera. 'Gate clear. Mag change.'

Cain pressed the tit and told the chopper, 'He's down. Go get him.'

They heard the machine wind up and soon it was slapping overhead. It kissed them with its shadow and did a near vertical down the face. It would take twenty minutes to pack the glider, lash it to a skid and bring it up from the valley floor. While they waited Cain asked the DOP what he'd got, wishing he had a video split.

The slapping sound again. They turned, surprised. The chopper was behind them — hovering high.

Cain grabbed the handset. 'What's he up to?'

'It's not ours,' the DOP said.

The thing dropped out of sight to settle on the mound behind the spine.

'Rich skiers,' the DOP said. 'Got more money than sense. They hire these four-blade turboshaft jobs to drop them off up here.'

'He can't sit there,' the grip said. 'Our lot'll be back in six minutes.' The flat New Zealand 'i' made it sound like 'sucks'. 'I'll tell him to sod off.' He struggled up the slope.

Cain followed more slowly, breathing hard. When he reached the crest, he saw a man stumbling toward them from the chopper, leaving deep holes in the snow. The grip met him halfway. The man pointed up at Cain. The grip continued toward the chopper while the man kept coming.

The visitor wasn't a skier. Apart from the parka, he seemed to be in ordinary clothes and was trying to wade through the drifts with his hands in his pockets. Then he fell and the hands flew forward to save him. He didn't even have gloves. No ski pants either, or boots.

Cain unzipped his jacket a little so that he could reach for the SIG if he needed it. Cold air poured in on his chest.

At last the man came up to him — shivering, panting, blue.

Cain said, 'What the hell are you up to? We're trying to do a shoot here.'

The man gasped — knee-deep in snow. He wasn't very dangerous. He'd been dumped 3000 metres up. No wonder he couldn't breathe. 'Cain?'

It wasn't the name he was using. He assessed the sodden clothes, the parka, probably borrowed, the pained soft face — said nothing.

The panting man blurted, 'Dragoons' chorus. *Patience.* Auber. Laughing song.' He had an American twang. It was all he could get out.

'What about it?'

'Need to talk.' He fought to breathe.

'You'll have to do better.'

The man gasped, 'Farewell my own. Only octet. Oh God, don't keep me out here, please.'

'Credentials?'

'Company.'

'Since when do we deal with the Company?'

'You do now.'

'Like hell.'

'Please. My feet are ice blocks.'

'And I'm in the middle of a shoot. And you're on our landing spot. So get that crate off it.'

'When you get back. Motel bar. Okay? I'll wait.'

'Okay. Now naff off.'

The man half fell back down the slope. Cain glanced at the clouds, cursed and waded back, trying to invent a plausible explanation for the crew.

They were weathered mid afternoon and it took three trips to ferry back the gear. On the last run, when they dropped out of blowing sleet, Queenstown was golden with late-afternoon sun. He watched the corn-coloured airfield coming closer and thought about the man.

Nine months into his exile things were going well. He'd graduated to medium-budget spots and established himself as worthy of a check-quote. Now this blast from the past. What the hell did the guy want?

In the motel room, he rechecked his shot list, showered, dressed comfortably and headed for the bar. He could use a stiff one and was determined the fellow would buy it.

The man was propped on a stool. He stood up and smiled. 'Harry Frost.'

'If you'd stayed up there much longer, you would have been Jack.'

'Yeah. Pretty dumb of me. Didn't think I'd be exposed so long. God was it cold!'

'I've been in colder spots.'

'Name your poison.'

Cain let him pay then walked to one of the tables by the window, knowing the crew would fly-blow the bar the moment they'd checked the gear.

He slumped into the booth, exhausted, sipped his drink and gazed out at the lake. The dying sun tinged the steep cliffs ochre, painting the beautiful scene with light.

'Great place, this,' the man said. 'Good shoot?'

'We'll know after the air-to-air stuff tomorrow. So what's up?'

'Yes, well.' The American smiled uncertainly. He wore half-frame spectacles now and looked professorial. 'It's about your new assignment. Rhonda said I could look at you.'

'If you're CIA, how come you're in bed with Ron?'

'It's a side job.'

'Our charter vetoes side jobs.'

'It's a delicate matter. Would you mind having dinner with me? She said I had to tell you it's the job you could do chained to a rock.'

Cain smiled.

'In the restaurant here at seven, then?'

'Fine.'

The crew were filing in. He excused himself and joined them.

Dinner was pleasant, the local red acceptable, despite the country being better at whites, and the conversation parabolic. Frost talked about the end of the cold war, displaying a mordant sense of humour.

Cain, warmly fuzzed and several glasses in, said, 'Okay, enough lovemaking. Give.'

'I'm told you're what I'm looking for — a highbrow hybrid — a hard man with a renaissance mind.'

'I mostly provoke less flattering descriptions. But at least I've earned my comparisons, not read them.'

'I believe you. Do you like women?'

'Generally more than they like themselves.'

'And I imagine they like you. Now you've been partly raised as Muslim so I doubt you object to polygamy.'

He shrugged. 'In EXIT, we're stuck with serial monogamy. But I could bow to business demands.'

'Good, good.' Frost looked relieved. 'Now your attitude to ghosts?'

Cain yawned. 'What's all this ghost stuff?'

'Specifically — poltergeists.'

'If they're polter they can't be geists. Contradiction in terms.'

'Ah, yes. Logical enough. But we know there are four possible forces — electromagnetic, gravitational, nuclear and radioactive. There may be an unknown fifth force. Would you accept that there could be some kind of nervous energy — not quite physical — that can manifest on this level?'

He shrugged. 'God knows. As we're on the subject of spooks, you don't seem to fit the CIA mould.'

'No. I'm a physiologist. The Company's reorganising, changing. The new emphasis is going to be transnational threats, economic opportunities. We have to become more scientific, technological, financial.'

'Or you'll be out of a job.'

He smiled and sipped his drink. 'We foresee the day when we'll be working with the KGB, the GRU or whatever they become. But there'll still be things we won't want our new friends to get too far with.'

'Like poltergeists.'

'Sounds strange?'

He nodded.

'No, I'm not Intelligence Division. I'm with Research — a branch called the Phenomena Unit. The USSR was into this early. Vasiliev at the Bekhterev Institute? You know the history?'

'No.'

'We have people working on remote viewing. But my group is focused on psychokinesis. The Soviets did a lot of work on that. Now they're broke and heading for a graft-based kleptocracy. The interest is military, of course. You know how the air force is working on thought-controlled fighters?'

He nodded.

'And SOFs are looking at what they call synthetic telepathy. A bit more practical are under-the-skin devices which are still a physical and training matter but things are moving that way. Now phenomena are simply a step beyond the limits we know. We're trying to expand our understanding — discover how it works.' He rubbed his eyes. 'Just so much one can cope with in a day.'

'And tomorrow's an early call for me.'

They got up and Frost held out his hand. 'Thank you for your time. This one's on me.' He waved his door-key tag at the waiter.

'I'd be interested,' Cain smiled, 'to see an intangible entity that creates physical phenomena.'

Frost looked at him quizzically. 'Everyone thinks it's a laugh until they're confronted with direct experience. But when they do, they don't find it funny. You're a resourceful and dangerous man. But I've seen men like you shocked into jelly.'

'Great. And I'm your new patsy?'

'You're it.'

20

BETA

The roaring forties buffet three lands, Tasmania's southwest, New Zealand's fiordland and southern Patagonia. All are rugged, wild places still, misted in a sense of foreboding. All once were joined. Fossils show biological links. In Tasmania's museums you can still see a relative of the South American prothylacinus, the Tasmanian tiger or thylacine — mounted and on display. The large marsupial carnivore with striped back and kangaroo-like tail was hunted to extinction by European settlers, as was the indigenous human population.

The inheritors of this terrible past consider themselves overlooked by the mainland and resent jokes about in-breeding. (How do you circumcise a Tasmanian? Punch his sister in the mouth.) But the island state still has one treasure beyond price — a huge wet and wild wilderness — one of the last on earth.

In an almost inaccessible mountain treescape, deep in the southwest, where some still hope a breeding pair of thylacines might survive, a narrow 40-kilometre-long fire trail winds beneath the rainforest canopy. The neglected-looking track is impassable, even to four-wheel-drives. It's cut by two deep river crossings, with collapsed wooden bridges, and a huge fallen tree. It ends at a rusty set of doors set deep in a rock wall. A faded sign reads: PROSPERITY MINE — CLOSED 1880. KEEP OUT. GROUND SUBJECT TO SUBSIDENCE. None of it explains why fresh tyre tracks reach to the concrete sill beneath the doors.

Cain braked the LandCruiser near the remains of the first bridge and switched the concealed FLIR to 360 scan. He checked the readout on the slide-out interactive display. A PROCEED cue showed that parameters had been met. Satisfied, he touched a square at the side of the screen and, in front of him, the centre of the bridge rose smoothly out of the torrent to form a dripping but drivable surface. Once he'd crossed, it sank back into the stream. Five kilometres on, the second bridge did the same. Further on still, the fallen tree rose, levered by hydraulics deep in the earth. It disturbed an echidna which, spines bristling, waddled across the road. The small creature paused between the ruts as if determined to stay there. Cain waited, watching its heat signature on the display and wondering if it had an egg in its pouch. When the monotreme left the track he drove on.

As he neared the 'mine', hidden active arrays and cameras observed his progress. He keyed in the day's code, waited for clearance. Finally the ancient doors, the facade of a blast-rated, vault-like entrance, slid into the rock.

He drove down the dimly lit ramp as the doors rumbled shut behind him. The tunnel, a kilometre long, took him under the bluff and under the next valley — a valley surrounded by steep, heavily wooded slopes, ringed by security fences, sensing devices and 24-hour patrols equipped at night with IR aimers only visible through night vision goggles. On the perimeter fence were signs: HYDRO ELECTRIC COMMISSION FACILITY. KEEP OUT.

In the valley were rows of barrack-like buildings several storeys high — featureless and painted to blend with the surroundings from the air. They had no doors and windows only at the top. One had a flat roof with concealed lights to assist night helicopter landings. A fenced-off gravelled area enclosed cooling boxes and vents.

Cain left the wagon in the transport bay and walked to Verification. Half an hour later he was cleared and in the lift heading for B4 — one of the seven underground floors. He now wore a metal wristband with a transmitter that tracked him and transmitted the codes that allowed him to enter each section.

'Welcome back, Mr Cain,' the duty surgeon on the B4 desk said with deference. 'A message from 2IC.'

Cain took it. Pat's handwriting:

Dear One,

I'm flat out like a lizard drinking. And Ronnie's not back yet. So settle in and visit Detainment. John knows you're coming today — been asking about you all week. We'll sort you out ASAP.
Love
P

He dumped his things in his berth on B6 and rode the lift down again to B7.

In the 'guest wing', as Detainment was called, not even a rat could move unseen. The level crawled with surgeons, surgeon instructors and cadets. The only creatures unchallenged were brown and had six legs.

He passed Zia's suite, not wanting to make contact, surprised they hadn't shipped him south.

He passed Stern's lab, still wondering what the guy was doing. The history of most of these people was 'need to know'. Stern was a likeable type. He went in.

Stern's domain was now an Amazon of drooping laboratory hoses. There was a spectrometer and so much test equipment it took him a moment to spot the scientist. 'Still at it?'

Stern, a small-boned Jew with a pleasant expression, looked up from the bench. 'I know that face.' He brushed through the festoon and shook Cain's hand. 'Been years. What have you been up to?' The standard joke. As if anyone would tell you. The man had a funny bone, a valuable quality for those robbed of their lives.

'I'm retired.'

'So why are you here?'

'They need a babysitter.' He waved at the tubes. 'What's this?'

'Same old shtick. It's a pilot plant. Just needs scaling up.'

'And it does what?'

Stern cackled. 'Ah, I have a secret too.'

Cain walked further down the corridor past the doors of more 'originals', preparing for the next encounter. He wasn't ready or worthy. But, as with most events in life, one rarely was.

He paused outside the pope's door.

A Grade One duty surgeon crept up to him as if confronting an icon. 'He's in the library, sir — alone.'

He nodded, continued to the originals' library, a long thickly carpeted room with a central row of tables, each with its brass reading lamp. John sat in an alcove, reading a book. He looked older, shrunken, but still wore a neat cassock and a cross. A good sign. He'd always been scrupulous. Cain stared at the grey face, feeling a stab of affection and concern. How old was he now? He'd been born in 1912. Almost eighty.

The old man looked up. A beautiful smile of delight. And Cain, authorised assassin, product of every religion and none, fell in front of him, bawling, grasped his hand and pressed it to his cheek.

The pope stretched forward, touched his shoulder. 'I knew you'd come.'

Cain remained on the floor before him.

The pope blessed him. 'I've missed you so much.'

'I didn't know if I'd see you again.'

'But we're here.' A twinkling smile.

Cain grimaced, 'Oh God,' mopped his face with his handkerchief. 'So how the hell are you?'

John smiled again in his disarming, timid way. 'Not terribly *ex cathedra* today. I have a cold. The legs are bad.' He had phlebitis. 'And the Hound of Heaven kept me awake all night.'

He laughed. The old man knew when to keep it light.

'And — I've been waiting for you.'

That started him bawling again.

The pope patted his shoulder. 'What you must have gone through.'

Cain pulled himself together. 'Your English has improved.' The priest's painful English — learned from a Linguaphone course — was much better.

'But my French has gone and my German and Spanish are rusty. My Latin still remains. The Lord giveth and the Lord taketh away.'

He wiped his eyes again. 'What's the book?'

'Something that speaks to me very much — *To Live Within*. Have you read it?'

'No.'

'I've ordered several copies for the others. Such depth. So clear.' He licked his finger, turned the pages for a moment. 'Ah yes. Here. "Awareness is freedom to see without entering into anything ... this awareness is called in the *Upanishads* 'knowing without content'."'

Cain nodded slowly.

'There are marvellous things here. I've marked many of them. Like this: "I am that I am!" It comes to that formula for which the Christ was crucified, the Sufi murdered. Only Buddha escaped that destiny, though he had many antagonists in his lifetime and still has.' He passed the book across. 'I want you to read this. To ponder it, absorb it. So,' he smiled, 'let me look at you. How have you been?'

He took the book with care. 'The "being" is the hard bit.'

John nodded slowly. 'Yes. Because it needs energy. But life bleeds us. Every thought, emotion, tension is a wound.'

'And I've had to kill more people.'

'Like Arjuna — without rancour?'

'At times there was anger — at what they'd done. As for Krishna and Arjuna ...' He remembered the extraordinary passage at the beginning of the *Bhagavad Gita*. 'Isn't it a metaphor for overcoming reactions?'

'Each reaction claiming to be "I". Yes. I'm glad you came to that. Of course, there will be several meanings. No scripture should be taken literally.'

'Can I quote you?'

'No. Or some fool will turn it into scripture.'

Cain laughed.

'But to stay with the field of Kurukshetra.' The pope, for all his meekness, was a persistent and methodical man. 'Everything we do has consequences. But we make the mistake of believing our acts are consequential. I don't know if you see the distinction?'

A Department D cadet had approached them and was now standing a short distance away, waiting to be addressed — too in awe to venture further forward.

Cain turned to him. 'Yes?'

'The CO's back on base, sir, requires you on G4, sir. She said only when you're through, sir.'

'Okay. Thanks.'

The youth backed away, as if from royalty.

Cain smiled, remembering how he'd venerated the great ones as a trainee. No wonder the lad was gobsmacked. He'd remember this all his life. The great Grade Four, cheeks wet, kneeling at the feet of the pope.

He turned back to his friend. 'Pat tells me you have morning sessions here.'

'Yes. The people are simple but genuine. Would you care to join us?'

'Very much. What do you try with them?'

'Basically the inner look. I want them to come to a sensation of themselves — as a beginning. Then of course, the relaxing from thought.'

'The breath?'

'Not yet. Well, not directly. One can't hurry.'

'So — energy ...'

'Yes,' he smiled. 'The energy eventually. And how it finds you. That book you have says much about it. But of course, there's really no approach. Each technique distorts. There are no methods.'

'One forgets.' He shook his head. 'Every moment.'

'So you need to begin every moment. Dogen-zenji's lecture on Being-Time. Remember?'

'Yes. Fantastic.'

'All true traditions are one.'

'You mean there's only one Void?'

The pope shook his head slowly, shut his eyes and a tear rolled from beneath one lid. He whispered. 'There is — only — Void.'

Cain's every pore was alive now, trying to absorb what was being given. It was amazing this, as if they'd never been apart, as if their relationship had simply paused.

The beautiful smile. 'I'm talking shorthand. I'm too much by myself.'

Except at EXIT Beta, Cain thought, you were never by yourself. All of this was being recorded as they knew. Just as they knew that no one at the consoles would comprehend.

The pope leaned forward, still intent on following the line. 'When I abandon myself utterly — there's an intensity, isn't there?'

'An energy.'

'You have it now?'

'A little.' He felt naked inside, and then the sweet deluge began — he was flowing with warmth, liquid gold. How had this come? From the pope's atmosphere that charged the room? 'But what ... knows ... this?'

'What can be said? The Substance knows the Substance. That's all.'

'There's no logic to that.'

'Truth can only be expressed as paradox.'

He nodded, intensely grateful for what had been said and what he was experiencing now — able from that to catch the insight. It wasn't the words. Only experience conveyed these things.

'You feel it?'

He nodded again, not wanting to disturb it with speech.

'Good. To quote the opposition, remember St Seraphim of Sarov? "God is a fire that warms the heart and the vitals." The motionless mind sunk in breath — flowing warmth right to the belly.'

'Are you sure he said all that?'

'I'm sure he meant to,' John chuckled.

That broke the spell. It was intentional. The old man knew there was just so much at any one time you could absorb.

Cain propped back on his arms. 'Phew.'

John laughed. 'Glad to be back?'

He shook his head as if getting water out of his ears. 'Hope I can stand the pace.'

The pope smiled. 'You better go and see her. We'll have plenty of time to try again.'

He grasped the aged hands, tearful once more. 'Thank you.'

John nodded, tired now. The effort had cost him as well.

Rhonda's den was worse than he remembered it. Despite modern furniture and communications systems it looked like the dispatch department of a correspondence school. All flat surfaces including the floor were covered with files, maps, manuals, lost coffee cups and scraps of food. She advanced to greet him through it all like a hippo learning hopscotch.

'*Anima mia.*' A perfunctory hug. She looked worn out.

'You okay?'

'Stuffed. The Great Dane's turned into my Caliban — more than Zuiden ever was to you.'

He picked his way forward. 'How's the worm in the apple?'

'Still there. But so are we. Curious, isn't it?'

He disinterred two chairs. It was safe to talk here. The room was electronically clean at least. 'Did Karen tell you about Murchison?'

'Yes.' She fiddled with a crushed pack of fags.

'And?'

'Forget it.'

'He wasn't assigned to her?'

'No.'

'Then ...'

'Ray, I'm on it.'

'I just want to help.'

'And you will. I'll inform you when. It'll be the biggest Blue Card job of your career.'

They sat and she lit a cigarette as if she barely had the energy to function.

'Oh — congratulations on Germany. Fantastic!' He shook her hand.

That pleased her. 'And now we're getting somewhere in South Africa. Quite enough to justify a life.'

'Shame about Benazir.'

'*C'est la guerre.*'

'Now they're back with the army and another Zia stooge.'

'Still, things have moved. I predict she'll squeak in again.'

He felt something under his foot, picked a squashed jellybean off his shoe. 'How come Zia's still here? Thought you would have topped the bugger.'

'I've got all the warrants except for the one from the UK. Muslim influence on their government. Never thought I'd miss Maggie but I do. Trying to get people to agree on an execution is worse than juggling ferrets.' She found another bean on the floor, picked it up, shoved it in her mouth. 'So how's Albino Luciani?'

'Amazing.'

'Is the pope a Catholic?'

'Good question.'

'I listened.' She dragged in nicotine. 'But, lacking the required supernal insight, found it as intelligible as a lecture on multiplexing systems. I was surprised you didn't both levitate.' She reached under her chair and pulled out a third-full bottle of scotch. 'Oh bother. It's not sacramental wine. Suppose you're too pure for hard liquor?'

'I'll risk it.'

'Such condescension. Two glasses under your chair, both dirty. But no doubt your sanctified touch will remedy that.'

He felt around till he found the glasses, held them out. She sloshed spirit into them. 'I think John's running this joint. Forty adepts ... dawn sittings ...'

He laughed.

'And you care for him more than me, fickle bastard. Now, if you're returned from the unmanifest long enough to attend to business ...' She swayed forward, legs apart, elbows on her knees. 'There are these two rich sisters who live in a mansion in the South Island of New Zealand. One has a teenage daughter. And wherever this brat goes, things fly across the room, doors open and close, clocks go mad, lights blow ...'

'Ron. The guy who I saw in Queenstown was CIA.'

'Even so. The sweet doves are leaning on us.'

'We're working for the Company?'

She gulped scotch. 'Funding crisis. Side job. Funds our more important work. Take no notice.'

'What about our charter? What about PARTISANS ARE PERNICIOUS?'

'Ray. Please. I'm barely coping here.' She dragged on her fag. 'Now, this nymph is to psychic phenomena what Rommel was to the desert campaign. She ...'

'Ronnie?'

An exhausted, 'What?'

'Why can't the person running this handle it?'

'Because, dear heart, it's Stromlo.'

'The guy who replaced the pope?' He was stunned. 'But he'd be in his sixties now — a prune.'

'Verily. The Great Stromlo. Sixty-two and rooted.'

'Shit, I'm working for the CIA — with Stromlo? You'd better bloody fill me in.'

She sucked in smoke, squinted at him for a time, assessing him. 'It was the first side job we ever did. The Vatican leaned on Wolf through a government I won't name.'

'Wolf did a *side* job?'

'You see the problem with information? Up to a certain point, knowledge is power. Beyond that it's disillusionment. Yes, Wolf did a side job for certain people in the Curia. They wanted two folks out of the way. John and one Amos Stern.'

'Why?'

'Gianpaolo had to go because he wouldn't toe the line. Wouldn't reject Liberation Theology, rattled skeletons in the Vatican bank and didn't see extending the natural period of infertility from 24 days to 28 as a sin. Then he was about to meet with a committee from the State Department on birth control. The Curia flipped.'

'Insane. I mean, nature kills human embryos. The endometrium resorbs them.'

'Ah, but one mustn't mess with a manufactured doctrine aimed at multiplying the faithful.'

'So why not the Italian solution? Haven't they popped popes in the past?'

'Because they're hobbled by this dark age of humanist democracy. No, they didn't want to kill him — just replace him.'

He nodded, frowning.

'But the switch went wrong.'

'It's getting confusing.'

'Bear with me.' She finished her drink. 'Stromlo was the same intake as Wolf and his best friend. God knows why. Stromlo's a grotesque creature — sensual, well-developed blood-lust and would have been a blast as a surgeon. But Tigon put him in D and streamed him as a priest.'

'Why?'

'Why indeed?' She threw up her hands. 'Stromlo then spent years warping his inhibitions in Brazil and ended as a full Grade Four. And our man in the Curia.'

'Then the switch was requested for the pope.'

'Yes. But Gianpaolo made waves too fast. That meant Stromlo lost his lead time and everything went pear-shaped. You see, the problem with side jobs is how not to let the left hand know the right hand's cutting it off. In this case, the left hand was the CIA, because Washington's big on third-world population control.'

'And now Stromlo's working for the Company?'

'With the CIA — and with you.' She snorted. 'Cruddy side jobs! Pains in the arse.'

He was still trying to understand it. 'So if Stromlo made the switch — then where's the duplicate pope now?'

'Buried in St Peter's. Terrible botch. Everything went wrong. Stromlo was sharp enough to scrape through, but it wrecked his nerve. As for Wolf — he'd been used, compromised, forced to go against the charter. And he'd turned his best mate, the Great Stromlo, into a raving, self-dramatising psycho. He topped himself three months later.'

'So *that* was why he did it. And what about Stern? What's he invented? The ultimate contraceptive?'

'Nothing so innocent. Nice man but he'll never get a job in pharmaceuticals.' She stood up with effort and dug at her dress to ease a bra-strap. 'Now we're off to Duplications. Time you saw what you're in for.'

21

ON ACTIVE SERVICE

Pat's domain was extensive. It included a TV studio two levels high used for recording duplicates' postures and expressions during rehearsals. From the control room they gazed down at sandbagged flats arranged into a set. The floor beyond that was marked out in chalk. Rhonda said, 'It's a mock-up of the house. It's too big to do it all here. The sisters are loaded. Their father left them millions. They work but don't have to.'

He pointed to a workbench. The floor around it was littered with white spatter. 'What's that?'

'One sister has a studio for moulding and casting porcelain dolls. They're still teaching the duplicate how to do it.'

They left the control room and went to the viewing room where Rhonda slumped on the lounge in front of the monitor and waved at the engineer behind his console. 'Run it.'

The soundless tape showed the dining room of the actual house. A girl entered the room, perhaps twelve, thirteen. Blonde locks. Up-tilted nose. Tanned lithe body with tight hips, budding breasts, perfect legs — a kiddy-porn starlet and lecher's wet-dream. But she was sullen, pouting, her movements angry.

As she crossed to the table, she banged her fist down on its top, yelling at someone.

A mirror on the wall behind her cracked, fell to the floor. She turned, still soundlessly yelling. An ornament on a sideboard flew across the room, hovered in the air, then went back to its original position.

Cain said, 'Is this for real?'

The table in the room began to shake. A metal candlestick lifted off it and stuck to the girl's cheek. She had trouble pulling it away, then wrenched it free and threw it across the room.

He blurted, 'Shit.'

Rhonda said, 'There's hours of this but that's probably enough.' She stood up. 'Next we meet the duplicates in person.'

They walked past the plastic surgeon's section, the operating theatre, the dental lab, training rooms, cosmetic workshop, reached Pat's office and knocked.

The door was opened by the same girl he'd seen on the video. Except she had bands on her teeth and a surgical bandage across her nose. She said in her breathy voice, 'Hi. I'm Nina. Come and meet the family.'

Pat's office doubled as a casting room. It had a light-stand facing a bare wall, a scattering of plastic chairs, a monitor with video player and a pin-board with a profusion of head-sheets. Pat was sitting on a plastic chair talking to two women. She looked up as they entered and came brightly forward to kiss him. 'Hello, stranger.'

He returned the kiss, delighted to see her, but surprised at her gaunt appearance. It had only been two years.

She said, 'So how's the thousand bucks coming? Remember our psychic phenomena bet? I take Amex.'

'Not a penny till I see it in person.'

She introduced the two women. 'Meet Eve and Jane.'

Neither duplicate was finished. The shorter, curvaceous one had two black eyes and face scars from operations. The taller, athletic one had a bandage on both ears, bandaged hands and a livid scar at the hairline.

The shorter one said, 'Wow, he's dishy.'

Pat said. 'Hands off. He's mine.'

The girl playing the daughter said, 'What about me?'

Pat said, 'You're supposed to be sexually frustrated.'

'Got it in one.'

'They wanted to meet you,' she told him. 'I know they're not completed but you're looking at the last of many operations. It hasn't been easy for them. All right, you three. You've met him now. Back to the voice-matching booth.'

The duplicates blew him kisses as she shooed them out.

When they'd left, she put an arm around him. 'Taking me to dinner tonight?'

'Don't I always?'

'Bloody wombat. Eats, roots and leaves.'

Rhonda said. 'Charming. Now if you lovebirds will accompany me to Logistics . . .'

Logistics was a barrel-shaped room adjoining the reference library with a circular central table and screens built into the walls.

The three of them sat around the table. Rhonda threw the jamming switch. Red lights came on above the door. She told Pat, 'You have the floor.'

'Okay.' Pat put on a Play School voice. 'Once upon a time in a big big house in the backwoods of New Zealand's brooding volcanic South Island, lived two rich, reclusive half-sisters and a daughter. The sisters slept in big beds and quite often shared boyfriends.'

He blinked.

'But the daughter slept in a small bed all by herself because she had emotional problems as you can imagine. And on bad days, she had invisible playmates — that flung things around the room.'

'Weird.'

'Now in a far, far country,' Pat simpered on, 'in a big walled compound called the Kremlin, people heard about the family — people interested in anti-bloody-gravity and psi-effects. Some wanted to visit them. Some wanted to kidnap them.'

'The whole family? Why not just the girl?'

'Because,' Rhonda cut in, 'if you disturb the situation the manifestations could stop. It could be a form of energy produced by the nervous system. The girl is certainly the focus, but no one knows the conditions causing the effect. It could be the girl alone or the family dynamics. So far, they know it's not the house because, if the family goes away, the thing follows.'

'Anyway,' Pat did a hand sashay for attention, 'in a big country called America a kind-hearted CIA man said, "Seeing the house isn't a factor, wouldn't it be nice to take the family to a cosy lab and study them? But in case that disappoints the people in the Kremlin, we'll make a duplicate family they can invite or kidnap if they want to."'

'Clever.'

'The problem's how to do it without upsetting them,' Rhonda added. 'A crude switch could affect the phenomena. So we need the family's cooperation.'

'You mean — tell them we're going to replace them?'

'We have.'

'Shit. Did they buy it?'

'No.'

'Which is where you come in,' Pat said. 'Because it's right up your street. You're a chick-magnet. Good at bullshit. Able to handle loopy females. Your religious background connects with Stromlo, you're psychologically strong ...'

'And,' Rhonda added, 'you're good at extermination.'

'Hold it. I'm supposed to *kill* people?'

She stroked her chins. 'Stromlo's an alcoholic, old and shot. Sharp enough to mastermind the switch. But he can't charm women or knock off storm-troops.'

'*Storm-troops?*'

She lowered her head as if looking at him over glasses. 'This isn't old home week, dear heart. We've just lost our key man in Pretoria. They've killed a Grade Two in Bosnia. Last month we lost the team in Yugoslavia — including the surgeons would you believe? And side job or not — you could be next.'

'So who's behind it?' He glared at them both. 'And if it's that bad, why aren't we blown?'

Pat glanced at Rhonda. 'Do we spill our guts?'

Rhonda picked her ear with a pencil, thinking. 'No.' She turned to him. 'It's not because we don't trust you, Ray. But if someone gets to you and grills you ... All we can say now is that things are changing fast. And you'll need to be ready for anything. All overseas assignments — even yours — are now Condition Red.'

'Condition Red? For a doddle with three females and a poltergeist?'

'Don't assume it's a doddle. Now we can't spare surgeon backup for this number. Vanqua's pushed for trained people as well, so you're it. All hands to the pumps. *Tu comprends?*'

He spent the rest of the day in ops, absorbing detailed briefings, then took the lift to the bistro to meet Pat. Unlike the canteen, the place had candles, fabric tablecloths and its windows overlooked the valley wilderness. Couples mostly ate there, despite the nominal charge.

She was waiting in a corner booth. She'd put on lipstick, done her best, but nothing could disguise her worn-out look. She pointed to the cliff and dusk-smudged trees. 'Isn't that beautiful?'

He nodded, sat down, uneasy. Life was rough sailing and reunions definite shoals.

'So how's the pet food and tampons trade?'

'Busy.'

'Enjoy it?'

'For a while. Now it feels a bit pointless. It's such a small tight push. People vanishing up their bums.'

'I told Rhonda you'd get jack of it.' There was great tiredness behind her smile. 'So ... women?'

'Just one. No intellectual giant but affectionate. Took a while to get my lies straight. It's over now. She had a child in Noumea and went back to the father for the kid's sake. So — how's life with you?'

'Ratshit.' She fiddled with her bread knife. 'I've had a double mastectomy.'

'Cancer?'

'I've been bald for a while.'

He took her hands. 'Is it ... ?'

'Too bloody right. DEATH IS A FACT OF LIFE. But we've still got tonight — if you can stand me.'

He stared at her and tears began.

She said, 'Don't. You'll wet the tablecloth.'

'Jesus. Why are you still here?'

'WORLD MAINTENANCE IS MORALITY. I want this outfit back on the rails. And I couldn't let Ron down. She's been in-bloody-credible — just plain heroic. You've no idea what we've been through.'

Their evening was all the more poignant because they didn't know if they'd ever meet again. She left the bedside light on, took the padded bra off with her back to him, shy about the scars, then turned. 'I look like a whore's drawers.'

'Those who matter don't mind and those who mind don't matter.'

He made love to her, surprised at the fierceness of her response. They cried a little, kissed a lot. Later, the peace on her face made him glad.

Sometime during the night they woke and he pressed her hand in the dark. 'You two can't carry this alone. You're both exhausted. Please let me help.'

'You're helping, love. Honestly.'

'By romancing two sisters in the sticks of New Zealand? Let me stay here and take the bastards out.'

'It's not that simple. But we've a counter-attack set up and getting you out of mothballs is a part of it.'

'You mean this job's a diversion?'

'Don't ask. And don't fret. You'll get your chance to spill blood.'

'For God's sake, Pat, fill me in.'

'Nup. Ronnie's right. Too dangerous.'

It often came to this. It was difficult sleeping with head office.

After a while she said, 'Do you think there's life after death?'

'Was there before?'

'I've had a fan-bloody-tastic life. Wouldn't have missed it for quids. You've studied all this stuff. What do you reckon?'

He gave the comforting reply. 'If there's not, you won't have a worry. If there is, it's a bonus. Either way you're in good shape.'

It pleased her. 'Hadn't thought of it like that.'

Soon he heard soft snores.

He stared for a long time into the dark.

22

DREAM OF FAIR WOMEN

Rhonda stubbed out the butt on the bed-head and tossed the report on the floor. She rubbed her eyes, switched off the light and forlornly prayed for sleep.

But her mind still churned with the questions that had kept her so often awake. If they wanted to get rid of her, why hadn't they attacked? If they knew enough to destroy EXIT projects, why hadn't the place been exposed? She was physically strong but couldn't take much more.

To soothe herself into drowsiness she thought about past loves. It was 1959. She'd been twenty-two — and Etta a flaxen-haired sixteen.

First love, so strangely sweet. The body that she loved, so fair and lithe. The rapture of a female heart and body responding to her own.

Nothing, nothing, could equal those brief months. She'd felt like an Olympian struck from the sun. But the lifespan in ancient Greece was thirty years. And in this age of medical dexterity and emotional aridity she was two decades beyond that — ugly, fat.

And the beautiful Etta was dust.

Better dust than the thing she'd found hanging from the beam in the laundry, the blood pooled in the ankles, glory gone. An unmoving thing that turned slowly on the rope. A broken thing.

Her love, stronger than time, scourging her with regret. She turned in the bed and groaned.

Mockery feasting on despair.

Sleep. She had to sleep.

Love — the most dangerous thing in the world.

23

TEMPTATION
AND BENT TIME

FIORDLAND, NEW ZEALAND

The house was a twenty-minute drive from the small township along a narrow road that wound between steep cliffs. Cain drove slowly in torrential rain, wipers on high. He crossed three wooden bridges — typical of this remote area — single lane with a caution sign each end. The rivers beneath the bridges thundered over jagged rocks and cascades sprayed from the high side of the road.

It was an ominous landscape, every turn revealing a new cloud-blurred peak gashed by thin waterfalls. He reached a cleared valley of tussocks and tree roots hacked from mossy beech forest.

The building commanded the valley, sat well back on the high side of the road. It looked more like a country hotel than the domain of a wrathful ghost. Behind it rose a precipitous backdrop of trees and sub-alpine scrub.

The curving drive was flanked by neat lawn and well-placed trees. He stopped the car beneath the entrance portico and the sound of rain on metal ceased. He'd expected a home this far south to have walls made mouldy by spring rains. But the ranch-style, two-storey building with its bay windows and elegant air was well maintained, its paintwork spick.

He got a bag out of the boot, crossed the terrace to the door and rang. A vacuum cleaner switched off. Through frosted-glass panels, someone coming.

'Cain?'

The Great Stromlo matched the briefing photographs. Shabby clothes, clerical collar, thin frame, pouched face.

'Mark West's the agreed name.'

'Yes of course, Mr West. Please come in.'

The tiled entranceway had stairs leading up.

He said, 'Impressive place.'

Stromlo's doleful look. 'There should be a sign: *Lasciate ogni speranza ...*'

Abandon hope?

A woman came down the stairs. The original was considerably better than the unfinished substitute. She wore tight black stretch-jeans and a woollen top open at the neck. She had a ripe curve to her hips and upper body, heavy breasts, soft lines to her shoulders and arms. The way it all moved was intriguing.

'So the parcel's arrived.' Her voice sounded like Baileys Irish Cream gurgling through a warm bassoon.

'This is Mark West, our new security man.' Stromlo introduced the woman. 'Eve Rinaldi.'

She stepped over the vacuum cleaner that Stromlo had apparently been using at the foot of the stairs, came forward to shake his hand. 'You're very handsome.' Then to Stromlo, 'I'll take him up.'

As he followed her she said, 'This used to be a conference centre. They couldn't make it pay. Too far away from anywhere. We got it cheap.'

He lugged his bag up the second turn of stairs, watching her rounded but neat rear straining her jeans pleasantly as she climbed. They walked to a bedroom with en suite and view out over the valley. As he put down the bag, he spotted a movement sensor at the corner of the ceiling.

She said, 'Father Roberto vacuumed in here this morning. He doesn't have to do it but sees drudgery as penance. He's a strange character — but a wonderful music teacher for Nina.'

She led him back down to the expansive lounge room that had been chalk-marks in the EXIT mock-up. It had a sprawl of comfortable furniture, a baby grand and a hooded central fire where logs smouldered in a pile of white ash.

'Central heating,' she said.

He gazed at the sweeping sodden view. The windows, true to the briefing, had security strips. 'A beautiful place.'

'It's converted well. Jane and I have made lairs of some of the upstairs suites. She has her workroom. I have my sewing room and materials storeroom. My doll studio's downstairs in what used to be a conference room. Then there's the pool, gym, sauna. We don't lack much. We have four garages in a separate building at the back with staff accommodation above them.'

'Cosy.'

'So you're here to protect us from the Russians?'

'I understand they paid you a visit.'

'Two of them. We said "no".'

'The next time you mightn't have a choice.'

'If you do your job properly we will. Coffee?'

'Thanks.'

'Follow me. Cook's off today. Jane's at work. You'll meet her later.' They entered a commercial kitchen. 'We haven't remodelled this yet. Too hard.' She fiddled with a mini espresso machine.

'Powdered stuff's fine.'

'In that case . . .' She spooned some crystals into a mug and filled it from a steaming electric urn. 'Milk?'

'Thanks.'

'Cow's milk's bad for humans. Ideal for calves of course.' She went to a fridge as big as a walk-in cupboard.

The sound of the rain and the hollow tick of a reproduction railway wall-clock.

'You've brought guns, I suppose?'

He nodded.

'We won't leave, you know.'

As he took the cup, the girl walked in. She wore a floppy jumper and jeans. Long fair hair hung down her back. Her sulkily beautiful face and slim frame made her classic jail-bait.

Eve said, 'Nina. This is our new security man, Mr West.'

'You going to screw him?' She spat the words.

'Behave yourself.'

'Suck eggs.' She grabbed a biscuit from a canister.

Eve shrugged. 'They're angels at two, contentious at five, savages at ten and demons at thirteen.'

Her daughter threw the canister to the floor. Biscuits scattered over the tiles.

Her mother ordered, 'Out. Now.'

The girl stood her ground, legs apart, holding her breath. Her eyes bulged slightly and she made a small grunting noise. The room, for no clear reason, became cold.

'No!' her mother cried. She clapped once and pointed at the door. 'Out.'

The girl glared a moment longer then flounced from sight.

Eve frowned. 'She's so destructive. I need to go and talk to her. Excuse me.'

As he stood in the empty kitchen, sipping coffee, he noticed the ticking had stopped and glanced up at the clock. The minute hand had bent until it was touching the glass. As he watched it bent further. He stared at it, incredulous, cold sweat starting down his spine.

Stromlo came into the room, squatted stiffly, began to pick up biscuits.

Cain pointed. 'The — clock.'

He glanced at it. 'Yes. Like Lazarus, we are trapped in the sepulchre of time.'

'The hands, I mean. They're bending.'

He looked again. 'Devil's child. I suggest we go back to the lounge room.'

'Why?'

'You never know.'

'Know what?'

The priest reached for the canister but it rolled as if retreating from his hand yet there was no draught in the room. He growled, 'Jesus Christ rebukes you oh demon, oh deceiver,' then lunged, caught the canister and dropped the biscuits back inside. He slammed the lid on it, stood and placed it back on a bench top. 'Come on.'

Cain was staring again at the clock. The hour hand had fallen off and now lay against the glass.

As they moved back to the lounge, there was a crash behind them. It sounded as if the tin had fallen and the biscuits were back on the floor.

'What's that?'

'The devil's work.'

'Shouldn't we ...'

'Best to ignore it.'

'How?'

'The trouble with evil is there's nothing easier to get used to.' The priest hunched into a chair by the fire and stared morosely at the rain.

Cain reluctantly sat, still churning at what he'd seen. 'How does she — do it?'

'I doubt she knows. I've talked to her but our relationship's mortified — a conversation with the dead.'

'Christ. It's ...'

'Unsettling.' His wintry smile. 'Yes, you can be briefed very well. But the actual thing. Always *imprevisto*. It's not under her control, of course. It comes when she reaches a certain emotional pitch. It seems to need the force of that to appear.'

He nodded. The best defence against the unknown was to keep things to business. He pointed to the ceiling. 'You switch the movement sensors on at night?'

'One can't with things flying around. I have a hard-wired seismic sensor grid that monitors the perimeter and another around the house.'

'Ten-metre spread?'

'Yes. Because the staff comes and goes by day, I switch it on at night.' He pulled something out of his pocket. 'This is the receiver. It has light, vibration or beeper readouts.' He worked the selector switches. 'Also shows grid and quadrant. I have a spare.'

'Any transponders for the family?'

'They won't wear them.'

'Is the Russian team still in the country?'

'No. But from what we know, they're making plans for the kidnap now.'

'So I don't have long.'

'Perhaps a week.'

'And you're ready to roll?'

'Just waiting for the duplicates.' He leaned close. He smelt of plonk. 'The postman, bank manager, accountant, solicitor — all transferred, paid off or changed. Eve's doll contacts are mostly American — made by post, internet, not a problem. The sisters keep to themselves so the local situation isn't hard.'

'Looks like you're on top of it.'

'The last people to change will be the staff. The gardener and housekeeper will be leaving before the duplicates arrive.' He poked again at the fire. His thin body still seemed wiry. 'Try to get Jane to give notice at the chemist. Her duplicate will know general pharmacy but obviously can't dispense.'

'So you're set?'

He lifted the poker, scratched at the fire. 'As set as a candidate for the inferno can be. *Corpore vili.*'

'Aren't you confusing your cover with your vocation?'

'Your cover, Cain, is secular. But I was ordained. Ordained! Thus I am a travesty. I long to separate the spirit from the body.' He swayed slightly, nursing his hyper-reflection. 'Tell me …' A breathy whisper smelling of port. 'What manner of priest removes the Holy Father from the Church?'

'You were doing your job.'

'A Judas,' he moaned. 'A Judas.'

Cain steered it back to business. 'The Rinaldis were from Palermo. But the sisters are hardly good Catholics.'

'Nothing here,' the priest hissed, 'is true. It's the devil's house.'

'I'm not convinced the devil fits a post-modernist world.'

A hollow laugh. 'It means you've never lived in Brazil.'

'Rhonda says it's condition red here. Seems over the top to me. How do you read it? *Quando comincia lo spettacolo*?'

'*Molto buono*,' Stromlo smiled, displaying gapped yellow teeth. 'We have time. I have excellent comms. I'm almost hard-wired into their intelligence.'

'Okay. So how do I get to the sisters?'

'You help them violate community standards. They're animals — cows that copulate with one bull.' He produced a silver flask from his back pocket, unscrewed the top. 'My medicine. *Scusi*.' He swigged, gasped with relief and said, 'Brown muscat. Very cheap.' He put the flask away with care. 'They tempt. They tempt.'

'Tempt you?'

'Punch and Judy. The twin temptations of a priest. *Mi capisce*?' He moved his head as if his collar were a noose.

Cain nudged it back on track. 'So whatever way they go, forcibly or willingly, the mechanics of the switch remain the same?'

'*Si*. We'll remain with the duplicates for a time. Also the cook — who is our partisan.'

He nodded, stared at the fire. Small explosions from the burning wood shot embers over the circular brick hearth. It was still pouring outside but the house seemed quiet. He'd been told that the staff had Thursday off.

Stromlo turned to him suddenly, face bloodhound long. 'Gianpaolo. Did you see him?'

'Yes.'

The priest closed his eyes, hissed through his teeth. 'How is he?'

'*Magnifico.*'

He shook his head and rocked.

'So anything else you want to tell me?'

The man just rocked.

'Right.' Cain got up. 'I'll check the house.'

24

HOUSE OF DOLLS

Cain knew the place was difficult to secure. He walked halls and corridors, peering into rooms, and eventually came to the humid central atrium with its heated pool and fernery. Spa and sauna one end, showers and gym the other. He looked up. The glass roof streamed with rain. He put the exterior recce on hold.

A noise from the back of the house. He followed his ears to Eve's workroom. It had cluttered work benches, an electric kiln and shelving stacked with doll parts and moulds. The floor supported bags of plaster, plastic-wrapped clay and mounds covered in damp cloths.

The beautiful voice. 'Come in.' Eve Rinaldi, in plastic apron, was working by the bench. Four smooth boards encased a mould. The frame was held by sliding brackets.

He asked, 'Can I help?'

She lifted a board clear. 'No, this bit's easy.'

'So you sell dolls to America?'

'Where the money is.' She walked to the end of the bench and his eyes slid to her rear. She was a doll herself, disturbingly so. She removed a wet rag to reveal a clay sculpture of a head. The face was beautifully done. 'It starts like this, then you make a plaster mould.'

'What if the poltergeist comes and ...?'

'Nina isn't allowed in my workrooms. I've told her if she wrecks anything, I'll send her back to her father.'

An effective threat, he decided. The father had tried to rape her.

'When the mould dries you open it like those.' She pointed to half moulds on the shelving behind. 'You take out the sculpture, put the halves back together, pour slip — that's liquid porcelain — through this hole and wait till you see drying rings.'

'Involved.'

'Very. I'm just giving you the overview. So when it dries to the thickness you want, you pour out the rest and it dries in the mould.'

'Why doesn't it stick?'

'Because porcelain shrinks slightly. Then you open the mould, get out the shell ...' She chatted about greenware, seamlines, multiple colour firings, dresses, shoes, gloves, wigs. 'Hundreds of hours of work go into an original porcelain doll.'

'What's one sell for?'

'I get $8000 each for a limited issue of five. That's $40,000 from one mould. And you people want me to walk out on this?'

'Just for a while. When the Russians pinch your duplicate, you'll come back. But if you don't accept our offer and get grabbed — you're out of business.'

'I'm not convinced.'

'If you'd been to Moscow you would be. Snow, slush, things falling apart. Not your scene.'

She took off the apron, looked at him speculatively. 'What are you like at plumbing?'

'Depends what it is.'

'I'll show you.' She led him up the back stairs into a bedroom and pointed to the en suite. The taps weren't dripping or stuck. The cistern seemed fine.

He went back into the bedroom to ask her what was wrong. She now sat on the bed, pulling the woollen top over her head. He stared at the full breasts, barely held by the light bra.

She said, 'Don't look so surprised. It's what they told you to do to us, isn't it?'

'Just like that?'

'Why not?' The dark chocolate voice. 'We haven't had anyone for months.'

She put her hands behind her and undid the bra. Her freed breasts hung lower but were full and firm with mouthable nipples. She pulled back the bed-cover, unzipped the front of her jeans. 'Your cue.'

He'd been propositioned many times but never so frankly. As he sat beside her she started undoing his shirt, his pants, then drew his head down to her breasts. He moved his tongue up between them, then round the nipples.

She lay back. 'Don't you like me?'

'Behave.'

She lay still and shut her eyes.

He undressed himself, then her. The peeled Eve was worthy of Eden — beautifully shaped, the hips and belly superb. He began with her slowly, stroking her, drawing it out. She shuddered at his touch, opened her eyes to look up at him.

'Close eyes.'

She did, obedient now. He kissed her lightly on the brow, worked down, avoiding the mouth, parted now for a kiss but left wanting. With the back of his fingers, he stroked every part of her, leaving the breasts and between her legs till last. Then he began with his tongue, feeling her tremble with each touch.

He brought her to the edge of climax, her hips and thighs squirming, arms tensing, before releasing her wrists and running his tongue up the whole of her — around her breasts, armpits, neck.

When he finally slid into her, her fingers dug into his back. Her eyes were open now, her hair across her face as she squirmed.

In less than a minute she arched and gasped out her release, then lay as limp as one of her dolls and murmured, 'God. You're hired.'

He flipped her, wanting to savour the shape of her from behind. She didn't need cuteness lessons, had a butt a surfing magazine would have paid for. Rock of ages, cleft for thee ... He slid back into her, let himself come. Sex — the hollow victory. Copulate or perish. 'Feeling better?'

She looked at him from within some personal bliss. 'You've just made yourself irreplaceable. 'Jane'll want some of this.' She curled inside his arm like a cat. 'Are you married?'

'No.'

'Why?'

'Married men develop what British airmen used to call "uxorial drag".'

Her throaty laugh.

He switched the subject to Nina and the poltergeist. 'How do you live with the thing?'

'You call it living? We cope.'

'What happens at her school?'

'Nothing. It's shy of other brats. Probably too much competition.'

They slept for an hour, then she went back to work. 'I'm behind on deliveries. No rest for the wealthy.'

After he'd showered and dressed he found the rain had stopped so checked the outside of the house then walked the perimeter fence.

It was six o'clock before Jane appeared — a severe-faced woman with an abrupt manner and the same low voice but few words. Apart from the blonde hair, she seemed not at all like her sister and he couldn't imagine her in bed.

The two of them offered to cook dinner and left to bang around in the kitchen. The sound of Eve's animated voice interspersed with Jane's terse comments suggested that they got on well.

He sat by the fire while Stromlo gave Nina her piano lesson. 'No, child! It says *legato*. *Legaaato* — smoothly, like this.' He demonstrated. 'Like a puppy dog running down the stairs.'

'Stop treating me like a child. It shits me off.'

He sighed and looked across at Cain. 'The doors of the heart can only be opened from inside.'

'You're so full of shit.' She grumpily attempted the passage again.

Eve emerged with a meal on a tray and the pouting Nina took it to her room. Stromlo, Cain noted, watched the girl's trim rear as she left, then saw he'd been spotted and intoned, 'They tempt. They tempt.'

'You don't have to look,' he grinned.

The priest furiously poked the fire, then, remembering something, felt in his pocket and handed Cain a perimeter handset. His pong was atmospheric. 'It's on now.' Cain nodded, switched it to 'vibrate' and put it in his shirt pocket.

Eve's head around the door. 'We eat in two minutes.'

'I'd better open some wine,' Stromlo said. 'One of our little traditions.'

They went into the dining room he'd seen on the video at Beta. No objects flew and the candles stayed on the table.

Eve gave a toast. 'To happy days and dirty nights.'

Dinner was an excellent roast. While they ate, the sisters chatted about people in the locality. Stromlo added comments like 'Hell is other people' and opened two more bottles of red, much of which he drank himself.

Cain brought up security. 'Jane works in the town and Nina goes to school. You should all be wearing transponders.'

'I don't want to be tagged,' Jane said. 'It's your job to know where we are.'

Eve said, 'I agree. Besides,' a twinkle in her eye, 'I've told Jane you have the skills we need.'

Cain, feeling uncomfortable, glanced at the dour-faced woman who said, 'Don't be concerned. I'm not like my sister.'

After dessert and coffee Jane stifled a yawn and glanced at Cain. 'Tomorrow I'll show you the local walking tracks if you like.'

'Could be useful.'

'Good. Let's leave about nine.' She began to clear the plates.

He said, 'We'll wash up. Won't we, Father?'

Stromlo stood unsteadily. 'Right.'

Eve got up. 'Then I'll see if my plaster's a disaster.'

As they entered the kitchen, Cain glanced at the clock. The hands were still as he'd last seen them. He looked at the commercial dishwasher.

Stromlo said, 'Don't bother. You need a pilot's licence. Detergent under the sink.'

Cain ran hot water and the priest found a tea towel. He said, 'Has she corrupted you yet?'

'Mattress mambo? *Si.*'

'Disgusting.'

'For someone who checks out their arses . . .' He let it slide. 'So is this place dry-cleaned?'

'I had it scanned two days ago. Our tennis partners aren't the Komitet. They're not after secrets, just phenomena.' He swayed to a drawer with a fistful of damp forks.

A drunken, self-pitying Stromlo. It was his chance to find out about John. 'Ron told me about your run but I found it very confusing. She said you'd fill me in.'

'Ah, yes. Security again,' Stromlo said. 'A case of it being too extreme.'

'How's that?'

'The Vatican is a nest of secrets and manipulations presented as piety and Church procedure. Certain curial *monsignori* I do not name ... One was a Jesuit. You know of the Arrupe matter?'

'No.'

The priest polished plates dry with a drunk's slow deliberation. 'John Paul was a practical man with an inquisitive, topical mind. He called people by their first names, waved at people from his window, talked to Swiss Guards, the gardeners. Such a gift with people.'

'Hasn't changed.'

'He wished to help the oppressed, the poor, to unite the Christian churches ...' The priest slammed plates on a shelf. '...and so some schemers in the Curia got to loathe his guts.'

'Why?'

'Because the pope is infallible. But — my God! My GOD! He mustn't do as he likes. Padre Albino was fresh air — an outsider they found uncontrollable.'

Cain started washing pots. 'I wonder what they'd think of him now.'

'Even back *then* he was beyond them. Most of them just want to preserve Church authority — see human rights and democracy as an invention of the devil. They grind obedience from people's pain — because original sin equals power over others. And Albino's progressive agendas undermined that autocracy.' The priest thrust pots into a cupboard. 'Albino wasn't afraid of the Curia — intended to reform it. There'd never been such hope, such promise in a pope.'

'Then you were ordered to nobble him.'

He groaned. 'No plenary indulgence will absolve this soul.' He dried another pot with furious despair. 'They demanded that we switch him before the meeting with Washington. That gave Pat no time to complete the surgery on the surrogate.'

'How'd you cope?'

'He arrived with a partial latex mask.'

'Shit.' It was worse than his predicament with Zia. 'He couldn't fool them for long like that.'

'He had no chance to try. The night he was installed, a faction involved with the Vatican bank, not knowing about the scheme, killed him with digitalis. Or thought they did. Too much security, you see?'

'Killed the duplicate — thinking he was John?'

'Then Sister Vincenza found him dead and raised the alarm.'

'How did you slide out of that?'

'We sent the nuns and secretaries away but the damage was done. Vincenza and Father Magee saw him before Villot could rearrange the room. Lorenzi had to be told, of course.'

Stromlo assumed that he was familiar with the pontifical household. It showed that the drama, echoing in his head for years, had been amplified into an apocalypse that blurred reality.

'We called the undertakers quickly and paid them well. Later we had to make the partial mask more waxen so it blended with the rest of the face.' He dabbed his brow with the tea towel although it wasn't hot in the room, touched the bench-top to steady himself. 'He had to be displayed on a bier in the Sala Clementina and the latex was a nightmare. It looks wrong on a dead, relaxed face.'

He paused, his pickled mind haunting the apostolic palace. 'Later we staged an autopsy and removed all signs of disguise before burial. We couldn't have him embalmed. Now what's left is safe inside three coffins which I pray will never be reopened.'

'So — without a presentable duplicate, and because of the witnesses — you had to say he'd died.'

'Yes. Total disaster. The Conclave convened again. And Wojtyla won the ballot.'

'And now the Church has two popes.'

'Not for the first time in its history.'

Cain chuckled. 'What a cock-up.'

'You think it *funny*?' Stromlo's affronted look. 'You think it *funny* that I've destroyed the greatest chance God's kingdom on earth ever had — dethroned a pope ... killed my best friend Wolf ...?'

'I think you did an amazing job — turned crud into apple pie. And Wolf wasn't your fault. He did it to himself.'

'In despair. In de-*spair*!'

'And you saved John's life. Without you, he'd be dead now.'

'*Che Dio le renda merito.*' He touched Cain's shoulder in thanks, dabbed a sudden tear, fumbled the tea towel over the oven rail with a sot's protracted attempt at care. 'Do you pray?' His sepulchral tone.

Cain said dryly, 'I'm secretly devout.'

'Then pray for this Judas burning in the furnace of his shame.' Head bowed, he dragged from the room.

For some reason the performance struck Cain as hilarious. When he judged the man out of earshot he spluttered with mirth.

Eve opened the door. 'Something funny?'

'Stromlo,' he laughed. 'Funny man.'

'He is? I must be dense.'

'He's dialectically defrocked. Reminds me of the French guy who said that his life had been full of tragedies — most of which never occurred.'

Her deep chuckle. 'Spot-on for Stromlo. The frogs see life pretty sharply.'

'It's the precision of the language. Has a downside, of course. Takes them nine words to say "flush the toilet".'

'This is becoming such a meaningful exchange I think we should continue it in bed.'

'I'm invited back?'

Her wicked look. 'Command performance.'

25

SAUNA AND LATER

Eve left him around six and headed for the shower. 'Deadlines. Got to hit the ground running.'

He went back to his room for his togs and walked down the back stairs to the atrium. As he passed Stromlo's room he heard him moan. 'Am I not myself when I'm asleep, oh Lord?'

The quote was from Augustine. Did the old boy have nocturnal emissions? Gandhi had confessed to them into his sixties, so it was physically possible.

He dived into the pool, struck out and, on the way back from the deep end, had a view of the gymnasium. Jane was seated on an inclined bench doing dumbbell curls, her slim body in a one-piece swimsuit.

On the return lap, he saw the red light on above the sauna door. Alpha, like many Antarctic bases, had a sauna and he enjoyed them. So, after four hundred strokes, he climbed from the pool and went in.

He was met by pleasing dry heat. He ladled water onto the coals, sat on the second bench up, closed his eyes and thought of Eve. She was proving the most sensuous of women — her body, moans, movements, a delight.

Muffled splashes outside. Jane was having her plunge. He let his mind drift, moisture pouring out of him.

The door clicked. The towel-draped Jane entered and ladled more water on the stove. She undid the towel and sat on it next to him, expressionless and naked. Slim strong legs and arms, trim hips, underdeveloped breasts. She was an exercise freak, his brief had explained. She looked like a bent schoolboy on oestrogen. She leaned against the wooden wall. 'You shouldn't wear a costume in here.'

'Want me to take it off?'

'You'd feel better.'

'Okay.' He stripped.

'How was Eve? Satisfying?'

'Very.'

'I suppose you know we share things.' She put her hand on him, working him hard. Then she moved over and impaled herself on his lap. He cradled her small moist breasts. 'You're an unconventional family.'

'You mean, honest about what we want?'

Soon they were lying on the bench. It was pleasant but odd. He had his fingers on her clitoris, but his knuckles were being mashed into the wood. She raised herself a little to help him. She was awkward, determined. No sound. No frills. Just the intention to be satisfied in the most practical, efficient way.

She said, 'On the floor. It's wider.'

They disengaged and she lay on her back on the floor. The boy's body, short hair, half-masculine face. He entered her again from the front. Her hands on his bottom were guiding him to thrust higher on her, harder.

She started to grunt, determined to come, body tensed, teeth gritted, hands clamped on him as if arresting him for possession.

After the savage delight of her climax, she relaxed and let

him finish in her. Although the floor of the sauna was cooler he felt as if his head would explode.

'Swim now,' she said, as if it was the next part of an exercise routine.

They fell into the pool, needing to cool off fast.

When they surfaced, Stromlo was standing by the fernery, sipping orange juice, the cord of his frayed dressing gown trailing on the tiles. He shook his head sadly, turned and shuffled away.

'Dirty old hypocrite,' she said. 'Tells us how sinful we are. But he perves.'

The staff were back and the capable Chinese cook packed them an excellent lunch. He left Stromlo holding the fort, Eve working on her moulds, and went bushwalking with Jane.

She was a practised tramper with a persistent steady pace and, on steep climbs with fewer toes, it was tough keeping up with her. She'd brought a machete and hacked at encroaching branches. For three hours they barely spoke. He tried to relate the trails to a walking map she'd given him of the area.

They ate near the peak of a mountain beside a tarn ringed by daisies where robins fluttered in the underbrush and squabbling parakeets drifted on the air. The view was impressive — thickening forest of beech and rimu dotted by huge tree ferns and mountain scrub.

'So what's your take on the poltergeist?' he asked.

'It's a fact of life.' She stared at mist trapped lower in the valley. 'I try to work around it.'

'Nina seems very disturbed.'

'Don't cry for that sneaky little minx.'

'You all need to leave here. The Russians have tried the polite approach. Next time they'll march in and grab you.'

'Leave this?' She waved at the opposite peak. A ribbon of white water cascaded down its rocks. 'Leave my job, the gym, the sauna, the pool?'

'But if they pinch you, you'll have nothing.'
She just stared at the stream of falling water.

It was an all-day tramp. Some of the track was overgrown and they saw no one. On a long descent during the afternoon, they reached a mountain stream, undressed and dunked. The water was very cold and they had no towels so sat on her space blanket, letting the weak sun dry their skin.

She pointed to his holstered SIG and the two clips.

'What's this?'

'Tool of trade.'

'Fully deductible?' The expressionless look that could be either dispassion or disgust.

He began to stroke her arms, wanting her again, licked the last droplets from her neck.

Almost irritably, she lay face down, legs apart on the blanket. Her attitude to sex had the rough practicality of a guerilla fighter on the trail.

He mounted her and it was good. Strong back and small neat buttocks — she seemed to prefer it from the rear. She lay as if uninterested for a while before she started to grunt, push back, then came in her repressed, explosive way.

After it, he tried to fondle her but her emotionless manner discouraged him. She pointed to his foot. 'You're getting a blister.' She rummaged in her bag, peeled a sticking-plaster, slapped it on his heel. He imagined it was the nearest she came to an expression of affection.

When they reached the house, it was almost dusk. Stromlo must have picked them up. He was framed in the back door, looking at his perimeter handset, the plonk smell heavy around him.

'*Buona sera*,' Cain said. 'Everything okay?'

'No. I'm glad you're back. Intelligence report. Five guests tonight. From Russia!'

Jane took her boots off on the back porch and walked past as if she barely knew them. Cain waited till she'd gone and said, 'Five? Hell. We'd better get set up.'

He got the large khaki metal box out of his car boot and lugged it to Stromlo's room. The Grade Four priest had his ordinance spread on the bed. It contrasted oddly with the crucifix on the wall and the statue of the Virgin.

As well as a BDA9 automatic, he had an M249 with a 300-round belt and five prepacked plastic boxes of thirty that rattled as Cain sat beside them. The MINIMI was a congenial and accurate weapon but Cain didn't know why EXIT had decided a machine-gun would be helpful. There were fragmentation and smoke grenades and a set of Bowman hand-held portables. The Great One was equipped for a field spat — not an ambush in a house.

One item was interesting — an M983 Gen III night-vision monocular that could be used as a goggle, hand-held viewer, pocketscope and day/night weapon sight. It would have been a blast, he thought, with standard red-dot aiming. Cain opened his box and lifted out two new P90s and some 50-round plastic mags. 'These make sense.' He handed one over.

'*Non posso più*. What is it ...?' Stromlo stared at the weapon — a hunk of oddly shaped black plastic casing with an almost fully enclosed barrel. A smoked plastic mag lay along its axis above the receiver.

'They call it a PDW. Not a pistol, sub-mac, carbine — new class. A simple high-firepower compact designed for tank crews.' He pointed at the finger holes in the slab-side for trigger and thumb-grip. 'Leaves your hands free because it's so short it hangs off your shoulder like a bag.'

'*Bizzarro*!' Stromlo read the calibre off the side of the bridge sight. 'P90 cal 5.7 by 28. Penetration?'

'Twenty-four layers of Kevlar or a steel helmet at 100 metres.'

'Then stops dead?' His hands caressed the strange moulded sides, his penitent's role fading fast.

'I asked them that. They say it drills an 8-centimetre permanent cavity in standard NATO gelatin. A 9mm Parabellum only does 3 centimetres.'

'You believe it?'

'Dunno. But I tried it on the Beta range. Fifty rounds at 900 a minute's quite handy.' He pointed out the fire-selector disk under the trigger guard, the magazine catch, the cocking handle.

Stromlo squinted down the sight. 'I may not be much help. My hands. *Tremante*.' He held one up. 'And it's been a long time since ...'

Cain had noticed the dead marines in brown paper bags under the bed but knew that EXIT training was so thorough it stayed with you, even when drunk. And, at 3-metre range, Stromlo's shake would be as effective as vibrato on a violin.

The man of God seemed intrigued by the weapon as if eager to test it on flesh. He stripped the barrel, receiver and bolt assembly without instruction. 'Interesting design. So — what do you suggest?'

The act put the cap on Cain's assessment of the priest Grade Four. A dismal, self-dramatising soak he might be. But even a blotto Stromlo would give a special ops hard-arse the trots.

He said, 'I reckon they'll come around 4 am. They could have body armour, carbines, image intensifiers and they'll head for the bedrooms upstairs. They'll know I'm a minder. Will they think you're just a priest?'

'*Signore Vita Angelica*.' The old fraud smiled and shook his head. 'No. They know I'm part of it. But not how much.'

'Uh-huh.'

'They'll also know about the motion sensors, the door and window circuits. But they won't pick the perimeter system.'

'Okay.' Cain factored that in. 'So they'll cut the power — get in quietly, spring us asleep if they can, take us out and grab the family.' He reached down to his metal box and lifted out two calf pouches fabricated by EXIT stores. Then the flak jackets, the balaclavas, the camo-cream. 'Good idea to look like them. The more confusion the better.' He filled the pouches with P90 magazines, pulled over the Velcro flaps.

A contemplative look from Stromlo, unconnected to piety. 'Would you engage them outside or ... ?'

'Too sloppy.' He slid his hand over the hammerhead stock of the MINIMI. 'If you hosed them with this or started tossing bombs you'd have a siege or a back-off. You'd take a couple out and the others would live to tell the tale.'

'Not good.'

'Less they know the better. No, I suggest we ask ourselves what we'd do if we were adults.'

Stromlo's face fell, his low opinion of himself re-engaged. 'If we were surgeons, we'd invite them in and surprise them.'

'... And trap them in the house and backburn.'

'Can I be the backburn?' He was like a child asking to hide first.

'Go for it. Ground floor near the back stairs. I doubt they'll bother with the front.'

'No. If we were doing it, we'd come from two ends — a window and near the back door.'

'We've got two handsets. We'll know when they're coming. So I'll be upstairs. You ... ?'

'In the gym,' Stromlo said. 'Good metal cover there. And it commands the back stairs and pool.'

'Fine. Now we can't smuggle the family out ...'

'Too obvious. They'll be watching us now. And we need bait.'

'So what if we hide them in the sauna?'

'*Splendente!*' He clapped. 'Then I can cover them as well as backburn.' He inverted his P90 and smiled at the ejection port. 'I'll tell cook to make sure the staff stay in their wing when it starts.'

'Good.' Cain divided up the remaining magazines. 'We'll need to chat up the family.'

Stromlo raked in his ammo. 'Perhaps as I've lived by the sword ...'

'Hoping to get killed?'

'With luck.'

'Whatever turns you on. Just make sure you take two of them with you.' He pulled the last object from his box — the piano wire with wooden handles. 'You never know.'

Stromlo fondled his gun. 'I thought this had passed me by.' His face contorted to a grin, returned to a guilt-ridden mask. 'I haven't fired at anyone for years. God forgive me, I've missed it so much.'

'My sympathies.'

Stromlo, he thought, must have been a hoot in the Vatican.

26

COALS OF FIRE

'All right,' Eve said, 'if we can't go outside, what's going to happen?'

Cain surveyed the council-of-war around the living room fire. 'We think they'll enter the house from two directions then head for the bedrooms and find you.'

'Find us?' Nina shrilled.

'We'll mock it up — bolsters in the beds. The lights will be knocked out. They'll have night scopes — image amplification, not thermal, and only Gen II.'

Jane said, 'Can we have that in English?'

'Three times less photosensitivity,' Stromlo said, 'and only half as much luminous gain. Far less resolution than the one I have upstairs.'

'Means it won't be that great for them,' Cain said. 'New moon with cloud. We'll get away with bolsters. No heat signature needed. It only has to fool them for a moment.'

Jane said, 'And where will we be?'

'In the sauna. I've switched it off.'

'Why there?'

'Thick door, double walls and Father Roberto can cover you from the gym. He'll need the light from the atrium roof and reflection from the pool. Because I'll be upstairs with the scope. You can leave the door open till he tells you.'

Jane's stolid look. 'If we have to stay in this house, I want a gun.'

Stromlo shook his head. 'There's nothing more dangerous than a gun you're not familiar with.'

'He's right,' Cain said. 'You're safer without it.'

'Well, I'm taking my machete.'

'Fine.'

The daughter cut in. 'How come a priest knows so much about night scopes, guns and all this crud?'

'A misspent youth, my child.'

'God you're a wanker.'

Eve slapped her leg. 'Apologise.'

She made a silly face and said smarmily, 'Sorry, Father.'

'You have an evil mind, young lady. I suggest you pray earnestly tonight.'

'I'll pray I'm not shot. If you're protecting me, I'm stuffed.' She turned to Jane. 'Have you smelt him?'

'Behave yourself,' Eve snapped.

Jane said, 'At least they don't want to kill us.'

'They could rape us,' Nina yelled. 'And I guess you'd think that was epic.'

'You'll be safe, dear. I promise.' Stromlo patted her shoulder with a not quite fatherly affection. His eyes flicked to her small high breasts, to the reddening thigh sprouting from her skirt.

'Who'd trust *you*?' She jerked her arm away. 'And get your hands off me, you perv.' She glared at the fire, tears budding.

Cain said, 'That's it then. We'd better dummy up the beds.'

Nina sobbed, 'What if we're killed?'

He felt something hot near his cheek, shied and quickly turned.

A grey-red glowing coal was hovering in the air near his eye.

'Shit.' He tried to knock it away but it seemed to avoid his hand and moved back like a dragonfly to hover near the fire.

The shock of it sent him reeling.

Anti-gravity!

No *wonder* they wanted her.

Now other coals were lifting from the fire and hanging in the air.

They scrambled back towards the walls.

Then the girl was on her feet, beside herself with rage, shaking her fists at them, breathing in harsh gasps while dull red coals circled her.

'Stop it,' Eve yelled. 'Right now.'

'Chicken-skinned shits. You go along with them. You *suck*.'

'Nina. Stop.' Eve's voice was a harsh command. 'Or I'll ...'

'... Send me back to dad? I'll *kill* you first.'

A coal sailed toward Eve and seared the front of her blouse. She shrieked and ran from the room.

'I command thee, ancient serpent, to depart from hence.' Stromlo was belting out prayers. 'We beseech thee, Holy Mary, to intercede for this prodigal child and adjure the Father to grant her redemption through the love and mediation of ...'

The girl turned to Cain and yelled above the racket, 'They're only half-sisters because their dad fucked two women for years — their bloody mums — in the same bed. That's what gave them the idea. So have you fucked them yet? Fucked my mother? Screwed her blind?'

Cain kept his eyes on the coals. One sailed slowly across the room, hit the carpet, which began to char.

The girl, face distorted, extended her rage to the others. 'You're all fucking scum. And that sick old wanker,' she thrust her arm toward Stromlo, 'wants to ram it up us *all*.'

Hot coals started to fly around the room, not in straight lines but erratically like flies, changing course in midair. Several landed on the carpet. Cain kicked the nearest back to the fire and stamped on the spots, knowing now, beyond doubt, that he'd lost his thousand bucks.

'None of you,' the girl shrieked, 'none of *them* — better come near *me*!'

27

AMBUSH

Cain sat in the dark on Nina's bed beside a toy goat stuffed with pyjamas. Her room, at the end of the hall at the front, was opposite Eve's sewing room. He'd closed all the blinds on the top floor to reduce ambient light. The NVG was good though hard to get used to. The monocular presented the night picture to one eye only so that the other pupil remained dilated and with 90-degree peripheral vision.

It was 4.20 am and the effect of three cups of coffee was waning. He kept alert by moving his attention through his body. He could die tonight if things went wrong — the strongest incentive to be inwardly attentive. To *be* — not just react.

His attempt at awareness was also a need to be worthy of John who combined all religions in his inner freshness and stability. They had often spoken of the importance of staying inside oneself, contained. Yet this almost impossible effort was only a beginning. Every moment one forgot. As the experience was always fresh, so by definition discontinuous, without an impulse continually renewed ...

The handset on his knee flashed red and vibrated — jerking him back — proving he'd disappeared again into thought.

He flicked the thing to silent and checked the dim LED readout. The outer grid registered two directions — side of house and back. This was it.

He switched to the inside grid and waited for them to show. They were registering now — one lot close to the back door, another at his end of the house.

A slight clatter. An aluminium ladder. Smart. The second group were heading for the upstairs sewing-room window.

He crossed the hall into the room, skirted the mounds of material on the floor and entered the disused en suite. It was stacked with cardboard boxes and bags of cloth. He peered around the stack until he could see half the window of the room — a window set into a section of tiled roof and two-thirds covered by a blind.

The muffled noise of ladder on guttering. The click of disturbed tiles. Now a black crescent of rubber sucker projecting just below the blind. The man was releasing the lever to fix it to the glass. He heard the graunch of the cutter. The scene through the NVG was a clear image in shades of green.

The circle of glass was extracted. A gloved hand reached in to trip the latch. Then the window frame slanted and the man had his head in the room.

The intruder's scope was also a monocular but its eyepiece-train covered both eyes. Cain backed behind the boxes as the man did his first scan. The floor creaked.

It could go two ways from here. And the more effective alternative was most dangerous. If Zuiden were doing this, he wouldn't shoot now. He'd let the man check the en suite, then silently kill him.

A silent kill? He had a chance — because the limitation with night scopes was 40-degree peripheral vision and, with a double eyepiece, the man couldn't look everywhere at once.

Cain, filled with adrenaline, dropped the P90 on its strap, stepped clear of the stack, the loop ready. He didn't know the current method but the technique he'd been taught relied on the garrotte. If you were fast and strong it sliced like a cheese wire back to the spine, severing nerves between brain and heart. The victim couldn't breathe or cry out.

The bulk of the man in the bathroom. He looked in the shower cabinet first. His mistake.

Cain got the wire around his neck, kneed him in the back to pull him off balance and hauled on the handles with full strength. The other was helpless in two seconds. Cain held him until the weight came on the wire, then lowered him onto bags stacked in the bath.

Then he was out of there, ready to fire.

The second man was in the room, standing behind the sewing machine bench, waiting for his companion to emerge. His carbine pointed to the door while his left hand adjusted his scope. He looked around, registered Cain's profile as the same masked and scoped figure who'd gone in, and waved him on. The mistake lengthened his life by 40 seconds.

Cain followed the man across the hall into Nina's bedroom. The bolster fooled the fellow long enough to have him pulling out a pencil torch.

Cain clamped the man's material-covered mouth and thrust his knife in from behind. Body armour couldn't stop a thin, sharp blade. It pierced the layered synthetic and sank deep into the chest. It wasn't instant or particularly quiet. A knifed heart took ten seconds to die.

Cain clamped one arm around the struggling man's neck, thrust from an undefendable direction. The snap could have been the crack of a stiff joint.

He pushed the twice-dead carcass over the bed. Zuiden would have marked him 'pass' so far. This was kill or be killed between professionals — no place for scruples or qualms. You relied on your training, functioned on automatic. He got back to the door, hoping the old phoney downstairs was on the ball.

He got the scope around the doorframe in time to see the second team. Two figures at the top of the back stairs, coming up to check the other bedrooms.

It gave him the required half second. The confusion factor again. He fired on auto, splitting the silence with the chatter of SS90 ball.

The slugs were small enough to get through armour, unstable enough to tumble in flesh. The lead man staggered against the wall, then fell back downstairs, carbine spitting at the ceiling.

The second man returned fire. But Cain, an instant before it came, had dropped. The heavier rounds zinging above him aerated the end wall. Bullets were fast, reflexes slow. The man was back behind the wall the moment he'd fired.

Noises from the staff wing. People were awake. They'd be trying to switch on lights, and the cook would be telling them to stay put.

Now, the dangerous part — the hall, the checking of rooms. He waited, listening.

The sudden racket of the heavier weapon, then the stutter of another P90. A firefight downstairs. Stromlo had engaged.

It stopped.

So who was dead?

He waited a minute until convinced the second floor was clear, then ran to the head of the back stairs.

A body floating in the pool.

He gave the agreed two-note whistle.

A three-note reply.

Stromlo's all-clear.

Cain came down, stepping over the body on the stairs and found the priest by the gym entrance — wearing a captured NVG.

Cain said, 'Two my end. Three down.'

'Three this end. Took out two.'

'That's five. Where's your second?'

Stromlo jerked a thumb over his shoulder.

The fifth man must have checked the gym on his way in. He was on his knees, dangling from the cord of a pull-down lats machine. The heavy weights on the end of the slide had cut the cord into his neck. His protruding eyes and tongue showed it hadn't been quick. A small dumbbell was near him on the floor. Stromlo had stunned him with it, then entangled him in the machine and watched the unconscious man strangle.

The priest held up the man's transceiver. 'Still must be one man with the transport. Mine, *va bene*?'

'Be my guest.'

Outside, the first thin light suffused the sky. The vehicle was far down the road — a windowless van with a driver behind the wheel, a driver preoccupied with his earphones and red-light VDU because he wasn't getting feedback. They discarded their scopes and managed to close without alerting him. Cain covered the rear doors and left the sacrifice to the priest.

When he heard the P90 stutter, Cain strafed the back of the van. Then the Great One fell back and covered him as he went in.

There was no one in the back. Just comms equipment, gun racks, a bench over ammo boxes. Ahead, framed by the blood-soaked windshield was the slumped form of the driver. Arterial blood pumped into the top of his scalp, which was upended like a bowl.

Cain got out of the van. 'Three-all.'

The priest removed his blood-spattered balaclava. The dark oval around his eyes, now exposed against the pallid face, made him resemble a starved panda. 'I've waited years for this.'

'But they didn't kill you. Tough.'

'All the same. A gratifying night.'

They shifted the bits of the driver into the back, wiped the worst of him off the seats.

Cain wiped a clear circle in the windscreen and drove the van toward the house. Stromlo, sitting beside him, hummed to himself, vastly pleased.

'Ever seen *Titus Andronicus*?' Cain glanced at him sardonically.

'I haven't had that pleasure.'

'You'd enjoy it, I'm sure.'

The sauna door was still shut.

Cain called, 'You can come out now.' He opened the door.

Jane stood rigid just inside, the machete held high above her shoulder, while the other two cowered in the corner of the topmost bench.

'All secured, dear ladies,' Stromlo crooned. He walked to the sprung back door. 'I'll tell cook we're mopping up.'

The family crept out to see the hunched shape in the reddening pool, the garrotted man's purple-blue face, the bloodied figure sprawled on the stairs.

The sisters shrieked. Nina screamed, crouched, covered her eyes.

The surface of the pool heaved. The body floating in it was inert but not the water. What looked like a long ripple began at the far end then advanced, growing in height, making the dangling carcass bob. It gathered in strength until it slapped against the tiles beside them. Water rose up, slopping over the rim. Cain watched incredulous. There had been nothing to cause it at all.

He said to Eve, 'Get her into the lounge room. Stay there till we've cleaned up.'

'She'd be better in her room.'

'I wouldn't go upstairs.'

She looked aghast.

It took an hour to get the bodies in the van — and EXIT alerted for the pick-up.

The blood-covered Cain clumped back into the dining room to find the family huddled over the fire beside empty mugs of tea.

He said wearily, 'All back to normal.'

A wrenching sob from Eve.

Jane glared up at him. 'Normal?'

'Well, until they regroup and try again.'

'Just ... get us *out* of here.'

28

MORTAR

It was a week since the switch. As usual the transition was uncanny. The people at the dinner table seemed the same, even to Cain.

There were subtle differences certainly. The new Eve couldn't quite match the original's satin voice. The new Nina acted sulkily pubescent but at heart was rather prim. The new Jane was identical but lacked her counterpart's practicality.

They didn't talk shop, kept the conversation general, discussed the mess in Yugoslavia, the skinheads in Germany.

After the meal came the evening routine. Stromlo handled the sked while Cain checked the grid alarms. Their function was now different — not to protect the duplicate family but to make it seem nothing had changed.

Cain strolled to the priest's room. He was used to the old fraud now, even fond of him. 'Still no word?'

The Great One shook his head and packed the headset back into the radio. 'I hope they haven't forgotten us because, without advance warning, we're dead.'

'Right. Next time they'll probably have a thermal imager. We have to be gone before they come.'

They knew their base was compromised. As they discussed the sabotage of EXIT again, Stromlo felt under his bed for a wrapped bottle. 'Would you care for a little . . . ?'

'No.'

'Don't mind if I go ahead?' He didn't bother with a glass.

'So, you're positive the Vatican's not behind it?'

'Yes. The Curia needs the *status quo*.'

'Is the CIA after Stern?'

'They don't *know* we have the pope or Stern.'

'So tell me about Stern.'

The priest swigged again. 'There was a certain organisation doing typhus inoculations in Manila. They added hormones to the injections. Also a trial done in Angola. Stern was involved. But his new project . . . You're trying to pump me, Ray. I've said enough.' He frowned and changed the subject. 'The duplicate Nina's . . . effective, don't you think?'

Cain smiled. 'Great arse. Fancy her?'

A pained look. 'Celibacy is the Church's gift.'

'And misogyny the nature of the priesthood?'

'No. Because the Church is the bride.'

'Ah!' He enjoyed these jousts. 'So Latin American priests commit adultery?'

'Your facile mind will hang you yet.' Stromlo's heavy sigh. 'John Paul himself said that we have made of sex the only sin — when it could be the least of sins.'

'Wonderful. He said that?'

Stromlo nodded sagely. '"Where does the bedroom end and the stars begin?" I quote the great Drummond de Andrade. What a pope I destroyed! God forgive me!' He rocked with remorse. 'What a pope! God! Oh God!'

'I'm sure you'll be forgiven. After all, they say God's a Brazilian.'

'*Deus caritas est*. So what else could he be?' The priest-assassin shut his eyes. 'Still, my best hope is annihilation — that afterwards there's nothing.'

'Life isn't simple. Why should death be?'

Stromlo's tortured look. 'Why are you cruel to me? I crave *not* to believe. And you still *do*?'

'Goodnight, my friend.' He gripped the man's shoulder, walked thoughtfully back to his room.

So it wasn't the Vatican. It wasn't the CIA. He went to bed still thinking about it, hoping to wake in a whole skin.

Something roused him. A sound?

He put his hand out for the P90, then checked the perimeter alarm handset by his bed. The backlit indicator blinked CLEAR.

He sat up slowly, freeing the bedclothes from the gun, slid out of bed, grabbed his flak jacket, got it on. No time for pants, or boots. He stood up in the dark room, breath suspended, listening, then edged out into the hall.

Broken plastic under his bare foot.

He looked up.

The hall skylight — shattered — open to the stars.

Something stung the inside of his throat.

The last thing he knew was the flesh of his cheek dragging back as it slid down the cold wall.

29

LIMBO

Cain felt as if he were being cut apart. He tried to open his eyes but had to shut them against the glare.

The next time he knew himself, he was feverishly cold and the unbearable pain remained. When he opened his eyes he saw red-streaked gauze. He gulped air as if he couldn't get enough. Then he seemed to be floating.

Later they described what they'd done to him.

First, the laparotomy. Bleeding points were ligated and, after peritoneal lavage, damage was assessed and the intestine resected. The surgeon performed an elegant midline opening and single-layer anastomosis of considerable facility.

The neurosurgical team shaved his shattered head, incised his scalp, drilled burr holes through the intact bone near the damage, then nibbled the bone away. The tangential bullet had caused a gutter fracture, subdural haematoma, contusion, and driven fragments into the brain. There hadn't been time for fancy tests. Relieving pressure was one thing. Finding fragments was another. As bone doesn't resist infection, debridement had to be complete.

Then, intestines resectioned, brain bruised and swollen, a mess of post-operative hazards, he was wheeled to the ICU. He was attached to nasogastric tubes, a drip, an oxygen sensor, ventilator. He had an ileostomy, abdominal drain, urinary catheter . . .

After days of sedation and checks for exudations and odour — bullets suck in bacteria and debris — he went back into the theatre for a delayed primary closure.

Eventually, two blurs, who were presumably people, persuaded him to hold up two fingers, follow a pencil with his eyes and say words. The words slurred and his left hand didn't quite work.

The bigger blur said, 'Obeys commands, opens eyes spontaneously, converses, has reasonable motor function. Now if we get him through biochemical and vascular changes, avoid peritonitis, epilepsy, myonecrosis, we're crash hot.'

He dragged at a tube that seemed part of him but the smaller blur plucked his hand away.

The bigger blur resumed the record of disaster. 'You're looking good, Mr Cain. You have a drain but the colon wasn't damaged so we've avoided a colostomy. You got a temporary stoma — be wearing a bag for a while. When the gut heals, we'll close it and you can shit the usual way.' He turned to the smaller blur. 'When's his next CT?'

'Tomorrow,' the sister said. 'And Dr Mead wants an MRI.'

The next weeks were discomfort and pain. He was restless, coughed a lot. When he was a little less out of it, an EXIT staff surgeon came and, finally, he got hard details.

'You've taken four hits. The cook found you, drove you to a doctor. We sent a chopper and handled it from there.'

'How did they . . . ?' He was slurring.

'Mortar. Gas canisters lobbed through the roof of the house. The gas was just to disable because they wanted the family alive. They plugged you and Stromlo.'

'Stromlo's . . . ?'

'Dead. You got one in the gut, one to the head. With all the blood from your head, they wouldn't believe you'd survive.'

'And my gut?'

'You've lost small intestine basically. Could have been worse than the head. When a bullet connects with body tissue it develops a yaw.' The man knew wound ballistics like all Beta medicos. 'You get a stress wave, millisecond pulsations ...'

'I had the vest on.' He couldn't get his tongue around the words.

'There's still cavitation on impact. It stopped two rounds but weakened enough to let through a third although it absorbed most of its energy. Did no more damage than a low-velocity pistol bullet. But a rough way to lose an appendix. The vest probably saved you a kidney and a pulped liver on the round that got through.' He replaced the clipboard on the foot of the bed.

'The duplicates?'

'In Russia.'

So it had worked. His mind was starting to drift but he mumbled the question that was haunting him. 'Were we meant to be taken out?'

The doctor shrugged. 'I'm not up with the politics. But Rhonda insisted we did everything to save you.'

He frowned under the bandage that was probably holding his head together. 'How will I be after this?'

'We're not so worried about your guts now. Your head's the iffy bit. We'll know more in a few days.' He waffled about secondary insults, BP fluctuations, torn bridging veins, blood absorption. 'Considering what you've been through, you're in great shape.'

'Don't snow me. Just tell me.'

The man nodded, strolled to the window, whistled tunelessly, turned around. 'Okay. You won't be the same. At best, you may have to walk with a stick.'

The shock of the statement went in. He knew a chapter of his life had closed.

After a month, the EXIT surgeon cleared him for the flight to Tasmania. He was shuttled to Beta by chopper and wheeled to a one-bed ward. He hoped Pat would come but they told him she was away having treatment.

Eventually Rhonda arrived, looking grave, her hair a mess. The ash and burn holes in the front of her dress told him how stressed she was. She put a hand on his brow.

His bleary look. 'So were we expendable?'

'We told you to get out, you mad idiots.'

'Like hell you did. We got nothing.'

Shock on her face. 'No signal?'

'Nothing. We checked the night before. They'd even found the perimeter system.'

'But the transmission was acknowledged.'

'Not by us.'

She went almost crimson with anger. The reaction couldn't have been faked.

'So it's still going on?'

She pressed his hand. 'I'm sorry, Ray.'

'I've been doing some thinking.' His voice still slurred like a drunk's. 'Rehana wasn't writing "Z". She was halfway through an "M". Murchison fixed the job in Chartres. And I reckon Vanqua's running him.'

She pressed his hand again, tears of rage in her eyes. 'Just . . . get well.'

30

EXPOSURE

BUNDANOON, AUSTRALIA, DECEMBER 1993

It took him a year to recover.

The walking frame went early, the ileostomy after two months. But he needed the stick three months more and the slurring was still there.

After eight months he was well enough to direct again but did it mostly from a chair — stop-frame animation, paintbox stuff. He wore the SIG each day, trusting nobody now.

The change was more than physical. He dwelt on his life a good deal — on the training that justified killing as a job. Now that he'd experienced directly through his body what bullets did, viewing death at one remove became hard to distinguish from brutality.

As for the second aspect they'd formed in him, the inner search — the respect for all religions, the capacity to commune with popes — it made him think a lot about Stromlo, that other unfortunate taught to pray and kill.

Would the ordeal of EXIT turn him into Stromlo's clone — tear him apart inside until even death became more terror than release?

He was physically damaged, ageing, less resilient to stress. During his flight to reality, his personal items had moved.

He bought a shack in a country town two hours drive south of Sydney, intending to repair it at weekends. But he pottered around the place unable to get on with things. He didn't even drive there but drowsed in the train, mind in neutral, a hypnagogic jerk.

One Sunday near the end of summer he made a simple meal and ate it watching the evening news. He'd heard nothing from base for months. The item was a slap in the face:

'...allegations,' the TV anchor declared with stock concern, 'that a covert organisation has kidnapped the controversial guru and replaced him with a surgically altered lookalike. A spokesman for "The Square" claims to have a tape showing one of Gustave Raul's closest associates teaching the substitute to impersonate him.'

Cain froze, fork in air.

A clip of the man followed and they supered his name: Peter Bell. He was described as a US Navy SEAL, dishonourably discharged. It was the man who'd followed him three years ago — on the night he slept with Jojo. Intelligent face, intense eyes — the man Karen Hunt had assured him she could trust.

An interview with Bell followed. He passionately declared that the cult would do anything to get Raul back. He mentioned the traitors who'd engineered the switch — two men and a woman — and implied that he'd cross-examined the men.

Was one Murchison? Had the bastard been caught in his own trap? Being grilled by the fanatical ex-SEAL wouldn't have been fun. How much had Murchison given them? With prompting it could have been a lot.

The interviewer then asked Bell if he'd interrogated the woman.

Bell said that she'd eluded them but they were keen to locate her.

And they punched up a still of Hunt.

Cain swore at the beautiful face.

The worm had poked its head from the apple.

EXIT was outed.

31

PRELATES PULL PLUG

THE VATICAN, ROME

The city-state seemed undisturbed. Bernini's colonnade still stood. The image of the saint's right foot was still being kissed by reverent lips. The decorative guards still patrolled with their halberds and the fountains, grottoes and hedges still resembled a landscape gardener's nightmare. There was the usual bustle at the Porta Sant'Anna but the helipad was bare and the ghost, in the second library of the English College, had not lately appeared. Like all deep changes, this one left the surface untouched.

The meeting took place in none of the 10,000 rooms yet appropriately close to the secret archives. Cardinal Sarrum avoided the library's black desks, uncomfortable chairs, solemnly ticking clock and walked through to the patio.

In the small garden, His Eminence, Cardinal Llosa, stood gazing at the flagging. He was a gaunt, chinless Peruvian with trifocals and spatulate hands who rarely looked at anyone directly. 'So it has come.'

'Yes. The Secretariat is manoeuvring to put pressure on four of the governments. We're only secure if both our guests at EXIT are disposed of.'

'It's not enough.' Llosa's mouth drew down. 'The exposure could compromise everything. My people want the whole thing closed.'

Sarrum felt the weight of the domain that bound them. 'The governments would never agree. Though perhaps we could persuade them to mothball the replacement side.'

Llosa, still staring at the ground, spoke as if in pain. 'Mothballing still leaves evidence. It has to be obliterated.'

Was he wearing, Sarrum wondered, a cilice, or a spiked chain around his thigh? Had he observed strict silence for an extended period after breakfast? Did he apply a whip to his shrivelled buttocks once a week? Did he cherish maxim 175: "It's beautiful to be a victim"? He glanced at the man, detesting him and his friends in Opus Dei, self-flagellating fascists all. But this was no occasion for prejudice. His enormously influential counterpart was today an emissary only, representing a further eight curial monsignors. And the purge wasn't in question. Only the *modus operandi*.

'That's your final position?'

'Yes.'

Sarrum nodded. 'I'll convey it.' He walked back out of the garden, out of the light, into the gloom of a bureaucracy now pledged to assassinate a pope.

32

BETA

TASMANIA

Vanqua entered the secure booth, the innermost concrete box, punched his card and waited for the checks. One by one, the ten green lights came on. Only then did he use his day key and pick-up.

Checks at the other end still ran. The security of bouncing off satellites was considerable, but had to be much augmented for such a sensitive real-time contact.

This time it was Washington — Senator Barnaby F. Pickett — a glad-hander with the mind of a snake. 'Vanqua? You got the 411 on what's goin' down?'

'Your original transmission is confirmed.'

'Questions?'

'Are the UK and France in?'

'No. It's still a three-tick rumble. You know what that means if you screw up?'

He avoided the test question.

'So what's the schedule?' Pickett prodded.

'A lot of people need to be recalled. We can't ship them all at once. But we'll get started.'

'Not a pretty assignment.'

'It's a routine Department S job. We'll begin with the support staff here at Beta.'

'You're a together dude. So how will you handle Rhonda?'

'Relieve her of command.'

'And if she gets wise to the rest ...'

'She'll be contained.'

'Better be. Lose it and we're toast. So you now assume full authority for EXIT?'

'Confirmed.'

'Keep me posted on all developments. I want a list of everyone in the pipeline.'

'You'll be informed.'

'With the grace of God and a fast infield ... Everyone they got. You with it?'

'Understood.' The new EXIT head replaced the handset and leaned against the wall.

He'd been appointed in '86. This had taken seven years to engineer. He'd felt triumph at first. Now a terrible joy mixed with pain. At last, he could complete this, avenge the one family member he'd known. Though not identical twins they were one in spirit, heart. They'd never known their parents, only ever had each other. 'She's ours, Etta,' he breathed. 'The last twist.'

33

CANCER CURE

TASMANIA

The northeast coast of the island was chilly in the late afternoon and the converted stable had no damp-course. Despite the heater, Pat felt cold. The cancer had taken all her strength. But her last job was her finest. There'd been time to do it precisely. Years.

When the duplicate had gone, she looked at Rhonda, her friend. A typical Aquarian, she thought — loving humanity but detesting individuals. Still, what she'd just witnessed had gone deep.

'Amazing. Strangest thing I've struck.' The big woman's face, though emotionless, had glistening streaks on both cheeks. The outer indifference that protected her feelings had cracked.

'It's how Wolf set it up. Bodyguards are trained to do it. Soldiers know they might have to.'

'But I expect she hoped that ...' She wiped her face.

Pat squirmed in the wheelchair. The sustained-release morphine tablets couldn't cope with pain peaks so she was self-injecting when she needed it. Tomorrow a Beta doctor had agreed to let her drift off. The kindest way. DEATH IS AN ASPECT OF LIFE.

Rhonda said, 'I need to look at the sea for a while. Will you come or is the pain too bad?'

'I'll give it a burl. You'll have to hoist me into the car.'

Rhonda drove her to the beach, a deserted stretch south of Beaumaris, got her out of the car and supported her so she could walk. Her shoes, sinking in sand, seemed not attached to her at all. She clung to the big woman, feeling her affection and strength.

Rhonda eased her to the sand, sat heavily beside her, stared out to sea twirling a lock of hair around her finger. Her hair had gone completely grey in a year. 'What we've come to.'

'Chin up. Good for the neuro-bloody-peptides.'

'I'm going to miss ... your tmesis.'

'My what?'

'The way you split words with "bloody".'

She felt love for the marvellous woman. So heroic, yet so British she dared not express affection in words.

'I'll miss you too, love.' She hugged her. 'But never say die. God, why do I say that when they're putting me down tomorrow?'

Small breakers crumped on the shore. Two seagulls faced the wind like boats in a storm. A lone fisherman further up the beach was driving a plastic pipe into the sand to make a stand for his rod. It was all so matter-of-fact. The world didn't care at all, she thought. The world never cared, just went on. And when people died, events closed over them as if they'd never been.

She plucked the scarf close about her head. Waves of pain were coming back. 'Well, we've given it a good bloody go. Wolf'd be proud of us, you know. And you could still win out. Except I won't be around to see it.'

'Time,' Rhonda grunted, 'the teacher that kills its pupils. Talk about adding calamity to disaster.' She glared at the waves, her strong face haggard with grim lines. 'Look at us. Two ghastly old clackers ...'

'... who've been steering the world together.'

That made her smile. Then the frown came back. 'So it's Vanqua. His anhedonia once inspired my irrational pity. He may live in a cloud of blight but I pity the bugger no more.'

'At least you know it's him.'

'But why this stupid, pointless vendetta?'

'Search me.'

Rhonda stared out to sea. 'I can't promise you Ray will survive. There's a chance they'll get him too.'

'Won't he suss the tip-off?'

'Yes. But probably too late.' The big woman picked up a strand of dried seaweed. 'You ... love him, don't you?'

'Much as I've loved any bloke. Thank God he can't see me now.' She stared at the buffeted seagulls, salt air on her skin, salt tears on her face. 'He owes me a thousand bucks, the bastard. Funny to think I've ... I've had the only time with him there was.'

Rhonda grunted, 'I loved someone once.' The words seemed torn out of her. 'Most dangerous thing in the world.' She wrenched the seaweed apart.

34

RECALL

The high penetrating whine of the Hercules was getting on Cain's nerves. The quip was that Lockheed had solved the aircraft's noise problem by putting it inside the fuselage.

He stood at the starboard side paratroop door, staring out the small window, wondering about the icebreaker. He'd spotted the red-painted ship thrusting through the pack ice. Normal enough. What wasn't normal was the tower. Ahead of its chopper landing deck, dominating the superstructure, was a column like a king-post that rose even higher than the funnel. Some kind of antenna? No. Far too strongly built. Whatever it was, it wouldn't have helped stability. The smooth-bottomed vessels rolled badly and seas down here could be huge.

He was wearing his inner gloves but had his hands in his parka pockets. The floor and skin of the hold felt like the inside wall of a freezer. The bird was pressurised, air conditioned. But it was colder back here. All the web-type folding seats along the sides of the aircraft were occupied by people from Beta — Department D technicians, research assistants, maintenance types. They'd told him they were the last to leave before the department was dismantled. They'd heard that D personnel worldwide were being recalled and sent south to the ice.

As a recently deployed agent he was one of them but had no firm information. He presumed Rhonda was already at Alpha. He'd asked after Pat but no one knew. So here he was, still dancing his strange history but glad about one thing. The pope would have been sent down, too. It meant the chance to see him again.

He stared down at the glare. Even at this height you needed sunglasses. The enormous, isolated icebergs he'd seen for some time were gone. Now floes and spreading pack ice made an unrelieved expanse of white. So beautiful. So treacherous. He'd never thought to see this again.

Karen Hunt emerged from the curtain-shrouded 'honey pot', her perfect body hidden by cold-weather gear. He watched her work her way forward unsteadily between the passengers and the palletised net-shrouded stores. She'd said nothing since coming on board and he'd stayed out of her way. He could imagine what she was feeling. If she wanted to talk, she would.

The transport lurched and banked. At this point, its magnetic instruments would be erratic and the crew would be concentrating on INS, radalt, probably GPS — if the third could be relied on. He'd heard there were dead spots on the continent and it depended where you were. Solar activity and ionospheric reaction compromised HF radio transmissions as well.

He moved back to his seat near the fuselage tanks, and ate the last muesli bar in his food pack. His digestion was back to normal, his body eighty per cent of what it had been. He was still prone to headaches, a little slow in his speech. He still limped but his left hand had come good.

He fiddled with his earplugs. The long, noisy flight had made him tired. A standard Herc flight would now be controlled by the Ice Tower at McMurdo. But the old EXIT four-fan trash can didn't have that option. No aid. No support. No PAR at the open-snow high-altitude Alpha runway. And they might have to land in one of the blizzards that, down here, sprang from nowhere. But then you only flew for EXIT if content with a short and thrilling life.

He tried to doze but couldn't. Restless, he climbed to the executive suite. Through the greenhouse of windows he saw a vast sheet of snow formed into wave shapes. He plugged in a spare headset, pointed down. 'Did wind do that?'

'It's not there,' the right-hand seat said. 'Just shadows from the cloud layer.'

'What's weather like at Alpha?' he croaked. The low humidity had dried his throat.

'Crud. Crosswind with rotten visibility.'

It wasn't good to land with drift. The C–130 landing-gear/ski-system conversion depended on complicated mechanicals and hydraulics. Side-stress could collapse it.

The navigator was using a periscope sextant, not quite sixteenth-century stuff but getting there. There was no en-route radar on the continent. Antarctica was one hell of a place to point an aircraft. Cain moved behind the engineer who was checking warning lights. 'How's she taking it?'

'Not bad for an old lady over thirty.'

'You're lugging lots of juice. Fuselage tanks, external tanks ...'

'We're topping up JP8 at Alpha.'

He ditched the headset and climbed back down the ladder, hoping the 'A' factor wouldn't kill them.

As they descended through buffeting winds and instability the head loadie checked his human cargo, seeing that everyone was kitted up and had a balaclava on under his hood. Cain peeked through one of the small windows. Nothing but the white haze they needed to get under. There were rudimentary markings and approach lights on the snow. And the ARA. That was it.

He sat in the drumming fuselage imagining the tenseness on the flight deck. The passengers seemed trusting. For most it was their first time south. He braced, waiting for the jolt, his little knowledge a disquieting thing.

They lucked it in — touched, pounded, then taxied for a while to dissipate the heat of the skis and prevent them welding to the deck. It was no fun digging skis out and meant shutting down inboard engines. He waited for the arse to open, for the shock of the frigid air.

Back in the big white.

What now?

35

ALPHA

The reception committee were anonymous shapes with faces covered against wind chill. They lumbered about in the katabatic wind, shouting instructions.

He and Hunt were told to wait while the rest were marched off. Then they were directed around a cargo sledge at the back of the plane. In five layers and 10 kilograms of clothing it was a struggle just to move and the effort of walking against wind carrying a duffel bag made him breathless. This wasn't the coast but the high plateau and being dumped in this thin air was murder.

As he puffed around the high orange and black striped tail he glimpsed a similarly painted Hagg. The Hagglunds — a Swedish four-track-drive all-terrain vehicle — was parked front-to-wind to prevent the doors blowing off.

They slung their gear on the back seat and Cain left Hunt there with the luggage. He got out and climbed in the front to sit opposite the driver. Thankfully the heat exchanger was working. The man engaged the transmission and the rubber tracks churned snow.

They passed the other passengers trudging along a flag line — staggering in their survival gear, leaning against the blow. They were taking them toward the fuel farm. Why? Had they built pre-fabs there?

As they churned toward the entrance he tried a diplomatic ploy — floated an exploratory comment. 'This is some business. How many down here now?'

The driver didn't reply. Ominous. Cain glanced back at Hunt and saw she was wary, too.

The driver stopped at the entrance ramp. 'Report to Vanqua at Command — immediate.'

They got out and the Hagg moved off.

The base was a lot deeper than in the old days when he'd been here. Newer ones were built on stilts to handle snow accumulation because older designs were progressively being buried. He slung his bag over his shoulder and followed Hunt beneath the dome to the guardhouse.

As they were processed, an addition to the rigmarole surprised him. They were relieved of their weapons. New orders, they were told.

Cleared, they crunched past familiar insulated metal buildings with small perspex box air-trap windows and thick doors secured by large levers — cool rooms that kept cold out, not in. They passed ops, the accomm block, the warm store, then entered the arched tunnel that led to the staff Command Centre. On the way he cautiously asked her, 'Know anything about this deal?'

'I know Ron's down here. I know I'll be crucified.'

But did she know about the sabotage — that she'd been spiked from inside EXIT? He doubted it.

Sound travelled in this place and there were pick-ups everywhere. He pointed to one wired beneath a pipe and was relieved to see her nod.

They reached Command annexe and got out of their freezer suits. It took minutes to de-ice and shed layers. When they entered the vestibule, Rhonda was waiting to greet them and he was surprised to see her hair was now completely grey. She looked haggard, worn, and her eyes were unnaturally bright.

Hunt glanced at her, biting her lip.

The big woman merely nodded.

Cain, more favoured, received a perfunctory hug. 'Welcome, acclaimed campaigner. You look almost back to normal.'

'Don't feel it.'

'Perfectly understandable. Right. Good egg.'

He found the silly-arse expression odd. 'So what's going on here?'

'Incarceration, ordered by Vanqua. I've been relieved of command.' She saluted the short corridor that led to his office door. 'We active verbs are now separated by — not from — our auxiliaries.'

Hunt's seamless frown. 'Did you get my report?'

'I did.'

'And ...'

'Treachery, no doubt, by one with affections dark as Erebus.'

Was it a reference to the continent's volcano? Hunt's frown deepened as she tried to isolate the message from the medium.

'Is John here?' Cain asked.

'In Block B.'

'I can see him?'

'You'll have to ask our new master.'

'What about Zia?'

'He's also down here, still breathing. The UK still haven't signed off on him.'

A door opened at the end of the corridor and a tall man with sandy hair came through.

Hunt froze.

Zuiden. He grinned at Cain. 'Hello, shitface.' Then leered at Hunt. 'And the super-bitch.' He brushed past them like a favoured employee gloating over workmates who'd been fired.

They entered Vanqua's office and the mournful surgeon CO rose to greet them. His immaculate sweater was hand-knitted and he still had the trademark tan. Be interesting, Cain thought, to see the meticulous one wintering over — to watch his skin become sallow, see him suffer from insomnia ...

'Hunt and Cain,' Vanqua said. 'Beauty and culture. Don't sit down.' He walked in front of his desk and perched on the edge, crossing his legs with self-absorbed care. 'As Rhonda's probably told you, I now command EXIT and your department is being dismantled. All D staff will be air-lifted down.'

You've got hopes, Cain thought. It was almost February. Soon flying in would be Russian roulette.

'Not only staff are coming,' Vanqua continued, 'but originals as well. That includes your Kiwi family, Cain.'

'And what does the CIA think of that?'

'They don't like it but have no option.'

'Pretty dumb idea.'

'I beg your pardon?'

'Importing a poltergeist to Antarctica is about the silliest thing I've heard of.'

Vanqua shrugged. 'Even if such a thing exists, the solution to it will be swift.'

Hunt cut in. 'How long do we have to stay here?'

'Permanently.'

She looked at Cain as if willing him to protest.

He didn't buy in. 'And where are you going to put these hordes?'

'That's my concern. Department S remains operational but your staff is decommissioned, your grades and privileges revoked. It means you don't exist and will do as instructed.'

Cain glanced at Rhonda. 'You endorse this?'

'I'm no longer your CO.' A characteristic eye-roll.

'I find this hard to take.'

'Perfectly understandable. Right. Good egg. But how you see it is irrelevant. As our executive assassin's just told you, we are *persona non grata*.'

Personae non gratae, he mentally corrected, surprised she hadn't used the plural. And why repeat the crass 'egg' line? She was crude but not crass and not prone to repeat herself. As her madness mostly cloaked method, he was instantly alert.

Vanqua was talking again. 'You have a temporary space in the old accommodation block. You'll only have one rack, so someone will be sleeping on the floor. You're dismissed. Rhonda will remain.'

As they walked back down the corridor he could feel Hunt's confusion like a force. She was still at the start of her career, purpose-trained for her single great assignment, young, fit. Now she'd been condemned to an ice-tomb for life. Worse, she believed that she'd wrecked EXIT single-handed.

She murmured, 'What can we do?'

'There's no "we" any more.'

She leaned against the wall, hands over her face.

He waited for her to collect herself, working on the repeated sentences. 'Perfectly understandable. Right. Good egg.' Second letters? Last letters? Start with first:

P. U. R ...

PURGE.

So obvious. Coincidence? No. The repetition said it wasn't. With mikes, cameras, movement sensors everywhere and Vanqua receiving the surveillance, Ron had warned him directly in the simplest, most practical way.

D staff were no longer needed and Alpha wasn't big enough to hold them. So as planeloads came in ... ?

He could predict the rest.

They'd put the newcomers at ease because there were too many to lock up. With insurrection avoided, they'd isolate small groups for covert execution because new arrivals wouldn't know how many had come before.

Then what? There'd be only enough acid for the originals.

Yes, originals would be dissolved.

The family?

And John?

What the hell did Ron expect him to do?

He was physically weakened and unarmed in a base crawling with surgeons. Their support staff would be useless. Even if he could arm them, they'd never pull the triggers. And even if they did, they couldn't hit moving targets. He needed field staff — people trained to kill.

Christ, he thought, I'm back in massacre mode again. The self-defence reaction had cut in.

Were other D field staff here? He and Hunt could be it. He'd need her help. But how to tip her off?

She joined him again, face carefully expressionless. As they reached the annexe, he said, 'You can bunk with me.'

She glanced at him, weighing the statement, knowing his motive wasn't sex. Threats shrank the penis wonderfully. But would she realise that sex could serve them as a blind?

As they started to kit up, she gave him a look that seemed to ask, 'Are they going to kill us? Is that why you want us together?'

It was a start.

They pulled on their outer gloves in silence.

36

BODY LANGUAGE

The accommodation block was a relic but they were permitted to share the same cubicle. It was designed as a single berth — its hanging space and small desk/table separated by open shelves which doubled as a ladder to the single bunk above. Heat was blown through a duct below the desk. But like most buildings here, it was no warmer than mid-winter.

The curtain that screened them from traffic in the corridor had enough space behind it for someone to sleep on the floor. There were bedrolls on the floor in other cubicles, so the rest were doubling up as well. He asked a man in the next space, 'How are the showers?'

'Turned off. They're short of water. Some problem about a . . . melt bell? It's our first time here. We don't know a thing.'

That made them support staff. 'What's your base?'

'Gamma.'

Gamma was in Argentina.

After they'd unpacked some of their stuff, he and Hunt went downstairs to the tatty lounge. It was packed with bewildered people — many speaking Spanish.

He glanced at Hunt's madonna face. 'See anyone you know?'

She shook her head.

They walked into the mess. Harried staff served a line of people. He spotted the bald head and luxurious beard of Pohl, the Alpha base commander. Good old Pohl. Serving food? Had Vanqua demoted him to slushie?

When Cain drew level with him in the line he said, 'Hello, Adam. Slumming?'

Pohl blinked at him over the counter, 'Hello, Ray. Some event.' He began to fill a plate with the one meal available.

'Got any new jokes?'

'I'm not feeling funny right now.' He spooned peas onto the plate.

I bet you're not, Cain thought and began verbal fishing. 'Stuffy in this old can. Thought I might stretch the legs later. Want to join me? Or is that off-limits?'

'Wouldn't advise it.' Pohl glanced nervously to the side.

'Seen any other D field staff?'

'No.' Pohl, blinking fast, handed the plate across. Two men came out of the kitchen and stood behind him. They weren't cooks.

Cain changed the subject. 'Seen Pat?'

'She got one of our doctors to turn her off last week.'

His reaction would have been visible.

Pohl said, 'Sorry, old mate.'

He took his meal and moved away, body flooded with emotion.

He joined Hunt beside the wall bench. He found it hard to swallow the food. He felt her watching him.

'She must have meant a lot.'

'Big sister. Lover. Friend.'

'At least she's out of this. Have you seen any of our field staff?'

'No. And, according to Pohl, we're it.'

* * *

When they'd eaten, they went back to the cubicle and drew the curtain across. Experience told him that the space was wired — that eyes and ears saw or heard everything they did.

They stripped off a couple of layers. She even looked superb in thermal underwear. He pointed up to the bunk. She frowned, then climbed up, displaying shapely flanks.

Strange, he thought, how affection transcended appearances. He would have given three of her for the scraggy breastless Pat.

He climbed after her and joined her in the bag. There was a duvet. He dragged it over them. The corridor light remained on. Pinhole cameras and pick-ups would be relaying their every sound and move.

She lay facing the wall. He turned behind her to face the same way, reached over until his hand was on her diaphragm, then used his finger to inscribe a 'Y'. She shied a little when he touched her, then understood, lay still.

Y ... O ... U.

He moved his finger straight across her ribs to indicate the end of the word, started the next word. READ. Slash. ME? He drew the question mark, then crossed her ribs twice to signify 'end of transmission'. If the watchers noticed any movement, they'd think he was feeling her up.

She reached down and back to his thigh, began her reply. He concentrated, trying to get it. It wasn't as easy as he'd thought.

Y ... E ... S. Double slash.

Encouraged, he started again. THEY INTEND KILL ALL D STAFF HERE.

Her hand moved again on his thigh. AGREE. GAMEPLAN?

WE STAY CLOSE. STRIKE TOGETHER WHEN CAN.

OK.

THEY WILL DO NOTHING DIRECT AS TOO MANY PEOPLE. SUSPECT THEY ISOLATING BATCHES FOR COVERT KILLS.

GOT IT.

TOMORROW WE RECCE.

OK.

The effort to communicate was tedious. They both needed sleep, were too tired to think well now. But he decided to tell her that she hadn't caused the fall of EXIT D. He needed her to believe in herself again. The emotional release would make her strong.

YOU WERE SABOTAGED WITH RAUL. INTERNAL. VANQUA.

Her body became a plank.

He went on. HE USED MURCHISON. HAS SPIKED D PROJECTS FOR YEARS. SO NOT YOUR FAULT. WAS SETUP TO DESTROY RON AND D.

Her every muscle tensed with rage. Her moving hand dug into his leg. WILL KILL HIM.

GOT ME TOO. STROMLO DEAD AND I WAS SHOT UP.

WHY DO IT?

HE HATES RON. ALL I CAN WORK OUT.

Then came a sentence that astonished him.

IS SHE RON?

WHAT?

NOT SURE SHE IS RON!

He was thunderstruck. A duplicate? Was it possible? If so, the double was amazingly good. Hunt was Ron's lover. What had she noticed?

She drew a query on his leg again.

He signed. AM STUNNED. WHY A DOUBLE?

SAVE HER LIFE? BUY TIME? GIVE HER CHANCE FOR COUNTER ATTACK?

It was possible, he thought. Just. The peculiar eyes ... The Latin slip ... Pat's last and greatest job?

A duplicate ready to die?

He signed. INCREDIBLE IF TRUE.

She murmured, 'I'm tired.'

'Goodnight.'

She said, 'Thank you, brother. Meant a lot.'

He squeezed her arm in reply.

She, too, had begun as a parentless child, seconded to the cause. They were orphans, he thought. Waifs. Monstrous ones certainly. But still . . .

She took his hand and held it between her breasts.

He appreciated that.

37

ACID DROP

Vanqua watched the big woman winched up. She hung suspended, feet just off the ground. The improvised rope harness cut into her bulbous thighs. She looked lewd trussed like this — stripped to inner field garments and bound.

This was the climactic act. The culmination of years. Obscene, but it had to be done.

Zuiden, the only other person in the gloomy space, stood holding the chain hoist's control stalk. He wore the attendant's protective clothing — overalls, helmet, acid-resistant boots.

Fitting, Vanqua thought. Just the two of them. The act, too intimate to be a spectacle, was like a sacrament in a crypt. He stared again at the gone-to-seed body that once had pressed against his sister ... corrupted her flesh, provoked her death.

'So, finally,' he said, 'you know why. Now you'll feel how.'

Rhonda's face remained a sneer, her voice a satirical lilt. 'I could forgive you for being a one-dimensional bourgeois twit — except you're so bloody boring.'

His whole body trembled. He suspected his hands were shaking. The effect of the moment was like wind chill blowing from his core. She hadn't given an inch. He was reluctantly impressed.

He signalled Zuiden to begin. The chain hoist whirred and dragged her up. Zuiden ran it along the overhead rail until she dangled above the vat.

Interesting that both 'department heads' were here to witness the dissolving, one intimately.

Unfortunately the alloy lip of the vat obscured his view, but he knew her swollen feet were only inches above the acid.

He called, 'You're about to suffer terribly. How do you feel?'

'Clad in the beauty of a thousand suns.'

'I don't take your meaning.'

'You're too dreary to understand.'

His shaking was embarrassing. He disliked Zuiden seeing him like this. It made him feel exposed. Disassociation, essential to killing technique, was part of Department S philosophy.

Zuiden said tonelessly, 'Your call,' his face death-mask sober.

This was the moment, the culmination of revenge.

The shaking. My God. He grabbed one of the metal chairs, turned it so he could prop a knee on it, then held the back with both hands. That was better. He took two deep breaths, called, 'Very slow. Begin.'

Zuiden prodded a button. The perverted bitch dropped 3 inches and stopped, her mass slightly bouncing on the rope. But she'd lifted her legs.

He motioned to Zuiden again. Her body dropped more. No matter how she writhed, her toes would soon be dissolving.

He waited for the agonised bellows.

They never came.

Her face contorted. Her legs dropped. Steam rose from the vat.

Cyanide!

He howled with rage and smashed the chair against the wall.

38

JOHN

The next morning the showers were on. They waited in queues to get clean. The naked Hunt was so stunning that no one in the bathroom, male or female, could drag away their eyes.

As they dressed, he said, 'You've got an amazing body.'

'And EXIT's fully exploited it, I assure you.'

They queued again for breakfast, then joined the crowd in the lounge while lists were posted on the board. Everyone had been allocated times when they were authorised to leave the building. Their time was 3 pm.

Cain said, 'Bugger this. Let's try and get out of here.'

They followed the first batch to the alcove for kitting up. Each person was ticked off at the door by two over-large young surgeons.

'Must be cadets,' Hunt murmured.

'Just shows how stretched they are.'

When they reached for their hanging outer suits, one of the youths confronted them. 'You two aren't scheduled till afternoon.' The thickness of his neck, the sloping set of his

— 199 —

shoulders, everything about him was hostile. The second cadet closed ranks behind the first.

Young punks, Cain thought — super-sensitive to hierarchy, measuring personal success by the degree of intimidation. He said, 'Stop strutting. I'm not impressed.'

'What are you on about?'

'Ever killed anyone, son?' He doubted they had. He knew that Hunt was probably wired enough to take them single-handed — chopping throats and poking eyes without them seeing it coming. But he could no longer trust his damaged body in a fight against young animal fitness.

Then Zuiden entered the porch, eyebrows encrusted, breathing vapour. The apprentice thugs snapped to attention.

Zuiden said, 'Two against the world, huh? Don't try it, Cain. You'll lose.'

'Been monitoring us, have you?'

'Yes, God knows why. You're an invalid and you've lost it. Without a gun you're stuffed. So what's your beef?'

'I want to see John.'

'Your wants don't count.'

Cain knew the surgeon had expected him to say Rhonda and that the request had surprised him. He also knew they didn't want fuss and were barely coping as it was. And that despite Zuiden's blustering, a dentist Grade Four was the biggest threat in the base. 'I want to see him, or I'll make things very difficult for you here.'

Zuiden weighed it up, then turned to the two thugs. 'Let him through. Not her.'

Cain flashed a glance at the savage-eyed Hunt that said, 'Hold your fire. I'll be back.'

He walked with Zuiden across the cold vault beneath the domes, his felt-lined rubber-soled boots slipping on the overtrodden ice.

'If you took the cadets,' Zuiden said, 'there's still the guardhouse. And if you got past that we'd come after you. And even if we didn't, where the hell would you go?'

Cain knew he was right. Sixteen countries operated over thirty permanent bases in Antarctica and all kinds of expeditions shared the ice. For an uninhabitable wilderness it was becoming rather densely populated. Even tourism was becoming a problem. But Alpha was as isolated as Vostok, 800 kilometres from anywhere, with the only workable egress by a full-scale traverse or a Herc. And two fleeing people couldn't organise either. He turned to Zuiden. 'If reincarnation exists, I bet you come back as a bird.'

'I'll bite.' Zuiden drawled. 'Why?'

'So you can shit on people.'

Zuiden chuckled. 'I'll piss on your grave before I go.' He walked up steps into the cold porch of a red-painted building and told the two cadets inside the entrance, 'This piece of Paki shit has clearance to see number three. He gets an hour in there. Any fuss, buzz me.'

The pope had a cabin-like room with a desk and a bed. He wore polar clothes too big for him and was correcting a typed manuscript. As Cain entered, he looked around, astonished. 'Ray!' He lurched up from his chair to embrace him, knocking papers flying.

Cain said, 'Thank God you're all right.'

'They said you were almost killed.'

'They've patched me up. But I'm not good.'

'How wonderful to see you.' He sat down again a little breathless, beaming with delight.

Cain helped gather up the papers. 'I think they're going to kill us. I don't trust things here.'

'No. But events don't matter. Only what we are.'

'But I'm afraid for you.'

John smiled. 'Leave what happens to God. Why complain? What we are *now* is all there ever is.'

'I know that theoretically but ...' He sat on the bunk. There wasn't a second chair.

John leaned forward and held Cain's hand in both of his, his face full of kindness. 'Relax. Come back inside.'

He tried to bring his attention back to his body.

'You remember when we were children? How we stared with such wonder at the sun? So naive. But the sentiment was true. Perhaps that youthful aspiration is the finest thing we have. Truer than our fashionable despair. Truer than the ruins of a life.'

The words went in as they always did with him, soothing, reaffirming, and the year since their last meeting dropped away.

'You feel it?' John went on. 'Why did primeval cultures worship the virgin?'

'What have you been doing?'

'Reading. Sufi poems. The Taoists. Gurdjieff.' He pointed to boxes stacked against the wall. 'They let me bring a few books.'

'Gurdjieff was a giant. A shame the Jesuits made a dog's breakfast of the enneagram.'

'Yes. The inevitable distortion. It shows how dry our doctrine's become and how desperate people are to infuse it. Gurdjieff offered practice but most people just respond to his theory. The approach to Being is incomprehensible to most because it belongs to eternity, not time.'

'May I ask you a daring question?'

'Daring?' John lifted something off his desk.

'Have you abandoned the concept of God?'

'Why name it? Labels shut you off. Fear God. Why? Because one attracts what one fears?' A smile. 'What a creaking construction.'

Cain nodded slowly. 'Concepts hiding truth? Is that the tragedy of the Church?'

'That depends on the level of perception.'

'So there are no steps to the throne?'

'Too sweeping. Read this — from here.' He handed over bound sheets of typescript.

Cain took the manuscript and read aloud: 'Religion is the ruse of the wise. It aims to bring the unsuspecting aspirant to a heightened inner vibration that reasoning can't reach. So it promotes irrationality — for a worthy aim. It is the only deception that can't be called untrue.

'This is beautiful.'

'I don't know. But it's the best of me. The need to express, you see? God's journalist.'

He skipped a few pages, read on, silently this time.

'When not "I" then AM. When the observer is abandoned, seeing simply is — an experience that reaches through diversity to unity in an enfolding verticality to time. "And there shall be time no longer." These words are literally true. Eternity is not duration but the infinite potential of all ages in the sunburst of unified awareness. We need to die to be born to that experience. But who is interested in inner death?'

He looked up, filled with the truth of it. 'What would the Curia make of this?'

'The dead would bury the living.'

He read on:

'Belief is superstition, piety straw and chastity without knowledge mistaking the means for the end. The end is the blind, true probing into that core predating time where knowledge and bliss are made flesh. The resurrection of the body is not a historical event but the central transformation of consciousness. We are asked to incarnate Christ. Not the spirit but the flesh must be transformed. The organism must be afire — the kingdom of God on earth.'

He looked away from the words, intensely moved.

The old pope smiled. 'You know what it's saying, don't you? And to know is a great achievement. But blessed are ye if ye do it.'

So this was what John had been working on through long years — distilling his wisdom far beyond the point of heresy. He knew the manuscript had to survive — for Ray Cain if for no one else.

He handed back the pages with care. 'Have you read Krishnamurti?'

'Life begins where thought ends. Yes.'

'I discovered such a clear expression of his recently. "In attention there is no centre. There is no me attending."'

'Exactly.' The old man put the manuscript into a scruffy padded postbag. 'Exactly.'

'Is your book finished?'

'As much as it will be.'

They sat in silence for a moment.

Then the pope murmured, 'And darkness was upon the face of the deep. The Buddhist view. Everything comes from nothing. Form is emptiness. Emptiness form.'

Cain looked into the wise eyes. 'Is that how you feel it?'

John's inward look, as if he were exploring it. 'The nature of that emptiness is so interesting. Death is the matrix of life. Not the other way around. Do you see it?'

He was trying to comprehend. 'Not yet.'

'The only knowing is being. But being is to be nothing. No memory. No anticipation. Blank.'

'It can't just be blank.'

'It can't and it can. Always the paradox. Everything flowers from nothing.'

He nodded, trying to keep up inwardly. 'But you say there are no steps to that.'

A bottomless look. 'Attention — the natural prayer of the soul. Or as the Diamond Sutra says, keeping the mind in its natural state. Remember Eckhart: riddance of goods, riddance of friends, riddance of self. But who understands that precise effort, that intensity? It's naive trying to be a finer person. Spirituality is not to be derived. That's working for wages — craving. It's an infusion of grace — induced by psychological death.'

As usual, with John, vistas kept expanding. 'I've missed this so much.' How quickly the pope had dismissed the danger they were in. Yet had that danger made this moment — this richness with him — possible? The old man used everything for his aim.

* * *

In exactly an hour, a cadet interrupted them.

Cain was taken back to the entrance and met by Zuiden who escorted him across the ice beneath the dome.

'How's it feel to be down the toilet?' Zuiden sneered. 'You're rooted, Cain.'

'Did he who made the lamb make thee?'

'You can forget those days,' the half-listening man said, focused as usual on his stomach. 'Now all we get down here is lasagna.'

Cain limped beside him, fearful for the pope, wondering if he'd ever see him again. 'You have a strange effect on people, Jan. They either hate you or loathe you.'

'Black bastard,' the surgeon guffawed. 'Never give up, do you? Well I hope the old boy saved your soul. Because your body's soon going to be fucked.'

39

TRIPLE CROSS

At precisely 3.30 pm Hunt and Cain were cleared by the guardhouse. A senior surgeon escorted them up the ramp. He walked ahead as if trying to put them at ease but probably had a weapon beneath his windproofs. They followed him in full kit, lugging rucksacks. They'd been told they were being relocated but didn't believe it.

Cain let his overmitts dangle from their harness. Gloves and glove liners would do until they got to the warmed Hagg. His limp was bad. He was breathless, felt vulnerable and old.

They walked from shadow into dazzling sunlight. For once the windiest continent on earth offered nothing but a light breeze but it was close to minus 40 degrees centigrade and breathing hurt. He glanced at the crystalline snow. If he removed the goggles it would become a field of diamonds — exquisite — and cause snow-blindness.

The man led them past the vehicle workshop to where a loader, a tractor and a Hagg were plugged into the power cable hitching-rail. The vehicles were plastered with snow, but only on one side, like iced cakes.

A man was uncoupling the cable from the front of the Hagg. It ran the cab-warmer and the in-line coolant heater that kept the engine from freezing. Several people stood around the back of the vehicle, waiting.

Their escort took their bags and heaved them into the front cab. As they reached the group of people, Cain recognised the two old men.

The bent figure was John, glasses beneath his goggles, the familiar smiling upward twist to the left side of his mouth. It was a shock to see him, engulfed in an overlarge freezer suit, standing out here in the snow. No *sedia gestatoria* now to bear him triumphantly through the crowd. Just an 82-year-old man with swollen ankles and low blood pressure — a man from a working class family who would have liked to have been a journalist. A man of warmth in a frigid hell. A man he loved.

And the other man, also small, but swarthy. Sly, obsequious eyes. Cain confronted his life's work — the president he'd plucked from power and inadvertently saved from a plane crash. Allah's little helper had been with EXIT — how long now? Six years. That would make him seventy.

'Rahib Badar.' Zia ul-Haq's smile displayed his huge trademark teeth, not so white now.

'Greetings,' Cain replied in Urdu, 'in the name of Allah, the Compassionate, the Merciful.' But Allah's mercy, he remembered, had not been conspicuous in Zia. He'd driven in a gold-plated Rolls and profited from arms sales while his minions jammed chillies into the rectums of his enemies.

'A brisk day,' Zia replied. 'I hope your health remains exceptional.'

'And yours, Inshallah.' What had Reich called it? Compulsive, contactless sociability? Zia drew it like a poultice. You couldn't get the better of the man. Even in this cold, even at this altitude, his manners remained impeccable and his sense of expediency acute. Did he still pomade his hair? Like most Leos he loved his locks.

The third man seemed to be a stranger. Then he recognised the voice.

'Karen. You can't escape me.' The *basso profondo* of Raul.

She stopped short. 'What is this? The confrontation waltz?'

Behind the notables stood Zuiden and another set-mouthed surgeon. Zuiden said, 'Everyone in,' and opened the rear door of the back cab.

Cain assisted the pope, helped get his boot over the sill and down to the well that ran between the side benches.

John settled on the bench and smiled at the dark-skinned president. 'So you are ...'

'Zia of Pakistan.' The old general would have bowed if the constriction of clothes and space had permitted it. 'And you, of course, are the Holy Father. I knew they had you. Strange they kept us apart so long, we People of the Book.'

John smiled again, no dupe of political politeness. History had shown how much hardline Muslims revered Christians.

'Popes and potentates,' Raul rumbled. 'Exalted company.' He got in and sat beside Zia, then glanced across at the mild, lively face of the pope. 'Al-Ghazali meets Augustine?'

The pope said, 'Two great men.'

Cain and Hunt got in, next Zuiden and his sidekick who sat either side of the rear door as the engine began its racket. In the front cab you got good views. In the rear it was harder to see out.

The oil pressure built. With a jerk, they were off, tracks squeaking on wind-hardened snow. They passed the generator house, churned past snow-covered surplus piping and stacked sections of wrecked huts, turned to follow the drumline as if heading out toward the strip.

They shivered. The heat converter didn't work well in the back. Cain glanced across at Hunt, not trusting this. It didn't look good. Four senior surgeons, counting the two in front. Could they take Zuiden and the other man? He knew it was a dream.

He looked out the back window. It was starting to fog but hadn't yet been covered by snow kicked up from the tracks. The ramshackle sprawl of Alpha had diminished in the distance and now they were passing two isolated freight containers on linked traversing sledges. Something red had dribbled down to the pivot of one massive runner. And there were drag marks for a distance sidewards. Were there bodies in the containers? Had they massacred people here?

The Hagg stopped, engine idling.

He couldn't see huts.

'Now what?' he asked Zuiden.

'We wait.'

The sound of multiple turboprops. A Herc coming in.

'So, my seditious friend,' Zia said in Urdu. The word 'seditious' was a threat. The Koran classed sedition as more grievous than killing, a precept dear to Muslim leaders who seized power. And to Zia, he was a seditionist. The man understandably hated him. 'My question is,' he went on, 'am I about to be killed?'

Cain smiled back, knowing the surgeons were watching, and answered in low Urdu, 'They're about to kill us all.'

'I thought so.' Zia returned the smile, nodded pleasantly, as if told the weather would stay fine. An accomplished performance. Not even a flicker of strain.

Raul still thought it was an excursion and an opportunity to play to the gallery. He surveyed the pope with a derisory air. 'A step into the unknown. How to move from time to space? Infinite choices then, you agree?'

John said, 'What is there to move from?'

Then, drowning the muffled tractor-sound of the Hagg, the roar of the landing plane.

They heard it reverse thrust, taxi. The Hagg moved forward again, twisting around. Its steering system was unusual — two servo-controlled hydraulic cylinders that articulated front and rear cabs around a central point. A curious vehicle, Cain thought, to spend one's last minutes in. DEATH IS AN

ASPECT OF LIFE. But to be gutted by bloody Zuiden ... Concentrate, he told himself. You're about to be shot.

They stopped again — and sat for almost an hour. Little was said, as if the impending event had killed speech. Once the pope glanced at him. He knows, Cain thought. Only Raul seemed oblivious to fate.

As they waited, other vehicles approached the still idling plane. They could shut the thing down above minus 40 degrees centigrade but perhaps the temperature was dropping. With just two old transports in the fleet, they tended to mother the hydraulics. Number three engine would still be running.

A loader went by, then a tractor towing a heater.

'What's that?' Raul rumbled.

'A Herman Nelson heater,' Zuiden said. 'You have to heat seals and gaskets or they contract and fluids leak.'

'I see,' Raul cut him off with a concrete smile and turned to Zia. 'What joy to have such well-informed abductors.'

The general refused to share in the derision of a military man. His indulgent smile was perfectly pitched to inform Raul he was the greater fool.

Eventually a tractor-drawn sledge passed them, returning stacked with stores — drums and dark metal boxes that might contain ammunition or explosives. Cain hadn't seen any people. Was it just a cargo flight?

A buzzer, the intercab phone. Zuiden answered. 'Right.' He opened the back door. Cold air poured into the cab. The two surgeons got down and Zuiden called, 'All out.'

Cain climbed down first with Hunt and looked around. The Herc was 40 metres away, its ramp still lowered. The heater trucks and fuel truck were returning. The flight deck looked crowded. And a man stood at the top of the crew door steps peering at them through binoculars.

Cain waited to help John down but Raul got out next, looked at the Herc, then stared harder, mouth moving as if astounded. Then he did an extraordinary thing — removed his cap and balaclava and waved at the plane with both arms.

The man standing in the crew door stared a moment more, then lowered the binoculars and yelled behind him.

Zuiden missed it. He was around at the front cab where his other troops were climbing out. They now carried buttless Ingrams.

This, Cain knew, was bloody *it*.

Raul was lumbering toward the plane when Zuiden spotted him.

'You. Come back here,' he yelled, ripping the Velcro tabs open on his ventiles, going for his gun.

Hunt's eyes flicked to Cain for a cue.

He yelled to Zia who was half out of the cab. Yelled in Urdu. 'Stay there. Both of you, down.'

Hunt, on the far side, hadn't seen the guns but read the diversion as a chance. She launched a roundhouse kick at Zuiden, hoping to drop him before he got to the weapon. But attempting an accurate foot to the face in five layers and a freezer suit was pointless. Her cumbersome felt-lined boot merely grazed his shoulder.

'Back off, bitch.' He had his Ingram half-out but was fighting a strap that had fouled itself around the barrel. In this cold, these layers of clothing, everyone was equally clumsy. It was life and death, yet they were stumbling around like drunks.

'You,' Zuiden's sidekick yelled at Raul. 'Get back here.'

Raul turned, saw the gun, stopped, held out his hands in a stagy way.

Why haven't they shot us? Cain wondered. Then he knew. Noise carried in this land like a shout across a glassy lake. So they took their victims to the strip and shot them during takeoffs when full thrust and the JATO drowned fire.

The surgeons were staring at the plane — at a man in khaki gear who was staggering down its ramp as if shoved. The man waved a desperate warning.

Gunfire.

His body tumbled into snow.

The sound galvanised Zuiden. 'Who was that?'

'Looked like Bowman,' his sidekick said, 'a loadie. Must've shot him from inside the hold.'

'What the . . . ?'

The man at the crew door, who'd briefly disappeared, was now aiming a rifle with a scope.

The yellow ventiles of the Hagg driver blushed darker with a laser dot.

Zuiden shoved him — but too late.

A single crack — high velocity.

The driver pitched back, hit the snow.

'Take cover,' Zuiden yelled.

Hunt and Cain, four paces behind the vehicle and exposed like bunnies on a rug, dropped flat.

She shouted across to him, 'What's going on? Who are they?'

'God knows. Stay down.'

The three remaining surgeons huddled behind the tracks of the Hagg. One let off a burst toward the plane.

Zuiden yelled, 'Fuck. Not at the plane.'

'But some mob's hijacked it,' the shooter complained.

'Tough. You fuck our planes, we die here. Who'll fucking come and get us?'

Cain knew he was right. Without the planes, all at Alpha would die. No one, on or off the continent, would dare lift a finger to help.

The sniper in the plane waited. Cain was exposed enough to be shot, but assumed the man was after armed troopers — the perceived threat to Raul.

Raul, halfway between the two camps, sank to his knees, lay flat, then looked back with a strictured smile. Headcase, Cain thought.

More engine noises joined the racket as two quads shot down the ramp. The ramp extensions weren't in place so the converted four-wheel ag-bikes bucked and slewed as they kissed snow. Cain didn't believe it. A man with a burp gun sat behind each driver.

The surgeons were shocked. They scurried as one of the fast, erratic quads circled wide to attack their rear.

Zuiden's men were now fighting on two fronts with cover only from one side. The Hagg sat lower than a snow-cat, with a towing point at the back of the rear cab, hydraulic steering linkage the other end, so there was no way, in bulky gear, to wriggle between the tracks.

Bullets pinged off wheels and splintered cold-hardened rubber as the circling bike strafed them. Then the second bike attacked from the plane side, its overlarge soft tyres mashing the snow-crust, kicking up crystalline white cloud.

Cain craned to look back at the open rear door of the cab — saw the dark head of the old general and the pale face of the pope peering just above the sill like startled cats.

The air sang with firing. Zuiden was pinned every way. The sharpshooter from the plane still methodically targeted movement. And he was good.

A cry.

One surgeon down.

Zuiden used the body as a bunker.

Cain called to Hunt, 'You set?'

The quad that had gone around the back did a 360, spraying snow, flipped. Zuiden had shot the driver and both riders were rolling in snow.

The two remaining surgeons now concentrated fire on the quad and took out the man with the gun.

Zuiden dragged out a two-way, was calling the base.

'Go.' Cain was up and running along the plane-side of the Hagg. He wrenched the driver's door open, leaped into the seat, felt under the dash, pulled the release catch on the park brake.

As the vehicle jerked ahead, it left the two surviving surgeons totally exposed. In the external rear-view mirror he saw Zuiden's last man, one knee up and firing, pitch over.

Zuiden lunged for the upended bike, took cover behind it, aimed.

Cain ducked as the right-hand side window filled with spider patterns, disintegrated. He dragged the wheel around, glad the thing was left-hand-drive.

A flapping rear nearside door. Hunt behind him on the floor.

The remaining quad was ahead of them, racing for the plane. Two men still on it. But the man with the gun was gone. Shot? He'd been replaced by Raul. The driver had picked him up.

Hunt, now leaning on the engine cover next to him, yelled, 'What are you *doing?*'

'You want to stay and play tag with Alpha?'

'That's Bell!' She pointed ahead. 'They're from The Square. If they get to me, I'm dead.'

'Deader here.'

Now he saw it. The cult had tortured facts out of Murchison, got the info on EXIT flights, done an insurgent strike the other end and . . .

Raul, on the back of the bike, turned around to wave them on as if leading a cavalry charge.

I'm onto you, bastard, Cain thought. You want Zia and the pope. You want to fly them back as evidence and feed them to the networks.

Cain half-jackknifed the Hagg, followed the spraying snow from the quad as it raced ahead toward the ramp.

Hunt yelled, 'This is mad.'

'Got a better idea?'

The quad was four-wheel-drive but too small to climb the lip of the ramp. The driver ditched it and ran inside with Raul. But the lack of loading ramp extensions didn't bother the four-tracked Hagg. It could climb steep angles, high obstacles, cross wide ditches. Its nose pitched up and it churned into the empty hold. From above them came the crunch of the radar and GPS antennae wrecking themselves on the overhead.

Two exhausted-looking crewmen — the engineer and

second loadie — stood near the forward bulkhead gaping at the approaching cargo.

The loadie bellowed, 'Jesus! Back that bastard out.'

Cain, no genius at reversing articulated vehicles, shouted through the shattered side window. 'You bloody do it.'

Bell, the man he'd seen in the TV interview, was flat against the hull with Raul. 'Leave it there. No time.'

The loadie moved forward as if functioning on automatic, glanced at the deck and beckoned the vehicle on with both arms. Cain inched it to where he wanted, then depressed the pedal that worked the park brake. He shut down, jumped out and searched around for straps. The engineer checked load-positioning before climbing the flight deck steps.

The frantic loadie recognised him. 'Aren't you Cain?'

Bell ordered, 'Shut the arse, lash this thing down and get us out of here.' He swung around to Raul. 'They'll block the skiway next.'

The loadie trotted back to the ramp, still looking at Cain as if the famed Grade Four would countermand the order.

'Do what he says,' Cain yelled.

The man hit buttons on the aft control panel. The door lowered and the ramp moved up. The crewman stumbled back like an automaton, started grabbing for chains, tensioners, strops. Hunt and Cain pitched in, attaching links to anchor points.

The sound of engines running up. The crack of the sniper's rifle from the crew door behind them.

Cain called to the loadie, 'How many of them?'

The man tried to think, mind in meltdown, 'How many shot outside?'

'Two.'

'Still six.'

They heard the skis being raised to break the seal so that the plane was supported on its wheels. Then the skis were lowered again. The air crew were delaying, doing it strictly by the book.

With the Hagg semi-secured, Cain glanced around — his first chance to check the terrain.

Zia helping the pope from the Hagg. The sniper closing the crew door, turning to cover the people in the fuselage. Raul standing by the forward bulkhead, watching the scene with his fixed smile. The wild-eyed Bell buttonholed him, probably asking whether to kill them.

Raul said something and went up the stairs. The loadie got more straps on the Hagg, yelled at them to sit down, buckle up. People were descending from the flight deck and heading for the troop seats. Zia, with courtly gestures, assisted the pope to a seat and strapped him in.

They were sliding. At last! The distinctive gritty feel of huge skis moving on packed snow. They turned the big transport slowly — nursing torsional load on the shock struts or still attempting to delay?

As Cain slumped back against the curtain of red webbing, the sisters, Jane and Eve Rinaldi, entered the bay. Good God, he thought. They'd been hijacked along with the plane?

Eve mouthed the name she knew him as. 'Mark?' Then Bell herded her out of sight on the other side of the Hagg.

He and Hunt were now flanked by two hard cases. The one on his side was probably under twenty-five, a big man with a coarse face shaded by stubble and an expression as thick as his body. The second man was older, with Slavic looks and inquisitive eyes.

Both had 9mm Spectre sub-machine-guns. Cain knew the M–4. Its double-action trigger dispensed with safety mechanisms for instant firing. You cocked, then the hammer moved forward to stop near the bolt. Press the trigger and bang. The young oaf, jaw out-thrust, had the gun-muzzle aimed at his ribs.

Cain glanced at the second man who had a bead on Hunt. Neither of them seemed like culties. Had Bell used his military contacts to hire mercenaries?

They were running up. This would be seat-of-the-pants. Up here, thin air and soft snow retarded acceleration. You had to pry the heavy plane from the plateau below minimum lift-off speed. A pilot had told him one technique. Start with fifty per cent flaps, pull full back-yoke at 60 knots to clear the nose ski, then lower it back just above the surface and pop flaps to full. He didn't care how they did it — as long as it happened before the cavalry arrived.

Stop stalling guys, he begged. Get us up.

As the JATO kicked in, he jammed his hands over his ears. With eight bottles adding 8000 pounds of thrust, they staggered into the sky.

He looked across at Hunt who glared back.

Well.

At least they were alive.

40

MAYDAY

They finished the climb-out, levelled off. The heavy airframe shuddered in turbulence and wind shear on the huge tail made it yaw. The loadie unzipped a flap in the insulation just forward of the port paratroop door. He pulled handles in one-to-four sequence to unhook the JATO bottles from the air deflector. Then he crossed the deck to do it on the other side.

Bell came through the bulkhead door, his M–4 dangling from its strap. He steadied himself against the Hagg, stepped over the tie-downs and worked his way back to Zia. He yelled in the general's ear for a while. Zia looked back once at Cain.

Then Bell moved forward again to the loadmaster, borrowed his headset, spoke into it, came back to stand in front of Cain. 'You.' He jerked his thumb toward the nose.

Cain unstrapped, went forward on the shuddering deck and climbed the near vertical steps.

The flight deck was like Grand Central. Riding shotgun over the crew was Raul in a headset and two other heavies with M–4s. The three interlopers crouched in a row, like crows at a feast, on the edge of the bottom bunk. In the top bunk lay a girl who seemed to be mumbling in her sleep.

Nina.

Asleep or drugged?

Drugged, he suspected. The CIA would have told EXIT to knock her out for the flight.

Raul handed a second headset to Cain. 'You can hear me?'

Cain adjusted the mouthpiece, nodded. The plane bucked and he grabbed for the top bunk rail.

'Name, rank and serial number.' Raul's trademark smirk.

'Ray Cain. EXIT Department D, Grade Four. Retired.'

'You're the one who replaced the president, I hear, and a very dangerous man.'

'No more. I've been injured.'

'I noticed the limp.'

'EXIT was going to kill me. That's why I'm here.'

'Does that put you on our side?'

'If it gets me away from here.'

The fixed empty smile. 'I wonder. Can you give me one reason not to shoot you?'

A scream from the top bunk. Nina — up on one elbow staring ahead, disoriented — betrayal on her girl-child's face.

One of the heavies rose and yelled, 'Shut up.'

She saw his gun and screamed again, kicking out at him with her feet.

He thrust her back.

She began to hold her breath.

'What's going on?' A new voice in the cans. Cain turned to see the copilot leaning forward to tap instruments in front of him. 'Ball's gone mad, my compass is spinning. And the bloody airspeed indicator's ...'

The engineer called, 'Number two generator out light.'

The pilot stared at the engine instrument panel. 'I think two's flamed out.'

Nina was still holding her breath, her face going red, her hands fists and the knuckles white.

— 219 —

'Confirmed,' the engineer said. 'Windmilling at thirty per cent RPM.'

The pilot eased the other three throttles forward.

'Engine shutdown procedure, number two engine.'

They ran through the checklist.

Christ, Cain thought. Was it the girl?

'Can't be fuel,' the engineer said. 'Tank three shows 2000 pounds. Quantity gauge could be ratshit. Pulling circuit-breaker. Going for cross-feed.'

The engine roar was now asynchronous, out of phase to the ear.

Cain looked at the solid pale overcast and the uniform snow below. It seemed to stretch far into the distance. It was technically called poor surface and horizontal definition. It meant a lack of depth perception.

The more ominous term was whiteout.

The engineer was reporting again. 'RPM on three fluxing out of limits. And the manifold switching's gone mad. And the main tank pump switches keep flicking off. Jesus, how can they *do* that?'

Cain looked back at the extended cheeks of Nina, wondering whether to knock her out.

The crew comments were increasing in pitch.

'Nacelle overheat light on three.'

'What the hell?'

'No visible smoke.'

Raul lurched to his feet, smile gone, 'If this is some kind of trick ...'

It clearly wasn't. Cain waved at him to stay out of it.

Nina screamed again and one of the heavies hit her across the mouth. She cringed back in the bunk, eyes bright, hand over her jaw. On the overhead systems control panels, the occasional toggle-switch flicked over without human intervention.

'Engine shutdown procedure — number three engine.'

The pilot was conserving airspeed, had the thing slightly nose-down.

Comments and commands became a babble.

'Overheat light still on.'

'First fire bottle,' the right seater said.

'Still on.'

'Isolating wing bleed air.'

'Still on.'

'Hell. Is the wing on fire or what?'

'Number four generator out light.'

'Procedure for restarting two?'

'Radalt's jumping off the peg. Got to climb.'

'Barometrics read twelve thou' and bloody going up!'

'Radalt two thou'. Dropping.'

Cain could see nothing beyond the windows but an unrelieved white. The ice could have been 50 feet below or 10,000. What was their position now? Probably 300 kilometres from Alpha and another 1000 metres higher up the plateau. God, if they went down here ...

'Firing bottle two.'

'Overheat light still on.'

'What's with the fucking cross-feed?'

Cain looked at the feathered inboard port engine, then stared beyond it — at something streaming from the dump-mast on the end of the wing.

He reluctantly added his voice to the yammer. 'I think we're dumping fuel.'

'Christ! The switches are ...'

'Got to turf that Hagg. Load, pilot.'

'Load.'

'No time,' yelled the navigator who was spotting out the starboard windows. 'Pull Gs. Pull up. Pull *up*.'

The last thing he saw before impact was the pilot hauling on the yoke.

41

HELL ON ICE

The first thing was shuddering, grinding. Then the plane shook itself into a blur. Above the yells in the cans, the sound of tearing metal.

He fought free of the headset, grabbed a handhold at the side of the cockpit roof, planted a foot against the back of the pilot's seat, which juddered like a paint mixer. There was no time to do more. The pilot was trying to pull full flaps.

They lofted once as if bouncing — perhaps launched off a pressure ridge — pancaked with a rattling smash and pounded, forward speed dropping, as lift bled from the big wings.

He knew the skis would have collapsed. From the sound, they were slithering on the belly. As momentum tried to suck him through the windows he fought lower until he'd wedged his back behind the pilot's seat.

The two heavies weren't so quick. One collected the back of the copilot's headrest in the chest. The other sailed above the central console. A third shape crashed rag-doll-like into the man skewered on the right-hand seat.

Nina's slight body was the last, landing against Cain so hard his vision went red.

Then the seat they were braced against broke loose, tipped forward. He slid up the back of it and was pressed into a body pile. The shaking was enough to loosen teeth.

He caught one glimpse, through an eyebrow-window, of the port wing with outboard prop still turning.

Saw the wing dip.

Its end shear off.

Felt the wreck wrenched around.

The inboard blades bent as they hit snow. The outboard prop carved down to ice, disintegrated.

Then it was quiet.

For five seconds.

He was lying on his back, could see a rolled black blind and a yellow T-bar handle. That put him near the cockpit roof. He moved his arms and legs to try them. No pain. He looked down at himself. Nothing seemed to have impaled him. He touched his face with his glove. No blood.

He was lying on top of people who were unnaturally still. Somewhere beside him Nina screamed.

Gingerly he slid off the pile. No pain yet. Everything worked. He couldn't believe his luck. He turned in the littered space as if dreaming and looked forward.

The pilots were under it somewhere and had to be dead. They'd been bare-headed and both seats had slid off their rails so the forward instrument panel would be wearing their brains.

One of the enforcers was half through the forward window, his neck cut and his face hanging from his skull. The other man was coughing blood. The navigator was bent like a contortionist — spine wrapped around the window frame. The face-down body lowest in the pile seemed to be the engineer. He must have undone his seatbelt to check something. The last thing to enter his head had been the throttle control of the feathered number two engine. Its bloodstained stem projected from his shattered mouth.

That left Raul and Nina. Both, he saw, were alive.

And in that disoriented moment it occurred to him how typical it was, in this greenhouse of slaughtered bodies, that the two most dangerous people had survived.

Like him, they had been cushioned by the death of the others, by the wad of corpses that would harden, like meat in a freezer, into a memorial to gear-up landings only a ghoul could love.

Bitter air spilled through the shattered windows. Nina crouched whimpering on the floor, which now had a steep starboard list.

He looked around for the guns. Raul was ahead of him, had the one still visible weapon in his hands. The other he couldn't see.

Then Bell staggered up the steps. He wheezed, 'Gustave. Gustave . . .' His drawn face changed to elation as he saw his imperator alive.

Raul had ignored the man behind him with rib-shattered lungs. He spread his arms with *ecce homo* bravura, gun in one hand, grinning.

'You're alive,' Bell panted. 'What happened?'

'I think the technical term's "pilot error".'

Cain looked at him with disgust, thought, when the cold gets you, you won't be chirpy.

Bell stared at the pile of bodies. His expression said it all.

'How bad is it back there?' Raul puffed.

'Two dead, two injured. We've got to get you out. It could blow up.'

'Couldn't it just catch fire? I'm freezing.' He eased himself down the stairs. 'Hard to breathe.'

Bell placed his M–4 muzzle against the back of the coughing man's head and fired.

The coughing stopped.

He followed his leader down.

'Don't leave me,' Nina howled and clutched at Cain's leg.

'This is your stuff-up, kiddo. You put the spanner in the spokes. You've killed us all.'

She started to sob.

Yelling at ferals changed nothing. Should he try to find the other gun? Why bother? Any fight he'd had in him had gone. They were definitely higher on the plateau. Even less oxygen than before. Every movement made him gasp for air. They'd all almost certainly die. He pointed a gloved finger at her. 'Put your hood on. And zip that parka.'

Her hands were clenching. She couldn't do it.

He adjusted her clothes like a parent, worked the hood around her. The perfect skin, up-tilted nose, sunbleached corn hair. She was jail-bait all right, more dangerous than bloody Zuiden. So where were his sun-goggles? He searched around and found a pair, wondering why he bothered. But snow-blindness wasn't fun.

He left her choking on sobs and went down.

The first thing he noticed was glare flooding in behind the front bulkhead. The nose of the Hagg had broken loose and peeled back part of the fuselage like a giant can-opener. The gash was where troop seats had been. Between its front tracks and the damage were the dead.

Jane was one — her face fixed in the agony her crushed body must have brought her at the end. The other body, the loadmaster's, hung through the rent as if frozen in a back somersault — which it soon would be. The red mess of a torn stump didn't explain where the missing leg had gone. Perhaps the disintegrating prop had sliced it. On the port side of the hull, shafts of light showed where blades had sheared through the guard skin doubler.

The main cargo deck was unbreached but he doubted much was left beneath it. The emergency exit hatches were untouched, the port paratroop door open. He could smell electrical wiring, aviation fuel. Cold was getting to him now.

He looked behind him. Nina hadn't followed. Bugger her, he thought. He stumbled along the listing floor past the bulk of the Hagg into the glare. No need to jump. The snow was almost level with the door.

He sank in up to his knees. Indistinguishable grey on grey. Just the sheet of low cloud and the plateau of frozen hope — the bleakest place on the driest, highest continent of all. This was the terrible interior — an ice pack up to 3 miles deep — where no one could survive without machinery, technology and luck. The wind seemed less than force 3 but wouldn't stay that way.

He waded toward the huddled figures, some lying in the snow, some on their knees, others standing, their Gore-Tex windproofs a spot of colour in the void.

Already out of breath, he paused, turned back to look at the hulk. Up front the radome was half cracked off and the shredded bodies projecting from the windows showed how fast they'd stopped. The fuselage seemed to be buried halfway up the main landing gear fairing but buckled panels along the snowline explained the illusion. The belly must have collapsed or been ripped off piecemeal on the ice.

From the rump of the broken port wing, JP8 dribbled, its enormous cold tolerance preventing it from freezing. Snow was porous to the fuel, which would go deep and be less likely to ignite. The outboard port engine hung from its spar, the mounting beams severed from their struts, nacelle tilting at the snow. He suspected the starboard wing had ploughed in and broken off.

The great striped tail stood proud and the rear fuselage appeared undamaged. A long skid-mark showed the way they'd come. They'd been climbing slightly on impact so must have matched the plateau's angle. For a shock spud-in, they'd done well.

He waded over to the gasping survivors who seemed in a fugue of disassociation. Air pressure was lower at the poles. And they had to be at 3000 metres — equivalent to around 4000 metres on Everest. So everyone was functioning on half the normal oxygen supply. It meant shortness of breath, dizziness, confusion, even nausea.

Zia sat in the snow, face contorted, shivering. Beside him was the grey-faced pope who was the worse for altitude sickness.

Cain touched his arm. 'You okay?'

The old man nodded, gasped, 'We think ... the general's ... broken his leg.'

'Pull your balaclava over your face. And always keep the goggles on. UV's extreme, even in this weather.'

Visibility was reducing. They could have been inside a large grey egg. The breath through his balaclava fogged his goggles and made the plane a blur.

He glanced at the hired heavies with their trigger fingers on their guns. Neither wore goggles and squinted against the glare. At least Zia had the sense to shut his eyes.

The oafish young mercenary had his M–4 trained on Hunt. She crouched beside Eve Rinaldi who lay on her back, unconscious.

He asked Hunt, 'What's wrong with her?'

'Knocked out, I think. We've got to get her conscious. Moving.'

She was the only other person here, he realised, who knew these conditions. The others were what they called 'fingies' — fucking new guys.

He waved a mitt at the assembly. 'Okay. First thing. Head-count. Eight here.' He tapped his windjacket. 'Nine. Girl's still in the plane. Makes ten. Everyone to stay close. Easiest place in the world to get lost. If you can't see the plane, you die.'

Christ it was cold. And if the wind got up it could drop another 30 degrees.

He turned to the mercenaries. 'Guns won't help you now.' He pointed to the big youth's outer gloves. 'Two sets of gloves aren't enough. Drop the iron and get your mitts on. And if you've got glare glasses, put them on.'

'Don't give them a heads-up,' Hunt panted. 'Let them bloody find out.'

Her strategy was right. Except they had two old men, one injured. An unconscious woman. A hysterical kid … If they tried a war of attrition, they'd win. But the civilians would die first.

'Tempting,' he told her. 'But we need their manpower now.'

Raul had been facing into the wind. He blinked with difficulty, eyelids frosted. Cain knew that even his meta-pop psychology would be vexed by cold seeping to his bones. He and his stooges looked as comfortable as nudists buried in crushed ice.

Bell turned to his guru. 'I'm up to here with Karen and this Indian smartarse.' He wasn't referring to Zia. 'I say we take them out now.'

Cain said, 'Without us, you'll die in hours. And I'm from Pakistan, if you don't mind.' He turned to all of them. 'If you don't have glasses or goggles, get back in there and find some. Mitts on, glasses on, hoods on. And cover your face with balaclavas, blizz masks if you have them. Or any way you can. Could save your nose dropping off. Probably save your hands. And face away from the wind whenever you can. And keep moving or your hands and feet'll shut down.'

It had been quite a speech for this altitude. He puffed to get his breath.

'He's right,' Raul said. 'It's mutually assured survival just now.' His words became frost on the fur of his hood. 'Our hitchhikers know these conditions so, for the time being, they live.'

'No one'll live,' Cain said, 'unless you break out the plane's survival gear.'

'What's it got?' Bell gasped.

'Tents, cookers, lamps, water, sleeping bags, shovels. And should be a week's crew rations.'

'What if the plane goes up?'

'We're dead anyway. So risk the plane and get these people in it.'

'But it's just as cold in there.'

'Warmer. No wind-chill.'

Bell glanced at the remaining hired help. 'Get the old men and the woman in the plane.'

The Slav plodded forward. But the young oaf seemed reluctant and kept the gun on Hunt as if comforted by what he knew.

'Forget it, Mullins,' Bell gasped. 'She can't go anywhere.' He turned to Raul again. 'You're sure you don't want to shoot her?'

'That would be too simple for dear Karen.'

'Stop fart-arsing,' Cain puffed. 'Got about two hours of light.'

Raul attempted a superior look. But in this vastness it just showed his insignificance. Here his adoring millions of followers were reduced to one man — Bell.

'Get wise, Raul,' Cain said. 'You're between a rock and a hard place.'

42

SURVIVAL

At that altitude, in that cold, every movement became an act of will. Constricted by their layers of clothing, they moved in the plane's ruined hulk as ponderously as deep-water divers searching for doubloons.

'We could pitch tents in here,' Bell puffed, 'if we got that vehicle out. The ramp doesn't seem jammed.' He looked at Cain. 'There's a pump handle for the hydraulics. If we can manually open the back ...'

'On a slanting floor? Frig around and you'll freeze. Gotta pitch the tents outside.'

'Why not shelter in the vehicle?'

'Ever tried camping in a Hagg? Death by carbon monoxide. Tents best. Got to get warm.'

'Tents are warm?'

'If it's done right.'

'Okay. Jakov. Mullins. Help him.'

Raul didn't condescend to help with the tents. He sheltered in the plane with the infirm, face half-buried in the fur-lined hood of his parka, the butt of an automatic pistol that Bell must have given him protruding from his parka pocket.

The wind was getting up. Fine drift settled on the tent bags, began to search for ways into their clothes and faded anyone a few paces away to a smudge.

Hunt and Cain showed them how to erect the first tent, probing the ground, digging out a square for the floor — the wisest way in this area of katabatic winds. They laid out the 30-kilogram contraption, driving the pegs in on the windward flap and covering it with snow. They attached a rope to the top and let the wind aid the raising of the peak. They packed the valances with snow, secured pegs, tightened ropes. The effort in that cold made them disoriented, exhausted. Each time they exhaled, the frost around their faces built up until their mouths felt wired shut.

They had three polar pyramids — the best tents for a gale. When they'd positioned the floor, he left Hunt to finish the set-up with the Slav. Jakov — was that his name? He wondered if she'd ambush him there and hoped she had sense to delay. He suspected she'd bought his manpower argument because the first thing to do was get warm. She'd show the man how to unpack the sleeping bags, get the stove on, hang the lamp, lug in the food box.

She called out, 'We've got seven sleeping bags — with left and right zips.'

'Good.' Two sleeping bags zipped together would accommodate three people. 'Zip three twos together. That holds nine. And one over.'

Cain worked with Mullins and Bell on the other tents, pitching them in the lee of the plane. It was hard, slogging effort with each step an agony. Their fingers and heads became numb while the rest of them started to sweat. Then their tear ducts became more viscous and stuck their eyelids together.

'Keep blinking,' Cain warned, 'or you'll end up blind.'

When Hunt and Jakov finished the first tent, they transferred the exhausted pope, the moaning Zia, his leg now roughly splinted between ice axes, and the now-conscious but hypothermic Eve. Hunt stayed with them as guide and mentor. He knew she'd help them thaw, warn them to change into dry socks, show them how to hang their boots and felt-liners up. And she'd get food cooking.

Raul said, 'I've done what I can with Zia's leg. There's nothing sticking out but there's swelling and bruising.' His eyes streamed with tears in the cold wind. The sullen Nina stood beside him.

Cain said, 'Does the leg seem shorter? Did you try rotating the foot?'

'It's too painful to move and I don't know how to set it. It seemed best to immobilise it. If you have better ideas ...'

'Find the plane's emergency pack. Give him two tablets of codeine. Elevate the leg. Check for frostbite. Get the girl to help you.'

By the time the other tents were up and fitted out, ground drift was piling up snow. In the darkening wasteland, the Tilley lamps suspended in the tents transformed each into a yellow pyramid.

Cain trudged from tent to tent checking arrangements. His breath had frozen on his face mask until it was metal-stiff, his goggles were almost iced over and his stubble, stuck to the jacket hood, made turning his head painful.

Hunt had left the first tent. But it was still so packed with people that he couldn't fully crawl inside. Zia, the invalid, had a sleeping bag to himself. Nina and the pope were in the double bag, cold and exhausted, while a sobbing Eve tended the stove.

The smell of cooking macaroni cheese made him instantly famished. They'd need 5000 calories a day in this weather just to survive.

'Any frostbite here?' he asked.

Eve's despairing face looking up. 'I'm frozen right inside.'

He cleaned his goggles. 'You'll be okay tomorrow.'

'How can you say that? Did you see Jane?'

He nodded.

She pointed to her daughter. 'Did *she* cause this?'

'The first real gremlin I've ever struck.'

Eve moaned and clenched her fists.

Zia sat in his single bag, his splinted leg protruding from the unzipped side and elevated on a pack. He sipped cocoa as dark as his skin but still managed to look like death.

'How are you?' Cain asked him in English.

'A lot of pain. Can we survive this?'

He said in Urdu, 'No. Down here, the tiger has wings.'

Zia nodded at the reference.

Cain held his hands by the stove. John seemed to be asleep. God's postman would bunk with two women tonight — the best way to keep him warm.

Cain said, 'Put your socks and water bottles in your sleeping bags. You get thirsty in this place and it takes hours to melt snow for water. And stiff socks don't help.' He pointed to a torch by the food box. 'That goes in with you, too. Batteries lose power if they get cold. And hang your boots at the top of the tent or they'll be like ice tomorrow.'

Raul and Bell, in the second tent, had told Hunt to join them. She hadn't liked it. He stuck his head through the entrance of their tent. Vapour crystallising on the inside was creating an ice storm. Bell was adding to it bashing ice from his parka. Their food was still frozen and they were trying to boil water.

Over the roar of the gas jet, Cain asked, 'Okay here?'

Hunt's return glance would have pitted bronze. But he doubted Raul and his hunter-scavengers intended to slaughter her that night. It might even go the other way. She still saw people as targets and killing as a game to be won — was too young, too recently trained, to know the cruelty and folly of it all.

He crawled into the third tent where he was billeted with Mullins and Jakov. Raul clearly intended to keep him supervised and separate from Hunt. Right now he didn't care, was at the end of his wick, body shaking with cold, hands and feet shutting down.

Mullins had made the usual discoveries — that matches froze as they came out of the box and saucepan lids froze to the pan. But he had the stove going at least. He still wore his balaclava. Frost had stuck it to his face and he was waiting for it to thaw.

The other hard case, Jakov, crawled in with them. 'Jeez, toilet in plane is like wind tunnel.'

Cain reached between the double lining of the tent and held up a plastic beaker. 'That's your toilet.'

'Like hell.'

Mullins cackled. 'We call him the phantom crapper 'cause his dick's so small he doesn't want us to see it.'

'Shut your face, big shitbag.' Jakov rubbed his hands together. 'Jeez, my hands sting terrible.'

'It's the sensation coming back,' Cain said. 'Good sign. It'll go in a while.'

He told them to change their socks and hang up the wet ones. He hung up his felt-liners and mukluk insoles from the apex of the tent to dry. Tents were warm at the peak but could be 60 degrees centigrade cooler on the floor. He explained how the body reacted to cold — reduced blood to hands, feet, limbs to keep vital organs warm. The other men had bunny boots — not as effective in this climate.

Mullins finally peeled off his headgear, said, 'My underdaks are wet.'

'Me too,' the Slav said. 'I sweat much.' They'd worked hard and the sweat that normally froze between the pile suit and the windproofs hadn't entirely wicked out.

'How you dry long johns?' Jakov said.

'Sleep in them.' Sleeping in wet polypropylene felt lousy but you did it.

'Yuk.'

*   *   *

It took them two hours to get watered, fed.

Cain had seen no guns for some time. Had they buried them outside the tent? At minus 40 degrees centigrade they could freeze up or hang fire. That could be useful later. He checked the vent, killed the lamp, burrowed into the bag.

'One thing,' the garlic-smelling Jakov said, 'we got to cuff you. Is orders from Bell.'

'Like fun.'

'Don' make it tough, fellah.'

He felt the man fiddling with plasticuffs.

'What do you think I'll do? Kill you?'

'Could be. Jus' 'cause you talk like uni poofter don' mean you not know how to kill.'

He let them do it, longing to sleep.

'So what about the girl?' Mullins said. 'Could use a bit of that.'

Jakov chuckled. 'I like to hump that Hunt bitch. If her body good as her face ...'

'That's Raul's bitch,' Mullins said. 'The one who done him in.'

'So?'

Cain said, 'You'd look cute with your dicks turning blue. Now can we get some sleep?'

He was woken by someone shaking him. Sunlight made the inner tent bright orange and the fabric was bellying in as if pushed.

A slapping noise.

Jakov had woken him. 'Chopper. Frien' or foe?'

'Foe.'

'You sure, fellah?'

'We were on an EXIT flight, damn it. That means no one but EXIT'll go near it. Get these bloody cuffs off.'

As they set him free he yelled, 'And get the guns.'

43

WASTELAND

He expected them to strafe the tent, was surprised as the rotor slap became more distant. He struggled into his boots and ventiles, dragging at closures and zips.

Mullins had released the drawstring and had his head outside the tent. 'Big twin.'

'Shift arse.' Jakov hauled him back and stuck his own head through the widening hole. 'Is Sikorsky S–76.'

ANARE, the Australian Antarctic Division, used those, Cain knew. But even give-it-a-go Aussies wouldn't meddle with an EXIT crash. 'Colour?'

'Orange and black stripe.'

'It's Alpha,' Cain said.

'How they find us?'

'Could be an EPIRB on the plane — probably still transmitting on the aircraft emergency frequency. But there'd be an EXIT classification on the signal.'

'Guns.'

Mullins lifted the matting off the air mattress that formed the tent floor. He pulled out the two M–40s and slung one to Jakov who struggled from the tent.

Cain got his head outside into the gold-grey light of morning. The chopper hovered far across the sea of snow against cirrus that radiated from the horizon like a fan. They'd taken a risk, he thought. They were a long way from base and pushing it.

The extreme clearness of Antarctic air made everything deceptive. The view across the compacted snow could have stretched for 60 miles, or 12, to the milky haze where ice joined sky.

Bell, Raul and Hunt were bunkered in a scour that had formed behind a piece of severed wing. Bell had the sniper's rifle and looked keen to use it. He called to Cain, 'What's going down?'

'I'd say it's a recce. They'll be asking Alpha for instructions. The wheels are up. So they're not going to land.'

'Can we negotiate with them?' Raul warmed his gloved hands under his armpits. 'If they think their plane crew's alive ...'

'They wouldn't give a toss. Lots of Herc crews around. They want us dead.'

'So what'll they tell their base?' Bell asked.

'Good news and bad news. We didn't escape but the Herc's a wreck. They'll report armed survivors. Then Alpha'll freak and order them home.' He pointed to the S–76, now a distant hovering speck. 'That's an all-weather, long-range job worth 2.5 million second-hand. They should fly them in pairs but they're stretched for planes so they've sent it out alone. And there's no way they'll let them up the risk by scrapping with us.' He shrugged. 'When we're dead, they'll come back for our bodies. In a year they'll mount a traverse — salvage engines, avionics ...'

'Which leaves us where?' Raul rumbled.

'Still dead.'

The chopper circled away, climbing, and soon was out of sight. The silence of the lifeless ice-scape, unfit for any warm-blooded animal, pressed in on them again. Raul slapped his mittens together. 'Well I don't intend to die here. So I suggest we hit the road.'

Hunt's look of derision. 'How?'

'In the tracked vehicle. I prefer being driven in warmth to walking in the cold.'

Bell said, 'Exactly. Exactly. One side of the front cabin's wrecked but we could patch that to protect against the wind. The tracks are okay.'

Cain said, 'And how will you thaw the engine?'

'Huh?'

'Thaw me first,' Raul said. 'I need hot food. Cain, you're joining us for a working breakfast. Mullins, Jakov, check our guests and get them fed.'

Cain bundled into the tent with Raul, Bell and Hunt. She already had oats swimming in half-melted snow. They took their parkas off in the comparative warmth, sat awkwardly, desperate to eat.

Bell tried to pick ice off his brows, looked at Cain. 'If the engine's an ice block, how do we start the vehicle?'

'On traverse, you'd plug it into a generator for two hours or use a Herman Nelson in condition one. But we don't have those items.'

'What if we soaked something combustible in aviation fuel, made a shielded fire under it and ...?'

'You don't light a match near a Hagg,' Hunt said with disgust. 'Do you know the flashpoint of JP8?'

'Well, the plane's engines have generators. Wouldn't the APU drive them?'

'If it's not wrecked,' Cain said, 'and you could hot-wire it. If you're an aircraft electrician, go for it.'

'I don't care how you do it,' Raul snapped. 'Just get us moving.'

'To where?'

He looked at Cain nastily. 'What?'

'I know where we are.' Bell reached beside the cooking box and pulled out a map. 'I found this with the navigator's stuff.'

He unfolded the map, spread it across their knees, pointed to a pencil mark. 'We're here. I've double-checked the GPS coordinates.'

Cain examined the mark — some 400 kilometres from the pole of relative inaccessibility. 'Great. Couldn't be further from anywhere. So, forgetting Alpha, your nearest chance is ...' He ran his finger toward the coast. '...Asuka, a Jap base over 800 kilometres away.'

Hunt distributed mugs. 'You couldn't carry the fuel. Even if you struck no sastrugi ...'

Bell held out his mug for hot chocolate. 'What's that?'

'Wind-scoured snow ridges. They can get as big as tank traps. So if you didn't strike those and got a litre per kilometre, you'd need 800 litres. It'd be closer to a kilolitre. That's 220 gallons.' She frowned, working it out. 'Five 44-gallon drums.'

'And we don't have the fuel.' Bell looked glum.

'Yes you do. The Hagg'll run on JP8. It runs turbines and diesels, too. And the plane's inboard tanks are full of it.'

'So we could siphon it out?'

Cain extended his mug. 'Into what?'

'There are drums in the plane,' Raul said. 'Certainly not five.'

Now Bell was a dog with a bone. 'How much do the vehicle's fuel tanks hold?'

Cain looked at Hunt. Haggs hadn't been around in his day.

She frowned, trying to remember. 'It has two 80-litre tanks plus the two jerry cans on the front of the back cab with about 20 litres each. So that's 200 litres.'

'There must be things we can use as containers.' Bell's eyes sparkled. 'Like water containers in the plane's galley or ...'

Hunt glanced at Cain. Her look said 'fingies'.

He said, 'Even if we got it started, loaded with fuel and ten people ...'

'Now you've got the spirit,' Raul said. Hot chocolate had cheered him remarkably.

'...and we don't slot it the first day, how do we warm it next morning?'

Bell said brightly, 'Never shut down. Drive night and day. Drivers take shifts.'

'I see. So you're going to have someone walking ahead all night, probing with an ice axe?'

'No,' Raul said. 'Life is risk and the riskiest policy is never to take risks. We drive fast, steer by intuition.'

Hunt snorted. 'It's lost a headlight and searchlights on one side. And you're going to drive at *night*?'

Raul looked coldly at his nemesis. 'If we drove twenty-four hours a day, how long would it take us?'

'If you averaged 20 kilometres an hour, you'd do it in 40 hours.' She sipped her drink. 'But you could strike a patch where you could only average 10 kilometres a day.'

'Still, it's theoretically possible?'

'Theoretically,' Cain said. 'Except that blizzards here can get up to 200 kilometres an hour.'

'We haven't struck one yet,' Raul said.

'This is a sucker break. It'll come.'

'The thing has radios,' Bell said. 'And radar.'

'Except we wrecked the antenna driving it in.' Hunt stirred the thickening oats. 'Anyway, if you transmit, Alpha knows your position. Has to be radio silence.'

'I can live with that,' Raul said. 'By the way, there's a set of skis in the galley up the front. Must have belonged to one of the aircrew. We take those, too. He beamed at them all. 'Life's full of solutions. After breakfast, we get to work.'

Solutions, Cain thought, remembering Rhonda's maxim, that are simple, neat and wrong.

After he'd eaten, Cain checked on the civilians. Eve was the only one up in her stale-smelling tent. Hair matted, face grave, she sat half out of her bag, priming the stove. 'I heard a plane. Are we going to be rescued?'

'No.' He lifted the pee tin near the entrance, disappeared to empty it outside, came back, replaced it.

She said, 'How do we survive down here? What do we do now?' She was a woman in despair — a woman whose child had killed her half-sister.

He passed her one of the small snow blocks Hunt had positioned between the skins of the tent. 'I'll get Hunt to come in and help you. How's John?' He nodded at the pope who still lay, eyes closed as if exhausted, beside Nina. Both seemed to be dozing.

'He's worn out,' she said. 'Finds it hard to breathe. And who on earth *are* you people? This is Pope John Paul I! I thought I'd seen him before. What have you done to our Church? My God, how could you ...'

'Can't always choose who you sleep with. Can you get Nina to make herself useful?'

'Impossible. Containment's the aim.'

The pope opened his eyes, gasped, 'Ray. How are you managing?'

'Ray?' Eve looked confused.

'We're still alive,' he told John.

Nina sat up and told the pope, 'He screws my mum.'

The pope turned to her. 'Have you ever felt someone loved you?'

'You've got to be kidding. No one gives a stuff about me.'

The pope smiled and took her hand. 'Don't be too sure.' Cain expected her to snatch her hand back. But the powerful presence of the man and perhaps the knowledge of who he was made it difficult for even Nina to deride him. She jerked her head away, not wanting her reaction seen.

Zia half sat up in his single bag and winced. His face had a sickly pearl-like sheen. 'The helicopter?' He spoke in Urdu.

'EXIT.'

'Why didn't they attack us?'

'No need. They know we'll die.'

He nodded. 'And which way is Mecca?'

'You can't make prostrations with that leg.'

'Your advice doesn't interest me. Which way?'

Cain pointed toward the rear corner of the tent. 'Consider your *mirhab* to be there. But best now to worship at the *Kaaba* of the heart.'

'You infidel. You upstart! Do you presume to tell Zia how to pray?'

'I'm trying to help, General. I feel for you and your injury. I mean no offence.'

'I need to — wash.'

He knew Zia wished to wash before praying and pointed to the splitting tips of the dark man's fingers. 'This dry air cracks skin. Washing isn't good.'

Nina said, 'Wankers. What language is that?'

The old general raised an arm, grimacing with pain. 'You are insolent, Rahib. The unworthy are promised fire, where they will ever abide without relief. You have profaned Allah and His Apostle and you will burn in fire.'

'God knows. Consider your own acts, Zia ul-Haq.'

'I cannot will except by the will of Allah.'

'Then may I point out that Islam forbids tyranny?'

'Do not sully this place with your arguments.'

Cain shrugged. 'Keep that leg up. I'll come back later. You have my good wishes, General. And I'll help you if I can.'

'And I will *kill* you if I can, Rahib Badar.'

'If Allah wills.' Cain backed forlornly out of the tent. The old soldier hated him but at least it was keeping him alive. Religions, he thought — all pointing to unity but made lethal by interpretations. He trudged toward the wreck. What did Seng Ts'an's poem say? 'Do not seek after the real. Only cease to cherish opinions.' Zia, who had grown up with state corruption, had probably done his best, as he saw it. And now, displaced, abandoned, dying, self-image was all he had left. Pride — angel and devil. Sometimes nothing was sadder.

'Cain?'

Bell and his storm troops padded into sight from behind the shattered radome. Mullins carried a piece of dented aluminium panel.

'Want to get that vehicle up,' Bell said. 'Have to find tools.'

'Then keep your inner gloves on,' Cain warned. 'No bare flesh against metal.'

He followed the ungainly figures into the plane, removed his goggles. The Hagg was a mess, the right side of the front cabin bashed in. The mercenaries discussed how to patch it against the weather. The front window was still holding together so it was drivable. He looked at the frozen bodies of the loadmaster and Jane. Their staring eyes were ice.

Bell said, 'I've checked the APU. It's wrecked. Was it battery start?'

'Yes.'

'The battery's where?'

'Forward of the crew entry door.' He adjusted his goggles and followed Bell outside.

They prised the bay open. The battery looked undamaged. The plane's starboard list had helped.

Bell peered in. 'You say the Hagglunds' engine has a coolant warming element. So could we wire that up to this?'

'Could try.'

They uncoupled the battery. Bell lifted it out, staggered. 'Heavy.'

'It's lead acid. Not nicad.'

'Voltage?'

'Around 20 to 30 volts DC, I think.'

'And what's the heating element in the Hagg?'

He shrugged.

In ten minutes they'd salvaged enough wiring to connect the battery to the vehicle.

'It's cold-soaked,' Cain said. 'Got to warm it.' Then he spotted a packing-carton-sized box in the cargo bay, opened the cardboard lid. 'Bingo!'

Bell puffed across. 'What are those?'

He held up colourful plastic envelopes. 'Chemical hand warmers. You pierce the plastic, scrunch up the sachet, blow into it, whatever, to get oxygen in and it starts a chemical reaction. They're a one-shot wonder but stay warm for hours.'

'So if we pack them around the battery. Then insulate it with something ...'

As they did it, the two mercenaries looked for things to patch the damaged cabin. With the battery warming, they helped the others strip lining from the cargo bay, then searched outside for more panels. Raul's troops, Cain noted, didn't seem to believe in face protection. For that they'd pay. On bad days here, exposed skin froze in minutes.

Bell went back to work on the ramp and waved Cain to follow. Aft of the port side paratroop door was a hand-pump and valve. Cain switched the pressure release valve handle to the manual position while Bell read instructions off a control plate. 'Move door valve handle to OPEN.'

He did it.

'Pump until door is up and locked.'

Cain pumped. The gauge pressure rose but nothing happened until he found and pulled the door uplock manual release. Slowly, the door began to rise into the upper tail. A black metal flag with a yellow circle swung out and down like some form of congratulation.

Cain said, 'You know Raul's not with it, don't you? That we're not going to make it?'

'Energy in all things — road to fortune.'

He was sick of Bell's dangerous zeal. 'Get real. We're stuffed.'

The other turned to him, eyes brilliant with conviction. 'Gustave Raul is the Master of this Age. We're tremendously fortunate to have him with us. And if he says we can do it, we can. There are thousands of people on this continent. Permanent bases everywhere. All we have to do is reach someone. There could be some temporary base or expedition just over the horizon.'

'In your dreams, pal.'

'I want us singing off the same sheet, Cain.'

'A requiem?'

'How do you think we rescued Raul? Against all odds?'

Cain laughed. 'You call this a rescue?'

'We did the impossible then. We'll do it now.' He turned back to the panel. 'Now handle to NEUTRAL and we start on the ramp. Move ramp lock valve handle to UNLOCK.'

'Check.'

'Move ramp valve handle to UP. Pump until all locks visibly disengage.'

Cain did it, watching Bell. The man's lips were splitting and there was frost nip on his cheeks. He apparently thought that being inside the plane was enough protection for his face although it had to be 40 below. I've told you once, Cain thought. Your next lesson is courtesy of the continent.

'Now lock valve handle to NEUTRAL.' Like many zealots, he had an officious streak. 'Ramp valve handle to DOWN. And pump up to 500 PSI.'

Cain pumped again. The ramp slowly lowered toward the vista of brutal terrain.

'You see?' Raul's disciple blinked at the glare of their graveyard, seeing nothing but a field of opportunity. 'Now our only problem's fuel storage.'

They gave the battery two hours but it was useless. The heating element warmed a little but the coolant was unaffected. Cain said, 'Won't do it. We'd need more batteries to get the voltage.'

'So why not pack the engine directly with the warmers? You've got enough.'

Cain nodded slowly, again surprised by the man's quick mind. 'Okay.'

'Always a way,' Bell grinned. He went off to check on the others as Hunt came into the plane holding a thermos salvaged from the galley. 'Cocoa.'

'Great.'

She dragged goggles from bloodshot eyes. 'How's it coming?'

'We might get the Hagg running. But we're still pissing into the wind.'

'They don't get it, do they?'

'How are you tracking with Raul?'

She cracked the ice around the plastic cover of the thermos. 'He's playing it cool.'

'You're useful to him right now.'

She got the top off, poured hot chocolate in it.

He gulped it down before the crystals spread through the liquid and it froze. 'What's the wattage of the Hagglunds' heating element?'

'The internal electrics run off 24 volts DC. The heater runs off 24O volts AC.'

He handed the cover back, grateful for the momentary warmth in his gullet. 'So how do we get Raul's head out of his arse?'

'You can't. He knew he was a phoney once. But now he believes his own press.'

'Are the civilians okay?'

'Zia won't live.'

'John?'

'He's amazing considering his age. He'll be all right while he's in the tent. But I'd like to kill that teenage bitch. And I know Raul's waiting to flay me. So — still want to hold off?'

'You want to try and take out four armed men?'

'We could do it.'

'Perhaps. But why bother?'

'So go along with their nonsense? Watch them die? Then knock off who's left?'

Cain saw Jakov emerging from the crew toilet. He seemed to think the plane was still an amenity. 'Incoming.'

She spotted the Slav. 'Nice knowing you, Cain.'

As she left, her outer glove brushed his.

*   *   *

The rest of the day was hell.

There were three 44-gallon drums and various containers. It wasn't enough. Cain told them to fill them completely to guard against condensation. Mullins climbed up on the broken wings to try and siphon from the overwing refuel ports. Eventually they discovered the small condensate drains that released water, then fuel from the bottom of the tanks. Mullins used a screwdriver to push the small inner part up and start the flow but got fuel on his gloves, which wasn't a good idea. By the time they'd finished, he was the worst of them — close to hypothermic, vision blurred, light-headed, hands stiff and unresponsive.

'Got another night here,' Cain panted, desperate to defrost his feet and stinging hands. His nose, runny with the cold, was now filled with frozen moisture. That made him gasp through the mouth and the cold air seared his throat. He'd worked too hard, too long.

Bell nodded. Snow had frozen his anorak hood to his balaclava and his goggles were layered with rime. He was shivering, stumbling, barely able to stand. He said nothing, just staggered toward his tent.

Cain followed, wondering about Eve and the others. As far as he knew, they hadn't emerged all day. He didn't have the energy to check them and hoped Hunt had. He knew Raul would be in good shape. The bastard had barely left his tent.

He entered his own tent and pulled the draw-cord tight. The wind was stronger, snapping the fabric and making the guy ropes sing. He slumped, too tired to remove his outer layer.

Jakov was pumping the stove. His face had tell-tale white patches and his ungloved hand shook as he lifted the kettle onto the flame.

All of them were shaking, which was good. At least their muscles still had the energy to shiver.

'Jesus, my hands are killing me,' Mullins moaned.

Cain said, 'Be glad. When they stop hurting, you graduate to amputee.'

Jakov glanced at Cain. 'So, fellah, you think we not make it, huh? So why we kill ourselves?'

'Because those two mad bastards want you to.' He wearily got his mukluks off and strung them up on the tent. The stinging was extreme. He could only think of one thing. Food. Soup. A meat bar. Pemmican stew. Like idiots they'd had no lunch — just survival biscuits and frozen chocolate.

Jakov felt his face as if exploring it for the first time. He winced with pain. 'Jeez, so cold. Is awful. Terrible.'

Cain smiled. 'Gets worse. Gets so windy that buildings and vehicles blow away. So cold that screwdrivers snap, tracks crack, teeth fillings fall out and if you aim high when you piss, it hits the ground as ice crystals.'

Mullins took his fingers from his mouth. 'I'll tell you now. I didn't sign on for this shit.'

Jakov said, 'What we do?'

'Eat,' Cain said. 'Best thing.'

'I could eat elephant seal.'

'If you'd seen them crapping in each other's faces, you wouldn't.'

The tent was getting warmer. He took off his inner pairs of gloves, examined his hands. They seemed in reasonable shape. He hoped his feet were as good.

During the long cold night, he woke. The wind had temporarily died and a thin moon made the tent a dark blur. He'd been alerted by a sound outside like something dragged through the snow. He looked toward the entrance but there wasn't light enough to cast a shadow. Then he heard a scratching. He half sat up, angry about the handcuffs.

Someone was out there in the snow. Had they flipped? Hypoxia was a menace, could make you lethargic or deranged.

He waited, watching the entrance.

Hunt? Surely not.

The cinched oval was being opened. Someone was trying

to get in. But quietly. Hands now undoing the double zippers on the inside layer.

Then the dark oval of a face, the flash of metal.

Zia had put the knife between his teeth to free his hands.

Flesh on metal. Too late, he knew what he'd done. His lips were stuck to the blade. If he wanted to stab someone, he'd have to wrench off his lips.

'Bad move,' Cain said, and elbow-jabbed the others. Mullins jerked up, half-asleep.

Jakov took it in faster. 'Where you going, old bugger?' He got his body half out of the bag. His inner gloves were still on. He picked up the kero tin, slammed the base of it into Zia's face. The face vanished with a muffled moan.

Jakov closed the entrance against the cascading cold. 'Someone not like you, fellah.'

A snigger from Mullins. The two men settled back.

Jakov said, 'Out there he die, for sure.'

Cain remembered a saying of Seneca. 'It's more honourable than killing.'

'But pay not so good.' Jakov's laugh.

Cain watched the entrance a long time, imagining the proud man outside, his final wish frustrated. After the effort of dragging himself through the snow by his arms, the old scoundrel wouldn't make it back.

He'd be disoriented already, his blood vessels clamping down, sacrificing his extremities to feed the heart, brain and lungs. He wouldn't even know the way back to his tent. Soon his fast-pumping heart would slow, his skin become mottled. He'd stiffen, his pulse undetectable, become comatose.

Would he see gardens with running streams? Would he recline on soft couches, in his face the glow of joy as he was attended by ever-young boys like sprinkled pearls? Would he be surrounded by virgins fair as coral and rubies — bashful girls untouched by man or *jinnee*?

God knew. God knew.

It was best for him this way, Cain thought.

44

SLOT

The Hagglunds — front cabin crudely patched, tracks squeaking on hardened snow — churned through the brief March night. With each shudder, the surviving headlight and spotlights bounced pools of whiteness on white. For hours the black finger of its shadow had lengthened on the ice but now contrast had faded into gloom.

Bell drove. Cain, in the front passenger seat, stared through the crazed half-covered windshield trying to spot irregularities. Even by day there was often no sign of subsidence or difference in sheen, texture, colour on the snowband that marked a crevasse. He peered ahead, half asleep — affected by the barometric pressure and sheer tiredness. He knew they'd be slotted or stopped by sastrugi long before the fuel gave out.

Behind him, packed in with gear, were Nina, Raul and Mullins. Jammed in the rear cab with fuel drums and tents were the others. He imagined them squashed against the load trying to doze — dirty, languid, unable to think clearly and suffering from lack of sleep.

Nine people in a coffin. As for the tenth ...

The ice sculpture of Zia in his long johns, knife still frozen to his mouth, was lashed on top of the back cab. In the delirium of hypothermia, the dying general had tried to strip. Raul wanted the carcass as evidence — more weight for the overloaded vehicle.

Above the noise of the diesel, Mullins yelled something and Cain turned back. The lout had one glove off and was prodding blisters on the back of his fingers. He displayed them in the dim light to Nina who sat opposite on a back-facing seat.

Bell put the engine into neutral. They slowed and speaking became less of a task. 'What is it?'

'My hand,' Mullins said. 'Look!'

'Gross.' Nina pulled a face.

'I signed on to fight. Not for this shit.'

Nina sneered. 'Major drag, huh?'

Bell called back, 'Better than taking a round.'

'Not if I lose my fucking hand.'

'Put your glove on,' Cain told him.

Despite the patching and caulking, some air still seeped through chinks. Yet the cabin was warm enough to make their inner layers feel wet and they were exhausted, uncomfortable, filthy after the effort of packing up.

Bell shoved the thing back into gear. He was pooped but his fanatic's eyes still shone.

Cain had spent the day preparing to start the vehicle. First, he'd activated all the plastic envelopes, packed them around the engine and insulated them with anything he could find. He'd jammed some around the oil sump despite limited room, positioned more over the engine head, the intake manifold, and packed the last of them around the batteries. He'd left it for six hours, then wound the engine in short bursts, trying to warm the plugs without burning out the starter. Then he'd removed the air cleaner — the fittings snapped off in the cold

— and sprayed ether from an aerosol can into the intake. A risk, he knew. Too much could break the rings.

When the thing kicked and kept going he felt an irrational sense of elation — then remembered he had to reverse the jackknifed cabs out of the plane. It took prolonged backing and filling, a few inches at a time, before the vehicle was straight enough to make it down the ramp.

Then they had to patch the front cab — using static rope to lash bivvy bags, plane lining and panels over the damage. Next came the loading of gear, topping up of tanks. The radar antenna was wrecked but they jury-rigged the GPS. It was torture in the numbing cold.

He was nodding off. To try and keep awake he glanced behind again.

Raul stared ahead, face in neutral, his eternal summer fading fast, body shaking with each jerk transmitted by the track assembly.

As Cain turned back to the windshield he spotted parallel edges of raised snow.

'Hold it.'

Bell hit the anchors, shunting everyone, everything forward.

'Back up.'

Bell hunted for reverse. The vehicle ground astern.

'Stop.'

He knocked the engine into neutral.

Cain pointed. 'There.'

'What is it?'

'Tracks.'

Raul chipped in. 'Company?'

'*Our* bleeding tracks.'

Raul was up, leaning over the engine cover to look.

'Not possible,' Bell said. He rechecked the sluggish needle of the oil-filled compass mounted on the dash. 'I've been watching this the whole time.' He checked the GPS, pulled out his map, spread it on the steering wheel, rubbed his red eyes, dragged his finger down the paper. 'Right on target.'

'They're ours,' Cain said.

'Bullshit. Must be someone else out here. If we only had the bloody radar.' He banged the useless VDU.

'Can we follow them?' Raul asked.

Cain yawned. 'Sure. And if you do it fast, you'll end up your own arse.'

Bell ignored him and answered his guru with his usual sickening respect. 'We don't know which way they're heading.'

Mullins leered at the sleepy girl. 'You're cute.'

'What's your name?' Nina said.

'Mullins.'

'Should be mullet.' She regarded him with contempt, well aware of her effect on men.

'See *her*?' Cain pointed to the girl. 'Why'd you think the plane crashed? Check the thing again.'

'See him?' Nina pointed to Cain. 'He fucks my mother. Motherfucker.'

Bell, close to collapse, did it all a second time then slapped the map. 'I don't get this. Now we're in the middle of the *ocean*.'

'Some cack,' the girl jeered. 'Are we going somewhere? Or is this intermission?'

'Shut up, bitch,' Bell said.

She made a lewd gesture. 'Suck hole.'

'I don't find any of this useful,' Raul rumbled with distaste.

Bell, at the end of his wick, checked the receiver a third time.

'Well?' Raul said.

'Now we're at the equator. Shit!'

Raul licked his splitting lips. 'Forget it and use the compass.'

A meek nod from his exhausted disciple.

Cain said, 'You still think there's another Hagg out here?'

Raul stared down his nose as if communing with his elemental. 'Avoid fixed opinions. A rigid attachment to any point of view is destructive.'

'Spare me the infomercials, Raul.'

'I must enter a state of self-referral.'

'What a crock of shit,' Nina jeered.

Raul snapped at Mullins, 'Silence her.'

Mullins shook her. 'Shut up or you get it.'

'Fuck off, mullet.' She held her breath.

The cabin chilled, light flickered.

An ugly-looking ice piton rose from the floor, hovered in the air, jagged sides gleaming, sharp point aimed directly at Mullins's left cheek. Astounded, he shrank back.

Bell yelped, 'Christ.'

Raul opened his eyes, saw the unbelievable, gaped.

Instinctively Mullins snatched the floating thing, perhaps to turn it on the girl. But his hand was jerked sideways and smashed against the window ledge. As he bellowed with pain and released the piton to hug his bad hand, the metal stake dropped harmlessly to the floor.

Bell rabbit-chopped the girl.

She grunted, fell forward on Mullins.

He shoved her off. She fell back into her seat like a corpse.

Mullins, muttering obscenities, found the piton, picked it up, looked at it amazed.

'Did you ... see that?' Bell was shaking.

Raul nodded. 'The paranormal. Yes. It proves we are parts of a unified field. A hologram. Give it here.'

Mullins handed the thing across. Raul examined it as if expecting strings. He handed it back, careful not to appear disturbed. 'The world in its true form is miraculous. The suspension of natural law is — at some level — natural.' He turned to Cain. 'Is that why she was with EXIT?'

Cain nodded.

Their tiredness, the extreme situation and the disorienting thin air made the phenomenon seem just another trial.

'Fuckin' hell,' Mullins grouched. 'I didn't bloody sign on for this crud.'

'Stop whining,' Bell said. 'If you want your second payment, put up with it.'

'Second payment. Big deal. I'll be stuffed.'

Bell, close to collapse, turned to Raul, his drawn face still respectful. 'What do we do?'

'Indeed.' Raul shut his eyes and leaned on the vibrating engine cover. 'I need to concentrate. Quiet!' His mouth moved and he presently rumbled. 'Then which way? Follow? Or go on?'

Bell watched the parody with weary devotion.

Raul finally opened his eyes and addressed the multi-vent heater before him as if it were a sacred relic. 'We continue as before — using the compass.'

Bell turned back to the wheel, palmed his eyes. 'Gustave, I'm dead. We've got to swap shifts.'

'Very well. You and Cain swap with Karen and Jakov. They should have got some sleep by now. Mullins, get the medical kit. We're going to inject that witch and knock her out.'

Cain said, 'Got a better idea. Put her in the back with the pope.'

Raul's derisory smile. 'You think he can cast out devils?'

'I think he can calm her. That's all.'

'Just get her out of my sight.'

It happened early next morning. Cain was in the rear cab, in a rapidly hardening sleeping bag, left shoulder propped against a drum. Bell was jammed beside him, Nina, the pope and Eve opposite. They were woken by a lurch, a crashing, a concussion. When he opened his eyes, Eve was on top of him, yelping, and the cabin was tilted 30 degrees to the side.

The engine had conked.

The sound of wind.

Slotted, he thought, along the crack line. At least they hadn't gone in.

Bell, buried beneath the weight of the Church, struggled to push the pope off his chest. Then everyone talked at once.

Cain, drowsy and stiff, freed himself from Eve and told the others to stay put. Bell, ever eager, unlatched the side door, now almost above them. Being a fingie, he used one hand and the wind wrenched the door from his grasp.

Cain clambered after him into glare. Sunshine seared through a gap in low cloud but they were almost socked in and all surface definition was obscured by a dense tide of blowing snow. There was no way the second shift could have seen the slot. Raul must have had them steering blind.

He joined the front cabin contingent who were already out on the ice and drift-obscured up to the thighs. He climbed up over the roof to get down on their side, clinging to Zia's frozen arm to lower himself.

Through gaps in the swirling snow he saw a slot more than a metre wide and perhaps two deep. But the floor was probably false. The Hagglunds lay along it, supported on one side by its tracks and on the other by its cabins.

'Jeez, we fucked,' Jakov said. His face was in bad shape — livid sunburns contrasting with ominous yellow patches that would eventually darken. Exhausted after driving for hours, he limped to the vehicle and leaned against it.

Cain said, 'What's up with your foot?'

'Think it die.'

'You drying your socks?'

'How? Jeez. First got to get boot off.'

'Forget about socks,' Raul snapped. 'We're wasting time. How do we get out of this?' The skin around his eyes was furrowed tight and he had frost nip on his nose and cheeks.

Hunt answered him. 'If you want the classic ploy, you dig a ramp.' She still seemed fit and wore her Batman-like face mask. 'Then you get two other vehicles and haul from the side. As we don't have those, you winch from ahead off ice anchors.'

'Can we use the tracks to help?' Bell asked.

'No. There's no differential lock. You'd just spin the free tracks.'

Cain left them discussing it and shuffled forward to look.

As he reached the front of the Hagg, the blowing snow lessened for a moment just as the side of the slot ahead of the front cab sheered off and slid down. The crack ahead was now wider than the vehicle. If they winched forward, it would go in.

The others had come up behind him.

Jakov said, 'Jeez. No way, José.'

Raul said, 'Fool. Negativity kills, not situations.' He turned to Cain. 'What now?'

Cain looked at the single feature visible — the tilted hulk of the patched Hagglunds with the bizarre shape on the roof. The roof seemed to be floating — a black and orange striped shoal in a white sea. Eve's face peered from the window in the back cabin door over the tide of waist-deep swirling snow. In minutes the wind had risen. The chill was painful. They were heading for Condition One. His hands already felt like wooden blocks and his nose was running. He pulled his inner hood lower down and leaned against the wind, head averted.

'Should we put up tents?' Bell asked.

'Too late. We could end up chasing them, could lose them.'

As if to prove the comment, a squall hit them like a wave. Raul and Hunt went flying and surfaced 2 metres away, as if dunked. When they stood, they were pale shapes, half-obscured by flying snow. Hunt adopted wind-walking mode, head down, arms in by her sides. Raul didn't, tumbled again. The sun had vanished in cloud.

Cain yelled, 'Right. Everyone back inside!'

While the others struggled to take shelter, he gripped the roof rack on the leaning front cab and walked back to check the heater hoses between the two sections of the vehicle. They'd looked brittle enough yesterday and at 40 below they could break. One hose seemed to have a surface crack but he couldn't spot a leak. The snow found the crack between his balaclava and goggles, stung his face. By the time he climbed up to the front cab roof hatch he was almost in total whiteout.

He dropped down out of the weather, secured the hatch against the blow and restarted the engine to get warm coolant flowing through the hoses. By then, the thin cabin was vibrating with the gusts. Luckily the patching was on the lee side.

The front cabin cast had changed. He was now cooped with Raul, Bell, Hunt and Mullins.

'Perhaps it'll die down,' Bell said. Then, spotting a look between Hunt and Cain ... 'No thanks to you pessimists.'

'Realists,' Cain said and parked his stinging hands under his armpits.

It became a hissing blizz that sounded like a passing train. He'd survived blows like it before, in container-huts tethered with chains. The wind had been strong enough to make them creak and shudder, to ripple the steel roofs and cause bottles to vibrate off shelves. Fortunately the slot held the Hagglunds firmly secured. But despite its positive connection with the ice, the fibreglass cabin trembled.

He turned to Hunt. 'Is the thing in gear?'

'There's no park position in the transmission.' She stomped on the park brake pedal to set the ratchet at the point of furthest depression for maximum stability. Then she called up the back cabin to make sure the others were getting warmth before helping sort out the confusion in the tilted cab. 'If we run the tanks dry we'll need the Primuses. Yellow boxes.'

'Why are you using our fuel?' Raul complained, shivering like all of them.

'If you let the engine freeze, what's the good of fuel?'

He pursed his cracked lips, his hatred for her showing.

'If you use a Primus in a Hagg,' Cain added, 'you'll do a Zola.'

'What?'

'Gas yourself. We need ventilation. This blow could go on for days and bury us.'

A fierce gust made the cab shudder. Above the rumble of the idling diesel, the noise was now a dull booming.

Nothing to do but wait it out.

He checked the blur through the side windows, braced against the engine cover, looked around. The boxes and sacks had been restacked to roughly simulate a level floor, and the people were perched on top of them in the tilting space. Hunt, Mullins and Bell searched among the mess.

Cain got his goggles out of his pocket, adjusted his balaclava. 'Keep the engine running. I'm worried about the heater hoses.' He checked his windproofs and hood, hauled his nose-wipers back on. 'I'm going to check the old man and the temperature in the back.' He got his hands on the roof hatch. 'If you need me, there's the interphone.'

Just then it buzzed. Bell picked it up. 'No.' His face clouded. 'He hasn't come in here ... How long? ... Half an hour? ... All right.' He shifted his mouth from the handset. 'It's the pope. He says Jakov went out to relieve himself and hasn't come back.'

Hunt said, 'Didn't he know to rope himself up?'

Bell repeated the question into the phone, shook his head, hung up.

'Well, as you're popping out, Cain,' Raul said, 'you can look for him.'

'In that?' Cain laughed. 'Did you know people down here get lost and freeze to death even between buildings at a base? Even if they have blizz lines? Forget it.'

'Are you saying we write him off?'

'He's your man. *You* look for him. Just rope yourself to the roof rack and walk in circles till you find him. Except you'll be blown off your feet. And there won't be circles because you'll end down the crack. And you won't see him till you trip over him. Personally, I pass.'

Bell said, 'You won't even look?'

'I'm heading straight across the roof, hanging on for dear life. If he's squatting there wiping his arse, I'll let you know.'

He put both hands on the hatch again.

The others waited for the shock of freezing air.

Hunt grinned. 'Then there were eight.'

Jakov had given it much thought. He was fastidious about such things. That was why he could never be an airman. Fighter pilots had told him that they often had to pee their pants rather than risk a false move that could cause them to eject themselves. And they were forced to sit in their shit. That's why the cockpits stank. He wasn't sure about guys in tanks. As a military man, he knew his place on the totem pole was low. But Antarctica or not, he refused to do it in a bucket in front of a woman and a pope.

He got out, hanging on to the vehicle, and was almost blown away, dropped to all fours for stability. There was nothing to see at all — like the inside of a ping-pong ball. He hugged the tracks of the Hagglunds, worked his way further back, then tried to unzip himself. The mean bitch called Eve had given him toilet paper taken from the plane. Not much. Four wipers and a polisher. He was shivering already, freezing. He'd have to be bloody quick.

He removed his big mittens so he could undo his clothes. Then a gust blew him on his back.

Mittens flying from their harness, ventiles half-undone, he struggled back onto all fours.

The blizz drove steel-hard ice crystals into his ruined face. The vehicle was nowhere in sight. He tried to crawl back in the direction he'd been blown. The Hagg could only be steps away.

Just more whiteness.

As he tried to get his mitts back on, his hood was ripped back by the blast. Snow instantly froze in his hair, and around his eyes. By the time he turned from the hail of ice and dragged the hood back he had no idea of direction.

Then he heard the engine start up.

So close.

The wind tearing at his hood drowned the noise. He turned in a futile attempt to hear it again. Numbness striking at his limbs. His legs were stiff, as if his kneecaps were freezing. Dizzy, confused, breathless, responses blurred and shaking with cold, he crawled into the wind.

And fell into the slot.

There it was warmer, quieter, sheltered. He'd fallen on soft snow. He could see a bit in here — ice walls either side. Not high. And a little ahead, eureka! Blurred like something seen underwater — the underside of the Hagg.

He could hear the engine going.

The slotted tracks were hanging low.

He could reach them and haul himself up.

How lucky could you be?

He crawled underneath the vehicle, rose to his feet . . .

. . . and increased his ground pressure.

The false floor collapsed and he plunged 60 metres to his death.

Just before he hit, terror made him soil himself.

45

TRAVERSE

The blow lasted two days.

When the engine stopped, Cain and Mullins roped up and, bodies slow and stiff, off-loaded fuel drums and refilled the tanks. They returned to the front cab, numbed, light-headed with the effort and the cold. The big diesel ran for an hour, then coughed, stopped, wouldn't even kick. Hunt told them that the fuel injection could have been damaged by frozen condensate.

They switched to Tilley lamps, Primus stoves and spent much of their waking hours cooking. The cabins stank of pemmican, salami, kerosene, human waste and fuel. By now they were filthy, ravenous, half-delirious and personal modesty was impossible.

Cain left the grim-faced militia in the front cab and went back to Eve, Nina and the pope. They were trying to beat layers of frost from between their inner and outer sleeping bags but the stuffing had frozen, too.

Despite the hardships, the pope still had his sense of humour. When Eve asked if he'd seen the All Blacks he replied that he hadn't studied secular religions.

After they gulped down food, they crawled into the stiff, chilly bags and the trapped ice melted with their body heat. They slept in damp, woke with aching backs — only to be showered from the tilted roof with their own frosted breath.

Eve moaned, 'I feel like death. I stink, can't breathe. And no one told me I'd have to defecate in front of a pope.'

John said, 'I haven't been looking.'

'But you can smell. Oh God, this is awful.'

'When you're this close to death,' the pope smiled, 'what's another smell?'

'Ignore her,' Nina spat. 'She's a user.'

'She's a person,' the pope said. 'And the only mother you'll get.'

'She doesn't give a stuff about me.'

'And you don't give her much chance. You may not live another day. Isn't it time to stop being cruel?'

Eve started crying. Nina lapsed into sullen silence.

'Here.' John handed the girl some wire. 'Can you fix the end of this to the roof near the door? It's hottest up there. We've got to dry our clothes.'

Nina glared at him and the pope scowled back the same way, then his mouth widened to a smile. The girl would have seen herself but didn't have the lightness to admit it. She grudgingly took the wire and secured it. The pope tied off the other end, then handed her clothes to drape over the wire. He knew his way around the teenage mind. Next, he showed her how to check the spot detector for the CO level and how to monitor the inadequate vents. The girl remained sullen, but the priest's powerful atmosphere had to be affecting her as a magnet might rearrange iron filings.

The pope napped when he could. The shortest sleep refreshed him. His breathing, though laboured, was not as bad as before. He also helped with the cooking. 'Whatever thy hand findeth to do, do it with thy might.'

Cain knew the passage, Ecclesiastes, and completed it. 'For there is no work, nor device, nor knowledge, nor wisdom in the grave whither thou goest.'

Eve said, 'You're so damn depressing. I don't know what I saw in you.'

'One thing about the ice. It brings out the worst or best in everyone.'

'Are you criticising me?'

'Just a comment.' He'd thought her sexy, talented, amusing. But trapped in this rancid space, stripped of comforts and facing death, her narrowness and bitterness had surfaced.

'Just a comment?' she persisted. 'What's that supposed to mean?'

Cain said nothing and checked the Primus flame. A yellow tinge was dangerous, meant incomplete combustion. They'd soon need more ventilation and opening the door wasn't fun.

Nina turned to the pope. 'See? He's starting to see her for what she is.'

The pope, stirring the pot, had a coughing fit and let the fork go. Nina took it and continued stirring. The pope recovered. 'Thank you.'

She reached for the zipper tag of the priest's padded waistcoat, jerked it higher. The roughness of the act was revealing.

Cain glanced at Eve.

She said, 'Don't look at me. If it takes a pope to get through to her, what hope have I got?'

After they'd eaten and the others had retreated to their bags, Cain asked John if he'd brought his manuscript.

'Of course. Would you like to read some more?'

'Very much.'

The old priest rummaged in his bag and produced it.

Cain started, this time, from the beginning. It was titled 'The Resurrection of the Body'. He was surprised to encounter complex Catholic metaphysics. Being. Change.

Act. Potency. Prime matter. Causality. The uncaused cause. *Ipsum Esse Subsistens*. God's permission of moral evil as a good. The intrinsic analogy of being. From this traditional basis the insight was expanded, developed. After a time he asked, 'So you're an advocate of Aquinas?'

'How could one not be? He's neglected now, of course. It's like ignoring the break of day. And there are many things he said that the Church never aired because it threatened its position — such as his view on individual conscience.'

Cain read more, trying to understand the precise meanings placed on the terms. 'I'm getting the impression the guy knew more than he's admitting. He seems to have adapted eastern insights to Catholic terminology.'

The pope's delighted laughter. 'Well done.'

During the second morning the wind died almost to a breeze. Through the upside windows they saw snow level with the sills. Cain heard voices outside, saw a flash of yellow parka. The front cab inhabitants were out. A scuffling at the side door — someone with a shovel, digging it clear. The door was opened by the masked Hunt who peered in like Batman, framed by pale sky. 'We've got company.'

'You're putting me on.'

He got into his parka and overmitts and joined her on the snow. It seemed a little less cold. The Hagglunds looked bizarre — half-buried, its sloping roofs and upper sides two triangles in the drift, the snow mound of Zia, the smashed radar antenna ...

Bell stood beside Raul, peering through binoculars while the snap-frozen Mullins staggered about swinging his arms.

Cain rubbed the towelling on the back of his mitt across his goggles, squinted at the horizon but saw nothing but vast blue-grey expanse.

Hunt's eyes were younger. 'Something's definitely there.' She pointed.

It was a long way off and seemed to float above the plateau like a mirage. Distance had robbed it of colour but not shape.

Cain said, 'It could be a temperature inversion — a reflection of something yonks away.'

'Looks like a lot of boxes.' Bell handed the glasses to Raul. All their actions now were slow — sapped by the constant fatigue.

Raul looked and handed the glasses triumphantly to Cain. 'Definitely a sign of human folly. So were we right to set out or not?'

Cain adjusted the right eyepiece. He could make out something orange but distortion obscured detail. 'Too big for a dump or a field base. Could be a parked traverse. You might've got lucky.'

'With Gustave it isn't luck,' Bell said, eyes shining. 'You should be thankful he's with us.'

'Don't make me puke.'

'I have enormous luck,' Raul proclaimed. 'But is it luck? Or something one attracts?'

'What you've got is delusions of adequacy. You're a showman, Raul. Just remember, your nonsense doesn't work here.'

Raul sneered. 'Such a need to defend your point of view!'

Mullins was excited about being saved. 'We got flares? Smoke bombs?'

'Haven't seen any.' Bell adjusted his neck gaiter and pulled up the outsized toggle on his parka to the limit of the zip. His face was blistered with deep ultraviolet burns. He'd tried sunblock — not knowing it was useless. In Patagonia, Cain had been told, the ozone hole was sending sheep blind.

Raul's face was angry-red as well. He asked Hunt, 'Can we get them on the radio without alerting EXIT?'

'With local-use low power. Could try raising them on 16 — the marine emergency channel.'

'Do it.'

'But if they see EXIT stripes, they won't come near us.'

'So we cover the thing with the tents as if we're trying to attract attention.'

'Exactly. Exactly.' Bell looked at him with adoration.

'Admit all possibilities.' Raul would have beamed had his lips been less cracked. He ordered Mullins to break out the tents and cover the vehicle.

Hunt clumped back to the front cab. Raul motioned Bell to follow her.

Cain went after them, back aching with the cold.

He called to her, 'What will you tell them?'

'Lies.'

The Hagg was fitted with VHF. She switched on, fiddled with the squelch, selected the channel, INTL, selected one watt, held the mike close to her mouth and pressed the switch. 'Calling trav. We're in a Hagglunds south of you and slotted. Have you in sight. Need assistance. Over.'

Crackle.

She transmitted again, repeated.

Nothing.

'Perhaps they're switched off.'

She repeated it again. Raul's frost-rimmed face now stared into the listing cabin from the roof hatch. 'Calling Hagglunds. Message received. Where are you? And how did you get here? Numbers, condition? Over.'

'We hear you, trav. Eight alive, fair condition. Over.'

'Where are you from? Please confirm. Over?' The voice sounded Irish.

She glanced at Cain, knowing anything she said would sound improbable. A lone Hagg 800 kilometres from anywhere. It made sense to play it straight. 'We were in a Hercules that crashed on the plateau. This vehicle was cargo. We're about eleven o'clock from you. Long way. You're only just in sight. Over.'

'Received. Please confirm your base, over.'

She looked at Cain.

'Say Scott Base. That'll square with the Herc.'

'We're from Scott Base. Over.'

The reply wasn't instant. 'Affirmative on base. We don't have you visually. Over.'

'We'll try to fix that. Over.'

'Received. We stay here for today. Too much drift obscuring the slots. Got a quad on board but we'd slot if we tried to visit. Forecast tomorrow is fine. We think we've got you on the radar and we'll try to get to you tomorrow. Sked tomorrow, 900 hours on channel 8? Confirm please. Over.'

'Thanks, trav. Very welcome. Looking forward to tomorrow. Nine hundred on eight confirmed. Out.' She looked at Cain. 'Could they be from Amundsen Scott?' It was the American South Pole base.

'Unlikely.'

'McMurdo?'

'Too far off.'

'And how come they don't ask difficult questions?'

'May not be locals.'

'Uh-huh.'

Raul crowed, 'You see? A step into the unknown. That's the way to live at every moment of your existence. Admit all possibilities.'

Hunt's jaundiced look. 'Gustave, you're alive because of us — not you.'

The next morning was fine. Clear skies with hard-packed snow and, further off, fields of low sastrugi. And the searing brilliance of the hazardous sun. Raul called a council of war. They conned Eve into handling the second radio exchange — hoping her accent would make it convincing.

'If you talk about the Hagg,' Cain told her, 'call it a haggis. Kiwis call them that.'

The sked went well but the response was now even more cautious. When Eve asked who they were they said a private expedition.

Hunt looked sceptical. 'They're playing it close to the chest.'

Bell and Cain took turns to monitor the far-off speck, standing back to the wind but turning every so often to check, stamping to try and keep warm. But the traverse didn't move.

During his downtime, Cain checked on the pope. The old man had survived so well because he'd stayed sheltered. He made sure John was as comfortable as one could be in a tilted plastic box on a white hell, then read more of the manuscript while John watched his frowns. The difficult second chapter was titled 'Effort versus Entropy'. The terms were unfamiliar and it was heavy going.

'You seem to be attempting a realignment of your Church.'

'Whatever thy hand findeth to do ...' John stared at the glare through the slanting window. 'I never wanted this job, but I haven't ceased to do it. The Church has abandoned its metaphysics for a sloppy feel-good approach that has no tone. I'm pointing that out.'

'At the moment you sound as much a hardliner as Wojtyla.'

'Far from it. Don't miss my point. I'm not preaching control and suppression. God knows we've had enough of that. Discipline and doctrine are no substitute for life.'

'I'm also starting to see that I've never understood your religion.'

The pope looked at him soberly. 'Good. Try to remember the means is not the end. But still, you change the means at your peril. An odd statement from someone they considered a dangerous eccentric, wouldn't you say?'

Cain nodded slowly. Every time he spoke to this man, new depths of understanding were offered. 'You make me feel a pygmy.'

The pope chuckled. 'You're not that. But there's always more to see. You have some idea of what I've come to but forget the tradition that produced me.'

'I misunderstood you?'

'No. But if you stumble on the last act of a play, don't be surprised that there was a first.'

Bell's shout from outside. Finally the traverse had moved. Cain got out and crunched toward him through the energy-sapping snow. They stood on the glaring expanse under the glaring sky, watching the specks crawl. The austerity of the scene, the quality of the light, the sense of space, stillness, loneliness, was astonishing.

'Grandeur. Isolation.' Bell lowered the binoculars, revealing white frost patches on his nose and cheeks. 'I have to say, this place is magnificent.'

'Pity it kills you. Where's your face mask?'

'Can't stand the thing.' He pulled up the adjustment straps on his gauntlets then used the pile-facing of one to warm his cheeks and nose. That nose, Cain knew, would soon be hard and, later still, black. His plastic surgeon wouldn't be impressed. Raul and his troops didn't understand what frostbite could do to them, the eventual, terrible stabbing pains. Later the red raw flesh. Then the blackening, gangrene. Well, he'd warned them — and respected their right to damage themselves as they wished.

Raul was in the Hagg's front cabin with Hunt and Eve handling communications. Mullins had gathered combustibles to make a fire. He'd poured kerosene over the pile and now had the plastic container from inside the back cab. As he emptied the last of their spare engine oil on the mound, his unwieldy gear, in profile, made him resemble a painted egg on legs.

Bell handed the glasses to Cain. 'They're moving very slowly.'

'It's big stuff. Converted wide-track bulldozers hauling up to 50 tonnes each. They'd average 4 kilometres an hour — a bit under walking pace.'

There were two trains. They shimmered and floated but looked real enough. By noon, one was far off on the horizon as if maintaining its original course and the other was heading towards them.

Cain and Bell went out again, numbness striking into their limbs.

'The one in the distance,' Bell said, 'looks like a mining rig. Seems to be carrying lengths of pipe.'

'That could be why they're so coy. The Antarctic Treaty vetoes mining and everyone bleats about doing pure science but the bottom line's political advantage — finger in the pie.'

Raul's head appeared through the roof hatch. 'They've got us on radar and seen the smoke. You can come in and defrost.'

While the mining train became a shimmering speck far ahead, the other grew enormous as it closed in. When they emerged again to watch it, it looked conventional enough — the sledges at the front stacked with fuel drums and heavy items to smooth out the track. Then came living vans, workshop and generator vans — converted shipping containers all.

Bell gasped, 'It's big.'

'Could have everything — even hot showers.'

'Fantastic.'

When it was a few hundred metres away, two men came out and stood on the metal catwalk that ran the length of an accommodation sled. All the sledges had a side catwalk with steps each end and A-frames steered the front runners. This was some rig — full scale, elaborate, no expense spared.

Raul, Mullins and Hunt joined them on the ice just as the snowplough on the dozer lost its glint.

'Shit,' Bell yelped, 'they're turning, veering off. Are they worried about crevasses?'

'They're suspicious more likely.'

'Get those skis on.' Raul waved an urgent arm at Bell. 'And get the guns. But keep them out of sight.'

His men freed the skis they'd strapped, days ago, to the ramp boards.

The train was now side-on to them, running parallel. Hunt had the binoculars. 'The guys on the porch are sussing us out. One's going inside.'

'They're changing course again,' Raul bellowed, 'heading away!'

Cain glanced back at the Hagg. The wind had lifted the corner of the tarp. A small section of the striped design was visible. That? Or had they radioed their base?

Raul, his chance of survival disappearing, yelled at Bell, 'Go, go!' He slung an M–4 across his back and squeaked across the snow, paused, panting, dizzy, then started to lumber toward the train as Bell went past him on the skis. Mullins was stumbling as fast as he could, carbine ready, desperate to live. Cain knew they'd soon be exhausted. The big oaf was already limping.

'Has he done his foot, too?' Cain asked Hunt.

'Deep frostbite. He's thawed it twice.'

'You didn't warn him?'

'Cluing them's bullshit. Once they're safe, they'll start on us.'

Bell was now far ahead of the others — powered by desperation. Despite the skis and the poles he was likely to miss the train. While the dozer, shackled to such a load, couldn't go faster — even changing gears, Cain knew, meant you either stopped or wrecked the transmission — its crawl was persistent and it didn't get breathless or tired. They watched the three straggling zombies under the deadly sun, trying to close the gap. Mullins was stumbling less but had slowed to a walk. A cooling foot lost sensation. You could walk with a frozen foot. Then both men reached a patch of sastrugi. They had no crampons. They slipped and fell. Bell had been forced to skirt the area, to divert far around on the snow.

Hunt turned to Cain. She'd left her mask off, had frost nip on her nose. 'I think Bell could make it. They'd better plug him before he does.'

'With what? They're civilians.'

'Oh Christ.'

Bell's now tiny figure reached the rear sledge. He clung for a time as if exhausted, then skied forward to the accommodation sledge, fell on the steps, jettisoned his skis, climbed up to enter the big container hut.

The train ploughed on.

It was minutes before they heard the shots.

Three sharp cracks.

Anything could happen now.

46

ALPHA

Vanqua thumped his desk with rage — keyed in the parameters again. The same flawed information — garbled names, addresses, reports — essential files doctored. It was expertly done, had fooled him for weeks. Rhonda was behind this. She was the only other person in EXIT cleared for level five encryption.

He cursed, stomped to the security booth, passed the hand geometry and iris checks, waited for the chemical atmosphere analysis. In the innermost box, he punched his card and tapped his foot, impatient for message clearance. One by one, green lights came on. He entered his day key. Checks ran.

A smooth face appeared on the screen. Kuneso Awa, the Japanese government's numbers man. 'Vanqua san?'

'I'm in trouble. I've referred these scrambled files to Washington but Pickett doesn't call back and no one will comment.'

'Ah so.' The dapper man nodded. 'I receive call from Vatican. They mos' concern.'

'But I can't eradicate this without working it back. That means encryption level six.'

'Ah. Difficul'. Clearance has come?'

'Negative.'

'No clearance. Mm.'

'I need six.'

'Ah, six.' The face on the semi-stop-frame screen remained impassive.

'You can authorise that. I'm requesting it.'

'Ah, not so easy.'

'I assume you want the project completed?'

'Your assignment mus' continue.'

'Then I have to trace the alterations. I can't reconstruct using five.'

'Level six not so easy.'

He attempted to hide his anger. 'I can't recall principal agents without a reconstruction. It's impossible.'

'Rely on you to take necessary steps. As wise man say: "Not to know is to be a Buddha." Am most busy at moment. So now please to excuse.'

The screen went blank.

He extricated himself, fuming, from the concrete box nest. None of them wanted to know.

They'd tossed him to the lions. He could almost smell the arena.

Rhonda and her 2IC dead. That left no one to interrogate. The only people left who might have the missing links were Cain and Hunt. Cain was Pat and Rhonda's crony and already a Grade Four — perhaps being groomed as next in line. Hunt was Rhonda's lover. But, by now, they'd surely be dead.

The screen of his computer altered as a priority message from Alpha Intelligence displayed over the previous data:

1. FOURTH INTERCEPT FROM FLYNN TRAVERSE ABOUT SLOTTED HAGGLUNDS.

2. SIGNAL SENT TO THEIR EXPEDITION AREA CONTROL ON CHARTERED RUSSIAN ICEBREAKER, *SVENAYA*.

3. TRAV ADVISED CONTROL THAT VEHICLE STRIPED.

4. WAS ORDERED TO AVOID.

Time and coordinates followed.

Were the survivors still alive?

He pressed the button that paged Zuiden, paced his office until he came, glared at the surgeon. 'I need Cain and Hunt for questioning.'

'They'll be ice.'

He jerked a thumb at the VDU.

The assassin walked around to read the message, grinned. 'Well, cut off my legs and call me Shorty.'

'They could never have made that distance unless Cain and Hunt helped them. So get out there.'

'No can. Unstable platform probs. Drive-train glitch in one chopper and vibrating tail rotor in the other. For now, we're whistling Dixie.'

Vanqua turned his back to hide his rage. 'Get airborne as soon as you can. Kill everyone but bring me Cain and Hunt. I want them here and able to feel pain.'

'My pleasure,' Zuiden smiled.

47

FUN TIME

The first thing that impinged was the smell. Meat casserole. Then the rough surface of freezing matting. He had his back to the noises, couldn't move. He tested the cords. They'd trussed him well. He knew better than to open his eyes, lay quietly, listening. The grating of the big runners below him, the dozer's growl, muted by the insulated walls. He had to be in one of the living vans but its propane-fuelled warmth barely reached the floor.

The sudden clatter of pots drowned by Nina yelling at her mother. The mother shouting her down. As the girl subsided into silence, the voice of Mullins: 'Want to shove some stuff into her?'

Raul's deeper voice: 'None left. I used the last on Cain and Hunt.'

He remembered what had happened. The dozer train looping around to pick up Raul and Mullins, then returning, they supposed, for the pope and the ice sculpture of Zia. He and

Hunt confronted with two M–4s while Raul injected them with some narcotic from the medical kit.

The last things he recalled were Eve and John's protests and Raul's reply. 'They're dangerous people. Under these new conditions very dangerous. For the welfare of us all, they now have to be restrained.'

A call button tone signal pressed three times. The other train would be trying to attract attention.

Then a transmitted voice with a Californian drawl: 'Calling freight train. Still can't hear you. We're setting up for docking. Baby could be in tomorrow noon. Need your fuel and supplies. Have you on radar. You seem okay and on our heading. Over.'

Mullins: 'Maintain radio silence?'

Raul: 'Yes. I'll check the dozer.'

Someone moving behind him. Steps on the floor.

A click.

Raul: 'How's it going? ... So long? No, I've persuaded Eve and her brat to cook lunch. It's almost ready ... Then come back, wash up and eat.'

Mullins calling: 'Tell him we've got booze.'

Raul: 'Beef casserole and scotch ... Right. Let him know that, if he doesn't, we'll be after him. Say we'll bring him food if he's lucky. Out.'

The mike replaced.

Mullins: 'The driver being good?'

Raul: 'He's one very scared diesel mechanic and he's now sure we're EXIT hit men. Bell says we can monitor him from this console and that if he diverges, we'll spot it. Come here and write down our bearing.'

The train slowed, stopped. Bell would be leaving the heated dozer's cabin and climbing down over the tracks.

A clash of plates.

Nina's whine: 'Why help deadshits?'

Mullins calling to her: 'Shut it, bitch.'

'Drugging people, tying them up. Killing people.'

'Shut up,' Eve's voice. 'They'll hurt you.'

A roar from the dozer. A creak of frames and shackles as the main cable beneath the sledge took up and jerked them ahead again. Bell would stand on the ice until the living vans drew level, then simply step on board.

Eve's voice, closer: 'I've made two lots.'

Cain opened his eyes, tried to sit. He found it difficult to focus. The drug still had him woozy. They'd taken off his parka to make it easier to tie him. He gazed blearily around the van.

A partition half-hiding a cooking space, a drop-down table with a cleaner Raul and Mullins on a bench beside it — Mullins fearfully removing his boot. Food and supply racks across from the table with windsuits roughly stuffed into them. At the near end, behind him, a field leader's work station set up for communication, navigation and probably the monitoring of fuel and stores. One high double window, the wind-out outer shutter raised to let in light.

He assumed John would be in the other van, retained as Raul's only living evidence, and that Zia's glassy corpse would be somewhere on the load. And the men they'd shot? Down a crevasse?

The barrels of two M–4s projected over the table.

Hunt? He couldn't see her.

'Ah!' Raul said. 'Cain's rejoined us.' He resumed rubbing ointment on the scabby frost-burns covering his nose — unaware that first-aid manuals warned DO NOT APPLY OINTMENTS, LOTIONS OR GREASY DRESSINGS.

'You're a work of art,' Cain said. 'I take care of you and ...'

'You needed our manpower.'

'I kept you alive.'

'And trusted me. Mistake.'

'Now you've killed noncombatants.'

'No. Bell did that.'

Cain blinked to try and clear his vision. 'You can't hide shooting civilians, Raul. Too much evidence. Too many witnesses.' He tried to sit again and pain stabbed up his spine through his head.

'Ignore him,' Mullins said. 'Bastard's past it.' The big soldier sat next to Raul, probing his swollen grey foot but the skin wasn't moving on the bone. 'Jeez, this looks ... There's no feeling.' He peered at huge blisters on his right hand. The hand itself was now swelling. He pulled out his sheath knife, thought better of it.

DO NOT BURST BLISTERS.

'You'll feel that hand soon,' Cain said, 'and it'll just about kill you.'

'Shit, I'm rooted,' Mullins said. 'I want compensation, Raul.'

The other looked at him with contempt. 'You were warned it was going to be dangerous.'

'But I didn't sign on to spend days in a blizzard. Not my idea of fun.'

'You wanted *fun*?' The other's arch look.

'Got it in one.' He used his good hand to pour scotch into tumblers.

Raul recapped his ointment. 'I'll give you fun.'

'You'd bloody better.'

Eve plonked plates on the table. A casserole with whipped potato, peas. 'We've kept enough for the others on the stove.' She had a bruise on the side of her face as if she'd been hit. She looked down at Cain, frightened to see him tied up. 'He has to eat, too.'

A scraping outside. The insulated door opened on what must have been a tiny slush-excluding cold porch. Against the glare, someone pushed back his hood and knocked frost off his clothes. The outer door shut, the inner door slid back. Bell came through, nose and cheeks scabbed. 'Food. Warmth. Wonderful.' He put his M-4 on the table with the others, dropped his balaclava, woollen gloves and goggles on a rack, shucked off his open parka, unzipped his ventiles, shoved them in with his other gear.

Raul handed him a tumbler of spirit.

Bell half-drained it, flopped on a bench.

Raul looked around. 'Joining us, ladies?'

The morose Eve and Nina came forward and sat.

Raul poured for them. 'To rescue.' He raised his glass. 'And to vibrant, unpredictable life.'

They swigged and attacked the food.

Bell ate, looking thoughtful, then asked Raul, 'So when we get to the other train, what then? If we grease the second crew we can't operate these rigs.'

'We've hours to ponder that.'

Eve moaned, 'You murdered those innocent men. You'll get life.'

Raul laughed. 'Odd that if you kill someone they give you life. But they don't if you have money and influence. The law's the lapdog of the rich.'

'You don't realise who he is,' Bell added. 'You don't know how many thousands of people would protect him. You don't know how many millions we have to fight with. He has governments in his pocket, friends in high places everywhere. No one can touch Gustave.'

'If he's got all that loot, he owes me compensation.' Mullins lurched up, went to the console, checked the heading on the compass. 'Driver's still being a good boy.'

'Good,' Raul said. 'And Nina's being a good girl, too. Aren't you, you living horror?' He glared at Nina who kept rebellious eyes on her plate. 'You're not in control of it, are you? It just uses you when you get upset. But it's nothing you can rely on.' He beckoned Mullins back. 'Come and have another drink.'

Cain recalled the manual — DO NOT GIVE ALCOHOL — happy to see the bastards screw themselves.

'So what about Karen?' Bell asked too loudly, whisky deadening his brain.

Raul piled food neatly on his fork, composing his words. 'Have you considered direct destruction of body tissue without immediate homicidal intent?'

Bell absorbed that. 'I have. For some time.'

'What's *your* wish, my loyal friend?'

'To anticipate your needs. To do your will.'

'Did I wish you to shoot three men?'

Bell protested. 'I shot them to save you.'

'But did I tell you to kill them?'

'No. But you ...'

'And have I told you to torture and kill Karen?'

'N-not directly.'

'So everything's your interpretation. Now what if I blame this whole demeaning excursion on you?'

'Then I'm ready to take the blame.'

'Excellent.' Raul nodded at him. 'You've killed three men. There are two EXIT agents here that could kill you. All of us are damaged — are going to lose fingers, toes, feet. Are we ready for life with a tin nose, mechanical foot, one hand? How do we live in the face of that? Are we prepared to take what comes?'

'Fuck no. Hell.' Mullins poured himself another slug. 'I want compensation.'

'So what do I do?' Bell pleaded. 'You know what's best.'

'You're a typical follower, Peter — always want to be told what to do. There's great security in that. And stupidity.' Raul smiled at him, aware Bell longed to bask in his approval. 'I thought I'd just suggested that you do what you think. That way, you create your life as you decide.'

'Touch Hunt,' Cain said, 'and you'll create your death.'

Mullins half-lifted his M–4, glanced at Raul. 'Junk him?'

Eve yelled, 'No!'

'You're a dangerous EXIT person, Cain,' Raul said, 'whom we can kill in self-protection.'

'Hardly logical when I'm trussed like a chook.'

'I agree there's an element of control without any notion of trust or consent. Just consider it as conflict resolution.' He chuckled. 'You've gone soft, my friend.'

'In the head,' Mullins jeered.

'You're a burnt-out case.' Raul was enjoying this. 'A worn-out warhorse ready to be butchered.'

'Exactly, exactly.' Bell gazed adoringly at Raul, eager for attention. 'And what animal am I?'

'A dog. Stupidly faithful.'

Bell swallowed his discomfort.

Mullins stared from one to the other, not sure what was going on or how to join in the conversation. 'So what's my animal then?'

Raul laughed. 'A bull. You want fighting. Food. Sex.'

'I wanna stuffa chicken.' He put a cumbersome arm around Nina.

Nina jerked back, punched him. 'Fuck off, mullet.'

He guffawed.

'And that would be — compensation?' Raul asked Mullins.

'You mean the chick? What you getting at?'

'Are you bull enough to ...'

'... snatch some snatch? That what you're saying? What if ...'

'... strange things start happening? Just drug her. Or knock her out. And they'll stop.'

'You're telling me to ...'

Raul's insinuating smile. 'This hellish place has damaged our bodies — could kill us. Aren't we entitled to some raw enjoyment? I suggest you drink up, relax, then ...'

Mullins half-grinned, drained his glass and wiped his mouth.

Raul stood, beamed at them all. 'Well, that was better than kero fumes and pemmican. Now I'm going to see the pope.' He reached for his boots, got his outside clothes from the rack. 'I might even discuss with him whether existence is an illusion. And I'll take him some food.'

Eve got up and went to the alcove. 'I've got something to put it in.'

'I'm sure you have, dear.' Raul appraised her rear. 'Now I see why gentlemen rise when a woman gets up from the table.'

The sloshed Mullins guffawed but Bell refused to interpret it as lewd.

Raul spread his arms. 'People are afraid to have fun. To live. They dream about it — never do it.' He kitted up, turned back to his troops. 'You have life's playground equipment on this very train.' His eyes rested on Eve, then Nina. Then he turned to Bell. 'And you have a certain female person who needs severe and protracted discipline.' He picked up his gun. 'So while I'm away — consider what I've said to you.'

'So I can rub Cain?' Mullins asked through a mouthful.

'Did I tell you to kill him? Or did I just point out what life owes him?'

The oaf's heavy frown showed he wasn't sure what he'd heard.

The now terrified Eve came back with plastic containers, forks and napkins in a bag. Raul looped the handles over the thumb of his overmitt and smiled. 'Pancakes and honey for afternoon tea?'

Bell got up to open the inner door for him.

'I just step off and on again?'

'Yes. There are steps on the ends of both sleds and it's only walking pace. When you want to come back, just jog until you catch up to us. You only have to go the length of the linkage.'

'Right. Have fun.'

Cain, immobilised, was starting to freeze. And as Bell let Raul out, the cold air from the small porch chilled him more. But not as much as the situation. Raul, just using words, had set a time bomb.

Bell slid the inner door closed again, swayed unsteadily, then retrieved his dropped windproofs.

'Going out?' Mullins slurred.

'Got something to take care of in the workshop.'

An unpleasant grin from Mullins. 'Need help?'

'No. You've got to stay here — keep an eye on things and

the compass. Or these two'll untie him.' He collected his M–4 and left.

Cain thought, just one man and one gun.

But how to get free?

Nina helped her shaking mother clear the table, hoping to get away from Mullins who sat finishing another glass. Eve glanced apprehensively at Cain, then the pair of them retreated behind the alcove to clear up.

Mullins drunkenly grinned at Cain, hand on his weapon. 'Fun time.' He grabbed the M–4, removed the four-column magazine and ejected the chambered round. He stuffed the round back in the mag, folded the gun-butt, then lurched up, almost knocking over the bench. He limped to the storage racks, stood on the bottom shelf and put the weapon and mag near the back of the top rack. He returned to the table, picked up his commando knife — a long double-edged blade — and limped into the alcove.

A scream from Nina. He emerged dragging her by the arm.

Eve followed him, shrieking, but he menaced her with the knife. 'Stay behind there. If I see you, I'll stick you.'

She looked at Cain, terrified.

He said, 'Do what he says.'

'He's going to rape her.'

'Do what he says or he'll kill you both.'

Beside the huge form of the emotional illiterate, the girl's compact body seemed a child's. Mullins hurled her to the floor, hauled her along the rough matting by one arm, dropped beside her and licked his raw lips. Half smiling, he ran the knife along her cheek. 'Payback.'

The girl now lay on her back, eyes bulging. 'Oh Jesus. Mum? Oh Jesus.'

'Do what he says, baby.' Eve's terrified voice. 'Just ... do what he says.'

Mullins said, 'All *right*!'

He forgot his damaged hand and foot, vanished into his task, dragging the pile suit off the girl starting on the inner layers, eager to see her naked, his pants bulging. Cain tugged at his bonds, could do nothing. But if the girl could summon her gremlins ...

When Mullins had her stripped he stared at her, stunned. She was more perfect than a retouched centrefold. Small uptilted breasts, a gymnast's long slim thighs, the miracle of a developing girl combined with the freshness of a child. He murmured, 'What a honey. You want fingers? Then don't you fucking move.'

He worked himself free of the thermal underwear until it was around his ankles, exposing big fair-haired legs. He searched around for lubrication, saw nothing, spat on himself, kicked her legs wide.

Cain's view of it was a wriggling hairy arse and the purple face of Nina — holding her breath.

It didn't take long.

The racks began to shake. Behind him, a logbook flew off the console. Then Eve screamed as pots and plates shot out of the alcove to smash against the side of the van. The end of one of the benches tilted into the air, then the entire thing rose slowly toward the roof.

Mullins looked up, dumbfounded, as the metal bench fell on his arm. Nina, shrieking, hauled herself up, clawed at his face. One of her fingers must have caught his eye.

He bellowed in pain and backed off.

Then Eve was around the partition with a skillet clasped in both hands, ready to smash in the man's head. He shoved her off, rose on one knee and thrust the knife up deep into her chest. She belched, staggered, and the iron pan fell from her hands only to float across the room. It smashed into the transceiver, wrecking the DC voltmeter, then sailed back and — in mid flight — disappeared.

In the bedlam, Mullins's yell of fear and rage. He twisted, half-blinded, looking for the girl.

Eve staggered two steps toward Cain, as if she felt he could still help her, glazed eyes staring at him with the astonishment he'd seen on so many dying faces, the sudden amazement at coming to the end.

Then she collapsed half on top of him.

That was his chance.

He backed against her until his bound hands met the edge of the knife. It was jammed solidly between her ribs, a section of the keen edge still protruding. He cursed the size of her breasts which made it harder to get the rope against the blade, thrust at the edge knowing he'd either cut his wrists or the rope.

He felt a cord give. Then it was simple.

The racket of screams, roars and phenomena told him Mullins was too occupied to notice.

He rolled, arms free, wrenched the knife from the woman's chest, turned.

Mullins, one eye bloodshot, was grabbing for the naked girl who had got loose again, was half up, her back to him, clinging to the table. He hauled at her bare legs, jerked her off her feet. She fell, slim bottom, goose bumps, her girl's form tiny beside his.

As Cain hacked the rope from his ankles a packet of dried onions hovered in front of him, blocking his view.

'Bitch,' Mullins roared.

Nina's scream. The onion bag fell to the floor.

Cain had the knife.

Too late. The girl lay still. Mullins had snapped her neck. With her death, the shaking had stopped and fallen objects had made the van a bombsite.

Cain, body cold-stiff, gasping thin air, dropped a knee onto Mullins's spine, yanked up his head — pig-slit him with all his force, howled, 'You scum.'

Mullins gurgled, rolled off the broken body, blood spurting, ruined face agape.

While the man's heart pumped his life out, Cain confirmed that Eve had gone. Then he climbed on the rack and got the gun, feeling the warmth that had eluded him on the floor. He shoved the magazine back in, pulled and released the cocking handle, depressed the decocking lever so that the hammer could move forward. That done, he placed the gun on the object-strewn table, retrieved his outer clothing from the rack, got his boots back on.

He was appalled to discover he felt disassociated, calm. Because of the extremity of the continent, the fight for breath, warmth, life?

He wiped the knife on the degenerate's long johns, located the knife sheath on the table attached to a discarded belt, sheathed the knife and slid the sheath onto his own belt.

Panting now with the effort, he retrieved his outer clothing and put it on. His joints ached with every movement. The time on the floor had almost wrecked him.

He found his mukluks, a balaclava. His goggles were gone but he retrieved another pair. He adjusted his mitten harness, snapped the big inner-lined gloves behind his back. He'd need them out of the way to use the gun.

He picked up the weapon like a carpenter selecting a tool. The action would be warmed after its time near the roof of the van. He got the strap over his shoulder. Forgive them for they know not what they do.

Bright sun slanted under the shutter through the high double window, imprinting the opposite wall with glare.

Execution time.

48

MOP-UP

Cain stepped off the sledge onto finnified snow like loose gravel. Searing cold and blinding light. On the ground, ice crystals shone like gems and diamond dust danced in the air. Above, stratus fanned from the horizon into a canopy of splendour.

The traverse slid ponderously past him like a shunting train, the one spot of colour in an infinity of white. Rusting yellow and red container vans sprouting H-shaped vents and masts, fuel drums, miscellaneous hardware — all perched on massive sledges. The train was elaborate, as the diminutive cold porch proved. Each van door opened onto a small railed landing formed by the flat ends of each sledge. A railed, expanded-metal catwalk extended down one side of the vans, joining the landings and steps at both ends. He let the steps of the next sledge pass him, waiting to check the following van. As it drew level, he swung on board like a pre-war bus conductor and clumped up to the next landing.

The insulated door of the big container creaked. He lunged inside, set to drop and fire.

Empty. An elaborately fitted workshop. There were spare

shoes for the Caterpillar tracks with special openings that stopped the snow compacting, spares for the hardware on the sledges, a lathe, drill stand, welding kit, pipe bending machine ... Then he saw the rope on the floor and masking tape on the bench.

He got out of there and off, waited for the last sledge to reach him, the one that would house the generators, grabbed the rail and swung back on.

He checked inside the van. Primary and secondary generators with ancillary equipment, three dead crewmen and the solidified Zia. He backed out and edged along the catwalk to the porch at the rear of the sledge.

Bell crouched at the back rail levering something with a length of pipe, his M–4 dangling on his belly, his snorkel hood obscuring his side view. From a winch bolted to the platform a length of light steel cable angled out. He was trying to force the cable more to the centre with a pipe he'd jammed against a stanchion of the railing.

Now Cain saw the weight dragging on the end of the cable — Hunt, tied by the wrists and gagged with masking tape. The cable, shackled to her bonds, was slithering her over the snow in a smooth track left by the runners. Bell was trying to move the cable across so that she'd rip apart on the hard uneven snow between the tracks.

She couldn't have been there long but her outer layers were shredding. She was twisting to protect herself but was too cold, had no strength.

Cain levelled the M–4 at Bell. 'Your turn.'

As the man swung around in shock, Cain dispensed one burst of three.

The impact slammed Raul's disciple against the opposite railing before his trigger finger reached the guard. He hung over the top rail, guts jellified, howling.

Cain closed, stripped the magazine from Bell's M–4. Rule sixteen: never discard ammunition. Then he lifted the dying man's legs and toppled him off the sledge.

By the time he'd winched Hunt off the snow, Bell was a lifeless yellow mound far behind.

Cain half-climbed over the rail and reached down to grab her legs. She was conscious but not connecting enough to help and it took all his strength to get her onto the platform. Panting in the thin air, he freed the cable, peeling off the tape.

She moaned but couldn't stand. Her hair, eyebrows, lashes were frost. He dragged off his polar cap and balaclava, got them on her head, pulled up the remains of her ripped hood. He was nearly hallucinating with hypoxia and rapidly losing heat. He replaced his double-lined hood, his starved muscles protesting. The air was so cold he expected to feel a crackle in his lungs.

He got her over his shoulders in a fireman's lift. It left his hands free for the gun. The weight of her made his legs tremble.

Now he had to run faster than the train!

He stumbled ahead along the length of the sledge to the front steps. There were no rear steps on the caboose. So if he couldn't trot faster than the dozer he couldn't get back aboard.

Could he jog on the hard snow, carrying a woman, and not fall?

He stood for almost a minute working up to it, sucked in all the freezing air he dared.

Bell and Mullins had been nothing. This was the test. The test of an ageing man who should have been out to pasture years ago — a shot-up man who couldn't trust his body to hold out.

He stepped off.

Stumbling, panting, he half-jogged along on the snow. The weight of the woman and two sets of Antarctic clothes made the task immense. He struggled, gasped, thin air freezing his lungs, the effort torture.

His bad leg was holding up but he was gaining too slowly on the sledge. He'd lose against the dozer as he tired. He powered forward desperately, knowing he mustn't slip. He made it past the steering linkage, drew level with the rear steps of the next sledge, grabbed the rail and hauled himself aboard.

He slumped on the lower steps, heart pounding, desperate for breath, one boot still dragging on hard snow. This was only the workshop van. One to go.

It was minutes before he was strong enough to stand and stagger along the catwalk to the front. There he waited, at the bottom of the steps, mustering his strength. Raul, in the next van, would have heard the bursts. Would he be outside, armed and waiting?

Exhausted, he braced himself, stepped off again, stumbled forward as fast as he could, eyes fixed on the front of the van. No one in sight, thank God.

At the limit of his strength he reached the next set of steps, collapsed onto the sledge, covering the catwalk with his M–4. When he had breath in him again, he left the ragged shape on the walkway. He had to get her inside. But first he had to deal with Raul.

He hauled on the rail, dragged himself upright and limped on rubber legs along the side of the rear living van. He lunged around the edge, barrel first. No one. The thick outer door was still shut. He lifted the big cold-store-type handle, pulled the door. The closet-sized cold porch was clear.

He pulled off his goggles and hood, crouched painfully, weapon at the ready, slid the inner door wide. Bliss. Warm air, defrosting his lungs.

It was the dormitory van — fold-down bunks, toilet, basin, shower. Raul, back to the door, was watching John eat his meal. On his canvas chair-back was screen-printed: BABY, Pole to Pole.

Raul didn't even turn, certain it was Bell or Mullins. He still must have been agreeably sauced and convinced he was invincible.

Cain tried to stand, almost didn't make it. 'You're next, Raul.'

As John looked up, relief on his face, Raul craned around, eyes saucers, then quickly composed his face to a smile. 'We've been discussing the devil, an invention that, fortunately, never got as far as the sub-continent.'

'What have they done?' John said.

'Killed three of the crew, Nina and her mother. What did he say when he heard firing?'

'That his men were high-spirited today.'

'And kept sitting here, calm as a swan? The parasitic turd.'

The pope said, 'I thought they'd shot you.'

'So did shithead here.'

Raul was determined to tough it out. 'Cain, you look all in. Grab a pew.'

'Fucking social terrorist. Your chat over lunch killed two women — almost three.'

'I haven't touched anyone. So stop posturing. You know you won't shoot. You're far too civilised for that.'

'Be careful,' the pope told Raul. 'He has authority to kill anyone he likes.'

'That's absurd.'

Cain played back the man's words. 'Admit all possibilities.'

'I'm unarmed and no threat to you, Cain.' He made an expansive gesture. 'I'm also intolerant of intolerance.'

'Too late for word games, Raul.'

'Come on, man. This is silly. I'm an unarmed civilian.'

'So were the crew of this traverse.'

Raul tried his winning smile then winced as his lips split further. 'Don't be tedious. Bell did that. Regrettably. Where is he?'

'Miles back. Gut shot out.'

Raul's damaged face sobered. 'Mullins?'

'Head's half off.'

A stammer breached his superior role. 'I'll g-give you money. Four million in US notes. Paid to a Swiss bank account. No tax trail.'

'I'm a rich man, Raul. Save it for your funeral fund.'

'This is madness.' His voice cracked. One hand went up, pleading. 'Please ...' It was an act — to mask a slight movement he'd made behind the canvas back of the chair.

But Cain had read the pope's startled look. Raul had an automatic pointing behind him beneath his arm.

The chair-back shredded as Cain riddled him. Raul fell across the floor, the pistol flopping wide in his hand.

Cain staggered out again for Hunt. When he dragged her into the warmth the pope was kneeling beside the dead man.

As Cain got Hunt onto a bunk, started removing her shredded windproofs, the pope looked up. 'Would you have killed him anyway?'

'Why not?' he puffed. 'Why excuse the generals that order the dirty work? He's already taken out five and had Bell torturing this one to death. Need warm water, med kit.'

'Even false prophets have uses.'

'You'd let the maggot live?'

'Vengeance is mine, saith the Lord.'

You couldn't please everybody. Cain found it prudent to shut up.

While the pope went looking for what he needed, he got the shredded layers off the woman, checking her face for pain, concerned about fractures. Why had Bell left all her gear on? To prolong her death?

It had saved her.

As he worked on her abraded body, he found no permanent damage. She was young, fit and had an excellent circulation because the frostbite was still superficial. Combat survival had helped her as well. She'd been trained in the four environments — arctic, sea/coast, arid, jungle — had been taught to endure intense weariness, hunger, thirst, heat, cold.

'Hurts,' she gasped.

'You're an OAE. You'll survive.'

'Mullins?'

'Dead. Area secured.'

Tears helped thaw her frosted lids.

49

TOWERING CONUNDRUM

When he had Hunt fed, thawed and patched up, he called the driver on the interphone and suggested he stop for food. But the man, frightened by the shooting, refused and hauled them on.

He left the pope with the swaddled, sleeping Hunt and dragged the dead onto the catwalks ... Raul, Eve, Nina — naked except for her socks — Mullins, the three from the traverse crew and Zia with the knife still a feature of his face. He would have jettisoned them except there was enough garbage on the continent already. Cold, tired, mind shutting down, he retreated inside.

He swabbed the blood stains back to smears, stuffed things back on shelves like some crazed housewife, then collapsed on a bunk and slept.

A jerk in the cable woke him. They'd stopped.

Shouting outside.

For the first time it struck him that the bodies would startle civilians. He peered through the small half-iced window, saw the other traverse, now uncoupled, and six gesticulating men.

He said, 'I'll try and sort this. You two lie low for now.' He placed the burp guns and the sniper's rifle out of sight on a top bunk, dragged on his parka and limped out.

Hooded masked faces stared up at him. He adopted the right body language, submissive, nonthreatening. 'Your crew are dead as you can see. Not my fault. I shot the man who shot them. He's back on the plateau.'

A big-framed man who seemed to be in charge stepped forward. 'So don't tell me. You're from the EXIT base?' The furious voice was Irish/American.

'Escaping the place. Been a lot going down.'

'That the best you can do?' He waved an arm at the carnage.

'To fill you in ...' He ticked the bodies off, told them the general history. How he'd been their prisoner, counterattacked.

The man's expression was invisible but his indignant voice said it all. 'This is a *private expedition*.'

'Life's a bitch.'

The other men stood warily as if expecting an ambush. None of them was armed.

'Just three left alive,' he told them. 'Me, a woman and an old man.'

A chorus of angry comments. But no off-colour words, which was odd. What were they? Christian Outreach? They kept turning around to gaze at the girl's provocative body, the skin now grey, the pubic hair a triangle of frost, the small nipples pointing to the sky.

He shrugged again, starting to shiver. 'Could we discuss this inside?'

Three men warily followed him up the steps. Two stayed outside the van while the leader cautiously entered. The sight of an old man and a stunning woman reassured him. He pushed out again and gave his backup the all-clear. 'Check the other vans, then get back to it. We've got to finish tonight. And line up the sledges. Met says we're due for a blow.'

The big man returned, took off his headgear, revealing himself as around fifty with a strong face and reddish hair. Cain introduced himself as Ray, the pope and Hunt as John and Karen.

'Peter Reilly, ground crew controller. Dear God, this is a terrible business.'

Cain gave the story again, while Hunt and the pope confirmed it. They regretted the loss of his men, insisted they were friendly, while the flabbergasted Reilly listened. During it, they heard sledges uncoupled and later were shunted backwards. It took time for Reilly to vent his protests and be persuaded by truth, lies and blandishments that they were other than rogues and marauders. 'So what do we do with the dead?' The man, his psychology massaged, finally aired the question nagging him.

'I'm happy to drop our lot down a slot. But keep your lot if you want them.'

'It's incumbent upon us to bring them back to their families for Christian burial. Terrible business. Terrible. And that poor, poor girl.'

'We were all very fond of her.' Cain faked sincerity while Hunt rolled her eyes.

'Why didn't you cover her? It's indecent.'

'True,' Cain said. 'Not enough oxygen and the brain's been drifting a bit. I'll do it. And what are you people up to? Or is it better we don't know?'

He looked affronted. 'It's perfectly legitimate. We're part of the Patrick Flynn expedition.'

It told him nothing. 'Uh-huh.'

'We're erecting the tower for resupply. Enormous project.'

'What project?'

'Pole to Pole!' He pointed to the inscription on a chair. 'A magnificent demonstration to the world. I have to go now.'

'Can I help?'

'Not unless you're a mechanic or qualified rigger?'

He shook his head.

'Well, there's one thing you could do. Cook up a mess of chow. Enough for us all. We'll need it in two hours.'

'You've got it.'

Reilly rose, donned his headgear. 'This van's now powered by the genny so the shower should work in an hour. You're welcome to have one but keep it short. Two minutes and out.' As he left he called back, 'And I'd thank you to cover that girl.'

Hunt said, 'What's with that guy?'

Cain shrugged. 'I'd better do a recce.'

The pope, tired of his long confinement, asked if he could go too. Cain made sure he put on all possible clothing including three sets of gloves, two sets of socks, a woollen undersuit over his double set of thermals, windproofs, polar hat, mask, balaclava and goggles. They left Hunt in the warmth of the van and braved the searing air.

The pope looked down at Raul's body. 'No one sillier than a clever man.' Then at Nina and the others. 'God forgive them. Why did you line them up like a morgue? No wonder the man was upset.'

'I couldn't think straight — was out of it.' Cain helped him off the sledge, offered his arm for support.

'What an astonishing sense of space.' The pope stared at the endless white desert, a mournful sight now, in the twilight.

The sledges were parked crosswind in lines of three — a defence against drifts and blizzards. Cables snaked from generator vans to power them. But the sound of generators was drowned by dozers. The sun was diminishing by twelve minutes each day and, by midwinter, would be an hour of apricot blush on the horizon. By now the two huge Cats should have been shut down for the night with battery blankets on, sump and coolant heaters plugged in. So why, he wondered, were they still working?

He steered the wheezing priest around the first line of sledges toward the noise.

The dozers, some distance from them and dwarfed by the plateau, fussed like beetles around a prefabricated cone-shaped structure of heavy metal pipes. From the apex a mast projected high above the snow. The support seemed set into the ice and, from it, low guy-wires stretched to belays. One dozer, headlights blazing, was using a crane-like structure, mounted behind its blade, to lift a girder into a trench. Shackled to the centre of the girder was a guy-wire. Men with wrenches stood near the hole, directing the move.

The pope panted, 'Is it for drilling?'

It was hard to see in fading light. 'Don't think so.'

The top of the structure was fitted with a half-sphere of metal that had some kind of inner mechanism and seemed mounted on a swivel. Cables hung down from it, one attached to a winch at the base. Near the mast was an empty sledge and another packed with equipment — wire crates holding tall pressure bottles, fuel drums, propane cylinders, a compressor, rolls of hosing, a motorised pump and a pile of canvas bags. They watched as the dozer pushed snow into the trench around the girder, piled more into a mound above it then rolled over it to compact it.

A megabucks traverse to put up some tower? What was going on here? He said, 'Want to look around some more?'

'Too cold,' John puffed, turning to go back. 'Was good . . . to get out . . . but now . . . have to cook.'

They walked back past a man erecting a blizz line between the tower and the encampment. He called, 'Could be nil tomorrow, folks.' He was referring to visibility.

'What's the tower for?' Cain asked.

'For Baby.' He continued hitting in the post. 'The belaying and guying's the hard bit. Down here it's got to be strong. You should see the specs.'

Cain left the pope in the van, sorting out packets of pasta, and went to check on Hunt. He covered the naked Nina with a sleeping bag then walked back to the bunk sledge. When he'd clumped up to its landing he rested on the rail for a moment and stared at the merciless landscape, trying to fathom what all this meant.

He'd called himself an exile, like the first Muslims. Why did that recur to him now? First an exile. Now a castaway. He'd lost everything — except John. When you lost everything you began to live, they said. The blessing of being near the pope was worth all the rest.

As he entered the warmth and light of the bunk van, Hunt sat up. 'What's happening?'

'They're building a bloody great tower.' He examined her face. Her nose and cheeks looked better.

'For drilling?'

'No idea. It's just a heavily guyed stalk. You should see the cables on it. How are your hands and feet?'

'Feet are okay.' She pulled off one of her gloves to expose a swollen hand. 'Stings like hell.'

'But looking good.'

'You got me in time.' Her seamless frown. 'Ready for a threat assessment?'

'Shoot.'

'Before we left the Hagg, we heard them radio their base about finding us. They would have monitored that at Alpha.'

'Agree.'

'Then they veered. That could have meant another transmission. Reilly knew we were EXIT. So Vanqua could know we're here.'

'. . . And have a fix on the trav. So why hasn't he attacked?'

'Don't know. But if the weather holds, Zuiden could fly in any time.' She shook her head sadly. 'LOYALTY TO THE CAUSE IS STRENGTH! What happened to us, Cain?'

'Slipped a cog?'

'I'm close to my event horizon.'

He sat on the bunk beside her. 'No training like a near-death experience.'

'I've been chewing things over for hours.' She stared at her hand. 'I thought I could handle anything emotionally.'

'Unemotionally, you mean. You were raised an emotional cripple, then landed with a sociopath.'

'Well, it hasn't worked. I mean, Raul dead, after all I've been through with him, all I've had to half-believe. Then Ronnie knocked out.'

'You can't pretend you cared for her.'

'There were times I could have throttled her. But she was a marvellous person. Of course I bloody cared for her. Was just too up myself to show it.'

'Take it easy, soldier. You've been through hell and this air makes us pea-brains.'

'Even you loved Ronnie. What a fool I was. I didn't know what I had.'

'Confirmed.'

She stared at the wall. Her eyes brimmed. 'When you got under her crust she was so warm. Am I right about her being alive?'

'Nice theory but — no.'

'Then ... EXIT. Destroyed. And I'm typecast as the trigger for it. Now they're going to take us out. So what's it all been for?'

'My situation analysis won't help.'

'You're a Grade Four. You're all I've got left. Please, I'm in damage control. What happened to us, Cain?'

'Simple. Everything becomes its own opposite. All it takes is time.'

'Oh Jesus.' She turned her head away.

'Sorry, *petite soeur*. Sometimes it's better not to ask. Got to go. I'm on kitchen detail.' He turned her head back gently. 'Remember, no combat-ready unit ever passed inspection. Now I suggest a nice hot shower before dinner.'

A brave smile.

TRAINING LEADS TO COURAGE. He'd never seen her smile. On her pre-Raphaelite face it looked odd.

He kissed her hair. 'I feel I've just met you.'

He left to help the pope with the meal.

* * *

The men came in for dinner, exhausted and ravenous. Stripped of outer clothing, they became basic types who seemed remarkably well behaved, although the smell of food and the warmth provoked their banter. But when Hunt joined them, they were gobsmacked to be confronted with such a superb-looking woman in that void. Their talk trailed off and they ate in uncomfortable silence.

'So,' Cain said to break it, 'we still don't know what you're doing. What's the tower for? What's this "Baby" thing on the chairs? And who's this?' He pointed to a framed photo on the cooking alcove wall showing an impressive man wearing a naval commander's uniform. The caption read: 'Kapitänleutnant Martin Dietrich, commander of L.22 and L.42.'

'Dietrich?' Reilly exploded. 'One of the *greats*.'

'So what did he do?'

'What didn't he?' The man's bombast revealed everything but facts. 'Martin Dietrich — the World War One Zeppelin commander.'

The pope's lopsided smile. 'That construction outside is for ... an airship?'

'It's a docking mast for Baby. She's circling the world via the poles. Surely you've heard?'

Cain scratched his head. 'Baby's a blimp?'

Reilly stiffened at the slur and his Greek chorus darkly muttered. Cain had once suffered a like reaction when he'd called an enthusiast's model railway a 'train set'. 'She's not a rubber cow. She's a *ship*. Rigid frame, high-tech, high gross gas cell volume. Internal cabin. Bow thruster. Carbon fibre construction. Vectoring ducted propellers. Latest diesel rotary engines. Fibre optic fly-by-wire. Computer-assisted stabilisation ...'

'Then why does she need to land here?'

'It's difficult for an airship over the poles. The altitude. The cold. Need a ground crew standing by. We'll top up her helium, her fuel. She's stripped down for the flight. No showers or amenities on board. Water's heavy, used mainly for ballast and 40 per cent antifreeze, of course. And their galley's just a cook-top. So we've got everything they need.'

'And who's Patrick Flynn?' Hunt said.

'Well may you ask, dear lady,' Reilly, charmed by her beauty, was delighted to digress. 'As you might know, the old country's now reversed the diaspora. The wild geese are flying home. New tax breaks. The wooing of high-tech industry. And when Flynn moved his company to Dublin, he became our greatest software genius.'

'And his hobby's airships?' Cain asked.

'*Hobby*? Good God, man. *Crusade*!'

He'd blotted his copybook again.

'The twenty-first century will be the century of the airship. And with luck, you might have the privilege of seeing Baby tomorrow. That's if wind-speed's below 30 knots so she can dock. But our base met officer's forecasting over 60. We might have flogged ourselves ragged for nothing, mightn't we, lads?'

His men made a disappointed sound.

'Still,' he slapped his knee, 'we shall see.'

Cain was hoping for a whiteout or blizzard. Anything to stop the choppers coming in.

50

BABY

It began as a distant drone unlike the sound of a conventional aircraft. Far across the snow at the docking tower, the ground crew gave a ragged cheer.

To avoid further alarming their hosts, Cain and Hunt hung the M–4s by their combat straps beneath their parkas and placed the remaining mags in inside pockets. Then they went out to see the ship arrive. It looked enormous, even from a distance, upper half white, lower red. And for a long time it seemed to hang static in the sky. But it steadily came closer, holding just below the cloud cover, crabbing into the crosswind, fighting drift.

Even the pope came out to watch. As he shuffled over to join them Cain was relieved to see he wore full Antarctic kit.

They left the encampment, taking the priest's arms to help him along, and followed the blizz line to the tower. The old man was as thrilled as the ground crew. 'What a magnificent sight.'

Had the weather been better, it would have been spectacular — a majestic craft with sun glinting off its hide, its great height and length set off against the blue. But the sky was grey and visibility decreasing.

'I'll try and get you on board it,' Cain told the pope. 'If EXIT attacks us, they'll kill you.'

'I've had my life,' John puffed.

'That's all very well. But you can't even get your breath. Your legs are bad. You're hurting. And I want you out of here.'

The giant shape approached, losing altitude.

Hunt said, 'It's enormous.'

Its size and slowness gave the impression of absolute calm and lack of haste.

As it made a slow sweep around to come up into the wind they could see its features clearly. The line of windows in the lower side. The protruding half-gondola near the nose. The vectored thrust engines on outriggers with their propellers in circular ducts. The side thrusters and, at the stern, huge rudders and elevators.

Ropes were dangled, ballast vented and a tricycle undercarriage lowered from the belly that had incongruous swivelling wheels. Almost immediately it was retracted as if they'd decided it was too dangerous to land. This had to be the vulnerable time — the great shape a wind trap, at the mercy of gusts and turbulence.

Reilly, standing near the tower, yelled commands into a field radio and gave signals to his men who lumbered after the ropes. Soon the thing hung above them like a cloud, the ribs of its frame clearly defined through its envelope.

As its low-revving main engines ticked over, the bow thruster roared. Slowly the great cigar approached until the connection on the front of its nose mated with the cup device on the tower. As clamps closed and the nose was secured, the whine of the bow thruster died.

But in the blustery wind, the tail began to lift. The ground crew hauled on the ropes like ants while the big rear thrusters swivelled on their outriggers until their ducts were almost vertical, the props inside them facing down, correcting aerostatic lift with dynamic. Slowly the ship levelled again.

Then a wind-shift buffeted the envelope and it began to swing. Two of the crew on the ropes were dragged in an arc across the snow. The strong tower's guy-wires snapped taut on the windward side.

Cain watched uneasily. The engines still ran. Could they feather the big props? He didn't know. The ship swung around its mast. Hoses with end couplings dropped from the belly.

Reilly called instructions through a megaphone. 'Ease her. Connect fuel and gas lines.'

In the thin air, the undermanned, exhausted ground crew fought to service the ponderous ship. Someone on the supply sled had the compressor going. Others pulled hoses towards the connections dragging through the snow.

Through an open hatch underneath, a winch lowered a man to the ground. He unhooked as a quad bike hauling a sled full of webbing-cinched stores arrived under the craft. A man on the sled loaded the hook with stores and the first consignment went up. A tag fluttering on each batch probably listed the weight.

The hook descended again with a second crew member. The airship now swung sluggishly, making the transfer harder.

The two men who had alighted crossed to Reilly, spoke for a minute. Reilly pointed at Cain. One headed over to him.

'Bit brisk.' The words became mist in front of his face. He held out a mitten to Cain. 'Ken Duckworth. Second Officer. Or First Mate if you prefer.' He was a plummy Brit with a nasal drawl that, unlike Rhonda's, seemed more practised than innate. The thin face behind the glare-glasses featured a long iced moustache. 'I gather you're from some dreadful covert outfit.'

'Yes. Ray Cain. Registered assassin.'

Duckworth's uneasy look. 'I'm told some of our blokes have bought it.'

Cain winced at the ancient expression. Did the flake think he was Biggles? 'Three.'

'And I believe you killed the prats who did it.'

'My job.'

'And now you want our help?'

He pointed to Hunt. 'We're both fit enough to stay here. But this man needs to go with you.' He indicated John. 'He's eighty. Can't handle the altitude.'

'Oh yes?' He was suddenly uninterested, a person put-upon. 'We have strict weight limits unfortunately.'

John put his glove on Cain's arm. 'I'll be all right.' A fit of gasping.

Duckworth said, 'Who are you, sir?'

John wheezed, 'A Catholic priest.'

'Priest?' Duckworth frowned. 'Have to confer with the Old Man on this.'

As the other man came over, Duckworth turned to face him. 'Spot of bother here, Skipper. Eighty-year-old Catholic priest requesting a berth.'

'Priest?'

'This is Captain Patrick Flynn,' Duckworth said. 'You are ...'

Cain suffered introductions. 'Ray Cain. Karen Hunt. Father John.'

Flynn, a tall, keen-eyed Irishman, in contrast to his second officer gave no display of self-image. He looked at the pope suspiciously. 'Could I trouble you to remove your face mask, Father?'

The pope struggled to do it.

Cain helped him get it off then undid the neck of his windsuit, got his finger around a chain, pulled out the crucifix he knew it held. 'He *is* a priest.'

John lowered his goggles and squinted against the glare.

Flynn peered at the aged face with a startled expression. 'And what would a priest be doing at this place you came from?'

'He was abducted for political reasons,' Cain said. 'He managed to escape.'

'I'd like to hear it from the father if you don't mind.'

'I was a cardinal in the Vatican.' John pushed the crucifix back in, breathing hard. 'They wanted me removed.'

Flynn's incredulous stare. 'And did they, by any chance, pretend — you'd died?'

'They did, I'm afraid. I'm told my funeral was quite elaborate.'

'I can't believe this.'

Duckworth glanced at Flynn, puzzled.

'My dear mother, God bless her,' Flynn explained, fighting for breath himself, 'is devout. Was in Rome for the coronation of John Paul I. Had tremendous hope in his pontificate, couldn't believe it when he died. Still has pictures of him in her house after all these years — pictures I've seen a hundred times. And ... when you took your face mask off ... I ... saw ... those pictures.'

That's torn it, Cain thought.

John looked at him for permission.

He said, 'Your call.'

The pope turned to Flynn, nodded.

'You're ...'

'God's postman, yes.'

'The ... Holy Father?'

'Albino Luciani, Patriarch of Venice. Then I drew the short straw.'

Duckworth's eyes popped. 'He's the pope?'

'My friend is right,' John gasped. 'I won't last much longer here. I don't wish to be a pest but if you could ... give me a lift out of this ... beautiful terrible place, I'd be grateful.'

Flynn dropped to his knees and grasped the pope's glove. John blessed him.

Cain muttered, 'Lid's off now.'

'I'm tired, Ray. I can't take much more.'

Flynn was up again, eyes wide with reverence. 'We'll get

him straight into the ship. We're not pressurised but we have oxygen.'

As they began to help him away, John turned back to Cain. 'Can you bring my manuscript, my things?'

'Travelling.' Glad and relieved, he shuffled toward the vans.

By the time Cain and Hunt saw the bag with the precious manuscript winched up, the weather was closing in. The more distant men in the team were intermittently obscured by ground drift. Visibility here was decided by the amount of blowing snow. The ship seemed fuelled but helium hoses still dangled. The last of the canvas bags were assembled below the hatch.

Cain said, 'One problem less.' Fine drift blew in his mouth as he spoke.

'Long as they don't know he's on board.'

'We'll have to slot the bodies so there's no head-count.'

'Too late. Listen.'

The noise of the airship's engines had been joined by a far-off *thock-thock*.

He yelled across to Reilly, 'Chopper coming in. It'll be EXIT. Tell your men to take cover.'

He wrenched at his heavily padded parka to get his weapon clear and ran for the supply sledge, wanting to steady the gun on its tray. He could see nothing yet. Just the airship floating above a white sea.

The striped Sikorsky came arcing over about 15 metres up, its downwash cutting a saucer of clear ground through the drift. It circled the airship at a distance, as if instructed not to impede the expedition. In a civil aircraft with no close support, and in such weather, he knew the hard-arses in the cabin wouldn't hang out of doors or rappel. The machine slapped off toward the encampment, checking the layout below.

Hunt joined him behind the sledge, gun out, yelling, 'Come back, bastards.'

She knew what to do if they got lucky.

EXIT choppers weren't designed for engagements or fancy insertions — had no Kevlar seat armour, boron shields, blast barriers. Apart from military style auxiliary tanks, due to procurement rather than defence, they were standard machines adapted for Antarctica.

Cain yelled, 'It's coming around again.'

The chopper, undercarriage down, still in clear sky above the drift, circled away from the encampment and back behind the ship. As it banked into a turn, close above, its belly momentarily faced them.

Their bursts were aimed behind the black and orange striped nose at the vulnerable spot just aft of the nose-wheel bay. If just one 9mm round holed the floor — and the pilot's gluteus maximus ...

Nothing.

The chopper straightened out and powered away, nose down, over the parked traverse.

Hunt stamped. 'Shit. Was sure I'd hit it.'

Cain waved a chilled hand. 'No stuffed panda.'

Not surprising. They were both excellent shots but this was similar to shooting skeet. A split-second window at a moving target. And the squat weapons were made for close combat.

He said, 'Short barrels — short expectations.'

'So they've checked the layout. They'll know they've been strafed. They'll land away in the drift and use the weather as cover to close in.'

'And we're drinking from a fire hose.'

Then they heard it.

If the crunch was a landing, the main blades had landed first.

A gust? Miscalculation? He doubted it.

The pilot had been hit — but had got the thing down.

Just.

The jubilant Hunt turned to him. 'Scored our panda. And it's stuffed!'

'Sounded expensive,' he grinned.

She yipped, 'First blood.'

51

FIREFIGHT

No encouraging explosion came. All they'd heard was the impact and the engines cutting out.

He said, 'Bad bend. But they'll be alive.'

He panted over to the flabbergasted Reilly who crouched behind the sledge near two of his men. 'Sorry. You're in a war. But the chopper's scrap. So if you uncouple those hoses and get the ship off, it's safe.'

Reilly grabbed the field radio, contacted the ship, called back. 'The skipper won't take off without Duckworth and Snodgrass.'

'Where are they?'

'Went to the bunk van to freshen up.'

'Then call them up.'

'They didn't take a handset.'

'Christ! Where's the quad then?'

'They rode it over there.'

'Hell.' He waved to Hunt who was covering the blizz line, filled her in. 'We've got to get back to the vans.'

'But we'll be heading straight for Zuiden's squad.'

'Tough.' He shuffled along the blizz line. 'Come on. We're dead anyway.'

'Is there a point to this?'

'I'm trying to save the old man.'

'First, you tell me to wet-nurse bastards who try to torture me to death. Now you want me to be a Catholic martyr?'

'Right. St Karen of Antarctica.'

'You're obsessed.'

'Quit belly-aching, soldier. After you cop a few rounds, you won't feel much.'

They worked out whistle signals on the trot. Visibility was now down to metres. The blizz line vanished before the next pole appeared as if veiled by gauze.

The sound of generators now. Through the swirling curtain, the first sledge loomed. They walked to its end past snow piled against its runners, plunged into whiteness, alert for any dark smudge that could be the approaching squad, cursing the ice on their goggles that made a wide field of vision impossible.

Their dead-reckoning plunge took them to the next line of parked vans. The bunk van was the second. The quad was at the foot of its steps, coupled to a small, now empty sled.

'Okay. You're holding the fort.' He left her crouched behind the bike and went up into the van.

Duckworth, all high shoulders and hanging testicles, was drying himself after his shower.

'We're being attacked,' Cain told him.

'My God! Thought I heard something.'

'You've got to get back to the ship and get airborne before they wreck it.' He dragged his goggles off to clean them, grateful for warmth on his hands.

The small dumpy second man had to be Snodgrass. He was pulling on his polar fleece. The crotch of his oversized thermal underwear hung near his knees. He said in a Midlands accent, 'We'd better slip our cable.'

Trust the Brits, Cain thought, to take their monthly wash at the least strategic time.

Duckworth grabbed his long johns. 'Who are these people?'

'Squad from EXIT. And if you don't pull your finger out, they'll gut you.'

'Gawd. Where are the others, Snodders?' Duckworth asked the smaller man, his drooping accent proving him a victim of the English caste system which Cain detested as much as the relic hobbling India.

'Sparks is still on board, sir. And the chief's checking trim and fuel weights with the skipper.'

A burst of fire from outside. Hunt — having a hard day at the office.

The two men exchanged frightened glances.

Cain said, 'I'll hold them off. Come out when I tell you, then get on that bike and go.'

When he cleared the cold porch, Hunt was still flattened behind the quad. He gave the whistle they'd agreed on. She didn't look around, put one hand half up to halt him. He listened, trying to stay alert. The blowing snow deadened sound and the generators had become white noise.

Once the rush would have clicked him into the drill. Now weary, breathless, weakened, he was an easy mark. His stiff, exhausted body just wanted to lie down. But the opposition, he knew, would be fighting the same disorientation as hypoxia starved their muscles and brains.

Still, they'd be fresher, well equipped. If they had a thermal imager he was sushi.

He glanced at Hunt, then up. Zero visibility. Nothing. Just the continent trying to kill them. He'd heard that tank commanders sometimes fell asleep between shots. You're drifting he told himself. Get with it.

Without food you'll perish in 30 days.

Without water you'll perish in three days.

Without oxygen you'll perish in three minutes.

Without the will to survive you'll perish in three seconds.

Hunt still crouched immobile, her yellow gear looking grey. In the grim world they now inhabited, colours faded with distance. Safer to attack than slug it out in one place. He gestured to her for a sitrep.

Her left arm went out. There was someone on that side and she was ordering a flanking move.

He edged back along the van, climbed over the rail, dropped and worked his way around the sledges. Now the skin was creeping on the back of his neck. Was Zuiden stalking him from behind? He had his hood down now, head protected by the balaclava only. He needed full vision, needed to attack before he froze.

Halfway along the second sledge, a smudge — as if the far runner had melted out on the snow. As he watched, it moved.

Then his vision became a green blur.

He fired, using the residual sight-picture, lurched back against the sledge, trying a roll.

Shoot and scoot.

But he was useless, blinded.

The green dazzle faded. Would he ever see again? Or had his goggles and the snow chopped the frequency? He blinked, helpless. Christ, his eyes!

A laser rifle.

Why not just kill him?

Some vision came back. The same smudge near the runner. When in doubt, empty your mag. He fired again.

Fighting the moment of shock, he moved forward, hugging the sledge. He was almost on top of the man before he could see what he'd done.

The surgeon was face down. On the back of his pile jacket, a perforation extended from mid-chest to neck.

Cain kicked him over, yanked off his goggles. Not Zuiden. The face lacked half a jaw and the wide eyes were silting with snow. He'd done his second-last mag on the sod.

He examined the laser pistol. The man had an Ingram, too. So why the hell hadn't he used it? He changed the mag on the M–4, slung the Ingram around him as well, ripped the mag pouch off the man's lower leg and wrapped its Velcro tabs tightly around his own where its jungle camo pattern stood out like a stop sign. Both guns were chambered for 9mm but the mags were different. No time for frigging around. Zuiden could be steps away and ready to give him a tracheotomy.

He waited, checking rear and side.

Nothing.

Whiteness.

He held his glove at arm's length from his face, testing his eyes. It wasn't just his vision. The blizz was worse. Although the wind wasn't strong, probing snow flew everywhere. The engagement was becoming a lottery in which the only thing that mattered was misfortune.

A burst to his right. It sounded like Hunt. Adrenaline, as combat instructors indelicately put it, would now be running down her leg.

He edged around the second sled, goggles riming, could see almost nothing ahead. Just the nearest runner and the vanishing lip of the tray. She'd be ahead of him now in the swirling grey. Where was her target?

Laser guns? Made no sense.

He moved ahead very slowly, knowing she might shoot him. The one thing more accurate than incoming enemy fire was incoming friendly fire. He gave the low whistle again.

An answer with the right note pattern. Crude but practical. He got past the first sledge runner, squirmed under the tray and waited.

Nothing.

His body was shutting down and his starved drifting mind told him he was a restless wandering ghost, a fugitive like his namesake in the Bible. Told him he was a shot-up relic being hunted by a Grade Three assassin. Bailed up in the world's worst environment with a femme dyke he felt sorry for. And trying to save the life of the 263rd pope ... And that it didn't come crazier than this.

He now had the M–4's stock unfolded and the stub barrel above the lip of the runner shoe. Without the protective overmitts, his gloved hands were turning to ice. He stared along the rudimentary sights.

Zuiden. Could he cream the sod?

Then — another break.

Bunny boots.

Yellow bunny boots padding past the runner — right in front of his face.

They stopped. The man was stooping to check under the sledge.

Cain waited till his pelvis was in sight and hit him with a burst.

A bellow. The surgeon crumpled, thudded on the snow, his gun bouncing on his chest, writhed, kicked. Cain riddled him and stopped it.

It didn't look like Zuiden and he had no energy to check.

A whistle.

He returned the signal, crawled to the back of the sledge, saw nothing, got out from under, retreated back to the bunk van and climbed up.

Nothing all the way.

A cocoon of nothing.

How many more were hidden in this soup?

He edged to the front of the container. Hunt was still just visible in position behind the quad. She'd heard him coming, briefly turned. He pointed to the van, then the four-wheel bike, flung his arm wide.

She acknowledged.

He went in, gave the pair their marching orders. 'You two on the bike. The two of us on the sled. Head straight along the sledges, then veer right and look for the blizz line. Go.'

The two crewmen got in position on seat and rear rack of the bike. Cain and Hunt kneeled in the sled, covering opposite sides, ready to fire.

The single cylinder four-stroke started.

No attack.

They churned to the end of the last line of sledges and

headed into limbo. Duckworth, steering — hands and face freezing — put the 250-kilogram vehicle into a slide that almost capsized them.

Cain cursed, 'Slow up,' and clung to the lip of the sled. Where was the bleeding blizz line? If they. . . .

It was wrapped around Duckworth's waist.

He freed himself, swung them left, headed through the void. Except for the slender line on their right, vision was nil. The bike's high-flotation tyres sprayed the sled with snow. As they approached the tower, they heard, above the racket of the quad, the welcome sound of engines from the ship.

Duckworth stopped them at the foot of the tower, which vanished up into nothing. Reilly, still crouched by his radio, pointed toward the noise. Duckworth turned the bike and went forward in low gear until the darker smear of the ship curved down to hang above them.

They reached the hatch, a shuddering lighter square in its belly with a crewman peering down. The winch-line hung from it, a metal triangle attached to the hook. Duckworth killed the bike, got his foot on the metal stirrup, grasped the wire and was hauled up.

Cain stood back to back with Hunt, gauntlets still off. His body was sluggish with cold and his hands felt like dead meat. Swirling snow and droning engines.

Last act, he thought.

The wire came down again and Snodgrass stepped into the stirrup.

Hunt pointed to the pouch on his leg. 'Got more nails?'

'Wrong mags.' He gave her the half-used mag from his Spectre, tossed the gun and got ready with the Ingram.

They stood back to back, ready to engage.

Flynn's face staring down, a handset held near his mouth. 'What's happening?'

Cain called, 'They're not after your men. They're after us and the pope.'

'Merciful heavens.' Although Snodgrass was on board, he was letting the cable down again. 'You'd better come up.'

Cain sent Hunt first.

Sporadic amplified crew-calls from above.

'Switching to manual.'

'Buoyancy?'

'Equilibrium.'

'Flippers?'

'Elevators neutral and stern ballast control standing by.'

Hunt was up there and the cable coming down.

'Clear away aft.'

'Reporting clear.'

'And reverse thrust.'

'Slow astern.'

'Release clamps.'

'Ten. Twenty. Forty.'

'Bow thruster and half left rudder.'

As he got his own foot in the stirrup, the shuddering above him ceased and the solid ice beneath him fell away. The huge envelope, no longer moored, was drifting astern and rising.

Flickers below. The surgeons had reached the tower, were firing up at the ship. Then he was too high to see anything but whiteness and the welcoming square of light above.

'Clear.'

'Forward thrust. Up ship.'

'Twelve degrees.'

He was winched from the freezing slipstream into the bay. The hatch beneath him shut.

Calm — and the low-revving engines' now muffled drone.

He stepped onto the vibrating floor of a cargo hold with surprisingly vertical walls and central carbon fibre web-struts travelling through floor and ceiling. Pallets secured at the rear. Doors fore and aft. Warm air wafting through floor vents. His ears popped. He felt light-headed.

Hunt stood in snow slush, holding onto a strut, her hood, mask, goggles off. She looked bushed and he wasn't much better, couldn't coordinate his movements.

Flynn said, 'Welcome to Baby.'

'You can say that again.' He felt a sense of expansion, freedom. Oxygen deficiency? The symptoms were lack of self-criticism, euphoria. 'They were firing up at us. You could have holes.'

A wave of frozen air as Snodgrass and two other men came through the rear door. They wore portable oxygen sets with small nose-masks.

Flynn said, 'Keel officer and sparks — on damage control. You're checking cells for bullet-holes.' Snodgrass and one man went back out through the aft door. Flynn said to the remaining crewman, 'Chief, sort these stowaways, will you. I'll be on the flight deck.' He hurried forward.

Cain presumed the remaining man was the airship's engineer, asked him, 'Will we lose much gas?'

'No. It's not under any pressure. We're not bothered by small arms fire. And we carry instant patches. The hard part's crawling around the catwalks and the frame in freezer suits.' He hung his parka on a hook. 'You're going to need breathing gear. Get your kit off and come into the saloon.'

Hunt tried to shed her outer gear, too exhausted to work the zips and tabs. She said, 'I've died and gone to heaven.'

The chief said, 'Yes, Baby's very comfortable — until she hits a storm.'

Cain dragged his gloves off to check his hands. Anything was better than the ice.

52

STORM WARNING

They struggled up the sloping deck toward the door ahead, grabbing for the wall-rails as the ship began to roll.

Hunt's exquisite face, fine-drawn now and sallow, looked more than saintly enough for what she'd done. Cain decided she was quite a woman. She said, 'Does our moving around affect things?'

'Not when we cruise under power,' the engineer told her. 'The computer compensates for weight-shifts.'

'I think I'm going to chuck.'

'Means you're seasick. This isn't a plane. It's a high-performance ship — same roll and pitch.'

The expansive saloon, probably designed for tourist travel, was stripped, utilitarian. Rime-rimmed windows flanking it revealed slowly drifting cloud. Although it wasn't cold, Cain panted, starving for air. He lurched between alloy work benches used for mechanical and electronic repairs then got to a broad area, bare except for six canvas chairs. They were on braked swivel-mounts and positioned either side of a low table. A mural on the forward bulkhead showed a duck, rooster and a sheep. Its significance escaped him. Stairs rose to a second deck.

The pope was strapped in a chair, breathing mask on, air bottle on his chest. As he raised a hand in greeting, the hull shuddered as if hit by a gust from the side. Hunt staggered, fell into a chair.

'We're climbing,' the engineer said, 'and you're a minute away from mental shut-down.' He got AVIOX sets from a locker and showed them how to put them on.

As Cain took deep breaths, he felt his mind start to function again. 'The Resurrection of the Body.'

The pope nodded. 'Wonderful just to breathe.'

A change in the tone of the engines.

'Have to go,' the chief announced. 'Belt up.' He left by the stern door.

The hull lurched again, tail swaying, gave a stomach-dislodging bounce.

'Oh God.' Hunt scrambled for something to be sick in.

Slowly they came back on course. Cain, thankful for the AVIOX, just wanted to flop, to sleep. He listened to the unobtrusive engine drone, felt the sluggish movement.

Hunt stared into a bag she'd found in the back of her chair. 'They'll radio Alpha, track us.'

'But they'll need their other chopper,' he said, 'to get the bodies and their squad back. So they can't come after us yet.'

'They'll still catch us up. This thing's so slow.'

'But it has huge endurance — because it doesn't have to hold itself up. So once we're out to sea, the chopper's stuffed.'

'We're still a long way from ...' She gagged.

The pope said, 'The toilet's upstairs.'

She unbelted and headed for it.

The rolling was less now and they'd levelled off. Cain unbuckled and limped to the forward door, wanting to find out their heading.

The flight deck was in a pod that projected like a half-gondola. It was surprisingly quiet and a mixture of old and new. It had work stations for comms, nav and two forward seats for the pilots. Through the big windows he saw a flotilla of approaching storm clouds. Handling-lines dangled from the nose of the craft which curved above them far ahead.

Flynn and Duckworth sat up front in World War II bomber pilot-style masks that covered their noses and mouths. Glowing displays in front of them showed multiple readouts for airspeed, rate of climb, altitude, pitch, yaw, roll. These were flanked by simple flight instruments that might have come from a light plane — artificial horizon, turn and bank ... An overhead panel appeared devoted to gaseous concerns — humidity, purity, temperature, pressure, altitude, ambient light ...

As he watched, one VDU switched to a skeleton-form of the hull showing numbered frames and longerons outlined in different colours that indicated shear-loads.

Duckworth was flying, if that was the word, threading them between ramparts of clouds that drifted past so slowly the ship seemed barely moving.

Cain asked, 'Can you get above this crud?'

Flynn glanced up from a weather radar display, pulled the mask half off to speak. 'We're considering that now.'

'Is it a problem?'

'Everything's a trade-off. You don't just decide to climb. The higher we go, the more the helium expands. We only have so much cell expansion before we reach pressure height. If we vent, we lose lift when we descend, and have to compensate by dumping ballast. Then sun on the envelope gives a temperature effect. Not as bad as a rubber cow, but significant.'

'Can't you compress the gas back into pressure bottles?'

Flynn shook his head. 'Helium's the hardest gas to compress and the most difficult to liquefy. No one's developed a practical way to conserve helium for airships by repressuring. But we have a limited propane system for heating air inside the envelope.'

'You get lift from hot air too?'

'Not much. It has a third the lift of helium. But we use it to warm the air around the cells and expand the helium when that's needed. But at these temperatures you have to insulate and preheat the tanks.'

'Sounds a whole new world.'

'It is. An airship's unique. It's part plane, part balloon, part ship.'

He watched the ragged clouds ahead as they discussed a multitude of things — diverting around the weather, crosswinds, down-draughts, shear-loading, cubic metres, ice caps, moisture freezing the valves ...

Then Flynn called the damage detail. 'We need to get above the weather. Your situation?'

An intercom cut in. 'Bridge, sparks. Cells two and three affected. Five holes located and patched. Estimated three sites to go. But locating and reaching's a worry. And we're pretty useless now with the cold.'

'Received. We'll be venting anyway. Come back in and get warm.'

Cain clung to a stanchion as they began to climb again. He was surprised to find how slowly the ship responded to the controls. They rose into sun-glare to hang just above a sea of cloud.

Duckworth checked the manometers. Cain could hear his muffled comment. 'Pushing pressure height. Starting to vent.'

Flynn scowled.

'And we're down to 50 knots. The diesels aren't efficient in this thin stuff.'

'Better than bashing her around in the clag.' Flynn punched coordinates into the flight computer. The untended controls gently cycled as the autopilot made fine adjustments.

Duckworth looked at his watch. 'Two more hours of daylight. Then she'll cool.'

'Yes. We can't maintain this at night and we'll need the burners or we'll be dropping too much ballast. But if we can get past this cloud, we're set. The plateau's falling all the time now. ETA?'

'With this wind, fifteen hours.'

'So we'll be over the Brun ice shelf in the morning.'

Cain didn't know the area. 'Where are we heading?'

Flynn glanced back, half-lifted the mask. 'Chile. Our last stop's a mother ship off the shelf.'

It clicked. The icebreaker with the tower he'd seen on the Herc flight down. 'How far to the ship?'

'Around 760 nautical miles.'

He knew the range of the remaining Sikorsky would be around 500. But it could do better with extra tanks, and Alpha could have fuel dumps. 'We could still be attacked with a chopper. They've got one left.'

Flynn said, 'Have to find us first. We look big but our radar signature's small.'

'They'll find us.'

'Maybe. But I can't worry about that now.'

Cain left them to their calculations and retreated to the saloon. Late sun now bathed the deck, turning the bare area into a futuristic stage set.

He asked the pope if Hunt was still upstairs.

'Yes, poor thing.'

'What's up there?'

'A small kitchen and cabins with bunks. Odd to have all this space. Can you believe we're suddenly above it all? Warm. Able to breathe.'

'I know.'

'Life never stops playing with us. I thank you for this, Ray.'

'Just confabbed with the helium-heads. They're taking us to Chile. With luck, I'll get you out of this.'

The old man shook his head. 'Not important. I don't have long to go. My legs, my heart … the thing's worn out. Just look after the manuscript if you can. It's all I ask.'

'I can't lose you yet. I'm still hopeless.'

'Yes. All that thinking, feeling, activity. All that life energy pouring to waste. How to bring the three together so that you ARE? You know, I AM that I AM is the closest statement of the truth. How to BE. But to be NOTHING. Do you see it?'

'The presence of absence?'

'In a way. I have to be completely naked — on the pinions of the wind, as Eckhart put it. The Kingdom of God is within — and for none but the thoroughly dead. But while you struggle with all that, remember the essential first step. Attention connects everything. Be — here — now. Present to your inner life.'

They sat for a long time in silence, listening to the engines' drone. And for the first time in some hours, Cain tried to listen to himself. But despite his best efforts, his mind dragged him back to EXIT.

Vanqua couldn't let them float free.

They'd be attacked.

But how?

And when?

53

DEAD WEIGHT

The chopper never came. They cleared the storm, descended. Cain removed the oxygen gear, found a bunk and tried to sleep.

Lulled by the rolling, he attempted to comfort himself by recalling women he'd known. The gorgeous Rehana. The bony Jojo. The seductive Eve. The remote but explosive Jane. And the warm and loving Pat. Comfort it was not. Three dead. One gone. Only Hunt remained, bent and seasick, two bunks along — his sister who, beside him in the wilderness, had placed his hand between her breasts.

Two crewmen passed the door and soon augmented the drone of the engines with their snores.

He thought no more, slept for hours.

Hunt woke him. 'We're over the shelf.'

There was a do-it-yourself breakfast on the central table in the saloon — fruit bowl, tureen of steaming porridge, packets of cereal and hot toast.

They now sailed like a stabilised cruise ship in thicker, less turbulent air. Through the sloping windows he saw, no more than a 1000 feet below, fast ice to the horizon. Its brightness filled the cabin with glare. This was the frontier of the continent, a vast sheet that, further out to sea, would calve into tabular bergs. Reflected on the underside of distant clouds a whitish light called iceblink signified that pack ice extended far beyond this petrified terrain.

There were four people around the table. The recovered Hunt, Flynn, the engineer and the pope, resting back in his chair.

Flynn smiled at him tiredly. 'Sleep well?'

He nodded.

'We've seen no other aircraft.'

'So everything okay?'

The chief shrugged. 'Boyle's law could get us yet. We're at the end of our weight/buoyancy trade-off. And you three are extra payload. May have to drop you out to stay afloat.'

'But the weather's still within limits,' Flynn said, 'and we'll dock with the ship in 40 minutes. Then we'll be regassed and over water.'

'And at the mercy of the cyclones that sweep around these latitudes,' the chief dourly added.

Flynn leaned close to Cain, murmured, 'Would the Holy Father care for an apple?'

He wondered why old people were treated as objects — hardly ever addressed directly. It seemed even popes weren't immune. 'Why not ask him?'

'Your Holiness?'

The pope didn't move.

Flynn plucked at his sleeve but the old man just stared through the windows.

Cain leaned forward. 'John?'

The eyes behind the glare glasses hadn't moved.

Flynn respectfully touched his arm again.

The pope slid sideways.

'Oh no.' Hunt got up, felt his neck, waited a moment. 'Nothing. He was just speaking to us.'

Flynn was appalled. 'Terrible. That this should happen here. On my ship. Dear God, my mother will never forgive me.'

Hunt removed the old man's glasses, closed his eyes.

Cain and the engineer carried the body upstairs and laid him on a bunk. When the other had gone, he squatted beside his teacher and sobbed. Then he took the priest's manuscript from his pack, went to the small galley, and hid it behind saucepans in the locker under the stove.

54

SNARE

The Russian icebreaker looked big — at least 10,000 tonnes — and badly maintained, its red hull mottled by rust. The dark water at its stern was being closed by moving ice. The eastern drift could move 80 kilometres a day. There were twin hangars behind the ship's flight deck and enclosed wings projected from the bridge. The raised hydraulic tower abaft the swept-back side-by-side funnels had a glassed-in pod at the top that could have been used for spotting ice leads, although the ship's choppers would be its main scouts. Above the pod, a windsock bellied out. Then a wisp of low cloud obscured the view.

The airship did two more circuits. Cain and Hunt watched from the saloon.

Their next glimpse was closer. They could see the ship's raked bow smashing through pack ice that reared each side of the hull, could see the jagged white clumps fall back and roll to expose fretted, algae-stained bases.

'Thick ice,' Hunt said. 'They must have huge shaft horsepower. I thought they'd be hove-to.'

'Could have to sail into the wind to stop the airship fouling the ship. Why don't we get up front? Be a once-in-a-lifetime sight.'

It was controlled-panic mode in the gondola. Flynn and Duckworth's leisurely flying style had gone. The ship's comms leaked from their cans. 'Baby, bridge. Flight quarters. Green deck. Wind 15 knots, speed three for approach and standing by.'

Flynn acknowledged. 'Ready and inbound on final.'

Duckworth called altitude readings as they closed the stern, drifting toward the tower so slowly they seemed to be hovering against the wind. As they nosed down, the ducted props swivelled on their outriggers. Sailors scrambled for a steel cable dropped to the deck and secured it to a cable hanging from the mast. A man in the tower-top pod directed operations as Flynn eased the nose of his craft back just above the stern.

The cable was winched in and they were drawn toward the top of the mast. The nose dipped unpleasantly once, then mated with the cup. The tethered craft shuddered like an animal trying to get free as they hovered above the chopper pad, fretfully swinging.

Flynn removed his headset, shook hands with Duckworth, elated. 'Made it. Everyone not on station's invited on board for sausage rolls and a hot toddy. Sorry, Ducky. You and keels stay on duty.'

Cain had never been winched to the deck of a moving ship. The damn thing wouldn't stay still. For long moments he dangled above ice rocks that rasped along the hull. As the envelope above him veered and swung him back over the flight deck, the cable dropped him lower with a bounce and a sailor signed him to let go.

He fell to his knees in the centre of the landing circle on a pile of canvas bags that gave as if filled with sand. Red-clad, red-helmeted crewmen beckoned him from a hatch but he waited for Hunt to come down. As she dropped he went to help her up. The insides of his nostrils were freezing but the air was breathable again.

They stood on throbbing deck plates and stared past ice-encrusted railings at endless pack ice.

She slapped frost off her parka. 'That hot toddy sounds good.'

'Let's do it.'

They entered a corridor smelling of fuel oil that ran beside one hangar. Bright-painted spares and tools were clipped to its cream metal walls. As they padded on black rubber beneath a maze of wiring and pipes they heard the hull drum as ice scraped and clanged along the sides. The crew waved them on. He suspected they only spoke Russian.

Through a clipped-back door on the left he got a glimpse inside the hangar. Wheeled cabinets with long red drawers, high shelves with lashed cases, hoses on reels . . .

. . . All mere background to the shock of the chopper.

Black and orange stripes!

The man behind must have seen his reaction.

Cain's head exploded with pain as he was coshed.

55

HIGH DIVE

It looked like the captain's stateroom, was probably high on the deckhouse below the bridge. The curtains of the two small windows were drawn back but it was still a gloomy space — dirty cream paint, dark built-in cabinets, scratched brown-leather chairs, a dartboard on one wall. Cain found it hard to see and the pain between his eyes was splitting his head.

He, Hunt and a burly, bearded man in a seaman's sweater were bound to the legs and arms of the chairs. Two surgeons stood in front of them, disguised in red crew waterproofs but identified by Ingrams fitted with long tubular suppressors.

'You walked into that one, Cain.' Zuiden's grin. 'Thanks for delivering the pope.' He tried to switch on overhead lights. They didn't work.

Cain didn't recognise the second man — broken nose, red hair — probably one of the senior surgeons recalled from assignments around the world. 'Bastards. So what are you waiting for?'

'Vanqua wants a word.' Zuiden's cruel smile. 'That's why we didn't retire you yesterday.'

'Big of you. Where is he?'

'Still at Alpha. I expect he'll tell us to fly you back. Then he's going to ask you some questions while I make sure you talk.'

'Questions?'

The red-haired man was happy to explain. 'Department D files are altered. Things don't square. We want to know what Rhonda set up.'

'Why ask me? I'm out of the loop.'

'You were her crony,' Zuiden said, then pointed to Hunt. 'She was, too. We'll get it out of one of you.'

'Pirates.' The heavily accented voice of the burly seaman. 'What you do with my crew?'

'We're minding them, Captain,' Zuiden said, 'while we collect our property. We've got no beef with your operation.'

'You destroy expedition, dumb shithead.'

'Bullshit. I'm letting your officer of the watch and the airship crew get on with their work.'

'You know half of fuck-all. Bergs to west. Temperature drop. Wind rise. We hit pressure ridge — airship is wreck. I have to be on bridge.'

'Tough.' Zuiden turned to his offsider. 'Watch them. I'm going to call Alpha.' He left.

The carrot-head pulled around the remaining chair and sat facing them, the sub-machine-gun across his knee.

'So how's the genocide tracking?' Cain said.

The man grinned. 'We getting to you, Cain? That's good.'

Cain tested the strength of the old wooden-armed chair. The right arm was slightly loose on its upright but he couldn't do much with that. He looked across at Hunt who was watching for the slightest diversion.

A knock at the quarter-open door. A man's deferential face peered around it and gaped at the trussed form of his captain.

'What the fuck do you want?' The surgeon aimed the Ingram. 'Get in here.'

The crewman came in reluctantly. He carried an electrician's kit and, outside his overalls, wore a belt-pouch holding screwdrivers and wire cutters.

When the surgeon challenged him again, he shrugged as if he didn't speak English. The captain muttered to him in Russian and the surgeon told the captain to shut up, then jerked the gun at the wall. 'Over there.'

The wary crewman placed his tools on the floor and stood against the inboard wall.

The captain drawled on in Russian, ignoring the carrot-head who levelled the gun at him and swore.

The sailor's blink rate rose. The two seamen were up to something. Cain tensed, ready.

Then the crewman snatched a dart from the board behind him and hurled it at the surgeon. He was good — just south of a bull's-eye. The spike flashed across the room and buried itself in the surgeon's right lower eyelid up to the brass.

A roar of pain from the carrot-head as he plucked it from his face, then the crewman was on him, gripping a screwdriver like a dirk.

This was the best it would get.

Cain wrenched the right arm from the chair's front upright and thrust his hand forward until the rope around his wrist slid off the end. He lunged until the chair toppled, grabbed for the tool-box.

Hunt and the captain were yelling.

The Ingram popped. The subsonic round and suppressor made the loudest sound the slap of the bolt.

The crewman staggered against the door, heading for the great dry dock in the sky.

Cain cut his second wrist free with a Stanley knife — expecting to be shot. But the surgeon was on one knee, a screwdriver planted in his belly and a hand to his bloodied eye.

Cain lunged, got his arm inside the gun before the half-blinded, grunting man brought it up. As he shoved it wide, bullets punctured overhead pipes.

Hot steam sprayed down as Cain cut the man's throat.

He retrieved the Ingram, used the dripping blade to slash his ankle bonds then free the others.

The captain lurched up, rubbing his wrists. 'Now we get these shitheads good.'

'How many left?' Cain grabbed the Ingram.

The captain shrugged. 'Eight? Ten maybe?'

Hunt frisked the surgeon and found another clip while the captain unlocked a cabinet and produced a pistol of his own.

Cain checked the Ingram, caught the spare mag tossed by Hunt. He gripped the forward webbing hand-strap that formed a rudimentary fore-grip. 'Okay, I go first. Back me up.'

Hunt's grim smile. 'Dentists forever.'

The outside passage. Clear.

The captain pointed up a ladder. 'Bridge.'

'Has this ship got a chopper?' Cain asked him.

'One. Is taking equipment on contract to scientist at Hally base.'

'So there's just the one helo in the hangars? Theirs?'

'Yes. They make us stow it to hide.'

They entered the chartroom, walked through to the bridge. The setup reminded him of a frigate — two raised chairs with readouts and a miniature engine telegraph between them. One display showed a high-res view of the pack ice ahead, probably coming from a camera on the tower. Two men were taped to the chairs and had tape over their mouths.

The captain muttered, 'Steering station, starboard wing.'

Cain looked along the glassed-in projection. It had a duplicate console at the end where an officer was conning the ship. The surgeon minding him was halfway along the wing, lighting a cigarette. He turned.

Too late.

Cain fired and took him down.

As Hunt retrieved the man's gun, the captain swore with satisfaction and started ripping the tape off the crew. 'Leave you with it,' Hunt said.

The captain nodded, lifted the bridge phone to his ear.

He and Hunt descended the musty creaking levels of the ship, feeling the engine throb, hearing the ice grinding the hull. They inched down a final ladder until they stood on thick black rubber.

He said, 'Looks like the main deck. Machinery spaces below here.'

They grouped at the next corner, covered the new angle fast.

A red-clad figure, Ingram lowered, climbing from an access trunk.

Hunt fired.

The man crumpled against the metal lip.

A dull crack echoed from below. Not a gun. The hull — under stress.

She went forward, kicked the body down the ladder out of sight.

They doubled back along the fore–aft passageway beside the starboard hangar, brushed past a frightened sailor wheeling propane cylinders strapped to a handcart. Loose items in the tool-tray under it shuddered and chattered. The general noise of the ship was giving them cover enough.

At the hangar doorway, they did the one-two entry routine. Just the pilot in there, his back to them, examining the Sikorsky's tail rotor.

Hunt shot him and, when he collapsed, Cain sprayed the tail blades until they splintered then emptied more into the rotor hub and the final drive gearbox.

A yell and firing from the passageway.

Cain was at the door. Too late.

Hunt was down. But she'd drilled the surgeon who'd done it. He lay gut-smacked on the deck, but alive. His second burst sang off the secured-back metal door near Cain's head.

Cain shrank back, held the gun around the edge and sprayed the deck.

A groan let him know it had worked.

He sprang out wide, finished the man, knelt beside the shot-up Hunt. She gazed up, couldn't speak but tried to smile. Her eyes said 'Thanks, brother' before her head fell to the side.

He blanked the pain out. Any distraction now and he died. And that couldn't happen until more of them had paid for this.

He reached the glare at the end hatch. Hoses snaking across the chopper pad were being reeled in. The frowning airship's engineer was directing operations, a two-way to his mouth. The racket of the craft's idling motors and a compressor had drowned any noise they'd made.

He peered around the door-frame. Two surgeons covering the crewmen.

He fired.

Both went down. Frantic crewmen scattered and the engineer hit the deck with fright.

He was in overdrive now, had all the time in the world — total coordination and focus, like a machine.

He wanted Zuiden, whispered, 'Coming for you, bastard.'

He switched mags and edged out on the pad, squinting, saw the movement above him in time — a surprised man with an unsilenced gun leaning over the railing above the hangars.

As he flattened against the frosted shutter, a burst chipped ice from the deck at his feet.

He'd have to expose himself to fire back.

Yes or no?

He instinctively knew it was right because it was desperately wrong. He ran out on the pad, firing up. The range was considerable for an Uzi-sized weapon but he'd always been good at this. And he now felt unassailable.

The two above hadn't thought he'd dare. One shrank back as the second pitched forward to hang over the railing like washing.

Then Cain, still firing, was backing through the disoriented crewmen. He dived over the bags, lay flat.

The tattoo of 9mm rounds.

But the sandbags buried them dead.

Through a gap between the bags he spotted the attacker in the open second hangar, crouching behind cylinders and hardware.

The man saw movement and the second burst came so fast that flying sand stung his face and a slug almost took off his ear. It might have done more. What was going on here? They were cleared to disable him but not to take him out?

Next time he looked, the scene was different. The surgeon in the hangar was face down on the deck. A crewman stood above him holding a wrench.

A bare catwalk above the hangars. For now, the coast was clear.

Terrified crew getting up from the deck and bolting for the safety of the housing. The chief crouching near a hangar door.

Cain glanced at the great shape overhead. The pop-eyed Snodgrass stared down through its hatch.

The engineer ran over, bobbed behind the ballast bags. 'What's happening?'

'They've killed Hunt. I've scrapped their chopper.' He scanned the deckhouse. 'There have to be two more left. Can you take off?'

'Got to. Ship's losing way and getting into thick stuff. If she rides up on the ice, we lose headwind, could foul.'

'Who's still down here from your crew?'

'I'm it.' He barked instructions at the crewmen now cringing at the edge of the pad, then yelled into the handset. Men scurried to uncouple the umbilical cords that still hung from the belly of the craft. The chief pointed to the cable dangling from the hatch. 'You better get aboard before you're shot.'

Cain got astride a hooked-on bag, feeling like a sitting duck, gripped the cable. It tightened as Snodgrass started winching him up.

It was hard to keep a bead on the deckhouse because the bag revolved as it rose. Where was Zuiden? Still in the radio shack? Feeding his face in the galley? On the can again? Cain, waiting to be knee-capped, felt enormous relief as the motor of the overhead winch pulled him inside the airship's bay. He got off, shoved the bag to the side and Snodgrass sent the cable back down.

'Flight deck, Chief.' The engineer's voice crackled from a speaker on the flimsy wall. 'Forget the rest. Ship reports thick ice with pressure ridges ahead. Have to slip our cable in five or we'll be jarred or swing. Got to get off now. They'll need to back and charge.'

'Flight deck. Have bridge report but not happy with equilibrium.'

Snodgrass got his mouth to the wall mike. 'Chief, keel. Ride another bag as you come up.'

Cain stared down through the hatch, gun ready, as the foreshortened figure of the chief snapped the link onto a bag and sat astride it. A burst of fire. He toppled off the ballast, staring up at them, mouth wide.

Men climbing on the bags, firing up.

The aluminium floor beneath the rigger helping Snodgrass became ragged perforations. The rigger made a hissing sound, pitched forward through the hatch.

As the two surgeons below scattered from beneath the falling body, Cain pumped his last two rounds into one of them, then rolled back and climbed on the one bag in the cargo bay that hadn't been emptied into a hopper.

'Are our guns still here?' Cain yelled.

Snodgrass, flattened against the wall, yelled back, 'They took them.' He shouted into the intercom, 'Skipper, keel. They've killed the chief and sparks and they're trying to hijack the ship. Release clamps now. Get her up.'

Another burst from below.

Were they shooting at the gondola?

'Acknowledge, keel. Equilibrium dicey.'

'Bollocks to that. Release clamps. They're chopping us to bits. Use the motors, flippers, anything. Get her *up*.'

Cain had nothing more to fire. It meant the men below would know he was out.

A klaxon sounded.

The airship's shuddering stopped.

'About bloody time,' Snodgrass swore.

There were no windows in the bay and it wasn't safe to be near the hatch so Cain could see nothing. If they hit the ice they were done. At least there was no more firing. And he was certain he knew why.

They waited long seconds as the stern of the craft rose crazily before the droning engines slowly pulled it down.

'Keel, bridge. What's hanging?'

'Ballast bag,' Snodgrass answered.

'Get it up or we could foul on the pack.'

Cain shook his head. 'Bad move.'

The floor tilted as the tail swung down.

Snodgrass said, 'Got to do it, laddie.'

He inched forward, hit the handle of the winch. The cable started to wind back into the overhead reel.

Cain picked up a pile of cargo webbing, waited.

Zuiden's frozen head and the muzzle of his Ingram appeared above the lip of the hatch ...

... as Cain threw.

It didn't stop the surgeon winging Snodgrass but did the job. After that slipstream, that wind chill, Zuiden's instant reactions were gone.

The surgeon swung snarling, trying to see through crusted lids.

Cain kicked him in the face, grabbed the gun and forced it down until the stub barrel pointed at the ice. Then he jammed his thumb on Zuiden's trigger-finger, riddling the bag, trying to shoot off the man's boot. A foot for a foot. Zuiden wasn't high enough to fight. With his right arm pinned and forced to hang on with the other, he could barely avoid the stream of fire.

Cain missed the boot but emptied the gun. Sand poured from the shot-up canvas bag.

The airship was lifting, lifting. A glimpse of the ship, a big toy below. The air washing into the hatch — utterly, unbearably cold.

Cain staggered back, hit the winch control.

Zuiden dropped out of sight.

He stopped the winch when the man hung 30 feet down and 500 feet above the ice.

As the craft churned through icy gusts, Zuiden freed himself from the net. He could do nothing more, just dangled, options gone, his furious face glaring up.

Snodgrass was cursing on the floor. It was a shoulder hit and he'd live.

Cain stared down from the hatch, watching the cable swinging astern, watching the surgeon Grade Three freeze.

Cain and Disable.

Now Disable was disabled. If he had another magazine he couldn't use it because the bag was going slack beneath him, and he needed both hands to hang on.

Zuiden had two choices — become an iceman or drop and get it over.

This was for Ron, he thought. For Hunt. For the dentists they'd shafted — an event he had to witness for them all.

Zuiden stared up, his encrusting face and clothing turning solid.

Cain remembered when they were young. When Zuiden had left him down a crevasse. Left him to die. Cost him three toes. Remembered Zuiden in the tent — sneering and raising his finger.

Cain raised a finger, slowly.

The freezing man grimaced back, then deliberately let go of the cable.

Cain watched him fall, was forced to smile and shake his head with admiration. Zuiden had assumed the skydiver's arch position — chest forward, arms back, aerodynamically stable and face down. The big-dick bastard was still proving he was top banana — putting the last touch to his legend. The supreme sensory-overload buzz.

Cain waited the brief seconds until the star-shape smacked high-speed ice.

'Bet you shat yourself, Jan,' he said.

He winched the slack bag up.

56

LANDFALL

With only two of the original crew left, the flight became forced labour. Furious side winds and turbulence obliged them to change height to minimise drift, which meant trading off lift against weight. Once, they descended low enough to trail a hose in the sea and pumped up water for extra ballast.

When they could, Flynn and Duckworth alternated in the gondola to work the rest of the ship. Cain became apprentice rigger and chief bottle-washer to the experts.

He spent hours outside the cabin in the half-light of the pitching, rolling envelope, freezing on the narrow catwalk above the spine of the carbon-tubed hull. He climbed high on spidery structures that surrounded the hose-entangled gas cells, wiggled past bracing cables to pass on patches and tools or de-ice valves.

He was shown how to operate pumps, how to free blocks in toggled hoppers, how to check inboard fuel and oil reservoirs and the exhaust water recovery system. He had to monitor the servo-turned worm gears that operated the huge control surfaces at the stern and check for ice on the outrigger gears that swivelled the propulsion ducts.

During rewarming time, he acted as steward and tended the bandaged Snodgrass. The bullet had gone through but the concern was infection. He used all the antibiotic powder but the keel officer steadily got worse.

At night he checked the systems in the hull's dark and lofty tomb, red-eyed, exhausted, unsteadied by the sluggish yaw and pitch, trying not to fall through the flimsy fabric to the wild sea far below.

They docked at the edge of the Punta Arenas airport in the still air of a pewter-coloured dawn. The tower was a converted mobile crane. There was no winching down. They lowered the rudimentary wheels and a ground crew manned the ropes and outside rails.

Flynn had offered to take him on the next leg but he knew it would be no way to thank him, would jeopardise the expedition, that he had to get off. Filthy, unshaven, exhausted, the pope's manuscript safe in his kit, he stepped onto snow-covered grass. His sea legs made the earth rock.

Snodgrass and the shrouded pope's body were carried with great fuss to the ambulance while the groggy but elated Flynn and Duckworth were enveloped by media crews. All attention was on the others as he limped toward the huddled spectators.

He reached the knot of people, too tired to be alert, hoping that EXIT wasn't there — no fight left in him.

Two men in padded windjackets fell in either side of him. He recognised the soft face and sharp eyes of Harry Frost, the CIA physiologist he'd met on the mountain-top in New Zealand. The other man had a thin head with large ears and sucked an unlit pipe. Half a dozen blank-faced men now moved with them, distrustful eyes on the crowd.

'Good morning,' Frost smiled.

'Hi.' He just wanted to sleep.

'Meet Julian Wilson. One of our senior people.'

The man with the pipe nodded. He looked like Special Group.

Cain said, 'Better you than them.'

Wilson's thoughtful expression didn't alter.

'We need a word,' Frost said. 'Got you booked into our hotel. Chance to rest, clean up.'

'Get me there.'

The trip into town was circuitous. Again they weren't taking chances. The four-car convoy detoured through slushy dirt roads past tin shanties with colourful roofs and stove-pipe chimneys, rusting cars and mangy dogs. The inner city's elegant square was surrounded by impressive stone buildings. Machine-gun-toting *carabineros* stood conspicuously on street corners. Frost pointed out features. 'Was an important place before the canal.' He could have done without the city tour.

They reached a hotel with an air of refined decay and escorted him to a room. It had a spa-bath, hot rail and could have been on 56th in New York.

They gave him an hour to fix himself up. He emerged a clean shaved shadow of his former self and the heavies outside his door escorted him to another suite.

'So,' Frost handed him coffee, 'we have the pope. Now we're interested in Stern, the sisters, Nina.'

He took the cup, hand shaking, eyes gritty with tiredness. 'So you knew about Stern and John?'

'We do now.' Wilson tamped his bowl-blackened pipe. 'You two-timers.'

'I just worked there.'

'So who's still alive at Alpha?'

Frost said, 'We need to know what's happened, Ray. Then you can sleep.'

Sleep deprivation was one of the most insidious tortures known. He had no reason to put himself through that, no reason to deceive. So he told them what he knew, which became an outline of the destruction of EXIT, and the two attentive faces became grim. He expected they were recording him but it hardly mattered now.

It took two hours. At the end of it, the part of him still awake was tripping on caffeine.

Frost cleaned his half-frames. 'A great pity about Nina.'

'But Stern's the money-shot for us,' Wilson said. 'Think carefully. Is there a chance he could be alive?'

'Pretty slim.' His eyes kept shutting. 'Look, I'm a threatened species, I'm whacked and I've told you all I know. Now can you guys give me a head start? Or some kind of steer on all this?'

'We're not authorised to assist EXIT personnel. I need hardly tell you that.' Wilson's pipe had gone out a fourth time. He probed it with a match. 'But, if it's any joy, we're flying back via Santiago. I can stretch a point and drop you off. Let you catch a commercial flight from there.'

'Appreciate that.'

'As for advice,' Wilson sucked his teeth, 'you're now Vanqua's favourite target. But if you're still alive in a month, you can kiss his arse goodbye.'

'How come?'

The man deliberated how to put it. The lines of his frown seemed to draw the sides of his skull together while his ears appeared ready to take wing. 'Let's just say he's had his run — but he doesn't know it yet.'

57

EXPECTED GUESTS

Cain didn't understand it. Nothing happened. Nothing at all. His credit cards and fake passports were still accepted everywhere. Santiago airport appeared free of surgeons. He was back in the world of posturing businessmen, agitated mothers, sullen shoppers, mortality-conscious suburbanites and the triumph of TV over tradition.

He flew Easter Island, Tahiti, Auckland, then switched airlines for the Sydney leg. He went first class, craving comfort and faked consideration — much as the hopeless or rejected would gamble, overeat or drink. He sat beside a concert pianist and, on the last leg, the Malaysian foreign minister. He didn't fraternise and comforted himself by studying John's book.

'Aquinas said that, at the deepest level, all things fade into mystery. At a certain level, life brings a wave that communicates joy — to be absorbed then radiated. When you feel that, have that, you are living in supernature — God. It means you deeply existentially are. But how to be? There's no approach because concepts kill it. It's organic — to do with energy-flow — an am-ness defying analysis.'

He chose Sydney rather than Lahore because the politics of a country that had spent half its years under military rule never ceased to depress him. He went to the shack at Bundanoon because wherever he went, they'd find him. And because in a box under its floorboards were weapons he'd need.

The big block of natural bush was unchanged but there was mould on the front verandah. He got the keys back from the neighbour on the other side of the hill and thanked him for watching the place. He switched on power and water. The dusty, musty rooms were as he'd left them.

He selected weapons, cleaned and loaded them. They wouldn't kill him — until they had their information. That gave him an edge. He waited. And he read.

'. . . and the Holy Ghost is always being sent. The greatest force in the world and we simply don't feel it, receive it. It's we who cut ourselves off — deprive ourselves of the Good.'

He remembered something John had said on the plateau days ago. 'The horizontal — life. The vertical — eternity.' He'd slowly made the sign of the cross. 'Our place is where they meet. Don't forget. We need to live both in time and in the space, expansion of the present. The denying force is as real as the affirming.'

'But if God's everything . . .'

'Yes.' The pope had joined his hands. 'In the expansion of manifestation, God becomes the devil. That means his force becomes increasingly automatic. But we're offered choice. To either drift . . . or fight back against the stream like salmon.'

'Fight God to rejoin God? Jacob's ladder?'

'If you wish.'

They came at four on a grey afternoon. None of his detectors went off. He wondered later if they'd monitored him on MDR. The transmitter could detect people through doors, concrete and brick walls.

He'd been in the shed, getting the ladder to clean leaves out of the guttering. Then he saw, through the cobwebbed window, the wrong end of a grenade launcher.

He ducked, turned. Silhouetted in the open garage door, a man holding a contraption with four splayed barrels capped by pods.

Before he could react, he was covered by the sticky net and disabled by the high-voltage pulse.

He hit the concrete, yelling with pain.

'Foam gun's better,' the man remarked, 'except the crud takes hours to remove.'

'Baby oil,' someone else said. 'Comes off with baby oil.'

'Non-lethals. Pain in the arse,' a third man said. 'Fucking rubber-pellet grenades. I signed on to kill. Not frig around.'

Cain remembered them stripping off his shirt.

'Fuck. Look at that. Get it off him.'

They took the breast-cannon and the underarm reverse-holstered pistols from him.

They stripped him to his underpants and taped him to a kitchen chair, then he was lifted like a parcel and put in the living room. They'd taped black plastic over the windows until the place was cellar-dark, then shone a lamp in his eyes.

'Now,' the big one said, 'we wait.'

Cain tried to see beyond the light. Four shapes. The biggest, bearded with curly hair, hulking body movement, pinned back ears.

'Know me?' the man asked. 'I'll clue you. I've had a bit of a make-over.'

'Murchison?'

'Got it in one.' He chuckled. 'We stuffed you lot good.'

A car bouncing up the potholed drive.

The men fell back as a fifth man entered the room. Vanqua's smooth face within the circle of the light — flushed with rage. 'Your turn, Cain.'

'So it seems.'

'Files have been doctored. Identities substituted. And funding for your absent department continues.'

'Encouraging news.'

'I've been sold a pup and don't like it. And you're going to tell me what you know.'

'Nothing.'

'We'll see. You were close to Rhonda. Talk, or we remove parts of you — slowly.'

'It was need-to-know with her. She left me out of the loop — never said anything vital. Now I see why.'

'Not good enough. But if it's true, you're going to wish she had.'

Murchison added, 'You're not our friend, Ray.' He unfurled a pouch on the floor beside Cain's chair. The tools in it were surgical steel. But antisepsis and anaesthetic were not part of the coming procedure. He selected a pair of serrated pliers with inturned, precision-ground tips. It seemed that his nails were to be withdrawn before his fingers were crushed. The cutters in the pouch implied that it went on from there.

'Well?' Vanqua said. 'Where will we start first?'

His gut turned over. He knew it was the end, either way. He hadn't been issued with one of Rhonda's cyanide capsules or the easier to hide sheathed curare-coated needles. He felt he might disgrace himself. He said, 'I don't know a thing.'

The sound of a chopper, a big one, coming fast. Murchison shot a look at Vanqua. 'Us?'

'No.'

Startled looks.

An act? An elaborate deception for his benefit? Otherwise, why cover the windows?

Vanqua said, 'Get out there.'

Murchison and the others dashed outside.

The thing hovering now. It sounded huge — a heavy lifter.

Cain said, 'Is this to impress me?'

The listening Vanqua didn't respond.

'Why the hell did you wreck EXIT, you small-minded, dopey shit?'

Vanqua struck him hard across the face.

Automatic fire.

The surgeon pulled out a Browning high power, hurried from the room.

Cain sat — alone, cold, frightened, puzzled — licking blood from his split lip.

The slapping, whining monster went away.

Sporadic firing.

Then nothing.

He sat.

And sat.

At last, the verandah creaked.

Men burst into the room from both doors, ripped the plastic off the windows, switched off the lamp. They wore black body armour, face masks and sprouted MP5s.

Then Rhonda walked in, holding Vanqua's Browning. Creased dress, dirty nails, straggly hair. She turned to the shock troops. 'Untie him.'

One unsheathed a knife and cut the tapes.

'Ron?'

Was it her — or a magnificent duplicate? Had they staged this to get him to talk?

She said, 'Thank God you're still with us. You know the drill.'

Christ. She wanted him to *verify*? He'd bloody make this good.

She waited, scratched under her breast.

He dragged his wits together. 'Okay. Who said, "Except at Wydecombe Fair in my youth I never saw anything so bad as *Pinafore*"?'

'Disraeli. Proving that the cleverest of men can be utterly wrong.'

The answer astonished him. No duplicate could have known that. But he wasn't quite convinced. He stumbled closer to her, stared. My God, she was the image. He dredged his mind for the most obscure G and S anecdote she'd told him. 'Sullivan said to someone, "Another week's rehearsing with WSG and I should have gone raving mad. I had already ordered..." Complete the sentence.'

'"... some straw for my hair." Yes, it's me.'

'Ronnie? Christ.' He hugged her, felt her big arms enfold him. 'What ...?'

'Long story, dear heart.' She pushed him gently back and handed him the pistol. 'For political reasons, as you're the only good guy around with a Blue Card, I need you to do unto others. They're outside.'

He followed her onto the verandah. Three surgeons were flat on the drive, flies already crawling on their faces. There were three more alive, huddled on the ground — Vanqua, Murchison and a third man.

Murchison cradled a shattered arm. Blood trickled between his fingers. Vanqua looked unharmed but stunned. The third man rocked with pain, hugging his shredded thigh and knee.

Cain stood in his underpants, blood running down his chin, the classic double-action pistol a familiar tool in his hand. He looked back inquiringly at Rhonda.

She nodded. 'The three, if you don't mind.'

He cocked the hammer and walked two paces from the group, aimed at the surgeon he didn't know, put a single 9mm round through his brain. Flecks splattered Murchison's shoulder.

As the man toppled he turned the gun on Murchison. 'For Rehana.' He shot him in the balls. As Murchison sagged forward, grabbing his crotch, Cain plugged him in the top of the head.

Vanqua, next in line, raised his hand in front of the gun, called to Rhonda, 'How did you do this?'

'If we can duplicate world leaders, why not department heads? We had your measure long before you knew.'

'That woman was a duplicate?'

'A brave one. She bought me time. Now certain governments have seen reason and I've blackmailed people, pulled strings. Department D never shut down. You only thought it had.'

He stared at the slit-eyed troopers. 'And where did you scrape up this circus?'

'CIA contra deal.'

'So much for edicts. What did you give them?'

'Stern.'

'You sick deviate. You destroyed the human race — for this?'

'Is your arse cleaner? What about *your* motive?'

'You still don't know?' His look of hatred. 'My sister. You corrupted her.'

Rhonda's eyes slowly widened.

Cain didn't understand.

A terrible sorrow contorted the surgeon's face. His voice when it came was agonised. 'See it now?'

'You're ... Etta's *brother*?'

'You pervert. I damn ... you ... to ... *Hell*.'

Rhonda's face crumpled and she half turned away. 'My God.'

'She killed herself — because she had principles. And what she did with you revolted her.'

'Bull. She was so desperately young she just didn't give herself time to come to terms with her own ...'

'Perverted bitch. She killed herself from shame.'

Rhonda grimaced. 'You'd never understand.' She nodded to Cain.

He couldn't know all that was between them and didn't much care. He said, 'This is for Hunt.' He shot Vanqua cleanly, walked clear.

The squad called the chopper in and the ungainly Sea King landed in his back paddock and shut down. While the troopers unfurled body bags, cleaned the site and loaded the evidence, he sat on the verandah with Rhonda and talked it through. Her expression was almost tragic and she seemed drained by some sadness beyond tears. Eventually, in a low, flat voice, she tried to convince him to return. 'I'm back running the whole catastrophe. Rebuilding's the problem. We've lost so many people. There's no Pat any more. I need you, Ray.'

'I'm thrilled for you. But no.'

'Please come back. I can't run the fucking world by myself.'

'I've had it, Ron. Been years in the front line. I'm not a killing machine. Too old and wrecked now. After this last lot, I'm junk.'

'Things got so grim, there was no way to back you up. As for Karen ...'

'You should have seen her. She was fantastic at the end.'

'Don't.' She screwed up her face.

'We couldn't have made it without her. And she thought you were wonderful — like all of us do. She cared for you, Ron.'

'Don't, love. Please.' She turned her head away. 'Been an ... absolute bugger of a day.'

The troop commander was at the bottom of the steps. 'Area cleaned. Cleared for departure, ma'am. Your call.'

They stood up but Rhonda didn't go, immobilised by some inner anguish. She glared at the weathered floor planks, yanked a skirt-fold from her rump, muttered, 'Most dangerous thing in the world.'

Cain glanced at the puzzled squad commander, turned back to the woman, said gently, 'Ronnie. Better disappear this outfit before the town arrives.'

A tight-lipped nod.

He took her arm and walked her around the back of the house. Her inner turmoil was so great she let him lead her like a child.

She gave him a ferocious rib-cracking hug, then lumbered toward the waiting chopper.

He called, 'Dentists forever.'

She waved but didn't turn around.

EPILOGUE

Cain's health has improved but he still limps. The cache of weapons is unused. He still potters around the property for part of the year, watches the sunset from the verandah, sometimes recalling those who died.

Mostly he travels — expensively, extensively. His relationships come and go.

Rhonda's brazen smoodging got him back to Beta part-time where he remains stubbornly emeritus and is regarded by the staff as a god. He's helped arrange several strategic deaths and substitutions in world leaders, has befriended Princess Di, is sad she won't see her children again. EXIT Alpha has been recommissioned but he hasn't gone back down.

Rhonda is still cryptic about Stern but Cain suspects the scientist developed a mass-sterilisation virus which the CIA is keeping in reserve.

He's considered publishing the pope's manuscript and sending copies to the Vatican. While he frets over what to do with it, he does his best to live as John taught.

Often he remembers the ice — the light, space, solitude, silence — the tumultuous events that are a legend at EXIT now.

His future? Each breath is enough.

An exile only has today.

GLOSSARY

70 Clifton: Address of the fortress-like Bhutto family residence in Karachi at the time of the story.

AC plasma: A high-resolution flat-panel display screen.

AKR: Carbine version of the Russian AK–47 assault rifle — a stubby sub-machine-gun.

ANARE: Australian national Antarctic research expeditions.

Anhedonia: Inability to enjoy oneself.

APU: Auxiliary power unit. Used to drive aircraft systems when main engines are shut down.

AR–80: Assault rifle made in Singapore.

ARA: Airborne radar approach.

ASAP: As soon as possible.

AVIOX: Oxygen equipment.

AWAC: Airborne warning and control system.

Ball: Aircraft carrier's optical landing system. The Fresnel lens emits a light-beam that tells the pilot whether his approach is high or low.

BDA9: Belgian-made automatic pistol.

Bingo: The predetermined amount of fuel needed to return to the place of origin at the same speed. Exceed that fuel level and there is not enough fuel to return and land at the take-off point. On a carrier, landing may require three passes and fuel budgeting is critical.

Bivvy bag: An outdoor sleeping bag.

Blizz line: Hand-lines provided as guidance between buildings or areas in Antarctica, for use during blizzards. A blizzard is classified as a wind greater than 35 knots.

Bolter: When an aircraft lands on a carrier for the arrested recovery or 'trap' it approaches slightly above stall-speed. As the plane hits the deck, the pilot applies full power as he could 'bolter' or fail to catch with the tail hook one of four arresting wires stretched across the deck. If these are missed, there is power to get airborne and go around again.

Boron shield: Light-weight armoured shielding — protects against high explosive or armour-piercing projectiles.

C–2A: Carrier based greyhound aircraft — same basic airframe as the E–2C but used as a workhorse for transporting spare parts, mail and personnel. A COD.

C–130: The Hercules medium-range high-wing military transport aircraft — powered by four turboprop engines.

CATCC: Carrier Air Traffic Control Centre.

Cavitation: A high-velocity bullet may cause a small entry wound but transfers its momentum to surrounding tissues when in the body. The shock-wave pulsations cause great internal damage — up to 40 times missile diameter. This is the area of cavitation.

CentCom: President Carter's Rapid Deployment Force (RDF) later became CentCom or Central Command.

CIS: Commonwealth of Independent States.

COD: Carrier on-board delivery. Applied to the greyhound C–2A aircraft.

Comms: Communications.

Comms op: A possibly covert communications mission.

COMOPS: Command operations.

Condition Blue: Some forces use colours to designate degrees of readiness. Condition Red. Condition Black. And so on.

Condition One: McMurdo weather classification. Three: normal. Two: caution. One: danger.

Conflag: A fire station.

CT: Computerised tomography.

CV: A conventionally-powered American aircraft carrier.

CVBG: Carrier battle group.

CVN: A nuclear-powered carrier.

DOP: Director of Photography.

E–2C: The 'Hawkeye' carrier-based Grumman early warning aircraft. A mini-AWAC. A large round radar dish mounted on its upper fuselage provides the 'eye in the sky' for a carrier battle group (CVBG).

EPIRB: Emergency position-indicating radar beacon.

F–14: The Tomcat fighter — a two-seat supersonic interceptor with 'attack capability'.

Fentanyl: A drug that can cause muscle rigidity and stop respiration.

Finnified: Finnified snow is snow crystallised with ice — resembles loose gravel.

FLIR: Forward-looking infra-red. An aid to night navigation. Can provide a real-time thermal image of approaching terrain.

FOD: Foreign object debris (and damage) — a constant concern with aircraft. A forgotten spanner, stray washer or nut can disastrously damage aircraft systems.

GCA: Ground-control approach.

GE: General Electric.

GIGN: The Groupe d'Intervention de Gendarmerie Nationale — French special forces.

GPS: Global positioning system — the satellite-based navaid.

Guard skin doubler: A strengthened strip in the C–130 fuselage in line with the prop arc. A broken prop will come through the fuselage as crashes have proved.

Hagglunds: A Swedish-made tracked all-terrain vehicle used in Antarctica. Twin cabin design.

Hangar queen: A problem aircraft that spends most of its time out of service. Often gets cannibalised for parts to support flight schedules of other planes.

Hawkeye: The C–2A aircraft.

HF: High frequency.

Hornet: The F/A–18 fighter aircraft (US Navy/Marine Corps designation).

Huffers: Engine-starting equipment.

Hypnagogic jerk: A bodily start experienced shortly before going to sleep.

ICU: Intensive care unit.

Ingram: A basic but robust submachine-gun.

INS: Inertial navigation system. Independent of external references.

IR: Infra-red.

JATO: Jet-assisted take-off. In fact, rocket-assisted, so a misnomer, and now termed ATO. The C–130 mounted eight JATO bottles, four on each side forward of the jump doors.

Joker: Joker is the fuel state above Bingo that would allow successful disengagement from an air-combat manoeuvre.

JP8: Primary fuel used in Antarctica — aviation fuel oil similar to diesel.

Karabiner: A strong metal oval with a spring-loaded gate in one side. An essential tool for rope work.

Kevlar: A light, immensely tough carbon fibre fabric used as body armour by special forces. Effective against most bullets including high velocity rounds.

Komitet: KGB (*Komitet Gosudarstvennoi Bezopasnosti*).

Lats: Bodybuilder's cant for the *latissimus dorsi* muscle.

Lollywood: Pakistan's equivalent to Bollywood.

LSO: The Landing Signals Officer or 'air boss' on a carrier.

M249: Bipod-mounted 5.56mm Belgian light machine gun. Mag or belt-fed.

M–4: 9mm Spectre submachine-gun.

MDR: Motion detection radar — detects movement through masonry walls and other non-metal barriers.

Melt bell: Some polar bases need to make water from ice. A heated metal bell-shaped object lowered into the ice forms a cavern with water at the bottom.

Mossad: Israel's central institute for intelligence and security.

MP5: Reliable and accurate Heckler & Koch sub-machine-gun.

MRI: Magnetic resonance imaging.

MSA: Minimum safe altitude.

Myonecrosis: Death of muscle tissue.

N–1: Gyro compass used at the time in C–130s. Two were fitted.

NFOs: The back-end boys in the 'tube' of an E–2C. (CICO: Combat Information Centre Officer, ACO: Air Control Officer, RO: Radar Operator.)

Nicad: Nickel cadmium.

Nip: Frost nip. A mild version of frostbite.

NM: Nautical miles.

NSWC: Naval Special Warfare Center, Coronado, CA.

NVG: Night vision goggle(s).

OAE: 'Old Antarctic explorer'. Term for repeat visitors.

Omega: Long-range hyperbolic radio navigation aid.

Pak One: The plane in which President Zia of Pakistan and the cream of his military staff died when it inexplicably crashed.

PAR: Precision approach radar.

Parabellum: A German term meaning 'for war'. Used to distinguish 9mm Parabellum cartridges from 9mm short.

PDW: Personal defence weapon. A conveniently stowed and handled sub-compact used as a subsidiary weapon, for instance by tank crews.

PIM: Point and intended movement.

Pri-Fly: Primary flight control on a CV.

Prusiks: Loops of thin rope which, when secured around a standing line, provide a moveable purchase or stirrup. Used in pairs. Now supplanted by jumars — mechanical devices with a gripping and releasing action.

PSI: Pounds per square inch.

PSM: A small, handy 5.45mm pistol first issued to Soviet Spetsnaz units. Its bottle-nosed cartridge has remarkable penetrative ability.

Radalt: Radar altimeter.

Ripped: Body-builders attempt to reduce as much body fat as possible before a contest so that muscles become more defined. The result is called being 'ripped'.

RPM: Usually revs-per-minute. But rounds-per-minute applied to weapons.

SAR: Not search-and-rescue but a compact assault rifle made in Singapore.

Sastrugi: Windblown and scoured snow and ice ridges.

SATCOM: Fleet satellite communications. More properly FLTSATCOM.

Sedia gestatoria: A portable papal throne carried on the shoulders of 12 footmen.

Shear-load: The force a body can sustain before shearing.

SIG-Sauer: Swiss handgun noted for excellent manufacture and extreme reliability.

Sikorsky S–76: Large commercial twin-turbine helicopter.

Sitrep: Situation report.

Sked: Scheduled radio contact.

Slot: Crevasse. Also known as a crack. A vehicle is 'slotted' if driven into a crack. Cracks are often invisible due to snow cover.

SNL: Sandia National Laboratories.

SOF: Generally sound-on-film but, in defence terms, Special Operations Forces.

Spetsnaz: KGB special forces.

Sponson: A structure projecting from the side of a vessel. On carriers, there are sponsons around the flight deck.

Spud in: Slang for crash landing.

SS90: Light bullet able to penetrate 48 layers of Kevlar at 100-metre range.

Transponder: Radio transmitter triggered by a received signal. Can be used as a positioning device.

Traverse: A convoy of vehicles travelling together for a considerable distance in Antarctica. Can refer to a train of large sleds supporting accommodation modules, stores, workshops and equipment. Pulled by converted bulldozers with very wide tracks.

Ventiles: Windproof outer garments used in Antarctica. A material developed by the Ventile Corporation.

VHF: Very high frequency.

VMC: Visible meteorological conditions. IMC is the instrument version.

WSG: Sir William Schwenck Gilbert of Gilbert & Sullivan fame.

Yaw: A bullet's base has more mass than its nose — a shape lacking static stability. When it leaves the barrel it develops yaw — tilts up in flight. The 'angle of yaw' is the angle between the axis of the projectile and the tangent to the trajectory. The gyroscopic effect of a spinning projectile fired from a rifled barrel partly corrects this.

AUTHOR'S NOTE

Any story set in many countries is a conundrum where measurement is concerned. The metric system is dominant throughout the world but America remains imperial, as do many older minds in other countries. US aircraft manuals, for instance, perpetuate their system. Shipping and particularly aircraft now use a curious mix: knots for speed and wind speed; feet, metres and nautical miles for distance. In Australia, runways are measured in feet but visibility in kilometres. Small boats are still so many feet but Lloyd's registers shipping in metres. Different flight zones require one system or the other. In *Exit Alpha* I have used both metric and imperial, adjusting for context — including the mindset of the characters — and hope this will not offend.

ACKNOWLEDGMENTS

This enormous project would have been impossible without advice from experts in many fields.

The services: Firstly, and fittingly, I acknowledge my great debt to warriors both active and retired of the United States and New Zealand Armed Services who bore my enquiries with their usual patience and grace. Particular thanks to Flt Lt Greg Caie, Master Engineer Brett Shanks (both 40th Squadron RNZAF), Daniel Brooks (Captain, 17th Squadron USAF and now Logistics Engineer for Lockheed). To the late, great Gerald Harris (Major, 17th Squadron USAF Rtd) whose tremendous enthusiasm helped power this book. As well to Flt Lt Robert Saxton (VAW–120, Virginia USA), Lt John MacMichael (Safety Officer, E–2C Training Command), Loadmaster Garry Quick (109th Airlift Wing NY) and crew members of USS *Constellation*. I acknowledge assistance from the Hawkeye Association and my debt to excellent articles in the US Navy Safety Centre's *Approach* magazine and the US Navy Institute's *Proceedings* journal.

Experts on and in Antarctica: Busy professionals who provided invaluable advice were Rod Ledingham (Field Training Officer, Australian Antarctic Division), Mike Mahon (Science and IT Support ANZ) and the long-suffering Fred Parsons (Mechanic, Scott Base ANZ). I was assisted by the International Antarctic Centre staff in Christchurch, by Antarctica NZ and the Australian Antarctic Division in Kingston, Tasmania.

Catholic studies: I was helped by Bede Draper and a perceptive teaching Father in the Catholic Church who prefers not to be named. I thank him.

Other professionals: Gratitude to Rex Dovey (helicopter operations, Queenstown, NZ). Glad you're still alive, Rex. To Anna Lewis (operating theatre techniques) and Siobhan McCammon (film production). For reading the manuscript, providing suggestions and corrections, I thank two brilliant friends — Diane Morgan and Jim Richards. Gratitude also to David Elfick for pointing out that the pope should interact with Nina in the tale.

I acknowledge brief quotes from *To Live Within* by Sri Anirvan and Lizelle Reymond, last republished, as far as I know, by Rudra Press, Portland, Oregon, USA.